The Damned Ones

Chris Miller

BLACK BED SHEET

The Damned Ones
A Black Bed Sheet/Diverse Media Book
January 2020

Cover art by Nicholas Grabowsky

ISBN-10: 1-946874-21-3
ISBN-13: 978-1-946874-21-4

The Damned Ones

A Black Bed Sheet/Diverse Media Book
Antelope, CA

Also by Chris Miller:

The Hard Goodbye
Trespass
A Murder of Saints
The Damned Place

Dedication

This one is for my daughter, Joanna. I would charge the gates of Hell for you, baby girl. Heaven and Earth cannot contain the love I have for you. You made me a daddy for the first time, and I will love you with all my heart for all of eternity.

Argument

In the fall of 1989, Ryan Laughton's dad went into the woods outside of Winnsboro, TX with his friend Mike on a hunting trip. The night before had been spent drunkenly battering Ryan and his mother, so when he came back from the woods covered in blood and raving about moving shadows in a strange house in the forest, most were happy to see him shipped off to the mental hospital, especially since Mike was never seen again.

A few months later, in June of 1990, Ryan and his friends Jimmy and Freddie are confronted after the last day of school on the playground by some older bullies. The altercation was broken up by the Middle School coach before Jake—the leader of the trio of bullies—could make use of his knife. As the kids rode away, Jake let them know they would be seeing them around later that summer.

Ryan meets a girl from their class named Honey whom he is instantly taken with, and soon he introduces her to the group and the four become fast friends, spending their days in the woods near town playing guns and building their fort out there into an impressive place to escape, all their own.

Jake Reese, Bart Dyer, and Chris Higgins, however, make good on their promise to catch up with the kids. Jake, the son of a preacher and an overbearing and wicked mother, leads the gang with visions of bloodlust. This bloodlust was born when he had taken dominance over his home when his mother attempted to enforce corporal punishment upon him, which turned to her being raped into submission by her eldest son. She had then turned to her youngest child and poured all her attention and love into Jake's little brother Norman. Jake's buddy Bart is also a teetering psychopath in the making, with a penchant for opening up things to see what they look like inside, be it frogs in science class or his family's pet dog at home. Only Chris seems to be just tagging along, not really interested in bullying anybody, but going along with his friends all the same.

The trio finds the four kids playing in the woods and give chase. During their flight, the kids come across an old house in the woods, the very same one Ryan's father claimed to have seen moving shadows within and where his friend Mike had vanished. But they don't concern themselves with the ravings of a madman as they look for a place to hide. While Honey dives under the house to hide and Freddie crawls into a tree hollow by a nearby creek and Ryan attempts to flee the woods altogether, it's Jimmy who rushes straight into the old house and hides in a closet. Jake and his friends are after all of them, and Jake wanders into the house and realizes he's cornered Jimmy, the leader of the pack of kids he's after. Before he can throw open the door to the closet and unleash his wrath upon Jimmy, the door incredibly locks itself, as though obeying Jimmy's wishes that it would do so. As he scoots himself further into the closet, he finds he's moved to yet another door that lets on to yet another house, much like the one he'd just been hiding in, but different as well. There are pictures of what he assumes must be people, only they're covered in a fine fur, with strange faces that seem to be a mix of animal and human, and they have cloven feet and four arms.

Jimmy rescues Honey from under the house using this ability to slip between the worlds and then she joins him in the other place where they come across a giant abomination of a spider-like creature and something else much like a slug, only far too fast and large and with dangerous teeth.

But then they come across the real monster.

The thing is big and intelligent and it can *speak*. But there's nothing human about it. Its vertical mouth is lined with razor-like fangs beneath its black eyes and protruding spines splay out from its back.

It gives chase and as Jimmy and Honey come back through into their own world—through the house—they discover Ryan and Freddie there, who have just dispatched the bullies using a large stick and a live copperhead snake.

They flee, seeing the moving shadows Ryan's dad had spoken of, hearing a hideous and menacing voice *in* their minds but not *coming from* their minds, a voice hungry for their meat. Strangely, the chase soon ends and the kids make it back to town safe. Jimmy and Honey tell the others about what they had seen and how they had slipped to the other world, and it takes a display from Jimmy moving things around with the power of his will at their new hangout before the others will believe him. Only, he is unable to slip between worlds here. It's almost like the fabric of space is somehow *thicker* here than in the woods where that old, strange house was. This puts Freddie's brain into gear and they all start to theorize about this anomaly. Finally, they decide it has to have something to do with the foundation of the fabric of time and space in a given area, that *thin spots* are made that way when some atrocity happens there and it wears reality thin enough to be able to be opened by someone with psychic abilities.

Freddie's suspicions are all but confirmed when he discovers an old journal at the local library from one of the people who lived in the old house in the woods back in 1906, but before he can tell his friends of his discovery, he's attacked and beaten in the alley by Jake and his friends, irreparably damaging one of his eyes in the process and getting lacerated all over by Jake's knife. A few days later when his friends visit him in the hospital—where Freddie is refusing to tell anyone what happened—Freddie tells them the story, showing them the journal and demanding they all keep quiet because he wants Jake for himself.

The kids learn that the Brogan family built and lived in the old house near the turn of the century, and the whole family fell slowly into madness and murder before Halloween of 1906. The journals describe a creature named Cloris who, Jimmy readily realizes, looks just like the pictures he'd seen in the house on the other side. Cloris is revealed to have the same ability as Jimmy to cross between the worlds. She and the Brogan matriarch, Susan, palaver frequently as Susan melts into madness, ranting about having a 'Brogan new'. Soon she is using her youngest son Richard to make her new child and Jonathan, Richard's older brother and the author of the journal, is falling apart after witnessing Cloris kill his father and later feed him, in a horrifying act, to a creature they called The Glutton...who seems to be exactly like the beast they had encountered while on the other side of their reality.

Madness falls upon them all and Jonathan finally takes an axe to his family to cleanse the world of their curse, accidentally trapping The Glutton on the other side with no one to help him slip through into the new world or to bring him meat. It is also discovered that the thing needs to eat the 'high-meat' of a new world to be birthed and incarnate within it, but once that has happened, it devours and destroys the world before making the leap to the next.

Desperate to make sure no one ventures near the place, especially Jimmy who has the power to open the door between worlds and let the creature through, the kids abandon the woods and try to set about their summer vacation like any normal kids might. But before long, Honey is taken by Bart at their new hangout while she is waiting on the other boys to come along. He contacts Jake who has him take her to the house in the woods where Jake and Chris meet them after calling Jimmy and demanding he and his pals meet them in the woods for a showdown. In the midst of their standoff, Jake reveals that he too has the power to open doors between worlds and he inadvertently allows The Glutton to slip through. Jimmy uses his gift to get them all into the other world, where The Glutton chases them, and the kids come up with a plan to slow the monster down by using Bart as bait so they can get back across and save themselves. Honey's father is with them too, a drunk who is in mourning for his dead wife and worthless all around, contacted by Chris Higgins, who had hoped to stop Jake's decent into madness without directly crossing his friend. But her father is mortally wounded by the monster as they all scramble for safety, and Chris flees in terror at the sight of the beast, only to be killed by one of the giant spider-like creatures that inhabit this strange new world. Jake soon finds Honey's father and, at the final tipping point, murders the man in a frenzied state, discovering just how much he likes it...*and* the taste of blood.

Before the kids can utilize Bart as bait, Jake catches them in the house and takes Honey hostage once more. It comes down to Jimmy's abilities to manipulate things with his will and to slip between worlds to save them. He and Freddie and Honey and Ryan end up mortally wounding Bart and injuring Jake as The Glutton rips into the house, tearing Bart in half as they escape back into their own world. But the monster isn't giving up and uses Jake's ability to reach back through for them.

In their final, desperate moments of survival, Honey barely gets away from a world-jumping Jake and they all bury spears into The Glutton, who jumps back into the other world where it is stronger. As the portal closes on the monster and Jake Reese, who is badly wounded but alive, the monster glares at them and says, *"Soon."*

Years after the incident, Cherry Reese, mother of Jake and Norman, is happy to be rid of her psycho-rapist son, pouring all her love and affection into Norman. She tells Norman he's called by God Almighty to lead God back into the world, that he will be the right hand of the Lord in His reacquisition of mankind. To bring God to the godless. Norman believes this, strangely drawn to his mother, and just as she lays bare her plans for him, the two embrace in a lover's rapture, feverishly kissing and petting each other as Cherry thinks of all the great things her *loving boy* is going to do in this world, and the now teenaged Norman believes her every word. He would be a new prophet for God, and by his actions would bring a specifically Reese kind of revival back to the land.

It's now been twenty-six years since Jimmy, Honey, Ryan, and Freddie faced down Jake, Bart, Chris, and The Glutton, and much has changed in their lives. As the summer of 2016 is winding up to its hottest point, something very bad is happening once again in Winnsboro, TX, and something ancient is stirring in the woods not far away...

Prologue:
January 1st, 2016

The cow shivered, huddling in his corner of the dilapidated house. A draft blew in, seeming to ignore the few walls that were left entirely as it whipped through the gaping hole that was once the front door. His gums smacked together audibly—there were no teeth left—wet, fleshy sounds, as he hugged himself. It was cold. It was miserable. It was—

All their fucking fault!

It was. *Them.* The authors and finishers of his misery. The ones who'd banished him to this frozen hell that sometimes wasn't frozen at all, but was always isolated. Food was a commodity becoming more and more rare every day, never mind year. And how many years had he been here? He didn't know anymore. The seasons didn't make sense. Hours didn't make sense. Night and day didn't make sense. Nothing did in this wasteland.

But what was he to do? He'd tried escaping through the door many times. More than he cared to remember, in fact, because each memory carried with it the dashing of hope and the horrors of pains the cow had never imagined possible. Pieces of him literally torn from his bones and devoured before his eyes, but never enough to cause lasting damage. A pinch here, a morsel there. Never more than the size of a silver dollar, but oh, the pain. He would scream in torment, wail at the thing, beat at it with his fists. But it never did any good. It never changed anything at all. He was forever trapped here. Trapped in this damned place, so far from home and everyone he...he...

Well, he didn't love them, that was for damn sure. He wasn't sure what his longing for home really was, aside from the fact it wasn't *here*, it wasn't this total isolation from all he knew and understood. His whole sense of reality had been changed, fundamentally *altered* that day so many, many years ago. Familiarity had never totally set in since he'd been in this place. There was air to breathe and there was the occasional meal—always some putrid, pus-filled refuse which hardly managed to keep meat on his bones—there was a hole to shit in. There were even trees outside and some alien sun which shone down on him. But none of it was *familiar*. Even after all these long years, familiarity had never set in.

The nights were another thing altogether. The moons. Yes, in the plural sense. Three, to be exact, though he'd never ventured out of these woods into the open to ever be sure if there might be more. But on more than one occasion when the thing allowed him to roam into the woods just a bit, he had identified no less than *three* separate moons, all glowing in the sky with an eerie iridescence. And none of them quite white, either. They all seemed to radiate dissimilar shades of blue and teal.

Does that mean there are multiple suns as well? he often wondered.

He didn't know the answer to this. He'd never been allowed to roam in the daylight. Always quarantined to the damned house which was falling down around him more and more each day. It was all such a nightmare. Such a nightmare caused by *them*.

But he would get them. This much he was sure of. His day would come. The deal had been made and his vengeance was assured to him. And what sweet vengeance it would be.

Another gust made the cow shiver all the more, and

he hugged himself tighter. He wished for a shirt or a blanket. Something with which to get warm. He guessed the temperature was somewhere in the upper fifties, which wasn't all that bad really, *if* you had clothes. But the cow had little more than rags now, and only on his legs. A pair of tattered and torn jeans, wearing through in many places. His shirt was long gone, victim to the thing when the cow had tried to escape one night. And he'd grown much too large for the jeans. From the knees down they were tattered ribbons, which betrayed just how short they were for him. He was amazed he'd managed to stay in the waistband, though he attributed this to his lack of food through the years. His stomach was a concave thing, sunken in like a pothole in a road back home.

Home...

He thought once more of that place of familiarity, though it was filled with people he despised with every fiber of his being. It was this hate which gave him just enough heat to survive these long, cold nights. His fuel to keep going, to not give up. He'd been here such a *long* time, and the only way to reconcile that was with the promise of the future. Part of the deal. The deal he had struck with the thing, in exchange for what he could do. What he *would* do, when the time came.

The cow heard a *thump* in the hallway and jumped, startled. He could hear a low growl and wet, dripping sound coming from the hallway just out of sight. But he knew what it was. It was the *thing*. That damned *thing*, holding another of its nightly vigils, head pressed against the wall, clawed hands digging into the plaster as it strained to hear. To listen for sound from the other side.

He sat there, in his cold corner, and shivered as he listened to the thing. He hated it, perhaps as much as he hated *them*. Sure, it kept him alive, if just barely, but it kept him *here*. Here, without hope of escape. With the tortuous bites. Just enough to keep itself strong for when the time came. The cow could feel the scars all over his skin and he bared his gums in a grimace. There were no teeth left. Those had long since rotted and fallen out. And though he had no mirror with which to see them, his gums were black around the empty sockets where his teeth had once stood.

He thought he could hear himself hiss.

"I-I'm hungry," the cow said in a croaked voice some time before dawn. The thing had been in the hall all night, pacing and thumping up and down its length. Listening. *Waiting.*

An aggravated growl was the only response.

"And I need water," the cow went on. "I can't do what you need me to do if I die of hunger or thirst."

His voice was shaky, and he cursed himself for that. But it couldn't be helped. The last thing he'd eaten was a full day before—*or was it two?*—and had consisted of little more than a repugnant jelly with some sort of cartilage inside, something the cow assumed served as a skeleton of sorts for the creature he'd consumed. But he'd eaten it. He hadn't any choice.

"I said I need something to—"

"Yes," the thing cut him off coldly.

The cow said nothing more, and listened as the thumps of the thing's hooves retreated further down the hall and then outside.

The sun rose, bringing little warmth with it, but the cow was grateful all the same. It was some time before the thing returned. There was no ceremony as it tossed the carcass of some horrible thing into his room and set down a crude bowl fashioned out of tree bark on the floor. There was a meaty splat as the thing hit and then rolled a few times towards his feet before coming to rest before him. This was one of the insect things, though the cow had no frame of reference with which to identify it. It simply didn't exist back home. It was a terrible thing, it's upper face consisting of a network of eyes, not unlike the compound eye of insects back home, but these seeming to be individual things, working independently of one another rather than in concert.

He had no reason to believe this to be the case, it was merely something he intuited. All the same, he knew those eyes were the best part by far. Most of the thing and its seven legs would be tough, covered in a thick exoskeleton with very little edible meat beneath. The abdomen offered some nourishment, but he had to be careful in getting the meat from it as it tended to tear the insides and spill terrible fluids from its stomach sack, utterly ruining the food. But what he could get was tender enough to chew with his toothless gums, and none more so than the eyes.

He scampered to the bowl first and drank deeply of the water. This seemed fresher than what the thing had brought him before, less stagnant, and the cow was grateful. After drinking his fill, he returned to the nightmarish creature on the floor which no longer gave him nightmares. Nothing gave the cow nightmares anymore, not after so many years living in one.

He pinched into the soft flesh around one of the eyes and worked his fingers behind it, getting a solid grip. Then he pulled and twisted. The eye came loose from the socket with a wet pop, then there were a series of moist snapping sounds as the stalk behind the eye gave way to his efforts. Then he was popping it into his mouth, squeezing down with his gums until the pressure caused the eye to burst and his mouth was filled with a salty, metallic flavor which had made him retch his guts out the first few times he had done this. But not now. The cow was used to it now. He could take it.

The slimy thing in his mouth squished and leaked

from the corners of his mouth, but it mashed up well enough and the cow swallowed. Then he was on to another eye, then another.

He ate his fill, the rumble in his belly satisfied for the moment. He drank still more from the bowl before settling back into his corner to listen to the thing in the hall as it waited, waited...

There was a scraping sound, likely the thing's claws dragging down the length of the wall, and the cow heard it speak.

"Soon."

Soon. It had been saying this one word repeatedly, nearly every single night, for all the long years the cow had been in this terrible place. It was always *soon.* He wondered if the thing had any idea of the definition of the word.

It wanted meat. Had to have it, in fact. Though, in all this time, nothing had come close enough to alert the thing to get the cow to perform his trick. Yet, despite this, it stood a constant vigil in a sort of limbo which the cow thought the thing had never experienced in all its long eons of life. He could tell it angered the thing that it had been bested. Bested by *them*, just as the cow had been.

This was the one thing they shared, the thing and the cow. *Them.* Just over there, yet so, so far away. If only someone would wander close enough, someone who might bring the thing what it needed, even if just a little. It would be enough. It would be enough to get the cow back home and closer to its vengeance. Closer to the one thing which kept it going all these years and had kept it from using the knife in his ragged pocket on his own throat.

The cow pulled the knife from his pocket and flipped the blade out. The moons had risen again, and the patinaed blade winked here and there where the metal still shone. And he could taste the metal in his mouth again, that old lust rising in him, and his long unused loins began to stiffen.

Soon, the thing had said, and the cow sincerely hoped it was right. As it was, they'd waited years. Decades, even, though the cow had no idea just how long. But *soon*—even if the term were a relative thing—had to be getting closer. Closer and closer every day. Closer to that door the cow was so eager to open and cross through without having his flesh devoured a nip at a time.

And *soon*, as it turned out, was merely a few months away.

PART ONE:

Bad Seeds

Thursday, August 4, 2016

Chapter One

Norman Reese clenched his fists.

His head was throbbing again. Another migraine. He was getting them all the time now, but he refused to take Doc Horton seriously on the matter and follow up with an MRI and bloodwork. The mass in his brain had been discovered when Norman had collapsed while in line at the bank a few months back. He'd been having one of those headaches like he was now, intense and all-encompassing about his skull, and the world had simply winked out for a while. His cranium had cracked hard on the marble floor, the skin splitting and oozing a lake of nearly black blood around him like a satanic halo. The doctors had been reasonably sure nothing had been fractured, but wanted to be sure.

But Norman had refused to accept what they'd discovered on the X-ray. He was a man of God, he'd informed the doctor, and men of God had their faith tested from time to time. That was all this was, and he wasn't about to dismiss his faith over some black spot in an X-ray. Even when the doctor had pointed out that the tumor was in all likelihood the source of his severe headaches, he'd scoffed at them. It was probably just too much sugar, he'd told them as he'd left the doctor's office. Too much soda. Too much caffeine, or maybe even not enough of it. Something like that. Men of God didn't succumb to cancer.

Norman hadn't been interested in discussing his theological conclusions when the doctor had told him God had nothing to do with whether people got cancer or not, and had finally renlented, urging him a final time to follow up with the specialists and writing him a prescription to deal with the migraines. They were merely putting a Band-Aid on a gaping wound, he'd explained, but handed over the script anyway.

For the pills to be effective, Norman had to remember to keep them with him at all times and to take them as soon as he felt one of the skull crushers coming on. His thoughts usually a scattered mess these days, he often forgot to bring the pills with him, and once one of the migraines set in, the pills were useless anyway. Still, he cursed himself for not remembering them.

Norman had a hard time remembering what he was supposed to do. His sense of direction in life had never been well focused, always relying on his mother's conversations with God to inform him of his great and mighty purpose. God had yet to speak to him on the matter, however, his mother had informed him that it was because he was *her boy*, entrusted to her to raise and guide. That was why God informed Norman of his great calling through her. The great, magnificent calling on his life to lead God back into a godless world.

But it hadn't happened yet, and he was pretty sure it should have, certainly by now. Norman was thirty-six years old, and if he were going to lead this divine charge, the Almighty had better get a move on or Norman would be too old to be of much good. Even his mother's rebuttals pointing to the ages of Abraham and Moses when their callings had come—much later in their lives than he was in his own—were starting to become a point of doubt within him.

Focus had become a fleeting thing for Norman. Even more so of late, as his life had begun yawing out of control. Not all aspects, of course, but one in particular which he could not let alone. Not when the Almighty had told him—*personally this time, not through his mother*—what was to be. This absolute and inerrant word from the Lord Norman had received was that his girlfriend—*ex* girlfriend now, though he'd yet to admit such—was supposed to marry him. It was God's will. His plan for *her* life. A man who was going to lead God back into a world from which deity seemed quite absent would *need* a good woman by his side for support, advisement, and—most importantly—to keep his ball-sack empty.

Only, she hadn't seen things quite the same way, which had led to their falling out and, ultimately, to this moment, to this late night visit to her home with his pounding headache turning into a migraine, palms ready to bleed from the pressure of his nails and a seemingly endless shudder rippling through every part of his body.

The silly cunt—*Jesus forgive him*—was denying God's will.

He stood next to the curb in front of Margie Johnson's house on Ward Street. It was just off the southern length of Mitchell Street, not on the corner but very near where it met Mitchell, and save for a sodium vapor street lamp at the far end, it was dark and quiet. He tried to control his breathing, which was becoming labored with anticipation, but his breaths continued to hitch out of despite his efforts. It was quite late—close to midnight, in fact—but Norman didn't bother to check his watch. He knew it was late. He had been working up to this moment for some time now. Several days, in fact. It had only been when he'd reassured himself with what God had told him that he'd finally decided it was time. Time to confront Margie about her dissent to the Almighty's will, no matter how late it was.

He was staring at Margie's front door.

Margie and he had been in a relationship for almost six months. She was a youth-worker at Revival Rock

Ministries, the church Norman's parents had started more than two-decades before. It was a small, non-denominational affair, situated on the south-eastern edge of town. Norman was the worship-leader, playing the rhythm guitar and singing in his nasal, huffy voice which seemed popular for the modern worship style these days, especially to the indiscriminate ear of the average congregant. The more you sounded like you had a cold, the better it was received, it seemed. Repeat the same three or four chords and a few lines about how Jesus loves you—or you loved Him, either angle worked with equal measure—and people would line up before you at the 'altar'. That was merely what they called it, 'altar', but it was no such thing. It was a stage. But, they would raise their hands and weep and fall to the floor in swoons of feigned—*or were they?*—adoration.

Whatever it was, it was powerful to Norman.

His father, George, was the pastor. George Reese had founded the church in the fall of 1988 after a falling out with the church they had been attending at the time, another non-denominational church by the name of Faith Creek. Funnily enough, there had been no creek anywhere near the church, never mind the fact it sat on an urban lot on Elm Street. It was just something that sounded nice and fit with the imagery of their logo, which depicted a stick-person dunking another stick-person into a creek in baptism. There was even a stick fish to witness the event with an obscene, aquatic grin. This church had been another small affair, almost identical to what George would later create for himself in obedience to the voice of God he had heard at the time of the split with the creekless Faith Creek.

George and Cherry Reese founded Revival Rock within a week of the split, a result of the dissolution of the elder's board at Faith Creek and the pastor there refusing to allow church governance to be attended to, or overseen by, *anyone* other than himself.

And God, of course.

So, the Reeses had started Revival Rock in their living room, and within a few months their membership had outgrown the small space and they had rented a small building on the Eastern length of Highway 515, just barely inside the city limits. They'd stayed there for a year or so, and finally bought a barn which used to belong to the city at the rodeo grounds near the town's community center. It was there they had set up shop—the potent scent of horse manure an ever-present reminder of their location—and still remained to this day. They'd rebuilt the interior to accommodate a sanctuary and fellowship hall, along with a few offices and a foyer, all with the help of volunteers from their humble congregation, and they had ebbed and flowed ever since.

There'd been yet another dissolution of an elder's board not long after their barn had been christened, this time at Revival Rock Ministries, but of course this was an altogether different affair because *this time* God Himself had spoken to George. It wasn't anything like the pastor at Faith Creek, who'd been out of line and totally out of control. No, this was *completely* different. And what was the *reason* it was different?

Because.

"I've got plans for this house of worship," God had said to George. *"And these men on the board are not hearing from me! They are hearing from the enemy! Be gone with them, and let me build my house upon this soil!"*

And so George had.

There had been yet another split, but this time no one had gone and started another church. They'd simply spread out and found homes at one of the three Baptist churches, the Church of Christ, the Methodist church, the

Pentecostal church, some converted to Catholicism, and a few even went back to Faith Creek. Others simply gave up on the whole religious game altogether.

And, of course, the Reeses knew—again, *because—all* of those other churches had it completely wrong. Yes, God had spoken to George about how wrong everyone else had things and had told him how to set it right. But even more than he, God had spoken to his wife, Cherry. It wasn't just that their *church* had it right, but that *they* had it right. Them. Their family. And God was going to raise up *their* family to save His church from the apostates and heretics, and it would be their boy who brought about the great revival.

Norman had started strumming at the guitar when he was around ten years old, and had never really progressed beyond that, contrary to the ravings of Cherry Reese about how amazing he was and what a great gift of talent had been bestowed upon him by God. His three-or-four-chord progressions were absolutely inspired by Christ Himself, she had proclaimed at their services—and more than once—as often as she could get the microphone from her husband. Which *was* fairly often. Her child was the one God was going to use to change the world. To bring God back into a godless world. She spoke of him as a near deity, as though Christ's return would occur in and through her boy as he strummed at the guitar.

And wouldn't it be? Why not?

But, despite his pitiful musicianship and his utterly narcissistic personality—an endowment granted to him by his mother through her years of worship to him—Norman had managed to woo Margie, and the pair had begun dating some months back. Margie had *not* thought Norman was the second coming of Christ that his mother was so convinced of, which was a bit of a problem, though one Norman had been sure he would rectify in time. She had liked him well enough, though. Even thought she might fall in love with him, as she'd told him only a month prior. She'd told him how kind he could be, and he had a great big smile that, when he was being genuine, warmed her soul. She hadn't been terribly attracted to him physically, however, a revelation which Norman couldn't believe, nor could he *understand* her need to tell him so. She simply had to be blind, he'd concluded, and had vowed to purchase her a pair of glasses once he got her sorted out in her spiritual life.

He was a tall man, about six foot two, and had sandy-blond hair above blue eyes. His teeth had been in braces from fourteen to sixteen years of age, but they seemed to have forgotten their barred imprisonment as they'd had no lasting effect at all. His teeth had managed to become crooked again and to overlap one another through the years, and no one would ever know an orthodontist had ever looked at his mouth. Norman was also very skinny—*lanky, really*—but had virtually no muscle definition anywhere on his body, even though he *was* reasonably strong. Stronger than a woman, anyway. He wore glasses most of the time, but Margie had thought his choice in eyewear was pretentious and rather hipster. She couldn't stand hipsters, so Norman began wearing contacts.

But, nonetheless, she'd begun to love him. Or so she'd said. He was kind to her, had bought her flowers and showered her with gifts. He had even written her a song.

It was in the same three-or-four-chord progression that all of the contemporary Christian songs he led on Sunday mornings were in, but she hadn't minded. She hadn't even minded that the lyrics could have been plucked straight from the shallowest of those in the modern worship music repertoire. All you had to do was replace *her* with *God* and you had another song for Sunday mornings. A shitty one, *but...*

It was sweet.

Then Norman had not only brought up, but had been adamant about, the fact that God had said they were to be married and Margie had simply not felt the same way. Not yet, anyway. It was something she was praying about, waiting to hear from God on, she'd said. But she hadn't yet. As a matter of fact, she had begun to think that he was simply not the one God had for her at all.

And finally, she had broken it off.

Norman simply wouldn't accept it. *Couldn't* accept it. He'd told her that God had said otherwise, and he would wait for her to hear from Him properly. There was simply no way that what she was hearing could be from God, because he'd heard the precise opposite. And he knew, from years and years of his mother explaining to him how special he was in God's eyes, what great plans God had for him, that there was simply no way he was wrong.

No, it was she who was wrong. There was no doubt. Women often heard wrong from the Lord and needed the men in their lives to set them on the right track. Well, most women, anyway. His mother seemed to have a most masculine intimacy with the Almighty that was typically reserved for the males of the species. But his mother was an anomaly, not the norm.

It had been a full two weeks since she had broken things off with Norman. He'd let her have her time and pleaded with God to pull the wool from her eyes so she could see she was simply being silly and stupid. Like most women were. That was why they *needed* men. So they could see things clearly. See things the way God *intended* them to be seen.

But his phone call earlier in the evening had indicated she was still resisting God's will. She would require a face to face meeting, and Norman had decided the time was now. A face to face reckoning with the man God had set aside for her. The one she was supposed to marry and submit to. It wouldn't be pleasant, but it was necessary. She was going to see things *his* way.

God's way.

Norman looked up and down Ward Street and saw no one. Didn't even see any lights on. There was nothing. The stars shone above the streetlamp at the far corner, which buzzed with the sound of electricity and the hum of moths.

He stepped up on her yard.

He made his way to her front door at an even pace. His head throbbed and ached. His fists clenched. He thought again of how Margie had broken things off with him. Over the phone. In a text message, no less. Sure, she'd spoken of it a few times with him in person, but she was so clearly out of God's will that he'd dismissed her completely. It was a man's job to direct his woman in the way she should go, and she was obviously going outside of God's will. Norman would set her straight.

But then she had sent the text message and asked him not to contact her anymore. She'd even stepped down from the youth-worker position she'd held at the church for several years, which had infuriated him.

You fucking bitch—Jesus forgive me, he thought. *Who are you to buck God's will?*

He got to her door. He thought he heard a shower turn off inside, and he blinked. When he thought of the shower, he thought of her naked. Not that he'd ever had occasion to see her naked, but he had to admit, to his shame, that he'd thought of it several times. Had even succumbed to touching himself to the thoughts, though he'd been sure to scourge himself with his knotted rope afterward.

God had forgiven him.

Still, he felt that firmness in his loins spring up as he

stood there. Springing up like a cuckoo clock.

Cuckoo! Cuckoo!

He knocked on the door.

He had no idea what he was going to say to her when she answered. He had no idea whatsoever. Maybe he would start with 'hi'. Maybe a 'how's it going, Marg'? But he would say *something*. She needed to hear the will of God.

Hey, so you heard from God yet? You get your shit together yet, Jesus forgive me?

Somewhere inside he heard a voice. *Her* voice.

"Just a minute!"

He imagined her again, naked, beads of water dripping from her pink flesh, pulling on a towel. He wondered if she had hair down there or if she was one of those modern women who shaved it. If she was, she was surely a whore. Only a whore would shave away the natural, protective fur God had given to every man and woman. Only a whore would do that. Why else would you shave it? It was only to please men. *Other* men. Men who didn't understand how God intended sex to be. Man and wife. *Only*.

There were footsteps within the house. His head throbbed. His fists clenched. The knuckles were turning white and the nails on his fingers were drawing blood from his palms.

Norman was hardly aware of any of this.

"Just a second, I'm coming!" he heard her say.

Then she opened the door.

She was standing there, her reddish-brown hair soaked and brushed back, her body covered loosely in a towel. It barely reached beyond her crotch. Norman stared at her stupidly, his face a rictus of confused astonishment.

Why on earth would she DARE answer the door in such a manner?

She was certainly a whore.

Norman's fist lashed out in a blur, smashing into her face. There was a crunching sound as her nose broke and a jet of blood began to pour from her crumpled cartilage in sheets. She chirped a groan of pain as her head jerked back and she stumbled backwards into the living room in an awkward gait.

Norman stepped in and slammed the door behind him, glaring down at her. He was as furious as he was confused. His lips quivered into a snarl, his eyes still stupidly confused.

How dare she answer the door so inappropriately, he thought. *Is she really such a whore? Why does God want me to marry a whore? I'm not fucking Hosea—Jesus forgive me!*

Her awkward stumble reached its climax when her feet twisted up and she collapsed to the floor, her towel falling free from her body, exposing her breasts and everything else in all their glory to Norman for the first time. Her jubblies—*Jesus forgive him*—were plump and round and perky. He felt himself harden even more. Then he noticed something else. Something which crawled up from his belly with such horror that, for a moment, he was sure he would cry out in terror.

Her crotch was shaved.

It almost glistened in the artificial light from the ceiling fan. Pink and proud. Maybe she'd been giving it a fresh haircut in the shower as he'd been on his way over. It sure looked slick enough. But for who? Certainly it wasn't for him, the one God had set aside for her. The apostate bitch—*Jesus forgive him*—was seeing someone else.

So she really is a whore, he thought. *How could God have let me believe this harlot was the one for me if she's such a whore?*

She started to sit up as he entered the room and she began grasping for the towel to cover her nakedness. Norman reached down and snatched the towel away from her and flung it to the door behind him where it crumpled into a heap.

"Why cover yourself now, you slut!" he barked at her.

She was terrified. He could read it on her features. It was all over her face, dripping from it like the beads of water in her hair.

"I take it you haven't been listening to our Lord?" he bellowed at her, continuing. "But then, how could you hear from him when you're so steeped in...in...*sin*?"

His arms had begun to whirl through the air as he was talking, and Margie's lips began to tremble. She feebly tried to cover her body with her arms and crossed her legs, fidgeting nervously as he glowered over her. Finally, she managed to speak for the first time since Norman had ruined her nose.

"N-Norman," her voice wavered. "Norman, please! I'm sorry about everything, I, I..."

She trailed off.

It was clear to Norman that she'd lost the words to say because she was so *clearly,* so *blatantly* outside of God's will. But with her shaved pussy—*Jesus forgive him*—gaping up at him despite her efforts to conceal it, it was abundantly obvious she'd strayed too far from God's grace to be reconciled now. His wrath would surely befall her.

Margie managed to stand and turn from him, attempting to run. Her bare ass cheeks clenched and flexed as she did, a vertical mouth with lips drawn into a tight line. Mocking him. His loins ached and he wasn't sure his pants would hold. Fury rose inside of him like a ball of nuclear flame and he kicked her in her ass hard as she started to flee. Margie sailed forward and began to fall. As she went down, her temple struck the corner of the coffee table in the center of the room with a *crunch*, and the table scooted away, the wood on wood chirp singing as the legs of the table squealed against the floor. It was a sharp thing, the coffee table's corner. All wood, metal, and glass. Fresh gouts of blood spewed from her head as she hit and sprawled out on the floor, face down.

Norman's eyes widened as he watched her. She began to twitch and convulse. None of her movements seemed voluntary at all, just spastic spasms as if her brain were malfunctioning. Something bad had happened when she hit her head. He hadn't meant to cause any real harm, only to teach her that good and perfect will of God, but it seemed a real number had been done on her. He had gone too far. Acted too rashly.

As she twitched and shook on the floor like a fish out of water, she shit herself. Feces spewed out of her with an abandon and freedom Norman had not known possible. It speckled her butt and the backs of her thighs and the calves of her legs as wet, spewing farts followed the debris, applauding loudly in the small room. He noticed only then that she was vomiting as well, a pool of grayish white gruel encircling her face.

And it stunk.

Norman was disgusted all at once. It still wasn't registering with him just what had happened, what he'd *done*, only that her shit smelled like rotten eggs and her vomit like rancid meat.

It was awful.

She twitched a few more times, the turds slowing their exit from her backside, her retches void of fluids now. Then she went still. No movement. Nothing.

"M-Margie?" he asked with a stammer. It was beginning to dawn on him what had happened. It had seemed as though he hadn't been there. Hadn't been the one to cause it. It was almost as if he'd just walked in here off the street and found her this way.

"Margie?"

Nothing. Stillness.

He moved across the room to her and stooped down

at her side. Norman thought he might have seen the slightest rise and fall of her back. Of her breathing.

Could she...is she still alive? he wondered in his clouded thoughts which were beginning to reach a chaotic speed.

But he couldn't be sure. His mind was racing now, darting here and there. What would he do? What would he say? How would he explain this? He thought he should call an ambulance but immediately cast this off, because with an ambulance would come cops and cops would put him in jail. They didn't care about shaved cunts—*Jesus forgive him*—and God's will and *they would put him in jail.* And how was he supposed to lead God back into a godless world like his mother had always promised he would if he were in jail?

Then, the voice of God came to him.

You'll explain nothing. You'll say nothing of this. Take her out of here. Clean up the house. Dump her body.

Was God was really saying this to him? Could it be real?

He thought not initially, but as he listened, he became certain the voice speaking to him was the Almighty Himself. The same voice that had told him of his marital destiny with this woman. The same reasoning. The same assuredness.

It was God, alright.

Yes, Lord! he thought, still panicked but hopeful now. *I'll do as you ask!*

Norman Reese looked down at Margie's bloody and beshitted body and smiled. His loin's appendage got even harder, aching and throbbing.

Jesus forgive me.

Chapter Two

Big Jim Dalton came into the station a little after nine that Friday morning. There were bags under his eyes and his skin was gray except over his cheekbones where it glowed in a pinkish hue. It had taken him two rather stout Bloody Marys to get his wheels turning properly that morning, but as they always did, they finally worked. After the drinks, he'd swished and gargled and swallowed half a bottle of Listerine to mask the fuel-like scent on his breath. These remedies, along with the mask of tomato-juice mix, left him confident—perhaps a bit overly so—that no one would notice the vodka on his breath. It wasn't like he planned to stand close to anyone while speaking, and his first stop would be the coffee pot, further quarantining the smell of his vice, but he knew he'd have to be careful.

He was thirty-eight years old and had grown into a full six feet, weighing in at two hundred pounds. He wasn't overweight, but his frame was large and solid, which had lent to the nickname Big Jim.

"Morning, Chief," his dispatcher, Barbara Leaks, said as he shuffled across the lobby toward the department proper. "There's a message on your desk from Charlotte Johnson. I think you should take a look at it."

Great, he thought. *Can't even walk through the fucking door, can't even get a cup of fucking coffee, and the shit starts.*

He sighed to himself, but relayed none of his disdain to Barbara. She was a kindly—if foul-mouthed—black woman in her mid-forties, her dark hair salted in a few streaks and strands. Her eyes matched her hair, so darkly brown they were almost black. She was probably thirty pounds overweight, and she carried it poorly.

"Any idea what it is?" Jim asked as he punched the code into the keypad next to the door which led in from the lobby. It *booped* and *beeped* and there was a metallic snapping sound when the door unlocked and he stepped through. A second after it closed, he heard it snap back, locking them into the station.

The dispatcher also served as receptionist. Barbara had been speaking to him through the window in the lobby when he'd first come in, but was now shouting out the door at the back of her office. Jim made his way down the hall, passing his own office, and rounded into hers. She had the coffee maker in there and he meant to have a cup of the swill. It was always swill, but it was hot and thick and had plenty of caffeine.

"She didn't say much," Barbara said. "Just that she needed to talk to you. I asked her if one of the other officers could help her, and she says no, gotta be you. I say okay, what's the message? She says tell Big Jim to call me soon as possible. It's about Margie. That's all she said."

"Margie?" Jim pondered aloud. "Did something happen to her?"

"How the fuck should I know? She ain't say, Chief. Just said it was about Margie and to have you call her soon's you got in. I done my part, shit's on you now. Pardon my French."

Jim nodded and poured coffee from the flask into a mug which read *#1 Chief* on its side. As he did this, he tried to hide the amused smirk spreading on his face. Barbara was one of a kind, and while he wouldn't let *any* of his officers speak so flippantly to him on the clock, he *did* let Barbara get away with it. She dealt firsthand with all the hell and shit coming through the office, and he figured she'd earned her cynicism.

He returned the flask to the warmer and blew gently over the steaming liquid. After several repeats of this ritual, he slurped a sip loudly from the rim. It was total shit, just as he had known it would be. Barbara couldn't make a decent pot of coffee to save her life, but it had the basic, and most important, ingredients: heat and caffeine.

He took another sip and winced as his tongue was scalded.

"Ahhh..." he sighed, scrunching his face in frustration, smacking a couple of times before turning to her. "Well, I guess I'll call her. How's your morning?"

Barbara snorted in mock disgust then laughed with equal distaste. "My morning? *My* morning sucks dick, pardon my motherfuckin' French, Chief. I got a dog who's a nocturnal little bastard. That's not French, he really is a bastard, *literally* by the way. Won't shut up all night long. So, I'm trying to sleep while this little son-of-a-bitch—again, that ain't French, Chief, he really is a son-of-a-bitch—he just howls all night. And you know what? It's at nothing! Nothing at all! I get up, I grab my Smith, I check the windows. Nothing there. Not a goddamn thing!" She paused for a moment, seeming to consider something, then finished in a subtle voice. "Pardon my French."

Jim was sorry he'd attempted to engage her in conversation now, but felt trapped. He wanted to turn from the room right then and head for his office, but he didn't want to be rude either. He *had* asked, after all.

"Sorry to hear that," he said. "But don't worry about the French, Barb. It really doesn't bother me."

"Well, it isn't fuckin' polite, so I apologize," she said and paused. "Pardon my French."

Jim smiled and nodded. Sensing a break in the conversation, he seized the opportunity and turned to go to his office.

"You won't forget to call Charlotte?" Barbara called

to his back as he was leaving. It wasn't really a question, though she'd intoned it like one.

He waved a free hand dismissively over his shoulder to reassure her he would and went back up the hall to his office. He went in and had almost made it all the way around to his chair when he turned and went back. He closed the door quietly after peeking out to make sure Barbara wasn't following him, then he went around his desk and sat down.

His chair creaked and groaned as he sat back and placed his mug of faux coffee on the desk. He looked around. Paperwork was piled in stacks here and there all over his desk. Arrest reports, citation copies, requests for time off, you name it. On the corner of his desk was a computer monitor connected to a tower under his desk, a dusty thing probably five years out of date, but it managed to accomplish what he needed it for. It wasn't as though the city was going to appropriate a dime for the PD to get some new computers, anyway.

Lying on the keyboard was the note to call Charlotte Johnson with a phone number printed in Barbara's neat, block hand. He stared at it a moment, grimacing. He'd only been Chief of Police for the Winnsboro PD a little over a year, and already he hated every moment of it. He missed patrol. Patrol was so much simpler. You just did your job, you filed your paperwork, you went home.

Repeat.

But being Chief was a whole new can of worms. There were the phone calls, the filing, the politics with the City Council and the Mayor. The babysitting of the officers. Dealing with the public. He longed for the days before the fiasco with Officer Tribbiani and the murders that had led to Chief Wilson's retirement. The days before he'd been thrust into this position by the Council and the Mayor.

You're the man for the job, they had said.

He exhaled.

He started to reach for the note and stopped about halfway to it. He paused a moment and thought about something he'd not thought of in a very long time. Something he'd not dwelled upon in well over twenty years. Something he'd done as a child, which had been integral to he and his friend's survival. He was unsure why it crossed his mind now, after so many years floating in the dormant part at the back of his mind, but it did.

Without any further thought, he tried it.

He extended his fingers toward the note, but kept his hand a good twelve inches away. He concentrated, his eyes narrowing to slits. He hadn't done this in years. He wondered again why, after all this time, it had occurred to him to do it now. But he had no answer. It just had. Something had urged him. It wasn't anything overt, nothing tangible, just an almost sub-conscious prodding.

The note on the keyboard rustled a little bit as though disturbed by a soft breeze. Jim focused his will, redoubling his efforts, and the rustling intensified, the paper softly scraping over the keys towards him. Then all at once, it slid off the keyboard, across a section of the desk, and floated into his fingers.

Still got it, he thought with an odd grin. *But why now?*

He'd discovered he'd been able to do this when he was a kid. When he and his friends had been playing in the woods outside of town. When the bullies had been coming for them.

Before that *thing* had happened.

He didn't like to think about it. It was really quite something, something only he and his friends from then had known about. And this thing he could do, which he hadn't even remembered he *could* do for so many years now, had proven to save their lives then. Had saved them from the bullies. From the...

The Glutton.

He shuddered at the memory and brushed it away. But the ability coming back to him just now brought the old memories, the old *nightmares*, back with it. Why had he stopped using such an incredible gift?

As strangely as it had started, it had just stopped. Not that he had become incapable of doing it, but he'd simply lost his inclination, his *urge,* to use it. It had vanished. After the *thing* in the woods, his need of it had seemed to be satiated, right along with his desire to use it.

And now, sitting at his desk, after more than two decades, all at once the urge had returned and the ability to use it as well.

But why?

He dismissed these thoughts after a few moments and reached for the phone. This time he picked up the receiver just like any regular person would and punched the number in for Charlotte Johnson.

The call was answered midway through the second ring.

"Chief?" Charlotte's voice came through the handset.

"Yes ma'am," Jim said. "What can I do f—"

She cut him off. "It's Margie," she said. "Something's happened."

Chapter Three

Norman had worked through the night.

Cleaning up the blood and shit had proven far more difficult than he'd imagined. Far more difficult than they made it look on TV, that was for sure. On TV, all you needed was a rag and a bottle of floor or carpet cleaner and everything looked like it was brand new. They didn't show you the smearing and the soaking into the pores of the wood, the discoloration even after the fourth, fifth, even *sixth* time you'd scrub, your arms screaming from the fatigue, eyes stinging with errant sweat. No, TV didn't show what it was really like at all.

But, in spite of all this, Norman thought he'd done an okay job. So long as no one looked too closely, that was. It wasn't perfect. He'd become convinced after his last tirade of curses—for which he had promptly asked Jesus for forgiveness—that it was *impossible* to really clean up a messy scene when there was blood involved. If anyone tried using any of those fancy forensic tricks he saw on the TV shows, they'd certainly find something. Especially in the bathtub drain. That was one thing he thought the TV had gotten right.

But, oh well. It was done, and to the best of his ability with what he had, and there was no sense in fretting anymore about it. It only made his headache worse. And after all, if they *did* find anything, they couldn't trace any of it to him.

Right?

He had pulled over on the side of an old dirt road just North of town with grass coming up down its middle to the level of his thighs. He dragged Margie's nude corpse out of the trunk of his car and rolled it into the ditch. Shut the trunk. Adjusted his throbbing member.

Jesus forgive me.

He checked to reassure himself the coast was clear. Both ways. It was just as clear as Ward Street had been when he'd gone to explain God's will to Margie; more so, actually. There was nothing out here. No houses, no cabins. In fact, he wasn't even sure why this road was here, if you could call it a road at all. He thought it might cut through to the highway a few miles further on, but he wasn't sure. Save for a couple of dilapidated barns—which clearly no one had used for decades—this little stretch of trail was completely deserted. It may as well have been on another world.

He smiled.

Norman hoisted Margie's lifeless body up on his shoulders and made his way into the woods. He remembered these woods from when he was a kid. Not that he'd been included in playing out here with any of the *other* kids around his age. Oh, no. Mother wouldn't allow that. It was the devil's work those kids had been up to. No good would have come from it. And there had been that poor man who had ended up in the nut-house and the teenagers that had vanished out here, his older brother Jake among them.

But he knew the woods here were a quiet place. Not many people came out here anymore. Kids stayed away. Hell, no one even hunted out here these days. It would be a good spot. And anyway, God had *told* him to bring her out here. That He would lead the way, and Norman Reese followed every word he got from the Almighty.

He pressed onward into the woods, dodging around branches and thickets. Margie hadn't been a large woman in life, but in death she seemed to weigh a thousand pounds. *Two thousand,* maybe. Norman decided most of the weight was in her tits—*Jesus forgive him*—and the thought of these brought that now-familiar warmth into his loins again. Made him imagine her on the floor of her living room, bare and bold.

Oh, and what God had allowed him to do with her after the cleanup. Oh, ladies and gentlemen...God was *GOOD!*

He smiled and trudged on.

Up ahead, he noticed a shape, a rather large one. It wasn't anything natural, certainly a manmade structure of some kind. It was, well, it was almost like a *house.*

A house? he thought through the pounding in his skull and the ache of his fatigued back. *Out here?*

He moved in closer and the shape shifted and enlarged inside the shadows, finally revealing itself to indeed be a house. There was no path to it that Norman could see. No driveway leading to it from the road. Nothing. Trees and bushes and thickets were grown up all around it, right to its edges. Like it had been built here but never used. Just dropped down right here in the middle of the woods. It certainly hadn't seen any company in quite some time, that was instantly evident. It was large, dusty, damp. Most of the windows were either busted into clawed shards or gone entirely, and a column rose into the trees to one side of the house where limbs from neighboring pines had grown through the walls in the course of time. The place seemed so utterly out of character with the nature all around it, Norman could scarcely remove the confused awe from his expression.

Then it occurred to him that this was the perfect spot for Margie. And it also occurred to him that God had led him right here.

That's right, Norman. This is my sanctuary. YOUR sanctuary. Come inside.

The voice. *Inside* his head but not *from* it. The voice of the Almighty.

"Yes, Lord!" he barked to the trees, and there was a flutter of wings as a crow flapped away from the area, cawing angrily in its retreat.

He climbed the steps, careful to avoid some obvious broken boards which looked to have been smashed in by someone's feet a long time ago. The place was in severe disrepair, and that was putting it mildly. The door at the top of the steps hung open and the morning light was beaming in through windows that were either there, half-shattered, or gone altogether, depending on which one you looked at.

I'm hungry.

God's voice again. But what the fuck did He mean He was hungry?

Jesus forgive me.

Norman walked inside and carried Margie's body to the back of the foyer which opened up just beyond the entryway. The boards beneath his feet groaned as he made his way, but they held firm enough. He dropped Margie onto the floor with a loud *thunk*.

That was when he heard her groan. Or, at least he *thought* he did.

He looked down at her and squinted his eyes, his pulse rising. She couldn't have moaned, could she? She was dead. All that blood and shit everywhere, she *had* to be dead. There was no way he'd just heard—

But he had. He had been right about hearing her groan, because now she was uttering another groan from her mouth and he could now see her beginning to move. She *wasn't* dead after all.

Oh, no...

"Wh-What's happening?" she mumbled, barely audible.

Norman began to panic.

What do I do? Oh God, oh Jesus, WHAT DO I DO?

The answer came a moment later, but not in words.

Margie managed to get up on her hands and knees. The gash on her temple was visible to Norman and he could see it pulsating, appearing thick and moist, though the blood was no longer flowing from the wound. Her arms quivered as she tried at first to stand, but when she couldn't get up, she settled for rolling over on her butt and propping herself against the far wall of the foyer.

Her eyes fluttered about, confusion and fear swimming in them. Her breaths were shallow and sharp, and her chest rose and fell with greater rapidity as she took in the surroundings. Norman could only stand there, locked in place by terror, feeling his pulse nearly bursting from his temples, his head aching worse than ever now.

She dropped her eyes and met his. Fear leaped out on her face like a startled animal. Terror welled in her eyes.

"Y-You!" she said, voice wavering. "You're a *monster!*"

Norman then laughed out loud, all fear melting away from him instantly as his mind fell on what he recognized as his purpose. That thing his mother had drilled into him his whole life.

You will lead God back into a godless world.

"I'm no monster," he said to her, faintly aware of a soft warbling sound kissing his ears, but ignoring it for the moment. "I'm doing God's work!"

That was when the shadows moved in around her and tore her head from her shoulders.

Blood sprayed from the stump of her neck. The head—eyes wide and mouth agape—rolled down the foyer and bumped to a stop at Norman's feet. It wasn't until the frozen, silently screaming head's eyes blinked that he reacted.

He stumbled back and his own silent scream filled his

mouth. Air hissed from his throat in rapid waves. He looked from the head to the shadow. It was now looking at him, though he wasn't sure just how he came to this conclusion. It was moving towards him. This hadn't been what he was expecting at all when he'd heard the voice of God calling him to this place. Had he been wrong? Had he been duped by a seducing, demonic spirit? What was this thing coming toward him, even now, if not a demon?

His mother's voice came to him then.

You be nice like Jesus, and as long as you have Jesus in your heart, the demons can't harm you. Because you're a child of GOD, Norman! My big, strong, godly man! You rebuke those things in the name of Jesus! The Jesus that Paul preached. And they have no option but to flee! You remember that and they will FLEE, Norman! My sweet, good boy!

Norman stared into the face of the approaching shadow-demon. A face had seemed to form on the thing, though it was made of nothing more than shifting shadows. It was in the area where a face *would* be, anyway, and he focused his gaze upon it. It seemed to be grinning at him, all smoky and vaporized.

Norman planted his feet. If God had led him here, then God would banish this demon from him. And he was God's chosen! His mother had told him so.

You're a child of God! his mother's voice screamed in his mind. *It has to flee!*

"I rebuke you in the name of Jesus Christ!" he shouted at the thing floating towards him, a mad twinkle in his eyes. "I rebuke you in the name of Jesus, of whom Paul preached!"

But the thing didn't flee. It didn't even flinch. It merely continued to stalk toward him, floating tendrils of smoky shadow trailing behind it.

Then, suddenly, the shadow flew toward Norman at speeds he was sure exceeded light. Something grabbed him about the throat and flung him up to the wall behind where he'd made his feeble stand. His feet dangled above the floor as he choked and clasped at the shadows, which oddly enough, seemed to have some substance. He was actually striking the thing, shadows or not. But it was no good. The grip on his throat was ironclad and his efforts only served to cause him to gasp out more precious air. There was a stink which enveloped him then, and Norman determined it was coming from the thing's mouth. If you could call it a mouth, that was. It stank like rancid meat that had been left out in the sun and spoiled.

Then the specter spoke and, to his horror, Norman recognized the voice. The voice of the one who had led him here. The one who had told him what to do with Margie.

It was the voice of God.

But it was coming from this *thing*. And it was laughing as it spoke.

"Jesus I know, and Paul I know," it said, its smoky face drawing right up to his nose.

It stunk abominably, and had Norman been able to breathe freely, he'd surely have gagged. Perhaps thrown up altogether.

"But who the fuck are you?"

Norman's bowels evacuated.

The pungent stench of shit wafted up to his nostrils as the thing let him go and he collapsed to the ground, his excrement splatting up his back like a toddler with a diaper full of the stuff. But Norman barely registered this. He instantly began to cry. Began to think of all his mother had said. How great he was in God's eyes. How much he was going to accomplish for the Kingdom of the Lord. Had she been wrong? *Could* she be wrong?

The thing began laughing again.

Norman shuddered and pressed himself against the

wall, willing himself to go right through the plaster and vanish inside. His trembling body began to quake with fear. He wished he could run. Run away as fast as he could. Go home. Go see his mother. Let her reassure him. Make sense of all of this for him. She could do that. She could always make sense of everything. Explain it to him. *Show him*. Then, with his fears and doubts put into proper perspective, she could show him again just how *much* she loved him.

But Norman's legs were as mushy as the shit in his pants and the thing continued to laugh.

"Norman," it said with a deep, inhuman voice. *"Norman, Norman, Norman..."*

He could only continue to cry and stew in his waste as he gaped up at the specter before him. He tried to form words, maybe scream, but the only thing coming out was a hoarse, rasping exhale which tore at his throat like claws.

Then the thing swooped back down to him, right in his face. The stink was back, but Norman could hardly register it now. He was on the verge of convulsing. His head pounded and the terrible rasping exhale that wasn't really a scream continued to shred his throat. Snot ran down over his lips and tears streaked his face.

The thing cackled again.

"Norman," it said one final time. *"I think we could help each other."*

Norman's rasp hitched and caught in his throat. He couldn't breathe. His body had stopped trembling, as though he'd been suddenly locked completely in place. All he could do was blink stupidly at the creature.

"H-Help each other?" he finally croaked, not more than an eon later. "Wh-what do-do you mean?"

The thing floated above Norman then. He thought he could detect a smile in the shadowy face, though it was difficult to be sure.

"You have appetites," it started, *"and I have appetites. These appetites need to be satiated. One cannot grow strong without nourishment, yes?"*

"R-right," Norman replied, a bewildered look encompassing his tear-streaked face.

"*Right, indeed,*" The thing went on, the shadowy head nodding. *"So what do you say, Norman? Want to feed our appetites together?"*

Norman's fear seemed to slip away. Not all at once, but like a tide slowly flowing back into the sea. It was receding because he was finally realizing with whom he was now speaking. The voice had been there all along, and while the form didn't seem to match at all with the pictures and mental conjurings his life had wrought, it dawned on him now just who this was. It filled him with not only hope, but pure, exquisite joy. This was no specter. This was no demon. No hellish abomination.

"Yes, Lord!" Norman said, his whispering voice cracking with delight. "Hear am I, send me!"

The shadow-demon that wasn't a demon cackled again.

"*I have such plans for you, Norman!*"

His mother's voice filled his mind again, her sure and confident voice which had told him all his life just how important he was to God's plan for the world.

You will lead God back into a godless world.

Then they were both laughing in the rotting house, Norman's pants full of shit, and the decapitated body of Margie Johnson gaping up at them both with an expression of permanent terror mere feet away.

They laughed heartily and long.

PART TWO:

Provisions

Friday, August 5, 2016

Chapter Four

Something had happened here. Something bad.

Charlotte Johnson had told Jim what she knew, which wasn't very much. Margie had gone home after a late dinner with her and was supposed to meet with her again this morning for breakfast at The Bakery, a local restaurant. Charlotte had been there at seven, prompt as ever, perusing the menu and even ordering her regular blueberry and pecan pancakes. However, Margie had never shown. Hadn't answered any phone calls or texts, either.

This wasn't like her daughter, Charlotte had explained, so she'd gone to Margie's house to check on her. She thought perhaps she had come down ill or something, so she wanted to be sure her daughter was okay. Charlotte had found her daughter's car in the driveway—not that she'd expected anything else—and gone to the door.

She had knocked for a solid five minutes, yelling in through the door. At one point, she had even gone around the side and knocked on the window of her daughter's bedroom.

No response.

After failing to get a response upon a second tour of duty at the front door, she had almost turned to leave when she finally thought to try the door.

It had been unlocked.

She'd gone inside. Something had been off, she'd told him, but she couldn't put her finger on just what. Nothing seemed *out* of place, per se, but several things seemed to be in the *wrong* place. The coffee table, for instance. It had been moved. And the rug beneath it was gone altogether. There had also been a strong smell of what she thought might have been Clorox Bleach.

Charlotte had checked the entirety of the house and confirmed that Margie wasn't there. Not at all. Margie's bed was made in such a way that it didn't appear anyone had slept in it the night before.

And the bathroom. It was so...*clean.*

That just wasn't like Margie at all. She was a bit of a mess, her mother explained, and it was never more apparent than in her bathroom.

Typically, the trashcan was completely full; swatches of tissues and wrapped up tampons, Q-tips, exfoliating pads, et cetera, et cetera. There would be dried toothpaste in the sink and the tub seemed to not have been cleaned since the house had been built way back when Ike had been president.

But now it was...*immaculate.* Furthermore, the strong scent of Clorox seemed to be coming most strongly from the bathroom itself.

"Maybe she went on a cleaning spree?" Jim had asked Charlotte on the ride over to Ward Street.

Charlotte had shaken her head.

"No sir, Chief," she said, her eyes distant and concerned. "You don't know my Margie like I do. I used to have to threaten her with a thorough hiding just to get her to pick her room up when she was a girl. Never mind cleaning anything with bleach. Just isn't her. You might think so, the way she's always put together so nice, but God help her, she lives in a pig-sty, I tell you what."

Jim had nodded and kept silent as she went on.

"I'm telling you, something's wrong, Chief. Something's happened. I don't know what, but it just ain't like her. I don't mind telling you I've about worried myself sick."

Jim regarded her sideways from the captain's seat of his Police Tahoe. She was an elderly woman, perhaps in her mid-sixties. A near perfect sphere of cotton sat atop her wrinkled head which shone almost an iridescent blue when the light trickled through at the right angle. She had deep lines of age all over her face, and a permanent frown was etched over her mouth. She wore a rose-colored tent of a dress that was common with older women of the area, which sported a wreath of flowers around the neck opening. Her hands sat folded on the top of her purse, the knuckles white and smooth, contrasting with the spotted wrinkling of her hands.

"Well, let's not get too worked up just yet, Mrs. Johnson," Jim said, returning his eyes to the road. "She's a grown woman, after all. I'm sure there's a rational explanation to all this."

But as he stood here in her living room, his sharp eyes scanning and taking everything in, he wasn't so sure there was anything rational at all about the situation.

The coffee table was a big problem. It was in the middle of the room, like coffee tables often are, but it seemed to be pushed so far back from any of the furniture that it would be rendered totally useless from a practical point of view. It wasn't anything definitive, he knew, but it was sure odd. And there was the pungent odor of bleach permeating through the house. Upon further inspection, he confirmed what Charlotte had told him. It was *certainly* coming from the bathroom. Mostly, anyway.

The bathroom seemed to sparkle. The whites were so white they almost hurt his eyes to behold beneath the artificial lights over the sink. Even the grout, from waist level down, looked brand new. Someone *had* been cleaning in here, that was for damn sure. He peered down at the drain and saw a sparkling chrome stopper, the twisting kind that drops in when you turn it. It gleamed and dazzled him with blue and yellow prisms as the bright light above danced off its slick surface. He leaned in, trying to block the light with his head to dispense with the light show, but then he stopped.

Something had caught his eye.

He leaned in further to get a better look. Charlotte was standing behind him in the hallway, clutching her purse and breathing deeply. She was agitated and upset, and Jim could understand why. Her daughter had vanished, with her car in the driveway, apparently after what appeared to be a rather rushed cleaning spree.

He stopped leaning in and squinted. The thing that had caught his eye was a small brownish spot on the lip of the drain, just beneath the twist-top stopper. It was small, and from a distance could've looked like a small rust spot. Just some patina forming around the drain. Nothing to get worked up about. Only now, from his new vantage point, he could see it was *not* rust.

A sick feeling hit him in the bottom of his gut.

He stood and returned to the living room. Charlotte politely stepped out of his way as he passed into the hall, then she followed him back to the living room, her hands still wringing the top of her purse. Jim made his way back to the coffee table.

It was just all wrong.

The coffee table was in the middle of the room, a good six feet from the couch and sitting chairs. And there was nothing on it. It wasn't littered with magazines or decorations of any kind. There were rings on the wood where glasses had sat and condensation had soaked into the panels. He could see a filmy, tacky spot where something had spilled and not been wiped up properly. And that made sense. Charlotte had said her daughter lived somewhat dirty in the house. Maybe she'd spilled some white wine and not bothered to do anything about it. She certainly hadn't been using coasters, the evidence was all over the top of the coffee table.

This thing has been used, he thought, *and a lot, but not from way over here.*

He also noticed a slight difference in the coloring of the floor.

The flooring was an array of thin, parallel wooden slats, probably over thirty years old. They were bunched together in spots and age and moisture had caused them to curl up into sharp peaks here and there. There was a large square area, directly in front of the furniture, that was a half-shade lighter than the rest. Like something had been there.

A rug?

And the area that was lighter would be where a person would normally put a coffee table. A coffee table where you sat your sweating glasses of water and where you spilled a drop of white wine. A coffee table that was *used.*

He turned back to the coffee table and noticed another discoloration. There, on the edge nearest to him and the front door, was slightly lighter than the rest of the table.

Jim knelt down and sniffed at the corner. His nose instantly scrunched and he blanched.

Bleach.

He noticed something else as he pulled his face away from the sharp odor. It was a thin string. A fiber of something caught where the wrap of thin metal edging met at the corner of the table.

A hair?

He turned back to the discolored floor. Then he

looked up the hallway towards the bathroom. Then back to the edge of the coffee table with the suspicious fiber.

Then he met Charlotte's eyes.

"Ma'am," he said somberly as he stood, "we need to back out of here. I think this just might be a crime scene."

Chapter Five

Three hours later, there was a full team of forensic specialists filling the house. Jim had called in the Wood County Forensics Squad and got things put into motion. Samples were being taken from the bathroom, the living room, the coffee table. The fiber he'd seen was indeed a single strand of hair. The rust spot he'd seen on the drain had indeed been blood. More had been found in the drain pipe itself, as well.

Something terrible had happened here.

Jim had taken as much information from Mrs. Johnson as he could before the team had arrived. Upon seeing the forensics team moving in, Charlotte Johnson had broken down into sobs for a while, and it had taken two female officers and Jim himself a solid thirty minutes to console her to a reasonable degree. Not that there was anything reasonable about their consolations. They were after information, and all Mrs. Johnson could be thinking was her daughter was either dead or had been taken. Whatever had happened, it had been violent, and her daughter had been involved. When Jim thought of it that way, the term reasonable seemed like an abominable thing to expect out of the poor old woman.

But eventually, she had pulled herself together. Once she had calmed down enough to speak coherently, Jim had started right in on his questions once more. Who did Margie associate with? Who were her friends? Did she have any boyfriends? Had she had any plans to go out of town in the near future? Did she have any enemies?

Anyone with a grudge against her?

"No, no, nothing like that," Charlotte had said, dabbing her eyes with a tissue. "Everyone loved her." She paused, hardening her face. "Everyone *loves* her."

Jim nodded, jotting notes down in a small flip notepad.

"She *did* have a boyfriend," Charlotte continued, gulping as she did. "But they broke up a few weeks ago. Strange young man, he is. His family has that weird church. Revival Rock, they call it. It's out on the edge of town, you know the one?"

Jim nodded, an involuntary grimace masking his face at the name of the church.

Charlotte continued. "Margie was going to services out there until recently. She was a children's ministry worker over there, you know. Just loved the kiddies. But she stepped down from her duties there and she's been looking for another place to worship these past few weeks. I told her a thousand times if I told her once she had no business in a place like that. They're crazy, I tell ya! All running around with their blasted flags and loud music. Speaking in tongues in public to boot!"

She stopped a moment, her brow furrowed in frustration and what Jim perceived to be resentment.

She went on. "They just don't have any order there at all! It just ain't Christian to not have no order, I tell you! I told her she needed to come with me to the First Baptist Church, that's where nice young Christian girls go. Nice young Christian men, too. Why, I know more than a handful of fine young men there who'd be a fine partner for her. She could find herself a good husband there. But," she trailed off, fidgeting with her tissue, which was now mostly destroyed with tears and snot. "Well. She ain't listened to me worth a hoot in years."

Fresh tears filled her eyes.

"You say she has a boyfriend?" Jim asked, trying to keep her on track before she went back into full hysterics. A part of him hated the callousness his job required, but there was no way around it.

Charlotte shook her head in the negative.

"*Had* a boyfriend," she snapped. "Margie broke it off a few weeks back. Crazy coot told her *God* had told him they were supposed to be married. Just dropped it down in his head. And he expected her to take his word on it! That's what I'm telling you about this place. They're just plain nuts, that's all there is to it! Always babbling about 'God said this' and 'God said that'. To hear it their way, God can't catch his breath from all the squabblin' He does!"

Jim was nodding, resisting the urge to roll his eyes. He knew George and Cherry Reese. Knew them all too well, in fact. He didn't know them *personally*, but he'd had run-ins with the family before. One from his childhood, in particular. Jim wasn't entirely sure about the rest of the family, but Jake Reese really *had* been nuts.

"Okay, so she *had* a boyfriend," Jim started, making sure he had the facts straight. "And you say this young man's family runs the Revival Rock Ministries church? Is it their son?"

"Sure is," Charlotte piped back without hesitation. "Norman's his name. Norman Reese. They dated for some time, but she broke it off when he got all funny. Seemed like a nice enough boy at first, but he was just weird. Kept asking her to change how she dressed and had all these weird notions. You ask me, he was trying to get her to be just like that mother of his. Cherry's her name, like the fruit. Or is it a berry? Is a berry a fruit?"

Jim's eyes were wide and confused at how the conversation had just derailed. He had no fucking clue what the hell a cherry was, at least not its scientific category.

"Ma'am, I have no idea," he said with an incredulous shrug.

"Well," Charlotte went on with a dismissive wave of her hand, the crumpled tissue wadded in her palm, "whatever it is, that ain't the point. Her name's Cherry, like the...the *food*. And that woman is crazy as a coot, you ask me. Seems they all are from that family, ain't no lie."

Jim nodded and jotted.

"As crazy as they are, I don't see them doing no harm to my baby girl, though," Charlotte went on, her gaze drifting off to nowhere. "They're just all wrong for my Margie. I think everyone has the right to serve God as they choose, but there's a right way and wrong way. People's free to be wrong, I say. Ain't no crime in being wrong. But it don't change the fact that they're *wrong*." She shook her head looking back to Jim. "She should have been at the First Baptist Church with me. None of this would have happened if she'd just come home!"

Fresh sobs burst forth now, and Jim reached out and put a hand on her shoulder reassuringly as he flipped his notepad closed.

"Now, now," he said, "we don't know *what* has happened, not yet. Maybe nothing at all. You gotta keep positive, Mrs. Johnson."

His face was soft and full of empathy. She smiled up at him through the tears, sniffing back clots of snot.

"You're right," she said, wiping the debris from her face with the destroyed tissue. "You're gonna find out, aren't ya, Jim? You're gonna find my Margie?"

Her face was suddenly full of hope as it gazed up at him, the webbed lines around her eyes seeming to shimmer from her tears. He wanted to tell her that, yes, he would find her and deliver her back in one piece, whole and healthy. He wanted to tell her anything at all that would give her peace and comfort. But he couldn't do that. He couldn't get her hopes up, only to possibly be dashed to ribbons later. Sure, they might find Margie okay, but he didn't think so. Something bad had happened in that house, and though he wouldn't tell Mrs. Johnson so, he was all but certain it had been a homicide.

Jim elected instead to smile at her, his most diplomatic and emphatic smile.

"I'm gonna do my best, I promise you that."

She nodded, her chin trembling. She was old, but she was no fool. Jim could see she understood what that meant, and damnit if he couldn't actually see her heart break in two just then.

Jim looked around and found one of the female officers who had helped him with her during her initial meltdown and motioned for her to come over. She came trotting over to them and stood next to them. He looked back to Charlotte.

"Now, Charlotte, you go with officer Seabolt here. She'll see that you get home. Is there anyone we can call to come be with you for the time being?"

Charlotte thought for a moment, obvious torment on her face as she thought.

"My pastor's wife. Shelly's her name. Shelly James."

"Okay," Jim said and nodded at Seabolt to make sure she understood to call them. "We'll get you home and have them come over."

"Thank you, Jim," she said with a sad attempt at a smile.

"Not at all, Charlotte," he said.

Officer Seabolt led Charlotte away to her cruiser and got her situated. Then the stout woman officer jumped into the driver's seat and pulled away from the curb.

Jim looked up and down the street after they were gone. People were standing out in their yards and on their porches, watching the big *to-do* going on in their little universe. He lost himself in his thoughts for several minutes as he tried to decide what his next move would be with the investigation.

"Big Jim!" a voice shouted to him from Margie's house, breaking him out of his daze.

Jim whirled around, slightly startled, and saw Jack Fletcher stepping down from Margie's porch, holding an evidence bag and coming towards him. Jim met him halfway.

"Whatcha got, Jack?" he asked, jerking his chin towards the bag.

"Well," the younger man said, "I can't say just what happened, but you were right to call us in. *Something* went down in there. We found a lot of blood and fecal matter in the drain of the bathtub, and evidence of the same on the floor of the living room. It's all been mopped up and bleach ruined most of it, but not all. We're bagging up a few samples for the lab."

Jack paused a moment, his stance uneasy.

"Th-There's something else, Jim."

Jim's eyes narrowed slightly. "What?" he asked.

Jack's mouth scrunched in a grimace and he looked around. "The old lady gone?" he asked before revealing.

"Yeah, yeah, just sent her home with one of my officers. What did you find?"

"Well, keep in mind, it's still not definitive. Margie Johnson's not the first person to live in this place, so until we can run some tests back at the lab we can't say for sure how old any of this evidence is, but..."

The forensics man looked to his hands, which were fidgeting aimlessly with the baggie he held.

"What is it, Jack?" Jim said after a moment, prodding

him on.

Jack blew his cheeks out like a blowfish and huffed an exasperated sigh.

"We found what appears to be semen. It was there with the blood on the floor."

"Jesus," Jim muttered through an audible sigh. He rubbed a hand through his hair.

Jack was nodding, that grimace still donning his face.

"Yeah. Like I said, we won't know more until we run some tests, and chances are the DNA won't be in the system. Hell, it rarely is. It's a great system, but most of the fucks we bust around here for stuff like this aren't serials. They're first-timers. So if he's not in the system, we won't have a hit. You'll have to gather suspects and take samples."

Jim nodded knowingly. "Great."

"You got anything to go on yet?"

"Not much."

"Any names?"

"One. Boyfriend. *Ex*-boyfriend, I should say."

"That's always the most likely suspect."

"I know it. I'm gonna try to find him and talk to him."

"Good deal. Let me know if and when you have samples for comparison."

"Will do. And you keep me informed on what you guys find."

"You got it. We're gonna run a match test on the blood and hair and fecal matter. I'm almost sure it's going to be from the same person, and we have the resident's blood-type, so we'll match that too. But you'll be my first phone call, Jim."

"Thanks, Jack."

Jack nodded and turned to the forensics van to stow

the evidence. Jim turned back and looked at the house.

What happened to you, Margie? he thought.

Chapter Six

Cherry Reese walked into her church around three o'clock that afternoon.

She liked to think of Revival Rock Ministries as *her* church. And it really was, if you got right down to it. Her husband George and she had been faithful attendants at Faith Creek for years when that maniac pastor over there had decided he no longer needed their input—or anyone else's, for that matter—on the decision-making of church business. That rattlesnake had even gone so far as to threaten taking them before the congregation on a Sunday morning for church discipline. He was going to take her and her husband, along with about five other elders who had been on the recently dissolved leadership board, in front of the church and 'expose' their heresy. *THEM!* They, who were faithful and were no doubt hearing from God every single day in the clearest of voices on the direction which they were supposed to be steering the church.

She couldn't help it if the pastor himself wasn't hearing from the Almighty. It was likely something he was doing in his personal life which had turned off his link with their Creator. Probably some *sin.* Perhaps he was having relations outside his marriage. Perhaps he was gambling over in Shreveport on the weekends.

He might even have started to take *drink.*

She wasn't sure exactly *what* he had been up to that had cut his ear off from the Lord, but she was sure it was *something.* Most likely it was drink, if she had to guess.

Nothing cut you off faster from Jesus than allowing alcohol to cross one's lips. Nothing on earth, and that was as sure as her salvation.

But, whatever the reason, he wasn't hearing from God anymore, and she and her husband obviously were, no doubt about it. They didn't take drink. They certainly didn't gamble—wretched, awful sin—or take up with others outside their marriage.

Well, not in a long time, anyway.

Her husband, George, hadn't *always* been a Christian, you see. Many years back, in the early years of their marriage, George had had what Cherry liked to refer to as a *wandering libido.* She couldn't call it merely a wandering *eye*, for if it were only his eye that had wandered, his phallic member would never have found its way to being buried in her sister's velvet hollow, balls deep. She never would have found him thrusting into her sister on their own marriage bed that day, Carla's breasts—much larger than Cherry's own, she had to admit, especially back then before she'd had her two boys—bouncing up into her face as she moaned, writhing her hips into his as the wet slaps assaulted Cherry's ears.

No, a mere wandering eye wouldn't have led to all that. It was that Goddamned—*no, that's not a curse, God really does damn it*—libido of his. Something which he'd not been able to exorcise himself of until sometime later, after weeks and weeks of good, godly counseling with a local lay preacher. George had tried repeatedly, time and again, to satisfy his urges with his wife, always rolling over to her in bed, his penis urging into the flesh of her buttocks. He would cup her breast, slide his hand down to her crotch, trying to awaken that sinful heat in her groin.

But she was simply stronger than he was. All women were, for the most part, anyway. Women didn't have that curse of testosterone dangling between their legs, torturing them for release, for escape.

She'd swat his hand away and rebuke his lust. After all, they weren't ready for children just yet, and everyone knew that good Christian people only allowed that act to take place for the procreation of families. She never understood why God had made the act of reproducing such an overtly grotesque action. He was *God* after all, He could simply have made it occur naturally or immaculately, the way He'd done with Mary, the mother of Jesus. Mary hadn't needed to allow some throbbing piece of flesh to enter into her to create the perfect Son of God. So why did she?

But far be it from her to question God and His ways. He'd made it the way He'd made it, and that was that. But she didn't have to like it.

However, after the weeks of good, godly counseling with the lay preacher they'd met at a tent revival, she'd come to understand that occasionally she would have to open herself to her husband to let him get the creamy demon out of his loins so he could control himself. After all, did she *want* to find him thrusting and fucking—*no, that isn't a curse either, that's what sex is when there's no love or procreation involved*—her sister? Of course not! He shouldn't be thrusting or *fucking* at all. That was supposed to be set aside for the procreation of children and rarely for the use of exorcising the swelling devil that resides in every man's crotch, but *only* in the marriage bed.

You could always repent afterward.

But she couldn't really say she'd never laid with another man. Well, she technically *could* say that. Because he hadn't been a man, not then. He was a man now, she knew well enough, but not when she'd taught him God's good and perfect will for how a man was supposed to treat a daughter of the Most High. And she had to admit she'd rather enjoyed it, especially when her sex had seemed to explode around his throbbing—albeit not terribly large—phallus.

Cherry was unable to distinguish all of the inconsistencies in her mind at all. If you had tried to point them out to her, you'd have to know about what she'd done with that young man. No one knew about that but she and him. And never mind all that, even if you *did* know about it, Cherry would argue it wasn't sinful to *teach*, now was it? You're supposed to raise a child up in the way that he should go so that when he is old, he will not depart from it. Wasn't that true? That's what *her* Bible told her, anyway.

Cherry walked past the reception desk in the fellowship hall of the church. The fat old lady—Rhonda Jacobs was her name—was there, clicking and clacking away on the keyboard of the church's computer, making a poor attempt to appear busy. Cherry knew better. Rhonda did two things well in this world. One, she knew how to sound pleasant and inviting on the telephone when people called the church, and secondly, she knew how to play a mean game of computer solitaire.

Cherry was sure Rhonda was doing the latter.

It didn't matter, though. She wasn't here to deal with that issue of poor stewardship on this day. There were more pressing matters at hand. There was a family to deal with. A *young* family, cursed with thinking that they could hear from God something contradictory to what she and her husband were hearing.

To what *she* was hearing.

The young patriarch was on their praise and worship team, and played electric guitar. He played well enough. *Really* well, if she were to be perfectly honest. But she wasn't going to be perfectly honest at all about that, though, now was she? Not Cherry Reese.

The young man had come to their church some years ago, he and his wife, and before long had been asked to join the team. He was about the same age as her Norman, who was the praise team leader. They had heard early on from God that Norman was going to do great things for the Kingdom, and that God was going to use him and his wonderful abilities on the guitar and his silky voice to lead thousands upon thousands to Jesus on their knees in weeping worship. That he was going to lead God back into this godless world. They had also seen dollar signs—courtesy of Jesus Himself—in their son's abilities, and that never hurt anything, either.

But this little shit-stain—*no, that's not a curse, not when it so perfectly captures the symbolism*—had felt led to start leading some of the worship songs himself! *Instead of* Norman! The nerve.

Such heresy was simply beyond her imagination. That *anyone* didn't see the superior calling on *her* boy's life to their own could be nothing more than willful blindness, if not outright rebellion against God Himself.

Of course, pride played a great part in it as well. That old devil pride. It had caused more than one issue in their tenure with Revival Rock, and more often than not it was always someone thinking that *they*—not the Reeses—had heard something from God that must be brought forward to the church. Some new ministry here, some new praise song there. You name it.

The fact that after the Reeses would run these people out of the church with their heels burning with hellfire they would often institute the very thing these people brought before them was beside the point. God had told *them* to do it, not some lay fool. If God wanted to move in a particular way, he could tell the *Reeses.* He didn't need to tell anyone else. He *wouldn't* tell anyone else.

And now she and her husband were going to have to send this little family down the road for trying to create division on their team. Their *son's* team, at that. Her special Norman. The one whom God set apart for His divine work in Winnsboro, Texas, and onward to all the nations of this sick and dying world.

She walked up to her husband's office door, knocked lightly twice, and then entered the room.

Her husband was already there, along with Dave Bowers, the young man in question. Cherry put on her best phony smile. It was always accompanied with the slight tilt of her head, the overly produced hair barely swaying with the motion.

She wanted to tear the boy's head off his shoulders and bathe in his blood, but she figured that wouldn't be very in line with modern Christian teaching. Still, she let her mind linger on the image a moment, relishing it.

"Daaave," she said, stretching the name out and bringing the pitch down in an even forty-five-degree maneuver. "How are you today?"

Dave looked at her stoically. She could tell he didn't like her very much. Dave never had much of an ability to hide his emotions or distastes, she had observed. You could always tell what he thought of a person right off the bat. He didn't possess her ability to mask distaste, another reason he had to go. Uniform happiness and devotion were required of anyone in a leadership role of the church. Anything less might let others see that perfect unity wasn't actually in play, and that could not be allowed.

Nevertheless, Dave forced a smile and nodded to her.

"Mrs. Reese," he said, "I'm fine, thank you. How are you?"

Cherry was sure the heat which had flushed her face was visible to some degree, but she simply hadn't been able to stop it in time. He'd called her *Mrs.* Reese. She liked to be called Pastor Cherry. It was what all of their good parishioners called her, the ones who recognized her authority in this house of the Lord, the ones who didn't go around questioning what they were doing or trying to justify their actions with the Scriptures.

But she managed to maintain her smile and move into the room, shutting the door behind her.

"I'm blessed, blessed, blessed!" she exclaimed as she let the door close with a moderate bang. She looked back at the door as it went home, wishing for a moment she had the strength to tear it out of its frame and beat the little bastard—*no, this isn't a curse either, this young man's father had never married his mother*—to death with it.

More smiles ensued all around and Cherry came to the corner of the office where her husband was sitting in a chair opposite Dave, who himself sat on a small couch. She sat beside her husband.

"Sorry I'm late," she began, the faux smile still beaming brightly, "I got held up on the way over. Bunch of police fuss over on Ward Street."

George looked over too her, his eyes raised.

"Oh?" he started. "Do you know what happened?"

"No," she said, shaking her head, "no I didn't get any details, just waited to get around the traffic. I was visiting with the treasury chairman over at the Pine Street Baptist church about donating to the rehab, so I was stuck for a few minutes."

"I see," George said, turning back to Dave. "Well, Dave and I have been discussing a few things here."

"Oh?" Cherry said, turning her head from George to Dave and nodding.

"Yes, ma'am," Dave said. "I was trying to explain to your husband that I was merely trying to bring a new song to the group to try out at practice and then maybe to play at Sunday worship eventually. You guys and Norman had a meeting about wanting some original work brought into the team and I've got stacks of original work. I'm not trying to trump anyone else, and I'm certainly not trying to cause division on the team. I honestly thought I was doing what was asked of us, and now I feel like I'm in the hot-seat for it."

He finished what he was saying and kept his stare firmly on Cherry. This little shit-stain—*remember, not a curse*—was so full of pride and envy for her son it was unbelievable. Sure, they had had this meeting he was referring to, and yes, they *had* said they wanted to start bringing original music to their team. God had, after all, called them to be the next big thing in Contemporary Christian Worship. They were supposed to start recording songs and concerts like some of the big non-denominational outfits in Dallas and New York and Australia. And God was going to show His unending power by doing it out of little old Winnsboro, population thirty-five hundred.

But what Dave and the *rest* of the team had failed to understand, what should have been intrinsically understood and glaringly obvious, was that God was going to use *Norman* to bring forth these songs. It was *Norman* who was going to lead the team to greatness. Not them. They were merely there to complete Norman's sound. It was about *Norman*, and how that had been missed was beyond her. Hadn't they heard him play? Heard him sing?

"Why didn't your wife come, Dave?" Cherry asked, processing all her baffled disbelief covertly in the background.

Dave smiled, unamused. "I told her to stay home. Didn't want her caught up in all of this."

Cherry and George exchanged shocked looks.

"Caught up in what, Dave?" George asked, almost

sounding genuine.

Dave looked back and forth between them.

"Look, I'm no fool, okay?" he said. "I see what's going on here. I didn't want to believe it for the longest time because I honestly thought I was just letting my thoughts get away from me, but I know better now."

"What is it you think you know?" Cherry interjected. That heat was rising back to her cheeks, and she was powerless to stop it.

"That this team, heck, this whole *church,* is all about you guys. You guys and Norman. And you know what? That's fine. It's *your* church. You started it, you grew it, I get it. But let's not play any games here, alright? You want your son in a spotlight. That's really the ultimate goal here, am I right? You want *him* in the spotlight, not Jesus, not revival, none of that. You want to promote him and you'll use anybody dumb enough to fall for it in the process to help make that happen."

The heat in her face was now blazing. She had no doubt that the thick, clumping layers of makeup on her face were no longer concealing her fury. Her eyes were certainly betraying her as well. She felt her lip quiver. Her inner voice was screaming at this insolent fool.

Well, of course it's about Norman, you idiot!

But she could never say that out loud. She just shook her head.

"I'm sorry you feel that way Dave, but I'm afraid you've got it all wrong."

"Do I?" Dave quipped back defiantly.

"You do, son," George said, a slow nod bobbing his head.

"This isn't about promoting any person," Cherry continued, ignoring her ignorant husband's interjection, "this is about following God's will. This is about making sure that the people being used in the church are working *within* their callings. If someone is trying to operate outside their calling, it's our job to reel them in."

She said this last part making a show of her hands as though she had just caught a fish on a pole and was pulling it in.

"You have to understand authority," she continued, "and you're going to have to get on board with the fact that God called *us* to recognize a person's calling and to utilize it in His Kingdom. He didn't call you to do that."

Dave laughed out loud now and sat forward, clasping his hands. He was shaking his head.

"I figured you'd say something like that," Dave said. "Hell, I could've written the script for this meeting."

"You need to watch your mouth!" Cherry piped up, referring to his misuse of the word 'hell'.

He looked at her befuddled.

"What?"

"I'm sorry, I think it's evident that there is a real problem here. We can't have people living in sin in leadership here at the church."

"Living in *sin?*" Dave asked, his hands spread wide now in utter confusion. "What are you—"

"I'm afraid so," Cherry said, cutting him off. "You're in open rebellion to the church's authority and you're using profane language on top of that. We have to represent Christ here, so I'm sorry, but you're going to have to be stepped-down from the team."

Dave's confusion was giving way to anger now. He looked from Cherry to George.

"You gonna jump in here, George?" he asked.

"That's *PASTOR* George to you, young man!" Cherry suddenly burst out. "You will address your authority with the proper respect!"

George was sitting back in his chair now, twiddling

his thumbs—*literally twiddling his thumbs*—and staring at the ground. He had taken his place behind his wife, the *real* chief in these here parts.

Dave stood and walked towards the door.

"You know what?" he said as he reached the door, his hand falling onto the knob. "I've been struggling with this for a while now, but you've just made it perfectly clear. You're nuts! You're out of your mind *nuts,* lady! You guys have stars in your eyes for Norman, and that's fine. Well, I don't know about George there, but you do for sure, woman! He can barely play a chord progression and the only tune he can carry sounds like a fucking nasal infection!"

He threw the door open as Cherry stood to her feet, rage permeating from every pore.

"How *dare* you speak to me with such language?!" she hissed at him. "You're off the team for good now, young man! You understand me? And you're going to have to stand before the church for discipline!"

Dave laughed as he stepped through the door.

"Get fucked, Cherry," he said calmly. "God curse the day I ever thought He was trying to move here. My family and I will find a new church."

He stepped out and slammed the door. It rattled in its frame a moment and then came to rest, forgetting the commotion.

Cherry was standing there next to her husband, who was *still* twiddling his thumbs and staring at the floor. She was shaking with anger now and her face was so red it looked as though hot, molten lava would erupt from her face at any moment.

She turned to her husband.

"Lots of help you were, George!" she barked at him. "You were going to let him talk to me that way?"

George finally looked up at her and shrugged as he stood.

"Honey," he said, "there was nothing to be done. If he wanted to act that way and leave the church, that's his prerogative. It's done. He's gone. Isn't that what you wanted?"

She glared at her husband for what seemed like a truncated eternity. Finally, her face softened and the heat dissipated from her cheeks.

"I suppose so," she said. "That boy was nothing but problems for poor Norman, anyway. Speaking of, where is our boy?"

George shrugged again.

"No idea. I haven't seen him all day."

Just then there was a knock on the door and Rhonda Jacobs stepped into the office. Her bespectacled face was wrought with concern.

"Yes, Rhonda?" Cherry asked impatiently.

"Sorry to interrupt, pastors," she said politely with a weak voice. "But someone is here to see you. Well, to see Norman, actually, but when I said he wasn't here, he asked to see the two of you."

Cherry could feel that familiar heat return to her face again as her patience wore thin.

"Who's looking for Norman, Rhonda?"

Rhonda gulped and licked her lips.

"It's the Chief of Police, Pastor Cherry," she said. "Big Jim Dalton."

Chapter Seven

While Jim Dalton was speaking with his parents, Norman was driving back into town. He had been out driving since his meeting with God that morning in the woods, where the true calling on his life had been laid out before him.

And what a calling it was.

His mother had always told him it would be his music. It would be him singing and leading the masses into the throne room of God Almighty through songs. *His* songs. Not many of those songs had come to him yet, of course, and the ones that had weren't very good, but his mother assured him that they would come. In God's timing. Always in God's timing.

And he'd never doubted her. After all, his mother was usually right. Hell, she was *always* right, wasn't she? It sure seemed that way. She had a knack for always pointing him in the right direction. When he was young, it had been she who had told him that God wanted him to start playing guitar. It was she who had told him how beautiful his voice was. It was she who had encouraged him to start writing his own music.

Once, after he'd written his very first song, he had shown it to her. Just the two of them. His father had been at the church working, and he and his mother had the house to themselves.

Norman had been dating a young lady in school for a while and, as most sixteen-year-olds are wont to do, he'd fallen head over heels in love with her. They had gone out to an old black-top road which was seldom used, especially at night. They went to talk and look at the stars together. Unbeknownst to his young girlfriend, Norman had brought along a promise ring.

A promise ring was like an engagement ring—sort of—but it was purely *pre*-engagement. An engagement *before* engagement. It was supposed to signify that the two people were going to be together, but they were too young for actual engagement and commitment just yet. It meant that the wearer of the ring was 'promising' to be true to the one who'd given it to her and that they would become betrothed in the coming years.

It was a fucking—*Jesus forgive him*—promise.

So Norman had given her the ring as they sat beneath the starry sky. She'd blushed and giggled as he put it on her ring finger and thanked him. She had liked him well enough, and Norman had felt drawn to her in a way he'd never known possible up to that point in his life.

But then Norman had tried to kiss her. And a great deal more.

They had as yet never kissed, as a matter of fact. It was rather unusual, actually, even amongst teenagers, to have any sort of relationship with someone of the opposite sex for virtually any amount of time and them to have not sealed their fondness with a kiss, but it hadn't happened yet. Norman had *never* kissed a girl, actually. His mother, sure, but that wasn't the same. The quick peck on the cheek or lips from mother to son was simply not the same thing as kissing your girlfriend.

Norman had seen kissing on the television. He liked how it looked. Wanted to try it. He had a girlfriend and all, so it seemed like the thing to do. If he was lucky, he might even get to put his tongue in her mouth. He'd seen that on television too, and he *really* liked how that looked. It made him get hard down there, and he'd discovered that he very much enjoyed being hard down there. Because when he got hard down there, he could rub it, and brother, that felt *really* good.

His girlfriend made him hard down there, too. Not by anything she did. Not deliberately anyway. She was a modest dresser, not like those whores in school who wore shorts that didn't even touch their knees and tops with spaghetti strings for shoulder straps. No, those sluts were *trying* to make all the other boys hard. But not her. She wore blue jeans, and usually about a half-size larger than she really needed to, so there was still plenty left to the imagination. The shirts she chose generally concealed her cleavage for the most part, except perhaps when she'd lean over to pick something up. She'd done that once in front of Norman and he'd had occasion to see the top of her cleavage and part of her bra. She was well-endowed for a teenager. *All* the girls in school seemed to be well-endowed, as a matter of fact. He'd heard it was something to do with the hormones being used to raise chickens these days, and all the girls in school ate a *lot* of chicken.

Seeing the tops of her breasts when she'd leaned over had made him so hard he thought it would show through his pants and he was afraid she would see it and think he was gross or a pervert or something. Panic had burst forth inside of him in an instant at the thought of it, so much so that by the time she was standing back up, the fear coursing through his veins had rendered his substantial boner flaccid.

So, as she giggled and blushed in the car, admiring her promise ring, Norman had tried to kiss her. He'd decided to start small, just a little kiss on the lips. He wouldn't go for the tongue. Not yet. He needed practice, anyway. This was his first time kissing a girl, a *real* girl, and he was pragmatic enough to recognize that he needed to work his way up to the juicy parts.

Their lips met. She was surprised at first, and Norman felt her draw in breath in surprise as he'd done it. But then she had returned the kiss. It was nice. A little rocky, but hey, what can you expect for the first time? So, after they had disengaged and smiled rapturously at one another for a moment, he tried again.

And that's where he'd fucked it all up.

Instead of a gradual build up like he had planned—all the way to *hopefully* putting his tongue in her mouth—and instead of letting it build naturally and organically, he'd thrust his tongue straight in and to the back of her throat. His cock had basically dictated this to him from its bully pulpit. The second she had returned that first kiss, it jumped up, pulsing and aware, and begun writing the script.

Give her your tongue! it had shouted to him from his groin. *That's what you want! It's what she wants too, even if she doesn't know it. Show her that she wants it! And put your hand on her titty, that'll make it easier for her! Chicks love it when you grab their titty!*

He rather enjoyed his cock, and it seemed to have pretty good taste. Generally good advice, too. Look at this here, check that out there. Rub me, stroke me, choke me. There, doesn't that feel nice?

So, he'd done it.

The poor girl had gagged almost at once from the force and depth of his inquisitive tongue and put her hand on his chest. Mistaking this for affirmation, he had reached up and placed his hand on her breast. He squeezed it through her shirt, surprised at how soft it was. He'd imagined time and again what a girl's breast would feel like, but his imagination was no substitute for the real thing.

Her hand began pushing hard on his chest. She was

mumbling something as well while Norman was trying to thrust his tongue into her mouth again, which was now closed tight, and he was succeeding only in licking her pressed lips and the minty taste of her saliva-slicked teeth. He was confused as to what was going on, so he followed slick-willy's advice some more and squeezed her breast even harder. His hand was bunched almost into a fist with the flesh of her breast balled inside of it like a rag.

That was when she screamed.

Of course, this hadn't been at *all* what he'd been expecting, certainly not what his now-throbbing member had promised would happen. He felt anger well up within him. Fury, the likes of which he'd never experienced up to that point in his young life.

Does she know who I am? Does she not know about the great call on my life? I'm God's chosen one to lead people into His Kingdom! She should be thrilled *to have my tongue in her mouth!*

She screamed at him to stop and pushed violently on his chest. The force of the push was enough to throw him back into his seat. He had been gnawing on her bottom lip by that point—*another solid pointer from his pointer*—and when he fell back to his seat he'd taken a sliver of skin off her lip. It tasted salty. It tasted nice.

He swallowed it.

As he did so, he looked back at her bewildered. He could see that her lip was bleeding too, from the place he'd gotten his tasty treat. He'd also let go of her breast and now she held it in both of her hands, sobbing.

"Are you crazy?" she asked him pointedly through her sobs.

Of course, Norman wasn't crazy, he'd explained to her. He was God's chosen one after all and God doesn't choose people who are crazy to do His work. He told her how she should be thankful that one such as himself should share his affections with her, but she'd heard none of it. She demanded to be taken home, right then, that very instant. There was another few moments of protest and lecture on all the ways she was wrong, but in the end, he'd done as she asked. He drove her home and she'd exited the vehicle without a word, slammed the door shut, and stormed into her house.

So, when Norman got home, he took care of his relentless boner, remembering the salty taste of her flesh as he'd swallowed it and the softness of her breast. It got the job done. Spritz, spray, almost as good as a lay.

Then he wrote a song.

The song was all about rejection and first kisses. It was total shit, of course, but Norman would never be aware of this. As he performed the song to his mother, he was acutely aware of the effect it was having on her. She swayed and smiled as he played it for her, and he even noticed a couple of times when her strong hand—her right hand was the strong one, he knew, because that was the one she'd used when giving his brother good godly discipline with the belt wrapped in her palm—had slipped between her thighs. It looked like she had touched herself. Touched herself down *there!*

This song MUST be good! he'd thought excitedly. *Mother is a woman, and look at what it's doing to her!*

Seeing his mother in this way had given him new confidence in the call on his life, and had given new rise to the thing in his pants. He played on, glancing up as often as possible to his mother as she swayed and touched herself, closing her eyes as she took in the ecstasy of the moment and his song. By the time he finished the song, the guitar in his lap was sitting an inch higher.

"That was the most beautiful song I've ever heard, Norman," his mother had said to him, actual rapture in her voice. "Didn't I tell you God has given you a wonderful gift?"

"Yes, mother," he replied, smiling sheepishly. He set the guitar aside.

"Where did the inspiration come from?" she asked him, moving next to him. *Close* to him.

So he told her. He told her everything, actually. They had that kind of relationship. Always had. He could tell her anything and everything, and she always listened. She gave great advice, too. She was so in tune with God, it was as if she had a direct pipeline to the Almighty. To His will.

She listened intently, her soft blue eyes narrowing as he got to the painful moments, the empathy for her son's rejection and hurt flowing out of her. As he spoke, she slipped her arm behind his shoulder and began to rub his back between his shoulder-blades. Soft, even strokes. Back and forth, up and down. A few circles.

Then she'd touched his thigh. He remembered how dangerously close she'd been at that moment to what was becoming a rather serious engorgement, and had a moment of fear that she would realize it and scold him for his sin. It was sin after all to have those feelings, outside of marriage anyway.

But she soothed his fears. She always did that. She encouraged him. Told him how beautiful he was, inside and out. What a great gift he was, to the whole world as well as to her. She told him that girl had been tricked by the devil. Anyone could see that. Any young woman who didn't recognize the greatness of Norman Reese—who didn't recognize the *privilege* of his touch, of his kiss—was obviously not someone who was listening to God. They were listening to the devil himself.

That had also been the day his mother began to teach him how to be a man. To teach him what women really wanted. What women *needed.*

And according to his mother, Norman had learned *well.*

Norman pulled onto the road leading to his parents' church, relishing the memories. A smile had spread over his face at some point during his mental replays, and it remained now. He wasn't even aware of the near-pain in his loins that the memories of his mother had wrought.

You're a man now, baby-boy, she had said after as they both sheened with sweat.

But all his memories and pleasure swept away when he saw the black and white Tahoe with 'Chief of Police' printed on the side of it sitting in the parking lot of the church. Fear flushed him all at once and his mind began an immediate reeling.

Do they know something? Are they trying to interfere with God's work?

He wasn't sure how they could know anything. He felt he had been pretty thorough cleaning the house. He'd even taken the rug. Bleached everything.

God had told him in their meeting that the enemy would certainly make attempts to stop him from doing the work of the Lord. The enemy *always* tried to throw a wrench into the machine that was building the Kingdom. He just hadn't realized how soon the enemy would mobilize.

Crafty fucking devil...Jesus forgive me.

He increased his speed and drove on by, craning his neck to look back at the menacing Tahoe as he went. He had a thousand questions now, and he would have to wait to speak with his mother to find out what was going on. How much they knew. She would understand, and she would be there for him, he knew that. She always was.

He decided going to his house was a bad idea as well. Until he had a handle on what the enemy was up to, better to lay low and stay off the radar. He figured he would go into town and stop at the store to kill time. To think.

A few minutes later, he was walking into the store. It was a Dollar General, located near the middle of town, and there were dozens of cars parked in the lot. Lots of people. Easy to get lost in a crowd.

He browsed the aisles, not really looking at anything. He didn't *need* anything, not so far as he knew. He was just trying to calm his nerves. Find his resolve. The work of the Lord was dangerous business, he'd known that his whole life. His mother had told him about the horrible ends many of the early Christians had come to, and how many still did outside the good old United States of America. Sometimes God's work required the ultimate sacrifice.

And he knew that if it came to that, he would die standing for God. There was no question of that. No two ways about it. He would stand to the end, follow his calling where it led.

He meandered out of one aisle and looped back into another, his mind lost in thought, when something on the shelves actually caught his eye. It almost stunned him, as if it had shouted out his name from its perch. His eyes gleamed as he beheld it.

It was a mask. A *Halloween* mask.

He thought it was completely odd that Halloween masks should be out this early in the year—it was just barely August—but nonetheless, it was here. He looked up and down the aisle and realized that it was a clearance rack where the store was trying unload all of the seasonal stuff they had been unable to sell throughout the year. There were Christmas ornaments and Easter baskets, a few American flags on small plastic rods with sparkling gold letters that exclaimed "Happy Fourth Of July".

And there were a few Halloween trinkets, among

them, this mask.

The mask was a rubber thing and bore the resemblance of a goat. Hard rubber horns rose out from the forehead and curled back and under the ears. The hollows where eyes should be seemed to stare into him. Into his *soul.*

This is for you, my child, they said. *My good and precious son. I will protect you, and hold you, and keep you. Every good thing comes from Me.*

He knew all at once that his aimless wandering hadn't been aimless at all. God had led him here, right here, to find this very thing. What God was calling him to do was dangerous work, and the enemy had already set about working against him. But God provided.

Here, in the middle of August, God had provided him with a mask that would conceal his work from the enemy. A mask that would *reflect* the enemy as well. He was God's sheep, and God would disguise him as the devil's goat.

It was brilliant, really. At least to Norman's mind.

Oh, ladies and gentlemen. Oh, good people...My God PROVIDES!

He snatched the mask off the shelf, manipulated it in his hands. Smelled it. He'd always liked the smell of rubber. Just another one of the many ways in which God takes care of His children.

He turned, heading to the front of the store, and passed a hardware aisle on the way.

God provided again.

He dropped the mask and an eighteen-inch hatchet down at the checkout register. He was smiling broadly, unable to remove the emotion from his face. But how could he, really? Sometimes God just shows up and reminds you of His goodness in such a way that the only thing you can do is smile and bask in the joy of the Lord.

He ignored the strange looks the clerk gave him as he

paid for his purchases and slipped back out to the parking lot. Once he was in his car, he pulled the hatchet out and hefted it. He liked how it felt in his hand. Though it was a Dollar General item, it seemed rather well made. Good thick steel and a sharp edge. Excellent balance.

Then he pulled the mask out and beheld it once more. Rubbed his fingers over it. Smelled it.

He put the mask on, pulling it over his head and down past his ears. He adjusted it a few times, getting his eyes lined up just right in the holes, breathing deeply. That sharp, sweet scent of rubber. He was smiling again behind the mask.

It was a perfect fit.

Chapter Eight

Jim checked at Norman's house after he left the church. No dice.

He walked around the house, a rather nice double-wide mobile home if he was being completely honest, about three miles outside of town to the South. It was located just off FM 852 on property that actually belonged to the senior Reese couple.

The house was white with green shutters, and it had lattice underpinning to hide the axles and towing tongue which resided beneath it should he ever decide to move. It was all tucked away neatly underneath, and you'd have to actually bend over and look in the way Jim was now doing to ever notice it. There was a quaint, custom-built porch on the front. It was nothing special, but did the job with a standard, rectangular approach.

Around back, there was another deck, this one more substantial. It was easily three times as large as the one out front, and had built in benches around its perimeter. There was a bar-b-que grill at the back, though Jim guessed it hadn't seen use in quite some time. Old grease had run down the sides and crystalized there, and a layer of dirt and grime glazed its exterior, adhered to the stainless steel from the muck left behind from a substantial cookout from long ago.

Norman's car hadn't been in the driveway, but Jim had decided to check around anyway. It wasn't as though he really had any other leads besides the fact that Norman and Margie had dated until recently. So he peeked around the house, attempted to peer in through windows where he could, but there was nothing to see. The blinds were drawn and the place was locked up tight. Mere suspicion wasn't enough to get a warrant, and even if he *did* get a warrant, he wasn't sure what he really expected to find here.

He hadn't liked the elder Reeses from the very start. He'd never met them, even with all his run-ins with Jake when they were kids, but he knew them by reputation. Most people in town either loved them or hated them. There was very little in between. Either they were the greatest of God's emissaries here on earth, or they were self-righteous sons-of-bitches feeding off the weakest of minds.

Jim tended to lean toward the latter.

None of it necessarily reeked of criminal behavior. Sure, they were the fundamentalist types, taking extremely hard lines on trivial matters such as R-rated movies, foul language, alcohol, Halloween, and the like. They would sometimes go to the movie theater up in Sulphur Springs—about twenty miles West of Winnsboro—and protest some movie coming out which had received an R-rating and make fools of themselves for a few hours in the evening with picket signs declaring the satanic influences that people were taking part in if they went and saw it. He'd also seen them doing similar things around Halloween, declaring it as the devil's birthday and other such nonsense.

But nothing criminal. And as much as Jim was *not* a religious man, he was certain of the existence of a spiritual world. He'd have to lie to himself to believe otherwise after everything he'd seen that summer in 1990. He'd not only seen another world beyond this one, he'd gone *into* it as well. It had to have some spiritual nature, didn't it?

Well, he'd gone into *some* world. Whether or not it

was the spiritual one, he couldn't really say. It had seemed real enough. Seemed pretty much like the one he lived and breathed and worked in day to day. But it was different, too. It certainly wasn't *this* world. Of that he was positive.

And that *thing*...

He shuddered at the memory of the *thing*. The Glutton, Jonathan Brogan had called it in that horrifying journal his friend Freddie had found at the library all those years ago. It had come from that other world, wherever it was, and it had been unlike anything he'd seen or heard of before. The most imaginative science fiction and horror movies he'd seen through the years never approached defining such a thing like the one that had nearly killed him and his friends that summer. The only thing he could think of that even brushed elbows with it was some of the imagery he'd seen in religious paintings in some of the old Bibles his mother had. She'd only taken him to Mass twice a year after his Confirmation, at Christmas and Easter, but she'd been deeply religious all the same. At least in belief, if not in practice. After his father had left, in search of that ever-elusive pack of cigarettes, their attendance in the Church had dropped off dramatically. His mother managed to go to her required once a year confession around Easter, and she'd always taken Jim with her so he could do the same. Jim had no belief in the deity of Christ, but it made his mother feel better when he'd go along, so he'd kept it up for a while.

And being Catholic in rural East Texas was actually a pretty rare thing. There was typically a parish in every town, if not every community, and the Tyler diocese that oversaw the area he and his mother lived in had everything in good order, but the vast majority of people where he lived, and throughout the deep South in general, were Southern Baptists or Non-denominationalist, sometimes calling themselves 'Full Gospel' churches. There were all sorts of denominations of course, but none that claimed as many souls as those.

Of everyone Jim had known growing up in school, he'd been *literally* the only one who had been raised Catholic. Well, the only white kid, anyway. There were plenty of Hispanic Catholics, but he'd never managed to make close friends with any. This wasn't intentional, just how things played out. But out of all his friends growing up, he was the singular Catholic among them. Not that it bothered *him* much, but it sure seemed to bother a lot of other people, especially those whose parents were raising them in the aforementioned 'Full Gospel' churches. There was a real disdain for Catholicism in those circles, to varying degrees.

But Jim had never been a real believer anyway, so he had always kept his religious upbringing to himself, for the most part.

In his meeting with the elder Reeses, he'd sensed that same sort of thinking in them. Not that anything about Catholicism had come up, and there had been no religious discussion at all, but it was at least a *vibe* of some kind. Especially coming off of Mrs. Reese. She made Jim's skin crawl. He couldn't put his finger on it, but there was something seriously off about her. And she was certainly the donner of the pants in the family. George Reese had barely spoken through the whole meeting when Jim had come trying to locate Norman and asking questions about his relationship with Margie. Even when he *did* try and speak, she would usually cut him off before he got the first word of a sentence out. What was stranger, though, was George just didn't seem to care. He wasn't frustrated, at least not outwardly. He didn't grimace, frown, rub his hand over his face. Just kept the ever-present, vacant smile on his face as he routinely deferred to his wife. He seemed happy to let her take over.

Satisfied that he would find nothing at Norman's house, Jim wandered back around to his Tahoe and got in. He fired up the engine and sat back for a moment, thinking. He wanted a drink. Something to balance him out. He always felt calmer and thought more clearly with a couple of drinks in his system. That was until he kept on drinking and blacked out, of course. Very little useful thought occurred once he got to that point. But just a couple of drinks would do him some good right then.

He looked to the radio mic hanging from his dash and reached for it. While he was still ten inches or so from grasping it, the mic rattled loose from its cradle and glided into his hand. He paused, staring at it. He knew all about his ability, the one that had come to him suddenly all those years before and had vanished from his thoughts in the years after. He hadn't thought about using it to pull the mic to himself the way he'd deliberately used it to move the note from Barbara about calling Charlotte Johnson earlier that morning. It had just happened. He wanted the mic, and it had come to him. Just like the lock in the door had snapped shut as a kid when Jake Reese was coming after him.

Jake.

Now *there* was a story which haunted his darkest nightmares. And he'd just been in with the long-since vanished boy's parents looking for their other son. It was as if every major event in his life was tied to the Reese family in some way. He also realized in that moment that his ability seemed to almost be *tied* to them as well. It had manifested with Jake Reese chasing him into the house in the woods and throughout the whole ordeal that summer. Even Jake himself had turned out to have the same ability in the end, a revelation that had haunted him ever since, if only at the very back of his consciousness. And now it had come again just as Norman's ex-girlfriend had gone missing under what were now emerging to be rather dire circumstances.

It also came in handy with The Glutton, he thought, pursing his lips.

True. But The Glutton was gone now. They'd made sure of that. They weren't sure it was dead, but they were sure it couldn't cross over without meat, and they'd made sure no one but them even knew about the place in the woods where the old Brogan house stood.

Jim didn't see any real connection to his ability and the *thing* from his childhood. It was the Reeses that had a tangible connection to it, not The Glutton.

Still, the thought wouldn't leave him. He pushed it back, but it wouldn't go away. Not altogether, anyway. It merely moved itself to the back of his mind and festered there like an infection ready to spread.

It's gone, he reasoned with the thought. *It's gone forever.*

But was it?

He remembered the mic in his hand and shook his head to clear his thoughts, then thumbed the transmit button.

"Winnsboro One to PD," he said officially into the mic.

There was a moment of static and squabble, then Barbara's voice came through the speaker.

"This is PD, go ahead W-One."

"Have we heard anything from WCFS?"

Another pause. More static.

"Nothing yet from the forensics squad, Chief."

Jim nodded, having already known the answer. But he had nothing. Nothing solid anyway. He needed something real he could point to and run with. It was worth a shot.

"Okay, PD," he said. He started to return the mic to

its cradle when he had another thought. He brought the mic back to his lips.

"PD, have patrol come into the office. Have them meet there in ten minutes."

There was another pause, then Barbara's voice came back on.

"I think you just let them know, Chief."

There was the sound of stifled laughter in her voice as she spoke. It hit him all at once. Of course the whole department had just heard everything he had said. They all operated off the same frequency.

Duh.

"Oh, right," he said.

Then there were three confirmations from his patrolmen affirming that they had received the message and would see him in ten.

He smiled to himself returning the mic to the cradle, his blushed cheeks returning to normal.

"Yeah, yeah, yeah," he said to himself, and dropped the Tahoe into gear.

In the drive back to the office, his mind wouldn't let go of that thought. The thought incubating in the back of his mind, refusing to go away. Refuting reason and logic.

He thought of The Glutton.

Chapter Nine

Honey Bascom pulled into town on Highway 37 from the South. She hadn't been back to Winnsboro in nearly ten years, though she only lived thirty miles away. When she'd finally gotten herself into a financial situation where she could get out of town, she had. Too many bad memories. Too many things that haunted her. Too many mistakes made.

But now she was on her way to see one of those mistakes. The mistake whose only redeeming factor was the daughter it had given her. Actually, if she were to give the matter some honest reflection, he had plenty of redeeming qualities. Somewhere, beneath all the depression and the harsh exterior, laid a man who would lay down his life in a heartbeat for those he loved. Hell, even for those he hardly knew. A kind man. A giving and caring man.

It was the past which had come between them. It ate at them both, she presumed, but even more so on him. A shared past that Honey had finally fled from. But he had stayed here, keeping his vigilant watch. Only it was a cancer to him, eating away his insides and leaving little more than a husk, reeking of alcohol and self-pity. It was his choice to stay, she'd often reminded him, but sometimes even she, with her own diamond-hard exterior, believed that really wasn't the case. He *had* to stay. If not him, who could face down their past if it ever managed to find its way into their present.

Honey's darkly died hair blew through the air as she

sighed, speeding along in her Jeep Wrangler. It was the four-door model, with all the bells and whistles. She'd taken the top off of it and was enjoying the wind as she drove into this town full of hate and misery and broken dreams.

She had received a call that morning from Freddie James, one of her childhood friends. Now he was *Reverend* Freddie James of the First Baptist Church of Winnsboro. He'd told her of one of his congregation whose daughter had gone missing. It was an elderly woman, he'd explained, and wondered if she could come in and help her through the ordeal. Honey was a counselor with Hospice, and was familiar with working intimately with people who were experiencing loss, with just the right amount of empathy and delicacy they needed. Her skills would fit right in with the situation, and though she was loathe to return to Winnsboro even on a compassionate mission of mercy, she had agreed. It would be nice to see Freddie again and meet his wife.

But before she went to meet with Reverend Freddie and the old lady, she wanted to stop by the Police Department and get a feel for just how bad things were. Victims could often jump to the worst possible conclusions and blow things completely out of proportion, so having a good solid perspective on the facts would help her in dealing with the woman and her needs.

The only problem was Jim Dalton. She would have to talk to Jim. The biggest blessing and mistake of her life. She did *not* look forward to that.

She edged up to the stoplight where the highway intersected with Coke Road. The light was red, and she rolled her Jeep to an easy stop. She realized the stereo was blasting, so she adjusted the volume to a lower level and 'Sharp Dressed Man' by ZZ Top faded into obscurity.

Glancing around the intersection—which was

typically what she did when waiting on a light to turn green—she took in the surroundings. There was a donut shop on the North-Eastern corner of the intersection that hadn't been there the last time she'd been in town. The building had been, and for the life of her she couldn't remember what had been there, but the donut shop was new. Directly to her right was a large and rather nice branch of the First National Bank. Lines of cars were waiting to get into the drive-thru lanes, folks making deposits and withdrawals and whatnot. Throngs of people were milling about, coming in and going out of the bank, and beyond the bank she could see the Dollar General store, its small parking lot jam-packed with cars and customers.

On the North-Western corner of the intersection stood the Shamrock station which had virtually become an institution of sorts to anyone who'd ever lived in Winnsboro. Ever-present and unchanging for decades, it stood ready as ever to sell you all the gasoline, cigarettes, snacks, and beer you could stand. The beer was a new addition, she reckoned. Wood County was still technically a dry county, meaning that alcohol sales were prohibited from occurring within the territory, but virtually *all* of the townships within the county had voted on new city ordinances that would allow for the sale of beer and wine inside the city limits in recent years. Liquor still had to be pursued out East in Camp County—or even Crystal County, if memory served—but it wasn't terribly far to drive. If you wanted to get fucked up, you didn't have far to travel.

Honey marveled at how much the town had changed while still remaining relatively the same. There were new paint jobs on some of the buildings and a few new businesses had popped up here and there, but it was still the same old Winnsboro, Texas, population thirty-five-hundred.

Her eyes looked to her left and saw the row of cars waiting on the light. Typical for Winnsboro, there were a couple of near brand-new vehicles—a silver Chevy Suburban and a white Toyota Tundra—along with dilapidated old things that were in such disrepair and of such an ancient vintage that she had no idea what models they were.

To her right, she saw much the same landscape and cars. She scanned over them, not really paying too close attention to them as her eyes drifted back to the light directly in front of her, which still gleamed red in the late afternoon sun.

Come on...

Then something dawned on her. She'd noticed something, something rather odd just before she had checked the light again, and she directed her eyes back to it.

It was the first car in line in the turning lane which took travelers coming from the East on Coke Road to head South onto Highway 37. It was a small car, nothing too fancy, but nice enough she supposed. It was a Ford, but she didn't recognize the model. It was gold in color, which was amplified from the low-lying sun beating its rays upon its sheen. But what had drawn her attention wasn't the car itself or even its sparkling paint-job.

The driver was a goat.

But that can't be so, can it? she marveled.

She leaned forward, her face becoming a comic rictus of curiosity, squinting her eyes against the glare and trying for a better look. The light for their turning lane had apparently turned green, because now the goat-driven car was moving forward, turning in a steady arc towards her direction. The car and its driver came nearer to her, and she now saw it was *not*, after all, a goat driving the car. It was a *man* wearing what appeared to be a goat mask. Some kind of Halloween getup from the look of it. She also noticed a white tag dangling and swaying freely this way and that from one of the rubber horns which curled up the side of the head. It appeared to be brand new.

Of all the things in the world, she thought.

Then the driver in the goat mask looked straight at her as the car pulled alongside her and accelerated to go out of town. The eyes peering through the mask locked with hers, blazing through the hollows in the mask, seeing her, *knowing* her somehow.

All at once she saw her mother's face from the night of the accident when she was ten years old, twisted and bloody, eyes wide and panicked, her mouth spitting bright red splashes of blood out onto Honey's face while she screamed in the back seat.

The vision startled Honey and a gasp escaped her lips as her hand shot up to cover her mouth.

She blinked.

Her mother was gone, as quickly and viciously as she'd appeared. And so was the goat-man. Honey glanced into the mirror on her door and saw the tail of the car speeding away, the silhouette of curled horns visible through the rear windshield.

Snakes slinked up her spine as she looked at the receding image of the goat-man's Ford, a sickening knot forming in the pit of her stomach. The man in the mask had been strange enough, but the image of her mother's bloody and beaten face was what *really* haunted her. She hadn't thought about those images for many years now. There was still the occasional night-terror that would jerk her up from slumber in a cold sweat alone in her room in the middle of the night, but it was extremely rare that it happened these days.

In fact, she hardly thought of her mother anymore. She didn't often think of her father, either. He was at once the greatest disappointment of her childhood and a painful sorrow for what might have been had he survived the woods in that other, awful damned place.

The knot in her gut tightened.

There was a honk from behind her which jolted her back into the here and now. She looked up and saw the light had turned green, inviting travel through this strange and mundane intersection. She took her foot off the brake and accelerated onward to the Police Station.

Pull it together, Honey-bunny. Keep your eyes open. Don't even blink. Control what you see.

She pulled through the intersection and glided up Main Street toward the mistake she'd made over twelve years ago.

Chapter Ten

Norman knew the woman in the Jeep. He didn't know how or from where, but he knew her. He remembered her.

But it was a strange sort of recollection. Not a familiar face, per se, but like a face you *used* to know that has aged and changed through the years. Yet the basic features were still there.

He wasn't even aware he was still wearing the mask. The electric feeling he'd had when he donned the mask had caused him to forget it was there. It was almost like it was a part of *him* now. A new face to go along with his new calling.

So when he'd turned through the intersection he'd had no idea why the lady whose face he could almost remember was looking at him so curiously. He'd begun smiling behind his mask that wasn't a mask at all in his mind and stared back at her. Then he'd headed off on his mission.

God had told him at the house in the woods, that cathedral of rebirth, that he needed meat. Margie was a good start, and what incredible luck that had been! Norman had had absolutely no intention of hurting Margie—much less killing her—when he'd gone to her house last night. And as it turned out, he *hadn't* killed her. He only thought he had. After he'd cleaned up her shit and piss and all that blood, he'd become so engorged with excitement that he'd praised Jesus audibly when the

Almighty told him what he could do with Margie, then. If people were nothing more than a spirit inside a meat-husk, then there was no sin in enjoying the meat when the spirit had left.

Only it hadn't left. God took her when you brought her to Him.

He ignored this reasoning, as it was ultimately irrelevant. God had told him in that moment it was okay. His head had been pulsing with another one of his migraines and, in that moment, he'd been given the word from the Lord.

And he'd acted upon it.

He reveled in the memory, soaking in every detail he could as he did so, and marveled at the completeness and mystery of God. God, after all, had indeed told him that he and Margie were supposed to be together. Margie had refused this, refused *God's will*, and then she'd paid the price. But even through all of that, Norman had still been able to be with her. Just as God had promised him.

Oh, friends and neighbors. Have I told you how great is our God?

Then God had led him—Norman knew now he had been led, it had all been too perfect to be anything but God's will—to that strange house in the woods. And in that strange cathedral, God had given him his mission.

Meat.

Yes, God wanted Norman to bring Him meat. As much and as often as he could. The supreme being had explained that He needed meat to nourish his spirit. Flesh to *become* flesh. Just as He'd sent his Son into the world, the Word becoming flesh, so would Norman act as his new Mary to help grow him from mere spirit into the God-man once again.

Norman Reese was so consumed with the twisted form of God he'd been raised to revere, it all seemed perfectly reasonable to him. And the tumor growing and pulsing inside his brain didn't help in matters of reason and logic either.

So Norman rolled out of town, still unaware of the mask hugging his face. He was going for meat. He had the hatchet in the seat next to him, ready to roll.

And he knew where he would get the meat.

He'd spoken to his mother on his cell phone while he sat in the parking lot of the Dollar General, and learned of what the Police Chief had been after. It wasn't much. Very little, as a matter of fact, but it was enough to get eyes looking in his direction. He also had learned of Dave Bowers's insolence in the meeting with his parents. Dave was a nice hefty chunk of meat. Plenty lean, but with just enough fat to add some good flavor to the palette.

Dave's wife was a bit of a fat bitch—*Jesus forgive him*—but it would be a good place to get a twofer.

After all, God needed plenty of meat.

PART THREE:

Feeding

Saturday, August 6, 2016

Chapter Eleven

Dave Bowers killed the light in the bathroom and went to his bed. Laura was already in there, wriggled in like a chunky burrito taking a significant portion of the covers on his side of the bed. She always did that. She always hogged the covers. Hogged *everything,* for that matter.

All too often he'd find the last *something*—be it TV dinner, sandwich meat, *slice of cheese,* you name it—would be gone. And he could always count on the fact that it would be, at that very moment, digesting into putrefied shit inside his wife's rotund belly. He loved her—he really did, despite his bitterness and disappointment—and he knew she loved him as well, but after ten years of marriage and an ever-expanding waistline, he'd grown to resent her. If he wanted to make sure she didn't get the last of something, he would have to literally sneak it out to the mini-fridge he kept in his shop behind their home. Because—let's face it—her fat ass wasn't going to get up and exert itself in a walk to go fetch food from his shop. That was *at least* forty feet from their back door. It was as safe in his shop as it would be if it were buried beneath Fort Knox, encased in lead, and buried in concrete.

He sighed as silently as he could as he made his way around the bed to his side and slid into the covers. It was after one o'clock in the morning and he was whipped. The meeting with the Reeses had gone even worse than he'd expected it to, and then after telling Laura all about it and her crying about losing her precious church and pleading, *couldn't you, Dave, oh couldn't you patch things up? We don't need to be on the worship team there, after all, but at least we could be at the church.*

Well, Dave's answer to that was a big *hell no*.

After all that, he'd gone out to his shop, taken the last piece of Italian sausage out of the mini-fridge, and devoured it victoriously. Then he'd plugged his guitar in to the Mesa-Boogie half-stack amp and cranked the volume.

He jammed out for hours, playing everything from U2 to Metallica to Bob Marley. Dave loved music. Everything about it, as a matter of fact. If there was one truth he'd found in playing music, no matter the genre or style, it was that you simply couldn't maintain a bad mood when you were playing guitar. All the shit, all the hypocrisy, all the anxiety he'd dealt with throughout the day shed away like a snake shedding its skin. He'd walked out of his shop after midnight, turning all the lights off and locking it up, with a huge smile on his face.

He really did feel a lot better. And he was happy about the prospect of never having to deal with the Reese family or their crazy little church ever again. They could start visiting other churches in town—there were plenty to choose from—and maybe find one that wasn't a pit of nepotism and self-service. He liked to hope they could, anyway.

It was good that they lived several miles out in the country, away from everyone and everything. He could crank the sound on his equipment as loud as he wanted and didn't have to worry about annoying neighbors or scaring dogs. Laura might be annoyed, but she usually watched her reality TV shows at such a volume that any sound he made would be like crickets in the background.

His smile was maintained all the way until he'd stepped out of the bathroom and saw that the eons-old battle of the blankets would be waged once again tonight.

Just go to sleep and forget about it, he thought. *After the day you've had, just let it go. It isn't worth getting into it with Laura over this.*

And he'd intended to do just that. But as Laura continued to wriggle and writhe next to him, hunting for that craftily hidden perfect 'spot', his temper had gotten the best of him. They argued about the blankets and he told her about how she *always* did this to him, which of course was met with indignant declarations that she most certainly did not. From there, it devolved to comments about their respective mothers raising cattle and Neanderthals instead of polite children, and then it predictably rounded back to the meeting at the church earlier in the day and their loss of a spiritual family.

It all came full circle.

That was the inescapable part of it all for Dave. He'd been unhappy at that church for some time, but was trying to be a good Christian and trying to serve the Lord the best he knew how. But virtually every step of the way, Norman Reese and his parents were trying to shut him down. And adding insult to injury, his wife always gave *him* grief for getting upset about the situation.

The truth was Dave was glad to be gone from the church. He wanted no part of that body of believers ever again, and was happy to shed them like a giant, steaming turd. But Laura was less enthused about the prospect.

And it was because of this argument, loud and boisterous as it was, that neither Laura nor Dave heard the small glass panel on the back door break and tinkle to the floor with an almost musical chime.

Chapter Twelve

Norman had sat in his car—which he'd pulled into the woods past Dave and Laura Bowers's home on the blacktop road—for the entire evening. He was fondling the hatchet most of the time, trying its weight and feeling its blade.

It really was a surprisingly sharp blade for a made-in-China hunk of steel. Typically, *anything* with a blade you purchased at the Dollar Store—unless it was an actual razor—would be dull. It was understood that you would have to take your purchase home and do some sharpening on it yourself. Just what did you expect for the price you were paying? But not this piece. No siree, Bob, this one had been done up just right.

The blade arced out from one side of the tool like a miniature version of a medieval battle-axe. The other side spiked out to a point that could be used to pry or dig with, whatever the need may be.

Norman could think of some other uses.

Even the top of the thing was useful. It was flat and smooth, wide enough for a person to get nails started if they chose. There was a skeletonized section in the middle of the blade itself for pulling nails out of wood. The handle was a full-tang piece of stainless steel. The whole thing had been painted black, save for about three-quarters of an inch back from the edge of the blade and the handle had a thick rubber grip on it.

It looked good and mean.

He was honestly astonished that the thing had been in the Dollar Store. You just didn't see this kind of quality at barrel-bottom pricing on anything, much less a tool such as this.

But that was the beauty of God's provision.

So he'd sat in the car, turning the engine off after a time when the needle indicating the engine temperature was getting uncomfortably high. It had been hot. When dark finally fell around eight, the air had cooled a good bit, providing some relief. Norman was still wearing the goat mask, the insides now slimed with sweat and reeking of it as well. But he didn't notice. Didn't care. He enjoyed wearing his new face very much. It reminded him of his mission. And he *loved* his mission.

There had been a rather annoying—and what Norman considered outright satanic—jam session coming from Dave's shop for several hours. Norman—who *never* listened to that devil music—was able to pick out a few tunes that he'd heard before, especially from when he'd been in High School. Metahlca, or some pagan shit—*Jesus forgive him*—had dominated the session for much of the time. It was no wonder his parents had been forced to remove Dave from their worship team. How could an honest to God Christian allow themselves to play such godless tunes?

Finally, after the day had passed from Friday to Saturday, Dave had shut down his Satan-worship jam session and headed into the house. Norman waited for the lights to go out. He could see from his position everything happening on the property. God had smiled on him once more, Norman took note, as he realized there were no dogs roaming around outside. He cared little for dogs, and didn't want to have to deal with one as he moved forward in his calling.

Norman started the engine and crept the car back out to the blacktop, keeping the headlights off the whole way.

He pulled onto the road and glided almost silently down the road toward the Bowers house. It finally struck him as incredible just how quiet modern car mufflers had become. His car made nary a sound, save for a squeak here and there from the suspension as he rolled over the uneven blacktop. Technology was an incredible thing.

He eased gently into the driveway, using the emergency hand brake located next to the shifter to slow himself. He was no brilliant criminal mastermind by any stretch of the imagination, but he did have enough rudimentary knowledge to know that taillights would light up like the fourth of July out here, and could possibly cause someone inside to take notice. He didn't know exactly where Dave's bedroom was, but it wasn't worth the risk.

He coasted to a stop and threw the car into park. There was a brief, bright flash behind him as the shifter moved through reverse towards park and the back-up lights came on. It was only a moment, but it had seemed like an explosion of light, like an alien ship in a movie.

Fuck...Jesus forgive me.

He froze, his heart caught in his throat, and looked for movement or notice from the house. He scanned the darkened windows, hardly breathing, his eyes squinted in strained concentration.

Nothing.

After two full minutes, he started taking in normal breaths of air again, and his heartrate dropped down to a more manageable level. He killed the ignition and reached for the door. His hand was on the handle, fingers tugging, about to pull it open, when he paused again, a new thought occurring to him.

He drew his hand back and turned to look up at the cabin light above him. There was a switch there, options for setting it from 'DOOR' to 'OFF'. He sighed heavily at the near fiasco, switched the lamp to 'OFF', then twisted his neck until the joints popped.

Norman reached back to the door handle and gently pushed the door open. Stepped out. Gingerly pressed the door back closed until it clicked.

He was immediately aware of shouting coming from inside the house. *Loud* shouting. It was so loud, in fact, that it almost sounded like the people arguing might have been outside with him. There were even some snarls mixed into the heated words, and at one point a high falsetto note—Norman thought this had come from Laura Bowers—pierced the night with a sarcastic vibrato.

He smiled.

Norman adjusted his mask again, breathing in deeply the rich, rubbery scent—now laced with sweat and body odor—and trotted silently around the side of the house to the back. His grip tightened and loosened on the grip of the hatchet as he made his way around the back corner of the house and tip-toed up the stairs onto the deck.

He worried momentarily about the wood creaking beneath his feet, but he needn't have. Dave Bowers was a construction worker by trade, and this deck was still fairly new and was plenty solid. Nothing moaned beneath him as he made his way up the steps and crossed the deck to the back door, silent as a cat.

The shouting was louder now, and he could even make out what they were saying.

"You always, always, *always* have to buck the system, Dave!" a woman's voice yelled. It was Laura. "It's *their* church, not yours!"

"You think I don't know that, Laura?" Dave Bowers yelled from inside. "And I *wasn't* bucking the system, I was doing *precisely* what they had asked! Only I was too stupid to realize the underlying message was that they weren't interested in what anyone but *Norman* had to bring to the table!"

"Here we go again, it's always *Norman*! *Norman, Norman, Norman!* You're so jealous, it's sickening!"

"Jealous?! You think I'm jealous of *him?* You really have lost your fucking mind, Laura!"

"Oh, wow! *Woowww!* Now you're gonna start using language like that? Barely twelve hours after getting us thrown out of the church and you're already talking like those thugs on TV!"

"Jesus Christ!"

"And blaspheming too!"

"Would you just shut up and have my back for *once* in your life?!"

The shouting continued.

Norman smiled when he'd heard his name come up in the conversation. He'd known Dave Bowers was jealous of him. He knew *everyone* was jealous of him, for that matter. And what was there not to be jealous of? Norman was tall and handsome; his mother had said so. He could play music and sing like an angel; his mother had said so. He was an incredible lover.

His mother had said so.

So he fully understood that everyone around him was green with envy every time they saw him. He'd probably be the same way if he were anyone else. People were always jealous of those who had such an amazing call on their life as Norman had. It came with the territory. It was just part of it, as his father would sometimes say.

The shouting intensified and the voices reached new heights hitherto not known achievable in the spectrum of human sound. Norman smiled behind his scowling goat mask and took advantage of the situation.

He broke the glass panel over the lock.

Chapter Thirteen

Laura waddled up out of the bed, her face red and angry.

It was a substantial effort for her to roll her girth out of the bed, and she grunted audibly as she rose. Blankets were thrown asunder in the process and the springs in the mattress squeaked and awed with relief as they attempted to return to their original size and shape, albeit unsuccessfully.

She was furious with her husband. He was always going against the grain, always seemed to have a different point of view from everyone else around him. Why couldn't he just go along to get along? He was always questioning every position *anyone* seemed to take on *any* subject, never mind those in the church. But he was never more vigorous in his opposition to leadership and authority in general than when it came to the church. Any doctrine, any *idea* the church put forth, he was immediately digging through his Bible, searching scriptures, holding it up to compare. He would take *nothing* at the pastor's word. Nothing at all.

This was perhaps the most frustrating part of the whole thing. Sure, the scriptures told them to work out their *own* salvation with fear and trembling, to study to show yourselves approved. Blah, blah, blah. Dave was always pointing those things out to her. But she would often retort to his reasoning by saying that if God put the pastor in authority, then he should defer to him. Should submit to him. Certainly, God had chosen a pastor for His church who understood scripture better than they could, why else elevate him to such a position?

But that was never good enough for Dave. That wasn't how things worked, he would explain. In such a fractured church world as they found themselves today, with literally tens of thousands of varying denominations throughout the world at odds with one another on various interpretations and doctrinal stances, it was up to them as individuals to search and know the scripture and be able to defend it against heresy and false teaching.

"You sound like a Catholic now, Dave!" she screamed as she stood.

Dave was rolling his eyes as he stood across the room from her in nothing more than his skivvies. He rubbed a hand across a face that was smiling bitterly in utter frustration.

"Yeah, yeah," he said, "I forgot. They told you at their church that Catholics were evil, the great whore of Babylon. If I use a word like heresy, I must be a Catholic now, and whoring myself out to religion. Is that about right?"

Her lips were quivering as her blood pressure rose and blossomed into bright petals of fury across her chubby cheeks.

"You know what, Dave?" she said, her voice quavering in spite of her efforts to the contrary. "You did this to us. You finally argued your point all the way out of the church. I hope you're happy now! Maybe now you *can* go and do what you want! Go be a Catholic now if that's what you want to do, I don't even care anymore! But I'm going back to Revival Rock, and I'm going to talk to Pastor Cherry and fix this so at least *I* can go somewhere where the Holy Spirit moves!"

"I never said I wanted to be a Catholic, woman!" Dave belted out to her, his hands spread wide in frustrated confusion. "I've *never* said that! I just don't buy that they're evil, that's all! And no, I'm sorry, I say we're done with Revival Rock. We're done! They're out of their mind and not trying to promote *anything* but themselves and their precious son, Norman. It's certainly not about Jesus over there!"

"I'll go wherever I want!" she spat. "And I'm not talking to you *anymore* tonight. I'm sleeping on the couch!"

With that, she stormed out of the bedroom and up the hall to the living room and the couch. Her thin silk robe swayed and bloomed as she went, her feet stamping a boisterous march all the way.

She was shaking her head, trying to understand how any of this had even happened. The fight had started over the *blankets*, for crying out loud! And it had somehow devolved into all of this?

But arguments were like that, she supposed. They start one place, then they spread out like mole-trails toward everything else that's bothering the arguers. From irritation about who was going to have the most covers to an uproar about church and scripture.

"That's fine, Laura, that's just fine!" Dave shouted to her from the bedroom she was leaving behind. "I hope you enjoy the couch tonight! 'Cause I'm sleeping in my *bed*! The one *I* paid for! Try not to break the fucking seat when you sit down!"

She twirled around in the dark of the living room and opened her mouth to respond, but then thought better of it. Something had happened to Dave, something in his spirit. The breakdown at the church and on the worship team had fractured something inside of him. He *never* would've used language like that with her back when things were good at the church. Before he started questioning everything and finding scripture to refute things left and right every Sunday morning. And he *certainly* would never have made comments alluding to her weight.

She shut her mouth so hard her teeth clacked and rattled. Tears stung the corners of her eyes. She squeezed her fists to the point that she thought the skin over her knuckles would split. Then she blew out a long, slow breath. Eased her hands back open.

Enough fighting for one night.

She turned again and went past the couch and on to the kitchen. She was angry, and anger demanded ice cream.

She strode across the tile of the kitchen, threw the freezer door open, and rummaged around until she found the tub of Blue Bell and pulled it out. Blue Bell was always there to calm her nerves, ease her frustration, and bring her solace.

Always there to spread your ass and join your thighs too, Laura, she heard a voice in her head say. It sounded suspiciously like Dave's voice.

Dave had never said such a thing, of course. Even at his most angry, she didn't think he'd ever say something like that. But in her mind, she was convinced that her husband despised her, was disgusted by her.

The heck with you, Dave, she thought in response. *And see? I didn't have to use any dirty language that would hurt Jesus's heart. Humph.*

She sat the Blue Bell down on the counter. It really was the best ice cream in the world. In fact, it was *synonymous* with ice cream. Every Texan knew this fact intrinsically.

Her mouth watered.

She closed the freezer door and the last light in the kitchen faded into the night. She felt in a drawer and produced a large spoon, then she snatched up the tub of the world's finest ice cream and started to make her way back to the living room. She felt a breeze slink past her arm as she walked in front of the back door, though she was still reeling with too much anger to pay it much mind.

Then something stabbed into her foot.

She winced and dropped the tub of ice cream to the floor. It thumped and rolled away under their kitchen table, the spoon skittering noisily across the tile. Her foot was throbbing and she could feel liquid heat oozing from her arch, something slick under the pain in her foot.

She hobbled backwards away from where she had just stepped and reached back for the refrigerator. She swung the door open. Light flooded out and revealed the scene before her. Her foot was bleeding. Bleeding pretty badly, too. She craned her foot around to get a look at what she'd stepped on and saw a shard of glass protruding out of the arch in her foot. It was streaked with blood and she could see spiderwebbed lines and splinters hanging off of it.

How in the world?

She turned her eyes to the floor and saw a trail of blood leading before her to where she'd just been. Right in front of the back door. It was smeared and messy. There were droplets of blood speckled around a snaking smear of the stuff that led all the way back to where she was now, where it was starting to pool.

Then she saw more glass. Several shards of it, in fact, scattered around the floor in front of the back door. She let her eyes follow up the door to the glass panel which was separated into eight sections above the knob.

The panel just above the knob was busted out.

Now how in the Sam-hill did that *happen,* she thought. *Heck,* when *did it happen? We've been home all night. Dave came in from his shop through that door. He didn't mention anything about it. And he would have, too. He would have made a big fuss about it and wondered how I broke the window, probably muttering all that dirty language he seems to have picked up here recently.*

Then a shadow moved from behind the table.

At first, her mind was refusing to process the images correctly. There was a tree-limb swaying in the breeze out back, or something like that causing the shadows to move. It wasn't the *shadows* coming alive.

But there *were* no trees in their back yard to cast shadows. This realization gave her brain freedom now to pursue all sorts of explanations, as the thought-gnome in her mind thumbed through millions of drawers, trying to find a file that would explain what she was seeing. Something that would make some rational sense of the situation.

The shadow moved in further and seemed to solidify into a shape. It was a more familiar shape now, no longer a blurring of dark lines cloaked in ink. The light from the refrigerator cast new eerie shadows across the kitchen, but the shape took form in spite of them.

It was a man.

Only, it *wasn't* a man. It was in the *shape* of a man, but the face wasn't human at all. The lines were all wrong and it appeared to have fur on it. Twin horns curled up from the sides of the forehead and went back behind the ears. The face had a blank appearance to it, as though there was no real life in it at all.

Except for the eyes.

The eyes. As soon as her eyes locked on the ones glaring out at her, she saw life there. They were dark, yet they seemed to blaze all the same. Like some dark fire was behind them, burning with intensity.

Then she heard it breathe. Oh, God, that breathing!

She would surmise in her subconscious during the last moments of her life that hearing the thing's breathing was the most horrible sound she'd ever heard in her life. Nothing had ever sounded quite so terrible to her. It was deep and seemed to be amplified and muffled at the same time. There were flapping sounds as though there were some horrible gasket in its mouth that had come loose and was now flapping loudly with each breath the thing drew.

Horrible claws dug into her spine and rendered her immobile. She may as well have been a paraplegic. A paraplegic who could nonetheless stand. She was rooted to her position, the pain in her foot and the blood streaked across the tiles were a distant memory now. She was faintly aware that she was trying to scream, but no sound would come out of her throat. Her airways were being choked tightly shut by invisible hands which seemed to be made of flexible ice.

All she could do was stare at the thing.

Then the man-thing with the animal face took a few more steps and she realized the thing had the head of a goat. A blank, white goat. It had the little goatee coming down off the point of its chin. She also saw that what she had thought was fur was merely shaped rubber made to *look* like fur.

It was a man, alright. A man wearing a mask. And as this realization came crashing home, she finally saw the hatchet in his hand.

At that moment, new power rose up in her from some deep well inside. She wrenched the claws from her spine and began to move. The hair on her neck was standing on end and her skin was riddled in gooseflesh, but she could move. She took a step on her injured foot and felt fresh agony shoot up her leg like a bolt of electricity as the shard of glass embedded in her foot buried itself deeper into her flesh. She tried to call out in pain, to call out for Dave, but though she had torn free of the claws on her spine, the invisible, icy hands around her throat were still present and accounted for.

Where are you, Dave? she thought. *Can you not hear this?*

But she knew he couldn't. She was on the other side of their house, and it was a rather large house. Further, what had there been for him to hear? The tub of ice cream thumping on the floor? Hardly. The clattering spoon? Perhaps, but that was no cause for alarm, not in the mood they were both in. Could he have heard her when she winced from the glass in her foot? Not likely, she'd hardly made a sound.

All the same, she was wishing and praying for him to come into the kitchen, perhaps looking to make amends for their argument, and find her. To stop this maniac who'd invaded their home.

But there was no sign of Dave and she was unable to scream.

The man moved toward her more swiftly now. She hobbled through the pain in her foot, which was now nearing excruciating, and reached her left hand out. She was going for the knife block. That's what she always saw the women do in the movies, and now, as if by instinct, she was doing the same.

She managed to cross the space of the kitchen to the opposite counter where the block of knives was before the man got to her. Her hand slid across the smooth Formica of the countertop toward the knives, both reaching out and steadying herself against the pain her foot.

Then her hand stopped dead.

There were new symphonies of pain raging from her arm. About two inches above her wrist, there was some black object protruding out of her skin. As her eyes followed the length of the black object, she could see the man's hand was attached to the end.

It was the hatchet.

It had buried into her flesh and cut deep into her. Her eyes bulged as she stared at it in horror and saw blood begin to flow out in jetting spurts. The man twisted the blade of the hatchet side to side a couple of times and wrenched it free. There were awful sounds of crunched bone and a wet, sucking *schlop* as it came free. Blood slung into the air as it arced away from her arm. But none of this compared to the horrific pain she now felt.

She *was* screaming now, only the sound of her screams still eluded her. Hot, wild breath was streaming out of her mouth as she saw with a totality of horror the wound on her arm. She picked up her arm, hardly aware of the man wielding the hatchet in her kitchen now. Where the hatchet had struck was a wide, gaping wound, blood flowing from it like a mighty river. The hand and wrist flopped over almost ninety degrees when she raised her arm. It hadn't managed to cut all the way through, but the bone was splintered and separated fully. Her hand now only hung by muscle and fleshy sinew.

She whirled around and started moving backwards toward the living room, staring at her ruined arm in wide-eyed terror. Her foot was slipping with every step as it continued to pour blood out of her in sheets.

Then something struck her face.

There was a painful, jarring sensation that went through her entire skull as the hatchet dug into her jawbone on the left side of her face. Shock was setting in at this point and the pain seemed to be less now, fading away into obscurity to be dealt with at another time.

She heard the crunching and sucking sounds again as the hatchet was wrenched free and she stumbled backwards. Somewhere down the hall she heard someone shout.

"What the fuck is all that noise?"

She knew she had to get to that voice. That was the only thing she knew anymore. She was bleeding horribly and she was hurt, oh *Jesus,* was she hurt! But through all of the pain and terror and choking fear, she knew if she could just get to that voice she might be saved.

She turned around and began to hobble through the living room, sprinkling it thoroughly with crimson. She felt herself starting to tremble as she made her way across the room and to the hall. The hall to her bedroom. To Dave.

To the voice that might save her.

Behind her, she could hear the man following her. And she could hear that horrible breathing.

Chapter Fourteen

"What the fuck is all that noise?" Dave shouted from his bed.

He had jumped right into the sheets when Laura left the room, waddling and stomping away in her self-righteous tantrum. He'd been too furious to follow after her, but managed that final warning to her not to break the couch, unable to click his mouth shut.

And he felt bad about it. It had been harsh and rash. Something a person says in the heat of the moment, trying to get one last dig in, one last *cut,* before the part where no one speaks for several days starts.

But it had been too far. And he knew it. Laura hadn't responded to it, and he knew that meant that he'd hurt her. Probably hurt her deeply. But none of that was what he really thought of her. In spite of the fact that she was a lemming for Cherry Reese and that awful damned church, Dave loved her. He loved her very much. Sure, she was off on some things, but who wasn't? No one was perfect, himself included. These were ultimately menial pet peeves he was striking out against.

However, making a remark about her weight was simply uncalled for. He knew she struggled with it, and she *did* make efforts from time to time to get it under control. Hell, he struggled with it himself, though not nearly to the same degree. He'd married her for better or worse, and her weight wasn't why he loved his wife. It was all the other things.

He decided he would give it a few more minutes, let

things cool off a bit, and then he would go in and apologize. She deserved an apology. So did he, for that matter, but that wasn't important. What was important was that he'd hurt his wife, and the relationship was more important than who was right or wrong.

Contrary to Laura's reasoning, however, he *had* heard the tub of ice cream thump to the floor. He hadn't known it was indeed ice cream that was doing the thumping, but he'd heard the sound all the same. It was faint, but the house was quiet and sound traveled. He'd heard the tinkling of metal as some utensil skittered across the tiles, but he hadn't paid it much mind. She was mad and flustered and had dropped something. No big deal.

He'd also heard the refrigerator door open for the second time. That sound was more identifiable and distinct. The soft *shucking* sound as it sucked open.

Then he'd heard a much louder thump a moment later.

It almost sounded like she was chopping up a carrot or something. That thought made him feel even worse, for if correct, she was likely trying to eat something healthier now that he had made the remark about her weight causing damage to the couch. Eating healthier was a good thing, but if his cutting remark were the reason...

He sighed and rubbed his face. It was late. All he had wanted to do when he came inside from the shop was to take a nice long piss—which he had done—and lay down with his wife. Feel her warmth and her touch. Her comfort.

But all this other shit had happened instead, and in spite of how tired he was, he knew he wouldn't sleep now.

And she's making so much noise *in there!*

New frustration had welled up in him as he heard thumping and rustling coming from the kitchen, and he let his anger get the better of him again, shouting at her and cursing for good measure.

As soon as he'd said it, he was sorry again. The language was explicitly aimed at pissing her off. More than she was already. As if he needed to do that.

Way to go, asshole, he thought. *You really know how to mend a relationship, don't ya?*

He threw the covers aside and rolled out of the bed. He was going to go in to Laura and commence with the apologies and repentance. Get it over with. Get her calm. Bring her back to bed. He wanted to sleep.

But he heard her clambering down the hallway now. She was coming to him. Probably hyped up mad, ready for round two to start, pink-cheeked and huffy, fueled with indignance at his cursing bark to her a moment ago.

God, you're an asshole.

He decided to just stand there instead and let her come to him. Let her have her say. Do his best not to react or respond with anything other than 'I'm sorry' and 'I love you'. He was just ready to get it over with.

Then his blood-soaked wife stumbled into the room.

Her eyes were wide and blood was streaming from her face and her hand. No, it wasn't her hand, it was her arm. Her hand was bent over and flopping at a horribly unnatural position. Her face was in awful shape too. There was a deep gash across her cheek and her jaw was hanging open and to the right in such a way that he was instantly sure that it had been completely knocked out of joint. Blood was everywhere on her, her thin robe bright with scarlet liquid.

He had no time to think, even if he'd been able to in that moment. No questions arose about what had happened, what she'd done to herself. If those questions *had* arisen, he might have had the state of mind to fetch the Sig Sauer pistol in his night stand and be more prepared.

But none of that happened. All he could do was move straight into panic mode.

"Jesus Christ!" he screamed and moved to come to her.

He heard something horrible and stopped dead in his tracks. It was something like...*breathing.* And there was an awful flapping sound joined with it.

Laura collapsed to her knees and sunk all the way to the floor before him. She was mumbling something now, but he couldn't make it out through her shattered jaw. Blood was shooting out from her arm in long arcs, and all at once he was certain that an artery had been ruptured. Curses to all that was good and holy arose inside of him about the fact that they lived ten solid minutes out of town and his wife was bleeding to death on their bedroom floor and her face was destroyed and *what the fuck had happened to her?*

He rushed to her side and knelt down next to her. She was still trying to talk, trying to tell him something, but he couldn't make it out.

"Shh-shh," he shushed her. "Don't try to talk, I'm going to call the ambulance."

But she wouldn't stop talking.

She reached out with her good arm and gripped his wrist tightly. She tried to pull him to her with what little strength she had left.

He heard the breathing again.

It wasn't registering with Dave to investigate the breathing sound, or to prepare for what it might be, not with all that was going on. His mind wouldn't lock in on the sound and identify it because of everything his eyes were seeing in front of him. Sight was the primary sense right now, and all others took second fiddle.

He leaned in close to her, trying to understand what

she was saying.

"Shumwen en couse," she muttered into his ear through her nightmare mouth.

He shook his head, not understanding her.

"Baby, I can't understand you, let me call the ambulance!"

She gripped his wrist tighter. Her eyes were getting wider as she struggled to form the words, desperately trying to get the words out of her mouth in a way that he would understand.

He heard the breathing again.

Laura lifted her head slightly. It was probably all she could do, he imagined. Dave watched as she strained the words out one more time.

"Shumwen en house."

She managed to get the last word pretty much right. And that was when it clicked.

Someone in house.

A knot formed in his stomach all at once at the realization of what she had been trying to tell him. His eyes spread wide and he lifted his gaze up and over her to look down the hall.

He saw feet standing in the doorway. And he heard the breathing again.

Dave lurched up to his feet all at once. His heart leaped into his throat and cut off his air way. There was some horrible thing before him. In his bedroom. An invader. It seemed to be a man with the head of a...*a goat?*

He shook his head and looked again, his face a mask of stupefied confusion.

No, not the head of a goat, he realized. It was a goat *mask*. But this was far from the worst part of the aberration standing in he and his wife's room. The worst part was that Dave could now see the hatchet in the man's hand, dripping with blood.

Laura's blood.

All at once he started to leap forward, trying to do something, *anything.* In the back of his mind he was cursing himself for not reacting sooner. For not grabbing his gun.

But it was too late for all of that now.

As he lunged forward, the hatchet swooped up and *shucked* into Dave's shoulder. Horrible pain screamed at him from the wound and he jerked back. The hatchet was yanked free and the wall was speckled with blood. Then the man in the mask was stepping over Laura and coming after him.

All Dave could think of now was how sorry he was about the fight he'd had with Laura. Such trivial bullshit. *That* had been their last moments together, and guilt threatened to drown his terror.

Dave looked past the man in the mask and down to Laura's bleeding body. He was crying. Tears streamed his face as he beheld his dying wife and the weight of guilt drove him down into a sea of regret. He managed a hissing, weeping sentence to his wife, the one he loved so much and had just treated so terribly in their final moments together on this earth.

"I'm so sorry, baby!"

Chapter Fifteen

Laura looked up at her husband, who was bleeding terribly from his shoulder now. His chest and arm were coated in a thick, red blanket of blood, oozing and spurting from the giant gash in his shoulder. Tears spilled from his frightened, astonished eyes. She was crying now too, the terror and pain finally flooding over her like a crimson waterfall, and when she'd seen the finality in her husband's eyes as he'd told her he was sorry, she'd felt her heart split open. She wanted to leap up from the ground and run into his arms, shower him with kisses, and tell him it was all okay. That all was forgiven.

That she *loved* him.

But she could do none of that. She was aware that she'd lost a phenomenal amount of blood. She was cold now, even covered from head to toe in warm blood. She kept trying to lift her head, to call out to her husband. But she couldn't. She was too weak. All her body did now was a sort of involuntary shudder. But she could see. Yes, she could still see, and worse, she was aware. Was there anything more horrific than stone cold awareness in a moment such as this, she pondered?

There was another horrible sound from the hatchet as it smashed into Dave's chest. He cried out in pain, tears streaking his face as more blood jetted from his body. Laura watched on, shuddering and aware, her eyes a blurring pond of acid.

Then Dave's free hand reached up and grabbed at the man's face. Laura could see the back of the goat mask pull free of the man's head as Dave sank back to his knees. The mask was now in Dave's bloody hand, clenched into a ball, his breaths coming in wet, gurgling gasps.

Dave's face changed.

It went from one of weeping horror to outright fury and realization in the snap of a finger.

"*You,*" Dave said quietly, almost a whisper, blood oozing from his mouth.

Then the hatchet came down again and slashed into his throat. Blood splashed and arced and squirted all over the room and on the man who had come into their home. The man Dave had just recognized. There was a gurgling sound from Dave as he began to spit up blood from his opened throat in sheets. He was twitching and writhing. But she could still see that anger in her husband's eyes as they bore into the maniac in their home.

More tears poured from Laura and she blinked as the shudders intensified. She could feel herself fading. The squirts of blood from her arm, which had been rather enthusiastic before, were now mere trickles as the supply ran low.

It was almost over.

The man pulled the hatchet free of Dave's throat and she watched her quivering husband collapse onto the floor in front of her. His eyes were locked on hers as he coughed up his life-liquid, his face a rictus of pain and rage and longing. She thought she saw regret there as well. She was full of regret herself.

With all the effort of her will, which was fading as fast as her blood supply, she tried to reach her hand towards his. It was little more than a crawling effort, her fingers clawing slowly across the carpet towards him. His mouth was moving, but only terrible, wet grunts came out. His hand moved towards hers then, and she mouthed words she no longer had the ability to give voice to.

"I love you."

A trace of what she thought might be a smile dimpled his cheeks and his eyes seemed to brighten. He too began to move his crimson-stained lips.

"I—"

Then he went still.

All at once. No more moving, no more rise and fall of his chest. Nothing at all. Even his crying stopped. Dave's eyes seemed to film over with the blank emptiness of death. She felt a gentle breeze glide coolly over her matted hair, and for a moment she believed it was Dave's soul, stroking her face as he made his way to the great beyond. But then she heard the hum of the air conditioner and realized it had just turned on.

Dave was gone. If his soul stooped to touch her, she hadn't felt it. All she could feel was pain and horror and guilt and despair. She desperately wanted to feel Dave one more time, to touch him, feel his skin. But her hand was no longer moving and no matter how hard she focused, it wouldn't move.

Laura's eyes moved up, dark rings encroaching on her periphery now. She would be gone soon as well, she knew, joining her husband in glory. At this thought, all the horror seemed to slip away. All the fear and sadness and pain. All gone. Now she was looking forward to the peace that surpassed all understanding, standing in the light of her Creator, next to her husband for eternity. A horribly disfigured smile graced her features then as her vision began to darken a little more.

She saw the man stoop down and wrench the mask free of Dave's lifeless hand. And when he did, she saw finally his face and knew why Dave had look so enraged.

It was Norman Reese. And the man was smiling.

If she could have laughed in that final moment, she

would have. Not out of humor, but out of realization that her husband had been right after all.

Funny, she thought. *Dave was right all along. They really are crazy.*

Then her vision faded fully into eternal blackness.

Chapter Sixteen

Jim had awoken at seven o'clock with a pounding headache.

The headache was no doubt from his body's dehydration from the five vodka martinis he had downed the night before as he sat alone in his recliner thinking of his life, his job, Margie Johnson.

Of Honey.

Thinking of Honey always brought back that day in the summer of 1990. Brought back the house in the woods and The Glutton and...and...

...and the reason you drink, Jim.

That too. What they had done to those boys. Maybe others could forgive him for allowing it to happen, to *use* those boys to get free. They were assholes, after all. *Psychotic* assholes to boot. But Jim couldn't manage to forgive himself, no matter what those boys had been.

Jim hadn't bothered to use actual martini glasses when he'd made his cocktails. No, he used a regular, wide and tall drinking glass. Made for drinking tea or milkshakes from.

He hadn't bothered with measuring his liquor out, either. He knew by sight about how much would work to mix together and fill his glass to the brim. He'd had lots of practice, after all. Lots of trial and error.

So, needless to say, he'd gotten shitfaced.

Now his head was pulsating with a relentless rhythm which was in perfect sync with his heartbeat. He groaned and cursed as he rubbed his temples and made his way to the kitchen in nothing but his underwear. He needed four Advil and a couple of stout Bloody Marys and he would be good to go. He knew what ailed him and he knew what medicine to take. He did this often.

As he rounded the corner into his kitchen, he was startled to see Honey Bascom standing there in one of his button-down shirts, mixing a Bloody Mary for him right then. His memory of the night before was fuzzy at best, but he thought he'd been alone last night. But here was Honey, in *his* shirt, hair mussed and frazzled, looking like she'd been ridden like a fifty-cent pony all night long.

"H-Honey?" he muttered, his senses returning to him.

She looked up from stirring his glass. She didn't smile.

"Morning," she said and placed the stirring spoon in the sink. "I assume you need this?"

He nodded. "Advil, too."

She slid her hand across the counter and placed four brown pills next to his glass.

"Figured that too," she said and nodded to the drink. "Made it strong, you were pretty far gone last night."

"I, uh," he started and trailed off. He wasn't sure how to start the conversation. But as it turned out, he didn't need to, because she could read him like a book.

"You don't remember me coming over, huh?" she asked, not *really* asking. She already knew. "Yeah, I guess that doesn't surprise me much. You could barely stand when I first got here."

"Did we, um, you know?"

"Did we fuck each other?" she asked curtly, a sharp look in her eyes.

He managed a chuckle. "Well, I was going to say *make love*, but yeah, I guess that's close enough."

She shook her head, apparent distaste on her face.

"Yeah, we did, Jimmy," she said. "Amazing what the body is capable of when you get the blood flowing to the right place."

Jim was shocked. She had come by his office the day before as he was having a meeting with his patrolmen about keeping an eye out for Norman Reese and to let him know if they found him. She'd come in, explaining that she was doing a favor for Freddie James with one of his parishioners, who just so happened to be Charlotte Johnson. She had figured, and rightly so, that Jim would have some idea of what was going on and if he thought there would be any hope that Charlotte would see her daughter again.

They had exchanged pleasantries in an uncomfortable sort of way and then talked about the case. Jim didn't have anything definitive back yet from the forensics team, but all indications pointed to the likelihood that the poor girl had been seriously hurt at the very least, and quite possibly it was worse than that. They did have a suspect, yes, but again, nothing definitive to tie him to the scene yet.

Then they had talked about their little girl and all the pleasantry ceased.

Joanna Dalton was the spitting image of her mother. The dark hair and hazel eyes could have been grafted onto her straight from Honey. Even the light and naturally occurring tan of her skin was identical to her mother's. The only resemblance to her father, Jim, was her last name. She shared a few of his mannerisms and quirks—DNA had seen to that—but in appearance, she was all her mother. Like an immaculate conception.

So she'd gotten his name, but he'd ended up with almost no rights to her. He would get to see her on occasion, *if* he came out to see them in Mineola, which was thirty miles to the South of Winnsboro, but she could never come home with him. And with work, especially since he'd become Chief, Jim found fewer and fewer opportunities to make it out to see her.

At least that's what he told himself.

But Honey was quick to tell him a different tale. One about when you're a parent, you *make* time to see your child, no matter what. What you did *not* make were excuses. You showed up to every recital, every tournament, every event. You came to see your kid as often as humanly possible. Period, end of story.

Of course, Jim's reply had been about his lack of rights and the fact that he could never bring her back here to his house for a weekend, or share custody in any reasonable way with Honey. And round and round they'd gone. Eventually, Honey had barged out and went to help Reverend Freddie with the grieving Charlotte Johnson and left Jim sitting alone in his office, red-faced, white-knuckled, and pissed off.

Yet, somehow, she'd managed to get beneath him in his bed last night.

"I didn't think we parted on very amicable terms yesterday," Jim said crossing to the counter. He put his hand out and scooped up the Advil. He tossed them into his mouth and gulped deeply from the Bloody Mary.

She had indeed made it strong. And spicy as hell. He coughed.

"We didn't," Honey said, watching him gulp down his medicine and slyly smiling at the burning in his throat. "To be honest, I'm not sure why I came over here last night. I could have guessed you'd be in the state you were in. You've been that way for years now. But I don't know, I got to thinking about how close we were as kids, and seeing Freddie again after all these years and visiting with him and his wife, it was just like old times, you know?"

Jim didn't say anything, just looked at her.

She went on. "Anyway, it got me feeling all nostalgic, and we *do* share a daughter together. I miss what we had, I guess. I can't explain it, Jim. It happened. It was a mistake, and it won't happen again. I...I just..."

She trailed off and didn't say anything for almost a full minute. Jim stood silently by, drinking occasionally from his glass, feeling the vodka and Advil working through him and easing his aching mind.

"Freddie says Ryan's still around, too," she said after the long silence.

"Oh?" Jim asked, raising his eyebrows. "I haven't seen him in quite a while."

"Yeah," she said. "He's drilling water wells at some place out of town not too far from here. Lives out in the country, Freddie says. Been going to his church, as a matter of fact. I'd have never thought Ryan Laughton would see the inside of a church house, but I suppose stranger things have happened."

They both laughed quietly at this. Ryan Laughton was the very last person you thought of when you thought of Sunday morning churchgoers. He and Jim and Honey had continued partying hard for years after Freddie had decided to go into seminary to become a minister. They had been close then, all those years ago. Ryan was working construction at the time and Honey was waiting tables and going to night school for her counseling degree. Jim had recently graduated from the Police Academy and was patrolling most nights. But they had gotten together as often as possible to throw a few back and have a good time.

And to forget.

That had been the real bond they shared, Jim figured. They *all* wanted to forget. The three of them were trying to do so with alcohol, Freddie with the church.

It had been during the time Freddie was studying in seminary that Joanna had come into being. She was the *only* good thing that had come out of the whole situation, and Jim figured Honey would agree.

The three of them had been out one night, drinking it up and having a good time. Nothing had ever gone on romantically between Jim and Honey. Or Ryan and Honey, for that matter, though Jim knew that deep down Ryan was completely and irrevocably in love with her. But Honey either never noticed or hadn't been interested in him, so they had remained merely close friends. Just like she and Jim had.

So the alcohol had flowed and one thing led to another. Before either of them knew what was happening, they were in bed together at Jim's apartment, writhing in drunken pleasure. The next morning had been terribly awkward, and they had decided to chalk it up to too many drinks and forget about it.

But babies are hard to forget about.

Their relationship had disintegrated over the following months and when Ryan learned they were having a child together, he'd withdrawn from them both. He hadn't gotten angry, hadn't acted out in jealousy. He'd merely been hurt, heartbroken, and with the baby coming, it was something he hadn't been able to bear. They saw him less and less, until one day they realized they hadn't seen him in years.

One disagreement after another had ensued between Jim and Honey. Where to raise the baby? Should they get married? So on.

Then the lawyers had gotten involved and Jim had lost.

"Well," Honey sighed, standing up from the counter. "I'll get my things and get out of your way. I'm sorry about last night."

She was avoiding eye contact.

"Don't be," Jim said, shaking his head. "It was good

seeing you again, Honey."

She got over her aversion to eye contact and stared at him with a crooked look.

"Good seeing me?" she laughed sardonically. "You don't even remember me coming over!"

"I do now," Jim said, squeezing his eyes shut and nodding. "I was just in such a fog I didn't remember at first."

This wasn't a *complete* lie. He really *didn't* remember her coming over or what they'd done, but listening to her tell him filled his mind with enough images to fill in all the blanks missing from his memory.

"Whatever, Jimmy," she said, rolling her eyes.

She walked out of the room to get her clothes. As she went, Jim's phone started to ring. It was sitting on the counter where it was plugged into its charger.

He walked over to it, gulping from his glass again, and picked up the phone. The screen told him it was the County Sherriff.

Ah, Jesus, he thought, and swiped the screen to answer the phone.

When Honey came back into the room, Jim was standing next to the counter, his tethered phone in his trembling hand. His face was white as a sheet.

He glanced up at her.

"What is it, is something wrong?" Honey asked him, genuine concern in her voice.

"Yeah," he said. "Yeah, something is bad wrong. Very, very *bad* wrong."

"Well tell me, won't you?" she pleaded with him.

He shook his head.

"I can't, Honey," he said. "Not until I see it for myself. I'm not sure if it's coincidence or if we have a real problem here, and until I know, I don't want to talk about it."

"Well, you'll tell me when you can, right?" she asked.

He nodded.

"I will. If it's what I think it is, we've got a shitload of trouble. Will you be in town?"

"Yeah, for a couple of days, helping Freddie out with Mrs. Johnson. Joanna is with my neighbor Jan until I get back."

"Good," Jim said. "I don't want her in town right now."

A sick feeling crept into Jim's stomach.

Chapter Seventeen

The scene was awful.

It reminded Jim of something out of a horror movie, where the slasher boogeyman has just laid waste to several teenagers in a house during a party.

Only this wasn't a movie.

This was somehow worse. *Much* worse. The kitchen looked like a bomb had gone off in a butcher shop. Blood was all over the tiles of the floor and on the countertop near the knife block. There were some chunks of what he assumed were bits of flesh which had come free of a body during a struggle and there were sprays of blood on the cabinetry and the sink.

And it only got worse from there.

Streaks of blood led into the living room. There were thin lines strewn all throughout the carpet and on the furniture. In the hallway leading to the bedroom were more thin lines, both in the carpet and on the walls, over pictures of the couple who owned the home and other various family members and perhaps friends. Some of the thin lines had streaks of blood that had slinked out of the confines of the original strokes and drizzled down the walls in awful, nightmarish crawls.

And the bedroom was a total bloodbath.

Walls, bed, blankets, carpet, television, *all* covered in blood. There were two large spots on the floor, perhaps four feet in rough diameter each, positioned about three feet apart.

"Is this where they found the bodies?" Jim asked

through clenched teeth. He didn't have a weak stomach, but the smell of the dried, congealed blood all around him was making him sick.

Sherriff Bocephus "Bo" Brock shook his head, looking down at the two massive stains. He was a large man. A *very* large man. He was in his late fifties, with solid gray hair that was rapidly thinning into nothingness. He covered this with the County Sherriff standard Stetson which loomed over deeply lined gray eyes that matched his hair. Above these eyes were salt and pepper eyebrows that looked like miniature wigs for a mad scientist. His cheeks and nose were permanently reddened from years on the bottle and beneath his chin was a substantial swatch of skin which dangled from too many fatty foods over the years and simple age itself. His belly preceded him wherever he went, rounding down acutely to a waistline that may once upon a time have been fit. He wore a tan Sherriff's Department button down with long sleeves buttoned at the cuff and black jeans with a large, golden belt buckle which displayed his department's insignia on it, though it was largely hidden by the girth of his stomach. Jet black cowboy boots rounded out his appearance of a Texas lawman.

"Didn't *find* any bodies, Big Jim," the Sherriff said, his arms spreading before him to the room, his accent the perfect, unhurried drawl of East Texas. "Only this. Peculiar, to say the least."

Peculiar, Jim mused. *There's an understatement.*

"Who found the scene?" Jim asked absently.

Sherriff Brock grunted a singular laugh.

"Damn Jehovah's Witness," he said, shaking his head. "Come 'round to peddle their brand of religion, don't get no answer, decide that ain't good enough. They's used to folks tryin' to dodge 'em when they're out proselytizin', and they seen the cars in the drive. So, they head on to the back to check for someone maybe millin' about outside, find the glass of the back door busted in and see a damn bloody mess inside. Called us. Never saw such a thing, they say. I say, *no shit, Sherlock, most folks ain't.* Anyhow, we come out then and find the place like this."

"Sherriff," Jim said, a hint of shudder in his voice as well as between his shoulders, "this whole thing is starting to look really bad."

"I agree, son," Sherriff Brock said peering out behind squinted eyes. "That's why I called you out. We been running the samples you found at that house in town. The Johnson case, I think it was? Anyhow, that's your investigation, and I ain't tryin' to butt into nothin', but I like to have an idea of what's going on in my county. I look into things from time to time. Especially things such as missin' ladies. You know that girl was churchin' over there at Revival Rock? Crazy sumbitches if you ask me. I attended just the one time, couldn't get my fat ass out the door fast enough. Anyhow, fella lives here, he and his wife attended that same church. Which is why I called you in. I ain't no conspiracy theorist, I tell ya what, but this ain't seeming too much like a coincidence to me."

Jim was shaking his head.

"I agree, this is no coincidence," he started, "but it's also different."

"How so?" Sherriff Brock asked, his bushy brows rising a notch.

"First of all, Margie's house—"

"Margie? Who's that now?"

"Margie Johnson. *Ms.* Johnson? My case from yesterday?"

"Right, right, right," Brock said nodding and catching up. "Didn't know her first name. Pardon my interruption."

Jim nodded and continued.

"Anyway, Margie's house was clean. Like *really* clean. Whoever did that took some time after. Cleaned the scene pretty well. Not perfectly, as you know, but well enough that it seemed like he was trying to cover his tracks. Just didn't really know what he was doing and wasn't thorough enough."

The Sherriff was nodding, his substantial second chin dancing and jiving along to the beat.

"But here," Jim said, spreading a hand out as if presenting the scene before them for the first time. "Here, he didn't do anything. No cleanup at all. And it also seems like this was more deliberate. A weapon was involved. At the other one, it seems like maybe there was an argument that turned bad and our guy panicked. Like maybe he wasn't going there to do any harm, but it just happened. Here, this was deliberate. The broken glass to get in the back door. All this blood everywhere."

The Sherriff continued nodding and said, "So you think we got two suspects? Two scenes where something bad went down and bodies go missing, people from the same church, direct ties to each other, but two different suspects?"

Jim picked up on the Sherriff's tone. He wasn't buying it.

"No, Sherriff," Jim said. "I agree, the coincidence is too strong to *be* a coincidence. I'm just saying the situations were different. Like maybe our guy *accidentally* did something to Margie, but then he liked it. Liked it enough to do it again, maybe. Only this time on *purpose*."

"I get ya, I get ya," Brock said with a slow nod.

Jack Fletcher walked into the room carrying a toolbox and wearing coveralls. He nodded to Jim, smiling grimly.

"Chief," he said.

"Jack," Jim replied with a nod of his own.

Jack went about his business, setting his toolbox on

the floor next to one of the large stains and went to work.

"Anything yet on my case, Jack?" Jim asked the man's back.

Jack craned his neck around to him, sitting back on his heels.

"Not yet, but I have my lab technicians on it. Hopefully I'll know something this afternoon."

"Lemme know," Jim said, flatly.

"Will do," Jack said, and went back to the grim business at hand.

Jim and Sherriff Brock left the techs to their work and went out to the front yard, breathed in some fresh air. The stink of the blood was sticking to the insides of his nostrils like a stubborn parasite.

"Got a suspect I hear?" Brock said after a couple of moments of silence.

Jim shrugged. "Sort of. Nothing solid yet, though. It's really more of a hunch. Ex-boyfriend of Ms. Johnson, worship team leader at the church in question."

"Norman, you mean?" Sherriff Brock said, again giving rise to his bushel of brows.

Jim nodded. "Yeah. Couldn't locate him yesterday. Caught up with his parents, though. They weren't any help, but man, that Cherry Reese gives me the creeps."

"You ain't tellin' me nothin' I don't already know, I tell ya what. That bitch is crazy as a cat in heat."

Jim laughed at this, though it was largely void of humor.

"Funny thing..." Sherriff Brock said and trailed off as his eyes drifted back to the house.

"What's that, Sherriff?" Jim prodded after a moment.

Brock shrugged. "Well, might not mean nothin', but I been lawin' long enough to know it's the little details that really tie things together."

Jim nodded.

"Anyhow, what's funny is, fella owns this place—Dave Bowers is his name—him and his wife weren't just members of that crazy church. He played guitar on their band. Don't Norman head that up?"

Jim's face was ashen as he nodded.

The Sherriff nodded grimly as well and went on. "Well, like I say, it's the little things what tie it together. Anyhow, you keep me informed if you catch up with Norman, alright? I'd like to hear what he has to say about all this."

Jim nodded in the affirmative. "I'll do it."

"Thank ya, son," Brock said as he hiked his belt up under his belly. "Now, if you'll excuse me, I got a turd tryin' to make a stain in my britches I'm gonna have to attend to."

Jim nodded again, looking at the ground, face flushed and awkward. Sherriff Brock was a good lawman, and a decent man in general for that matter, but his bedside manner was lacking in droves.

Jim looked back to the house through squinted eyes as Sherriff Brock ambled toward his vehicle.

God, if you're there...I need some help.

Chapter Eighteen

Getting the bodies to the house had been no small matter. Dave was a solid mass and probably weighed a good two hundred pounds, but in death his weight seemed to have tripled. Norman had wisely chosen to take him second, because although Laura was technically lighter than Dave at around one-seventy-five, there was simply more *of* her. Rolls of fat on her belly and around her tits. *Huge* tits, though they weren't of the type Norman typically liked. He liked them to have a little more perk to them than these sagging bags of flesh. More like the ones Margie had. Or like the ones his mother had had, before age had caused her nipples to point down like the eyes of a chastised puppy. But despite their not being to his taste, the graceful brushing of them against his shoulder as he carried her to the house managed to awaken his trunk.

However difficult, he had still managed well enough, all the same. After leaving Laura in the foyer of the house and returning with her husband, he'd found that the Almighty had not shown up to feed. Norman marveled at this, thinking surely his Lord would be anxious for a feast. But Norman didn't see Him.

Not at first, anyway.

After poking around the house for a few minutes, Norman heard an odd warbling sound accompanied by the creak and groan of boards, straining to support weight. Clopping footsteps floated through the house.

That's odd, Norman thought. *He was gliding when we met.*

Then he saw a hulking shadow come around the

corner of the hallway leading to the foyer. It was very tall, about seven and half feet, and the shoulders were about four feet across. The thing's body was covered in a gel-like slime, and there seemed to be no skin at all. Organs were visible and they quivered behind a cobweb of ribcage. Norman could see bone structures that were reminiscent of a human skeleton, but with some marked differences. The knees went the other way. The *wrong* way, although they seemed sturdy and to operate all the same. The hips were extremely narrow in stark contrast to the ultra-wide shoulders. There was no sex between its thighs that he could see, but then again, there was no skin. Tendons and muscles were writhing around the bones and he could see cartilage compressing and expanding as the beast moved. Its face was a strange shape that Norman simply couldn't identify. It didn't seem to follow anything his mind had ever learned about planes and lines and arcs. It wasn't an oval shape like most human faces, and it wasn't square or circular either. There were several jagged lines around its perimeter and tiny horn-like spikes jutted out from the meat of its flesh. The eyes were black as ink. And the mouth opened and closed horizontally instead of vertically like his own. It looked like a battered vagina lined with razor sharp teeth which were as black as its eyes.

Norman was frozen in awe. His Lord looked very different from the shadow that had come before, but somehow he knew it was the same being. He marveled at the thing's back when it bent down, wordless, and began to devour first Laura and then Dave. Huge bones protruded from its back, like spears which had been stabbed there and left. Only the points protruded outward rather than inward. Almost like tentacles, only these were rigid spines.

God is a marvelous being! Norman marveled with wet eyes.

He listened in pure rapture and watched as the thing ate. Sounds of tearing and ripping flesh, of splashing intestines as they spilled from the bodies onto the floor, sent sensations all over Norman's body that he'd never experienced before. He had no fear, none at all, only ecstasy as he watched his God feed. The activation of his penis, which had started with the gentle brushings of Laura's massive breasts, was now a raging thing. He could feel every sensation as blood pulsed through his member, and there was no surprise at all in him when he began to ejaculate. He embraced its flow, shuddering with the pleasure. The pleasure only achieved when in the presence of God Himself.

The beast ate everything. Skin, meat, bone, organs. All of it. It even sucked the blood from the floorboards in an almost comical slurp. When it was done, the foyer—which should have been covered in a crimson pond—was as clean as it had been when Norman first brought the bodies inside.

And then a curious thing happened.

As the monster which Norman thought was God was finishing its meal, Norman could see new muscles forming beneath the gelatinous coating covering its body. Fibers formed and writhed into place, tightening over the bone structure. New tendons wrapped up from joints and cartilage seemed to puff larger from between the bones like silicone filling a hole. And it seemed to grow in height and breadth. Not much, but enough that Norman noticed it.

It was truly marvelous.

"I need more meat," it said to him, its voice sounding more wet now than it had before. A small piece of flesh hung from one of its vertical lips.

Norman was nodding. "Yes, Lord," he said, his eyes

wide with amazement. "I can get you more! As much as you need!"

"Good," it said. "Bring me more tonight. I'm growing stronger. Soon my body will be whole in your world and I can bring the new Heaven into existence."

Norman was nodding vigorously now, his hands clasped before him in adoration. Norman was utterly mad, the tumor in his brain and the mania of his false religion pushing all reason and logic so far from his thought processes that he was snorting up this line of shit like a coke addict with a mirror.

"For your glory!" Norman hissed sharply and fell to his knees. "Thank You for using a vessel such as me!"

Then the thing smiled. Or what passed for smiling with a creature such as itself. The razor lined vagina-mouth spread from the center in a diamond shape, revealing the black knives in its mouth. As it spread, it made Norman think of the flesh around a cobra's head.

It was beautiful.

"I'll have fresh meat tonight," he said, staring up at his false god. "I have just the ticket in mind for a fine feast!"

The thing's smile broadened. A black, forked tongue slinked out and fetched the loose piece of flesh hanging from its lips.

PART FOUR:

A Confrontation

Sunday, August 7, 2016

Chapter Nineteen

George Reese tore the picture of the baby Jesus off the wall of his church office and smashed it across his desk. Shards of glass danced brilliantly through the air and tinkled to the floor in a jagged mess, the light from the fixture above him reflecting back accusingly in the broken blades.

He was breathing hard, a startling vein protruding from his forehead, throbbing like an angry worm. His eyes blazed with fury and frustration.

"Bitch!" he hissed under his breath.

His fiery eyes clamped shut and he drew in a deep and deliberate breath. Let it out slowly through an *oh*-shaped mouth. Then he did it again. And a third time.

She did this to him often. Got his blood pressure up, his anger, his wrath. But what George Reese was incapable of doing was confronting Cherry with his issues. His issues with *her*. He wasn't, in fact, very good at confronting *anyone*, but this was especially true with his wife.

He figured it all went back to his affair with her sister, all those years ago. He often lamented internally how he wished Cherry would have just left him then. Not stuck it out with him. Not counseled with him and that lay pastor.

He wished often she'd have just shot him dead.

It wasn't so much that he *wanted* to be dead, but simply that death was preferable to living with her in a post *'I-fucked-your-sister'* world. And he could forget all about leaving now, thank you very much. No, everything they had was tied up in the church, in the belief of their flock in the sincerity of their pastors. Everything. Leaving her now would destroy every bit of what they had built. Their livelihood came from this place, and it had turned into quite a lucrative livelihood at that. Between the ministries and the tithes and offerings, along with the books they had written together that were selling rather well—*books on successful marriages, ha-ha!*—they were bringing down quite a bit of money. The dissolution of their marriage at this point, under such a microscope—which the leeches were always peering down upon—would destroy it all. He'd be left with nothing, irreparably destitute.

Hence, the preference of death.

But what of his children? If she had killed him back then when he was playing hide the bone with her sister, his children would never have been born. Well, no great loss there. None at all, as a matter of fact. Jake had been an absolute nightmare—one he was all too thankful had vanished—and Norman was such a carbon copy of Cherry that it was frightening and sickening all at once.

Norman...

Yes, he seemed to be the focus of their current issues now. Norman. That god-forsaken nut. George had no illusions or delusions about his boy, not the way Cherry did, anyway. He knew Norman was nothing special, and he knew good and well that the *only* reason Norman was heading up their praise team ministry was the fact that he'd fallen out of Cherry's cunt. In her eyes, there was simply no one else. Her boy, her boy, her *precious little boy.*

Despite this knowledge, George had resigned to the notion easily enough. After all, it wasn't as though he was going to argue with Cherry. He'd relinquished his masculinity to her decades ago, and he was happy enough to let her have it most of the time. But days like this, on mornings only hours before he had to go up and give a sermon and pretend to be happy and saved in Jesus Christ, the she-demon would raise her ugly head and bring this shit down on him.

He opened his eyes and looked down at the shattered glass. It gleamed and mocked him.

Pick me up! the shards were saying to him. *Pick me up and bury me in her fucking throat!*

If only.

She had come to his office just a short while ago. Neither of them had heard from Norman all weekend, not since Jim Dalton had come by and informed them of Margie's disappearance and of his knowledge of her recent breakup with their son. Should've been an easy enough thing to clear up, if only the little motherfucker would show his goddamn face. But no. Norman had vanished. Vanished right into thin air. Then there had been the second visit the day before. The bloody but bodiless scene at the Bowers house. The house of the same Dave Bowers who had stormed out of this very office in a fit of anger mere minutes before Jim had come around asking about Norman in relation to Margie Johnson. Norman had been due to be at the church around that time. They'd been expecting him any minute, as a matter of fact. But he'd never shown up. Cherry had spoken to him on the phone that afternoon, but that had been the last contact either of them had with their son.

And the bitch had had the nerve to come to *him* like it was his fault. Like she believed *everything* was his fault in this post *'I-fucked-your-sister'* world.

"If you'd have just stood up to Dalton like a *man,* none of this would be happening!" she'd spat at him. "But what do I expect from a dog like you? Honestly, what do I really expect? You've never seen the greatness in Norman, not the way I have, and you've never had much of a spine either!"

"Cherry, I—"

"Shut up!" she'd yelled. "Don't you Cherry me! Do you have any idea how bad this looks?"

George remembered nodding and looking at the floor, the same spot now occupied by the debris of the baby Jesus picture.

"So, you realize how much trouble Norman is going to be in, right?"

"If he'd just come forward and talk to the man, I'm sure—"

"Stop interrupting me!" she bellowed. "You'd be *glad* to be rid of him, wouldn't you? Glad to be rid of your own *son!*"

George found a tiny fragment of spine at that point, and had tried putting it to use.

"You mean like you were glad to be rid of Jake?" he had asked and almost instantly regretted it.

Crimson wrath replaced her eyes.

"How *dare* you bring up that name!" she hissed like a serpent. "Who do you think you are that you can mention that name to *me?*"

The fragment of spine crumbled into powder.

"I'm sorry, I—"

Then she had slapped him, open-palmed, across his face. Red fingers of pain exploded up his cheek and into his temple and there was a sharp needling of agony on the soft flesh of his ear. His hand instinctively leaped to his face for aid, though none could be administered. He was wincing and actually felt involuntary hot tears stinging his eyes.

"Don't you *ever* mention that motherfucker to me again!" she said coldly and without regret. "Out of the same mouth flow blessings and curses, like our Bibles say. Norman has been my blessing. Jake was the curse. Never mention him again."

George had nodded, still trying to nurse his sore face in a pitiful display.

"Now," she said, more calmly, "I talked to Norman. With all that's happening, I've convinced him that skipping service this morning would be a mistake. He's going to be here. The church needs his leadership in worship, anyway, but if Dalton or one of his goons shows up looking for him, he should be here. We need to contain this. Three people are missing from this church, all with a direct connection to Norman, and he's been missing as well. Meeting with God, he tells me, but who knows. He's a very spiritual boy, my Norman..."

She trailed off, looking to the picture of the baby Jesus where it had been hanging. George had no doubt she was placing Norman's face over the baby Jesus in her mind. It was sick. *Truly* sick. He knew much more about her relationship with Norman than she realized, but he would never say anything to her about it. She was as crazy as Jake had been, maybe even more so. And Norman was cut from the exact same cloth as she.

A family of psychos, he thought, but did not dare say.

Cherry's eyes refocused and she looked back at him.

"We'll say he's been with us," she said, going on as though there had been no break in the speech. "We'll say he's been studying the Word and praying for Margie all this time. Dave and his wife too. We'll say he couldn't be disturbed in this time, so we kept it secret."

"Won't that sound, I dunno, *phony?*" George had asked.

She shook her head. "Not to anyone who knows Norman, it won't. And those who don't know him will come to know him through us as we tell them about him. About his loving spirit and kindness. His holiness and devotion to God."

That crazy look was back in her eyes as she spoke of her son. George realized that she could just as well be speaking of Jesus of Nazareth at that very moment. Evangelization was what she was talking about when you got right down to it, but evangelizing for their *son.*

You twisted bitch, he thought, but once again did not dare say.

"And you need to have an altar call to pray for the missing people. To pray they will be found safe and sound and free from harm."

"Cherry, the Bowers' house was *covered* in blood," George said. "Literally covered. The evidence Jim talked about finding at Margie's house suggests the same!"

"They don't know that," she said, nodding to the wall which separated the sanctuary from the office. "The congregation doesn't know the details. *Won't* know the details until at least tomorrow when the newspaper comes out and the media starts to speculate. And no one knows that *we* know those details either. It will look good, like good Southern Christian people should look. Now you do it, and for God's sake, clean yourself up."

That had been when George had realized there was a trickle of blood coming from the corner of his mouth. Cherry had smiled that phony smile—the one she always had ready for quickdraw—turned, and walked out. Her three layers of clothes swaying behind her and hiding any hint of a figure—*George had to assume she still had a figure under there somewhere, though he hadn't seen it or fucked it in many years now*—and he watched the door close behind her.

He grabbed a tissue from his desk and soiled it thoroughly cleaning up his mouth, just like he'd been told to do.

As he was doing this, he happened to look up and see the baby Jesus, smiling and laughing at him. Then he saw

Mary, holding the baby in swaddling clothes, adoring her son with tearful and joyful eyes.

Then he'd seen baby Jesus's face turn into Norman's in the picture. He also saw Cherry's face materialize over the Blessed Virgin's.

He smashed it.

Chapter Twenty

Jim pulled into the parking lot of Revival Rock Ministries just before 10AM. He was driving his police Tahoe, though he wasn't wearing his uniform. He was dressed in dark gray slacks, a black button-down shirt tucked into the waist, and a pair of black loafers.

His Sunday best.

He hadn't been to church in many years. So long, in fact, he couldn't remember the last time he'd actually gone. Of course, when he *had* gone, he'd always gone to Mass at the Catholic Church, never to any of the other denominations. His mother, while deeply flawed, had always maintained and instilled in him a reverence for the Mass, and though he didn't really believe in much anymore in the way of religion, he did maintain a healthy respect for the structure and beauty of the Mass.

But from what he'd heard and seen of this church, he was able to muster very little respect. The meeting with George and Cherry Reese—which may as well have been with Cherry alone—had instilled this prejudice within him. The lack of sincerity was the biggest thing, but also the worship of their son—and *not* of the Son of God—was another red flag to him. Jim had felt metaphysical *slime* actually seeping onto his skin and into his pores during the meeting, and he had no desire to experience that again. However, his inability to locate and interrogate Norman Reese had brought him here. There was serious circumstantial evidence tying Norman to the disappearance of *at least* Margie Johnson, but the coincidence of the Bowers' disappearance in relation to this was overwhelming as well. In fact, he believed coincidence to be such a rare thing, that it was almost nonexistent. Coupled with the fact that, as it turned out, the angry man he'd seen leaving this very building a few days earlier as he'd come to speak with the Resses had turned out to be one of the missing—*and almost certainly dead*—individuals Dave Bowers himself, it was impossible to ignore his suspicions.

Jim sent a text to the on-duty dispatcher that he would not have his radio near him for the next couple of hours and to text him if anything of significance occurred. He received a thumbs-up emoji a few moments later and dismounted his chariot.

The parking lot was full. More than full, actually. Cars were stacked so closely together that Jim thought those with a handicap of circumference would be forced to wait for the cars to clear out before they would be able to get into their vehicles after the service.

People were milling about, heading to the front entrance of the church where a pair of greeters stood holding the doors open and smiling broadly. They were handing out printed programs and shaking hands as people came in. These smiles contrasted those that he'd received from the Reeses themselves, however, in that they seemed to be utterly genuine. These weren't people who were trying to promote anyone or anything other than Christ Himself, it seemed, and Jim felt a pin-prick in his heart. Though the leadership of this outpost was almost certainly in it for selfish and misguided reasons, the parishioners did not seem to be.

He made his way to the doors and shook hands with a man with a wide smile who displayed a perfectly colored and tailored set of what Jim believed to be dentures.

"God bless you this morning!" the greeter stated as he handed Jim a program.

Jim smiled and nodded to the man, careful to keep his mouth closed in a subconscious attempt to hide the scent of liquor on his breath from his morning ritual of overcoming the previous night's debauchery. He moved past the doorway and into the foyer. There was a large wooden Cross over the mouth of the hallway that led to the sanctuary, and a dove was resting atop the crown of thorns which hung askew at its top. In his own church, there was always a Cross, but upon it hung the crucified Christ, crowned in thorns and a grimace of anguish upon his face as it struggled to gaze upward toward the Father.

This version obviously wanted to look upon the Cross as a symbol of Christ, rather than upon the sacrifice which had been made upon it.

None of this bothered him, it was just very different from his own upbringing. He moved into the hallway, passing a men's and women's restroom on his left and what seemed to be children's nurseries on his right. There were two doors ahead of him, leading into a darkly lit sanctuary, and the hallway teed off in either direction beside these. These hallways also led to the same room at the corners. Jim walked into the doors in the middle and found a seat at the back of the sanctuary, right next to those doors.

Easy escape out the back, he thought as he sat down.

No sooner had he sat than he looked up and saw George and Cherry Reese smiling—these smiles lacking the genuine qualities of those the greeters at the church entrance had donned—shaking hands with some people at the front. George turned and left his wife and the parishioner they'd been greeting and headed to a lectern which was positioned on the floor in front of a rather large stage adorned with red carpeting and—*was that plywood painted black?*

It was.

Upon first glance it was rather elegant, but a seasoned eye would notice the poor workmanship that had gone into the building of the stage. Large white sheets hung upon the walls behind the stage, the two outer ones in triangular shapes, the one in the center closer to square, but arcing inward about its four edges. Jim had no clue as to their purpose.

"Good morning and welcome to Revival Rock!" George Reese announced into a microphone which snaked around his face from his ear. "We're so glad you chose to worship Jesus with us here this morning!"

The crowd began to clap and whistle and cheer. George smiled and looked about the room, clasping his hands in front of him. Jim thought he saw a red spot on George's face for a moment, but dismissed it as he considered the lighting in the room. There were colored lights dancing about the room and upon the stage while the sanctuary proper was nearly pitch dark. There was a clear focus on the front of the room and on the people inhabiting that area.

"I'm going to lead us in a word of prayer as our worship team comes up on the stage to lead us into the throne room of Almighty God. As I pray, I want to ask all of you to join me in prayer for some people who've gone missing in our town this week. People in our own *church*. We're working closely with the local police on this, but we know Who's *really* working on it: God! Can I get an amen?"

The crowd cheered their 'amens' and 'absolutelys'. Jim looked around the room astonished. Hands were waving in the air and fingers pointed to the ceiling. This was *nothing* like the Church of his youth. Aside from the Jesus they claimed to worship, the two churches could be wholly different religions.

He supposed they really were.

As George started his prayer, Jim saw several people come up from the crowd and climb the stage, grabbing up guitars and basses, a woman sitting at a piano, and several people grabbing microphones. One man went through a door to the left of the stage and into a glass-encased room containing a drum-set. The man grabbed up a pair of sticks and sat down.

George finished the prayer and returned to a seat at the front of the sanctuary. Then one of the people on the stage, donning an acoustic guitar, stepped up to a microphone.

"Good morning!" the man said loudly as he smiled, holding his hands in the air. "We're not here to promote anyone but Jesus Christ this morning, and I hope you'll follow me into his throne room!"

"Son of a bitch," Jim muttered under his breath, too quietly to be heard by anyone near him.

It was Norman Reese.

Jim hadn't met him before, but he knew it was him because he knew Norman was the leader of this worship team. And never mind that, the guy looked like someone had taken Cherry Reese and shaved off her tits and twenty-five years or so. He was her spitting image.

Norman closed his eyes, his hands in the air in faux exaltation.

"God, we come before you this morning to offer up to you a sweet incense!" he began. "We pray your spirit will fall on us like never before and move in and through us as we praise you and worship you. Father God, fill us with your Holy Spirit and break the chains of bondage upon us all, as you've broken them in me as I've met with you this week!"

Met with you this week? Jim thought.

Then they began to play.

Jim noticed immediately how awful they were as musicians. It wasn't that they couldn't play music, but it was as though they simply couldn't hear each other. The timing was off, voices were off-key, and the drum set seemed so quiet that it may as well have not been there at all in its tiny tomb off-stage.

And then Norman began to sing. Through his nostrils.

People were running down to the front of the sanctuary and grabbing large, silky flags from either side of the stage and then they were running about the sanctuary with them, waving them in the air like Olympians with a torch. People were raising their hands and dancing at the front of the stage—if you could consider bouncing around and flailing your feet out wildly dancing—while others were on their knees weeping. Others still were falling to the ground and people were coming to them and laying their hands upon them and praying out loud, their eyes squinted shut, their faces a grimace of what he supposed was passion. Jim could hear some of them and they were speaking in what they might refer to as *tongues*, but in all reality came down to nothing more than pure, babbling gibberish.

This excruciating display went on for nearly an hour.

Towards what Jim hoped would be the end of this pitiful display, Norman put his hands out in either direction across the stage and the music calmed to nothing more than a quiet piano progression. It was actually quite nice, as when the piano was on its own, the timing mattered less and it almost sounded like music instead of chattering nonsense. Then the sound of the piano faded quieter still and Norman once again stepped up to the microphone.

"Can you feel Him in your presence, church?" he asked the crowd in a whisper.

They all issued their 'amens' and 'absolutelys'.

"He's here in this place," Norman went on. "He's here, as He's been with me this week. He's revealed so much to me the past few days, and He wants you to know He is coming. Not just to the world, not just to our nation, but right here, to Winnsboro, Texas!"

There were cheers and applause. Hands flew up into the air and danced upon shaking arms above the exultations of weeping parishioners.

"He wants you to know that to abide in Him, He must abide in us. We eat his flesh and drink his blood, but if he doesn't have our flesh and our blood, he cannot truly walk amongst us. He is all-powerful, but if we're not willing to give Him our very lives, *our very flesh,* He cannot walk amongst us as He wishes to do!"

More cheers and applause. Jim sat, enraptured by this display, not because he believed any of it, but by how these poor people were in such awe of this sideshow.

"So I ask you," Norman continued, bringing his hands to the microphone, his eyes fluttering open, "as He has told me, *will you offer Him your flesh and blood that He may become truly alive in our world?*"

At this point the cheering became a deafening din. Jim looked about, losing the assurance he thought he'd had about these people being decent folks serving under some indecent leaders. Tears were ejecting from every oculus in the room, it seemed, and Jim felt a shiver go up his spine.

Offer Him your flesh and blood? What the fuck?

In Mass, it had always been about Jesus offering *His* flesh and blood to His followers, not the other way around. Yet nonetheless, here was this young heretic—Jim had no problem referring to him as such even though he lacked faith in his own Church—spouting off that very idea. And with the missing people from this church and his deluded ideas of *meeting with God* this week, Jim became all the more suspicious of this man, this glorified *man*, Norman Reese.

After the rambling of the worship leader had ended, George Reese came up to the podium. The musicians—for lack of a better term—descended the stage and returned to their seats about the sanctuary. George went on for ten minutes about tithing your money—*a minimum of ten percent, mind you*—and about how their money would literally be cursed if they withheld it.

Then he preached. A solid hour of asking for 'amens' and 'absolutelys' after every third sentence was uttered. At the end of it, he made a closing statement.

"So we can see that, through all of this, God's Word is *alive!*" George said. "We can see that God wants to work *in* our lives and *through* our lives. Wants us to be His hands and feet, to go out from this place and make disciples of His church! But not just *any* church, you have to remember!"

His finger was wagging in their air as he made his point.

"*This* church," he continued, letting his voice trail off as he said it to make the effect he was after. "God called *this* church. I'm sure you've heard this in all the Baptist and Methodist churches you were saved from, and praise God, snatched from the very fires of hell in the Catholic Church!"

There were more applause and whistles. Jim squirmed in his seat, looking around at all the ignorance before him.

They really believe this shit? he wondered.

"But," George went on, "God didn't call those churches. Didn't establish those churches. Those churches are all just trying to make a *form* of religion, but denying the power therein! You know that Scripture? That's what He was saying. *This* church. *Revival Rock*. We are the ones He's called to change the world!"

The crowd cheered incessantly, hands raising in the air, some waving flags and tambourines, others with sodden tissues clenched in their fists.

"Now," he finished, a wide smile splitting his face, "if that don't get you fired up, your wood's wet!"

The crowd went nuts. Which Jim thought was fitting.

Chapter Twenty-one

Norman had noticed the policeman at the back of the sanctuary when he had taken the stage. He wasn't surprised to see him. The man had been looking for him since the morning after he'd gone to show Margie that good and perfect will of God. Norman hadn't been especially *avoiding* the cop, per se. Not in the traditional sense of avoiding someone, anyway. He'd been about the Lord's work all weekend, and the Lord's work was, quite simply, time-consuming. That was all there was to it. His call was higher than earthly laws and Norman had been about his Father's business.

Somewhere in the deep recesses of his mind, Norman had known that if the cop got too close he would try to interfere with God's will for Norman. And that couldn't be allowed. No sir, not at all. The cop was an agent of Satan himself, sent by the dark lord to stand in the way of God's perfect plan.

After all, hadn't he always?

Indeed he had. Everyone who'd ever read a Bible knew that. The easiest place to see that was when Mary had been visited by the angel, proclaiming to her that she was going to bear the Son of God in her womb. He'd also told her—or was it her husband?—that she had to flee to Egypt for a time and all over as the forces of Satan were after her and her boy.

And wasn't *Norman* the new Mary?

He certainly liked to think so. He'd been uniquely chosen by the Almighty to feed and nourish and cultivate the Lord into this world once again. Once again, God was becoming flesh itself, and flesh required nourishment to flourish. Jesus had given them His body and His blood as food. Now He was using the flesh and blood of His creation to re-enter the world and set it right.

And God had chosen *Norman* to help Him do it!

What an incredible honor it was! Norman's mother had always told him of the greatness he was destined to, and he'd never doubted it, no sir, not for a minute. He could feel the power surge through him every time he watched his Lord feed on the body and the blood, becoming more and more flesh in this world, His spirit covering itself with muscle and sinew and bone.

Even skin now.

Yes, the previous night had brought his Lord almost all the way into His new incarnation. He needed only a little more of the precious body and blood of His creation and He would be able to fully enter into their world, Norman had been told. He would no longer be trapped in the new womb, which was the old house, and He would be reborn unto the Earth.

Behold, the return of the Lord!

Norman had donned his guitar, waiting for his father to stop his blathering before the service began, and stepped to the microphone. He surveyed the crowd and smiled as he came across a pair of empty seats. Dave and Laura Bowers' seats. Margie's seat was still vacant most Sundays, though she'd been gone for several weeks now. No one had bothered to commandeer it yet—people were such creatures of habit—and with all the talk going on around town about her missing, and now the Bowers' home as well, people were avoiding those seats which had been the regular parking places of those fallen asses—*Jesus, forgive him*—as though they were holy relics.

Then there were the empty seats of Charles and Meagan Collins and their two children.

Norman was thankful for the guitar which hid his engorgement as he relished the memory of the night before, acting in his fresh calling as the new Mary, feeding the womb and person of his Lord.

He had been wearing the goat mask again last night. He found he could hardly stand to remove it, as a matter of fact. He could feel the power of God in that hollow of rubber, a talisman of the Almighty. And He'd sent it to him, hadn't He? Of course He had! The hatchet, too, another item he found it hard to stay away from. Earlier that morning, after his work was done, removing the mask so that he could shower and get ready for church had been almost painful. His head had been throbbing, too. *Pounding*, was more like it, actually. He had looked in the mirror, noticed the reddening of his eyes, like one of those filthy addicts who needed Jesus so goddamn bad, praise the Lord—*and Jesus forgive him.*

The work had been strenuous. The Collins family had proven to be quite a bit of work. Waiting for the lights to go out, giving them time to fall asleep, sneaking into the back yard, careful to avoid disturbing the neighbors' animals, blah, blah, blah. All the tedious shit that went into the work of the Lord.

Jesus, forgive him.

The children had been relatively easy. The Collins family had a large home. Thirty-seven hundred square feet had been what Norman had overheard Charles say one time in a conversation at the Revival Rock Fellowship Hall after church. The master bedroom was at the opposite end of the house from the children's rooms and spare guest rooms. And the house was in the Del Rey Heights subdivision as well, which was a plus. The subdivision was on the edge of town, heading West on Coke Road, but it had never really taken off like the developers had hoped it would. It was full of potential and beautiful, half-million-plus dollar homes, but most of the lots were vacant, and there was a huge field in the back of it that was accessible from a blacktop road in town. The field had been where phase two of the subdivision was to be developed. But since the whole thing had relatively failed, it had been left empty and forgotten for many years. Norman had been able to pull his car into the field, completely hidden from view.

The back yard of the Collins' property had a stone wall around it, but it was short enough—and he tall enough—to get over it with relative ease. His vision had been skewed briefly as the mask twisted on his face, and his audible, flapping breathing had increased in volume. But it was an easy fix, and his blindness had only lasted a few comedic moments as he struggled to right it on his face as he tumbled over the wall and let out a quiet *oomph* as he'd thudded to the grass beneath.

In spite of the high-dollar homestead, there had been no security system installed. That had been another plus, and an obvious provision from the Lord. Norman managed to tap on the back glass and eventually break it free with the heel of his hatchet and gain entrance very quietly.

He had stepped into the living room with twenty-foot vaulted ceilings. Beautiful patterned furniture lay about on the floor, facing a rather large television mounted on the wall above a gas-log fireplace.

All had been quiet. Quiet as a mouse.

And so was he. Yes, Norman could move with the silence of a cat on the hunt. And he'd utilized this God-given talent—*he had so many, his mother always told him so*—to creep through the sleeping home toward the children's bedrooms.

The only sound had been the quiet hum of a refrigerator in the kitchen, and the soft ticking of a large grandfather clock by the entrance to the hallway to the rear-most bedrooms of the house.

Norman crept ever so silently to the first open door and saw the rise and fall of little Charlie Junior beneath his covers. The walls were a light shade of blue, and there were pictures of airplanes—Junior's daddy was a pilot and the boy meant to be one himself when he grew up, something the brat brought up constantly, interrupting conversations after church meetings—and lots of painted clouds.

The next room was a female version of the first. Pink walls instead of blue, but the same cloud prints were there. Instead of pictures of airplanes, there were pictures of little ponies and some magnificent Colts. Her mommy was an accomplished equestrian, and the little girl meant to be the same when she grew up, which she'd often pipe up about when her brother had taken a break interrupting adult conversations.

Over the next few minutes, some other sounds—quiet but distinct—joined the hum of the refrigerator and the ticking of the clock.

Mostly chops and splats. And one short cry.

That cry had been unfortunate, but ultimately unavoidable. After dealing with Junior, Norman had come into Beverly's room. Just as he'd raised the hatchet to do God's work, his foot had bumped one of the legs of her bed and she stirred. She had just enough time to start what would surely have become a full-on scream before the power of God—moving through the instrument of the hatchet and Norman himself—had silenced her.

He finished his work quickly, savoring every slash and chop. His breathing had increased, and the flapping sound of the rubber hole in front of the mouth on his mask had peaked.

"Beverly, that you?" a man's voice had called.

Shit! Fuck! Norman had thought, and then of course asked Jesus to forgive him.

There were footsteps. They sounded like they were coming from the hallway beyond the kitchen which led to the master bedroom. They were soft things, only audible because of the relative silence of the house. They were bare feet on tile, making light slapping sounds as the feet came down, one after the other.

"Are you alright, honey?" Charles Collins asked into the dark.

Norman slipped into the hallway and down to the next room. This one was empty, apparently set aside for guests. He eased the door to shut it, and then cursed the devil as the hinges made the announcement that they were on the move.

Creak!

Norman froze. His heart had begun thrumming in his chest and he could feel his throat pulsate with the rhythm. His head had begun to ache again, throbbing in time with his heart, and he held his breath.

A light came on in the kitchen and cast through the darkness down the hallway. Arms of shadows reached toward Norman like informants pointing the way to the intruder.

"Bev, baby, are you—"

The sentence had stopped and was followed by a long silence. It may have only been just a few seconds, but to Norman it seemed to stretch out for an eternity. His heart began to leap in his chest, and he was unaware of the rising sound of the flapping mask as he began breathing again.

"Oh, my God!" Charles's voice cascaded down the hallway, the pitch rising and wavering. "Oh, my God, Meagan!"

He was shouting now. Norman could hear the slapping footsteps retreating down the hallway, then muffled voices conferring for a moment and what sounded like *boops* and *beeps*. Where had he heard sounds like that before? They were strikingly familiar, but the source just wasn't—

Then there was the distinctive *crunch-crunch* of a pump-action shotgun.

A gun safe.

Yes, that's where he'd heard those sounds before. A digital keypad to gain entrance to a gun safe, where any reasonable person would keep firearms, especially when there were children in the home.

"The back door is busted, we need to get the kids and call the police!" Charles's voice was crying.

There was obvious fear in the voice. Norman realized he liked that, but he didn't at all like the introduction of a shotgun into the mix. That wasn't fair at all. The hatchet was a wonderful tool, but it would be no match for the shotgun head-on. None at all.

Norman had a brief image in his mind of charging down the hallway, hatchet raised over his head, screaming behind the mask, and then he saw his intestines splattering out around his spine and decorating the wall behind him.

No, that simply wouldn't do. But he had to do something, didn't he? He couldn't just sit here in the room for very long, not with the surety that within the next minute or two either Charles or his wife would be on the phone with 9-1-1, calling in the dirty policeman and his posse, Satan's crew, coming to end the work of the Lord.

He couldn't let that happen. No sir, not for one minute.

He heard the footsteps again, trotting now, coming down the far hallway. Then the slapping sounds became muffled and Norman knew the man was now crossing the carpeted flooring of the living room and nearing the mouth of the hallway.

Perfect, Norman thought, and gripped the hatchet tighter.

He finally noticed all the noise he was making through his mask and made a deliberate effort to calm himself.

"I'll get the kids!" Charles yelled. "Call the police!"

Shit! Fuck!

The prayer for forgiveness.

Norman peeked through the crack he'd left between the door and the frame and saw the backlit silhouette of Charles Collins, wearing nothing but a pair of pajama bottoms and carrying a large shotgun, sprinting toward the rooms of his children.

There was little time to act, and Norman, his heart racing, decided to go for it.

Charles had come to the door of Junior's room and reached in to flip on the light. He was looking back down the hallway toward the living room and kitchen as he did, calling to his wife.

"Get the phone, Meagan!" he screamed.

"I'm trying to find it!" she hollered back.

Then Norman saw Charles look into the room of his beloved son.

Nothing happened for a moment. Charles seemed frozen in place, unable to move or act. After several seconds, a low, guttural moan had begun to emit from the man. There were no words in this moan, but it communicated the horror and devastation that only a person who's lost a child can fully comprehend.

It was utterly delicious.

Norman threw the door open, the hinges shrieking in protest, and charged forward, hatchet raised. Charles never turned, never seemed to notice or care, all the while his groan rising to an eventual scream.

A scream which was never fully realized.

Norman brought the hatchet down into Charles's skull with a loud *crack*. The groan continued for a half-second longer before his body seized and began to tremble. Blood flowed like a fountain from the wound in his brain and his eyes began to roll up into their sockets.

Norman ripped the hatchet free with a wet crunch, raised it for a second chopping, but missed as he swung it down. Charles had stumbled backwards a second before and the shotgun was rising from his waist as if hinged there. His whole body was trembling now, and his mouth hung open, the sides of his face coated in a brilliant display of crimson as it flowed over him in sheets.

Missing with the second chop threw Norman off-balance and he stumbled forward. As he was regaining his footing, there was a thunderous, deafening *boom.*

The shotgun had gone off.

Norman turned in time to see the front of Charles's face rip apart and the top of his head transplant itself to the ceiling. In his convulsions, he had managed to accidently whip the barrel of the gun—which was shorter than most Norman had seen—up to his face. One of the convulsions must have caused his finger—which had been tight around the trigger—to squeeze.

And that was that with that.

Charles's faceless body fell back against the wall and slid down to the floor, leaving chunky smears of blood, brain, and bone on the wall above it.

A moment later, the convulsing stopped.

There had been a nerve-rattling scream from the kitchen then, almost equal to the shotgun blast in volume. Well, not really, but what the hell is poetic license for anyway?

Norman had turned and saw Meagan Collins standing in the kitchen, her mouth agape in terror. She was wearing a silk nighty, one of those thin things that barely covered her crotch, and nothing else. He could see the protruding nubs of her nipples trying to fight their way through the material and suddenly felt that old feeling once again in his loins.

She was *really* pretty.

Then Norman had noticed she had a phone in her hand. He had no way of knowing if she had dialed anything on it yet, but there was simply no time to waste wondering. He leaped to his feet and charged her. He saw her eyes meet his, through the mask, and the look in them caused a metallic taste to erupt in Norman's mouth. It was sharp and sweet all at the same time, like copper.

Like blood.

He charged into the open kitchen, raising the hatchet. He brought it down, and the hand holding the phone fell off her arm cleanly.

Norman had been amazed at how sharp the hatchet had been, but had still taken time to fine-tune the edge of the blade to a razor point over the weekend. Her hand and the phone it held fell to the floor with a meaty clatter. The one made a splatting sound, the other a *clack*. Blood was jetting from the stump at the end of her arm, and a scream finally made its way up her slender throat and erupted from her mouth like a long-distance ski-jumper.

He cut this short with a quick chop to her throat.

After he had finished, he took stock of his game. There was a little bit less meat on Charles's head now because of the incident with the shotgun, but that couldn't really be helped. Norman had checked the phone in the separated hand and found it had not yet made a call. That was good. Things had started to go to hell there at the end, but God had provided.

Friends and neighbors, God provides!

He made quick work of loading the bodies into his car after taking a few minutes for himself with the late Mrs. Collins. She was much better stock than the Bowers woman had been, and after the near catastrophe with the shotgun, he felt entitled to a little taste.

He'd been lucky that no one had seemed to hear the gun blast, but he figured that late at night, in such a large and well-insulated home, it wasn't that unusual. The houses weren't that close together either, and they were *all* well-insulated.

As he stepped to the microphone later that morning, his eyes falling back on the policeman, Norman smiled. He smiled remembering the feel of Mrs. Collins all around his member. The drive to the woods. The trek to the house. And of course, all that followed after.

The feeding.

The watching.

The incarnating.

Chapter Twenty-two

Jim was leaning against Norman's car when he finally came out of the church carrying his guitar case. Most of the rest of the church crowd had dispersed already, and they were alone in the large parking lot.

Jim had slipped out at the end of the service when Norman and the team had reclaimed the stage and played some poorly executed ambiance while people at the front were laying hands on people and speaking in tongues. The clincher had been when folks had begun falling to the ground and shaking as though they were being electrocuted. That had been quite enough for Jim.

As he had looked around the car, he'd noticed a smear of some sort of red substance on the back of the car, very faint, near the trunk. He'd used a cotton swab and a plastic baggy to gather a little evidence, but he knew what it was. There was no doubt in his mind. And after what he'd witnessed in the church service, all the weirdness and narcissism, he was convinced that Norman—and his parents, for that matter—were perfectly capable of doing everything he suspected had been done.

That, and Jack Fletcher had texted him that the samples from Margie's house had finally come back, and they were a positive match to her blood type.

"Can I help you, officer?" Norman asked calmly as he walked toward his car.

"Is it that obvious, Norman?" Jim asked dryly.

"Everyone knows who the Police Chief is in a small town," Norman replied. "I've heard you've been looking to harass me for several days now while I've been trying to draw closer to the Lord and pray for these poor people who've disappeared."

Bullshit, Jim thought and almost laughed out of disgust.

"Not trying to harass you, just trying to get to the bottom of it. Seems like some real bad things are going on."

"Well, I wouldn't know anything about that," Norman said with a shrug. "You know, Margie and I dated for a while, but she wasn't hearing from God like I was, and she tried to flee His will. No telling where she went off to. Folks tend to try and hide from God when they're out of his will, just like Adam and Eve in the Garden of Eden."

Jim nodded along with this, staring hard into the bloodshot eyes of Norman Reese. He wasn't buying one word of it, and he wanted to make sure his face conveyed this.

"I don't think she's just missing, Norman," Jim said, crossing his arms over his broad chest.

"Oh? Why do you say so?"

"Blood," Jim said matter-of-factly. "There were traces of blood and hair in her house. Positive match to her blood type."

Norman's face remained firm, but seemed to ever-so-slightly crease around the edges. He was getting to him, Jim knew, all he needed was evidence to tie him to the scene.

Norman said nothing.

"Anyway," Jim went on, pushing himself off the car, "if you know anything about that, it would be a good thing to tell me now. If I find out later, it would be bad for you. *Really* bad, if you follow my meaning."

Norman's edge-creased face broke into a smile now.

"You're kidding with me, right?" he said with a soft chuckle. "I'm a man of God, not some crazy person. You were in the service. You saw how God moved. That's because my family and I have *surrendered* to His will, and God isn't going to move through unholy people, am I right?"

"You're wrong," Jim said, a bewildered look on his face. "I didn't see anything in there but a bunch of weak people falling for a bunch of narcissistic horseshit."

Norman's smile broke and morphed into a frown.

"I don't think there's anything else for us to say here, Chief," he said. "Now, if you'll excuse me."

He went for the handle on the door of his car and Jim grabbed his wrist forcefully. He gripped it tight and leaned in close to Norman's ear.

"I know what you did," Jim whispered to him. "I don't know what you did with them, but I know it was you. And I'll prove it, too. Keep that in mind."

Norman's smile returned as he turned to Jim and whispered back.

"Seen Jake recently?" he asked menacingly.

Now it was Jim's turn for his face to crease. He hadn't thought much about Jake Reese in many years before the last few days. The alcohol and work had seen to that. But he'd also been sure that outside of his circle of friends from that day, no one knew what had happened. No one but them and, well, The Glutton. And it was gone. *Had* to be gone.

Right?

Norman was nodding. Then he winked.

"Before long," he said, still in that horrible whisper, "you'll get a chance to see Jake again. I'm sure of that.

Missing for quite a long time, but, sometimes the prodigal son returns."

Norman looked down to the hand gripping his wrist, then back to Jim's eyes. Jim let him go and took a few steps back. He watched Norman throw his guitar in the back seat, get into the front, and start the car.

Norman smiled at him in that chilling manner once more as he pulled away. Winked at him too.

Jim stood alone in the parking lot, watching the receding taillights fade away, and pulled the plastic bag with the cotton swab in it from his pocket.

He stared at the bag.

"What the fuck do you know, Norman?" he said aloud and to no one.

He felt completely alone.

Chapter Twenty-three

That evening, Jim met with Honey, Freddie James, and Ryan Laughton.

It was time to bring Honey up to speed, but more to it, it was time to discuss with them all what they had sworn to never speak of again as long as they lived.

As he drove along, he thought about his relationship with Honey through the years. The childhood friendship. The adult companionship. The one-time fling resulting in their daughter. The bitterness and hatred which had followed.

And the new fling. Well, what he was *told* was another fling, anyway.

He couldn't wrap his mind around that one. He'd been so smashed that he didn't even remember it. Just waking up in his drawers and finding her nearly naked, wearing only one of his shirts, making a Bloody Mary for him. Speaking so matter-of-factly about *fucking* him the night before, the terminology her own.

But why?

That was the great question. *Why* had she, as she put it, fucked him? They'd had nothing but bitterness and disdain for one another for many years now, then she shows up in town, they have it out arguing over their daughter, he gets hammered, she shows up and has her way with him.

It was like a porno plot, only thinner. Yet, it *had* happened. The only thing he could conceive of on the matter was that crawling, gnawing pain which lived in the back of his mind, and no doubt in the back of her own. Likely in Freddie's and Ryan's as well. The pain and horror of what they'd done that day so many years ago. The day they had faced The Glutton in the woods, along with Jake and his bullying entourage.

That had to be it. Of all the things that medicated pain, sex was the most potent. By far. Alcohol and drugs were okay, and work helped, too. Staying focused on something outside of yourself, putting your nose to the grindstone, kept your mind moving outwardly rather than inwardly, and that was always a good thing. Jim had utilized this very tactic his whole adult life, coupled with the alcohol, of course, for the times when he was off-duty. And the work he'd chosen was to try and help others, to do the opposite of what he'd done that day, so long ago now.

But none of it compared to sex. Especially sex with someone who not only sympathized with your pain, but actually *knew* it themselves. Pouring into one another, comforting each other, *knowing* each other in the most intimate way possible.

That had been why Honey had come, he supposed. Had to be. There was simply no other reasonable explanation for the phenomena. Her work, like his own, was to work outwardly for the good of others. She also had their daughter most of the time, and having a child was an exercise in constant outpouring of love and thought, leaving little room for self-reflection.

Or self-damnation.

That was really what it was when you came down to it, Jim supposed. They condemned themselves for the horror of that day so many summers ago. They had been scared little kids, thrust into an incredible situation, and they'd made a choice which couldn't be undone, a choice that had killed other children. Children who were awful in so many ways, but still children all the same. And now Jim and Honey carried that weight, as well as Ryan and Freddie. They had damned those kids to an awful fate in the summer of 1990, and now *they* were the damned ones.

So perhaps Honey coming back to this town, this damned place, had broken through the walls she'd built around her heart. Even seeing the man who'd led her to her pain, who had taken her by the hand and bid her to participate in that which haunted them all, had not been enough to keep her away. Of course, she'd gone to see Freddie, too, and he certainly knew their pain. But Freddie was a married man, and a Reverend to boot. A man of God. She couldn't go to him for the comfort she needed. And Ryan wasn't around. Not that poor Ryan had ever gotten more than friend-zoned by Honey, despite his obvious longing for her. Jim mused that, had Ryan been around, had he bumped into her that day, she'd likely have tried making love to him rather than *fucking* Jim.

But perhaps she wouldn't have, either. Ryan was no Reverend, but if reports were true, he'd become a man of God himself. Men of God still had dicks, and they enjoyed using them as much as the next guy, but when a man truly surrendered to the God of Abraham, they tended to at least pay lip service to reserve their cocking for marriage. Sometimes.

So that had left Jim—bitter, depressed, overworked, alcoholic, self-loathing Jim. One of the truly damned ones.

She knows how to pick 'em, eh, Jimmy?

But none of that really mattered. What mattered was that Norman Reese was killing people. Jim was sure of it.

He didn't know how, or why, and he didn't have any evidence yet. Nothing concrete, anyway, but he knew it.

Or maybe he *did* know why.

Seen Jake lately? Norman had asked him, a devilish smile playing across his face. *Sometimes the prodigal son returns.*

These cryptic words had driven an icy fear into Jim's heart. Not fear of Norman, he could handle Norman, but fear of something else. Something otherworldly and infinitely more powerful. More powerful than Norman or himself.

The Glutton.

But how the hell would Norman know of the thing? Well, the answer was obvious, wasn't it? Jim knew, as well as Honey, Freddie, and Ryan, what the thing needed. What it had to have.

Yes, all those years ago in their battle across the dimensions, they had seen into its mind as it gazed into theirs.

When you look into the abyss, the abyss looks back into you.

They knew. The thing wasn't of their world, that was blatant, but the fact was it wasn't of *any* world. It was eternal. Or at least nearly so. Jim and Honey had been able to pass between the worlds, in that place that was thin from the evil it was built upon, in their own bodies. But The Glutton? It hadn't been able to. It could only project itself into their world from the one it was in. Like a new age hippy with the astral projection. It could project its essence, but not its body. Because all the bodies in all the worlds came from a singular source. Some say it's God, the man Jesus, whatever. Others say it is simply nothing more than a great energy that binds all things together. So, in any case, those *of* that creation, shared a bond, even between the worlds.

But not The Glutton.

The thing was not of creation. It was of something else, something more ancient than the foundations of the universe. It was as old as God, but unlike all other things it was not *of* Him. Thus, the need for the flesh of the world to *enter* that world. To rebuild its abominable form and bring death upon thc planet.

It had tried, too. Oh, yes, it had tried and damn near succeeded. Had it not been for Jim and his friends, coupled with Jim's strange gift, The Glutton might have succeeded. And it was likely that nothing that stood—nothing which Jim could see all around him now—would be standing had it not been for them.

Jim, pondering all these things, decided to call Freddie. Freddie first, and see if he could get hold of Ryan as well. All four of them needed to meet. If Jim was right, much more was at stake than a nutcase serial killer on the loose in Winnsboro, Texas. Something far worse.

If Jim was right, Norman Reese was feeding the thing back into existence. It meant that they hadn't succeeded all those years ago in banishing it. And it meant they would have to return to that damned place before it was too late.

Soon, the Glutton had said to them as the portal closed and Jake Reese had screamed on the wrong side of it.

Soon.

And for an ancient demi-god, twenty-six years was plenty soon enough.

Chapter Twenty-four

"He knows," Jim said grimly to the group.

They were all there. Jim, Honey, Freddie, and Ryan. On his drive earlier, while he pondered the mysteries of women and all that the four friends had been through, starting in the woods all those years ago, Jim had pulled his phone from his pocket and called them. Called all of them. Freddie had gotten him in touch with Ryan, and he convinced them all to meet at one of Winnsboro's finest Mexican restaurants—there were a plethora of them to choose from—because they needed to talk about their shared history and what the recent events in town might mean in relation to it.

Jim had made no bones about the gravity of the situation. Nor about what it pertained to. They all had understood what they were facing and what they may well have to do about it if Jim's suspicions proved correct.

But first, they had to talk.

They met in the back room of the restaurant, smiles and shaking hands going all around. It had been years since Jim had seen Ryan, and he'd not kept in contact with Freddie very well in recent years either. But like with all genuine friendships, it transcended time and hurt, and they all got on as if nothing had ever happened. As though they had just been playing guns in the woods by their fort only the day before.

There didn't even seem to be any dust to be knocked off of their roles, either. Freddie slipped right back into the role of funny guy—though now with his new vocation as a Baptist pastor, his funnies were cleaner, as was his general language—Honey into the cohesive feminine glue that drew them all together, Ryan the quiet, strong presence, and Jim, the stoic leader.

It all fell together so naturally. Jim couldn't remember the last time they had all been together in the same room. Certainly couldn't remember the last time they'd all been together without trying to mask shame and fear in gallons of alcohol. But it was nice being with them again. Like coming home to your family after being in a war overseas, fighting God-knows-what for God-knows-who, and falling blessedly into the presence of those you loved most.

They ordered food, digging into the obligatory chips and salsa that was offered free of charge whether you ordered anything or not, and then Jim had started.

He told them everything. Everything he *knew*, anyway. As soon as he had started, the smiles and good cheer seemed to find a seat at the back of the room where they sat quietly and respectfully. Still there, but no longer front and center.

Jim started with Margie's disappearance, then with the Bowers. What they had found at both places, both concealed and left in the open. He told them about Norman's ties with Margie and Dave and Laura Bowers through the church. About trying and failing to track down Norman over the past several days, and about his meeting with the elder Reeses before.

There had been shudders all around at the mention of those names. To anyone in the know, a shudder was the minimum requirement of a sane person's nervous system to keep things clipping along rationally when discussing the Reese family.

Then he told them about going to the church that morning and his cryptic encounter with Norman. And what Norman had asked him at the end of the confrontation.

Seen Jake lately?

Shock fell on every face at the table then.

"He knows," Jim said, his face hard and ashen. "I don't know *how* he knows, but the look in his eyes...well, there's just no doubt."

"But *how*?" Honey asked leaning forward, snatching another chip from the bowl and scooping up a copious amount of salsa. "We never came across *anyone* in the Reese family back then, aside from Jake anyway. I don't think I ever even *talked* to Norman all through school."

Jim nodded, regarding her. She was dressed in a minimal but elegant dress, dark green backgrounds with bright flowers and vines in the forefront. Her hair was pulled back with a clip, and a small lock of hair hung across her cheek.

She was absolutely radiant.

Jim had also noticed just how much Ryan was noticing her as well. To his knowledge, Ryan and Honey hadn't seen each other before today in quite some time, but nothing had really changed between them. Ryan pined for her inwardly and Honey, always sweet to him, seemed to be oblivious to the fact. She never seemed malicious about this, and though Ryan had proclaimed his love to her that day they'd escaped the woods in 1990, she'd never taken it as a romantic proclamation, instead believing it to be one of plutonic affection. At least that was what Jim believed.

Ryan was wearing a fine, black button-down shirt tucked into a pair of blue jeans with fancy stitching down the sides which poured over a pair of black leather boots. He'd grown into a rather handsome man with well-developed muscles under his shirt sleeves, no doubt achieved from slinging wrenches and hefting hundred-pound gravel and cement sacks around jobsites at the water-well company he worked for. The look on his face was skeptical.

"I'm not sure he knows anything," Ryan said, fetching a chip for himself.

Honey was crunching down on her salsa-conquered chip. The sound seemed amplified in the deserted back room of the restaurant.

Jim looked to Ryan. "I'm telling you, if you had seen his eyes, Ryan...He knows."

Ryan shrugged, biting down on his chip and creating a surround sound with Honey of the crunching bits.

"I just don't see how," Ryan said through his chewing. "As far as anyone knows, Jake, Bart, and Chris just went missing. That was it. There was never a connection with any of us, and Norman would have been even younger than we were back then. None of us have ever talked about it, right? So how could he know?"

Jim shrugged. "I don't know how. But I've got a theory."

Freddie leaned forward now, conforming to the ceremony of chips and salsa destruction. He was wearing a button-down shirt too, this one navy blue and tucked into a pair of black slacks over polished loafers. The quintessential small-town pastor.

His good eye seemed to sparkle behind the thick glasses he wore, not altogether different from the ones he wore as a child, though these were rimmed with large, thick, black plastic borders. His glass eye seemed to trail his real eye in its motions, though it did eventually find its way to where it ought to be. It almost made Jim's own eyes water.

"A theory?" he asked as he scooped and chomped on his chip. "I'm always down for a theorizing. Gets the brainy bits moving. Lubes the old intellect. Let's hear it."

So Jim laid it out. Told them about the crazy speech Norman had given on the stage. About God needing to feed on *our* flesh and blood, rather than the traditional other way around. How that was the only way God could really come into our world and dwell amongst us.

"That's a bunch of crap!" Freddie spat, a fine mist of salsa detritus flying from his lips as he did. "Do they even read a Bible over there, or do they pull it out of the toilet?"

Ryan and Honey laughed at this, and Freddie grinned his familiar, self-satisfied smile. He always had enjoyed making people laugh, and that hadn't changed.

But Jim's face remained void of humor.

"I agree it's a bunch of bullshit," Jim said, then winced. It was easy for him to forget that Freddie was a preacher now, and it dawned on him as soon as the profanity escaped the clutches of his mouth.

"I-I'm sorry, Freddie, I didn't—" Jim started.

"Oh, pish-posh," Freddie said as he waved a dismissive hand in the air. "Don't apologize, you're not offending me. If I got offended by curse words, I'd be pretty useless in ministry."

Jim nodded. "Anyway, it got me thinking of back then, when we were in the woods. You know, *that day...*"

All residuals of smile began to fade from their faces as their memories carried them back to a time they'd rather forget. Had all *tried* to forget. But it was still there, a malignant cancer just beneath the surface of their polished veneers.

Jim reminded them of what the thing had been attempting and about its need for *meat.*

Ryan shuddered visibly at this point, no doubt remembering the ravings of his abusive, and thought-to-be-insane father.

"If I'm right," Jim went on to the conclusion of his theory, "and Norman really is doing what I'm all but certain he's doing, that means—"

"That means it's back," Honey said, finishing his sentence for him. "After all these years, it found a way to get back."

"And that we didn't stop it by keeping quiet and staying away from that damned place," Ryan added.

"Holy crap," Freddie said flatly.

"Yeah," Jim said, nodding. "And there's this."

Jim looked over his shoulder to make sure they were alone, and judging by the speed of this kitchen, he figured they were for a while longer. All the same he checked, and saw no one around. He turned back to the table, every eye on him, and held his hand over the chip bowl.

A single chip leaped out of the bowl and into his fingers.

He moved his other hand and opened it into a C-shape in front of the bowl of salsa in front of him. It slid into his hand without ever being touched.

He dipped the chip and ate as he observed his friends.

Every jaw hung open. Every eye was wide. It wasn't that they didn't know about his ability, only that they had forgotten all about it. Just as he had. Once the thing was gone, or at least when they *thought* it was gone, the impulse and desire to use the gift had vanished, not only in practice, but also in memory. They all recalled the battle with the thing, the horrifying conclusion with Jake and his friends, but they had all forgotten about Jim's unique and out of nowhere ability.

Well, forgot *isn't really the right term, is it?*

No, it wasn't really forgetting, at least not in the sense that it had *literally* vanished from their collective memories. As amazing as it was, the memories of it were nonetheless relegated to a place in the mind where insignificant bits of information went to collect dust in the recesses of their brains. The place a person would store the look of a certain coaster they had seen in a store as they browsed. Something you saw, but merely glanced over as insignificant. It was technically *there* in the memory, but unless you saw it again, knocked the dust off it, it would never be thought of again.

And here, Jim was blowing the dust off this old memory with an industrial air-blower.

"Holy shit!" Ryan and Honey said in unison.

At the same time, Freddie said, "Holy crap!"

Jim was nodding. "Yeah, *this* is back. Out of nowhere. The day I got the call from Mrs. Johnson concerning her daughter, even as I was going to make the phone call, *this* reappeared. I hadn't thought about it in decades. Not since that day in the woods. Then, I'm reaching for the note with her number on it, and *boom.* It all floods back, and I try it out. Turns out I've still got it."

"I can't believe we forgot about that!" Freddie said, his eyes enormous behind his thick spectacles.

"And I can't believe it's back," Jim said. "With all that's going on and my theory about Norman, I just can't believe it doesn't have some sort of connection."

Freddie was nodding now.

"You know, God gives us what we need when we need it," he said, slipping suddenly out of his funny-guy mode and into something more pastoral. "We put it all sorts of ways, like 'God doesn't call the equipped, He equips the called', and the like. It's sort of a cliché, but there's truth to it all the same. God gave you this—this *gift*—and all those years ago it manifested and saved us. *All* of us. And now it's back, Jim."

"Exactly why I'm so scared," Jim said pointing his finger at Freddie. "Because if any of this holds water, it means Norman Reese is as crazy as his brother was, maybe crazier, and he's killing people and feeding them to a monster that we've all spent the last twenty-six years running from, using to justify what we did to Jake and his pals. And now, it's all coming full circle."

"Karma," Honey offered.

"Reaping what we sowed," Ryan interjected. "Same basic principle, but without all the new-age crap."

They all laughed at this, a much-needed respite from the mounting tension Jim's story had created.

A moment later, their food came and they all dug in. Jim got enchiladas, loaded inside and out with cheese. Ryan had ordered a Mexican burger, replete with avocados and caramelized onions. Freddie had tacos, Honey, a salad.

When they had eaten enough to slow down on the initial onslaught such flavorful food seemed to incur—they all seemed positively ravenous—Freddie looked up from his plate at Jim, then around to all of them.

"So, what do we do?" he asked.

Jim glanced around the table and moved forward, taking point as the leader he'd always been to them.

"*We* don't do anything," he rebuked mildly. "*I* am going to check things out. If there's danger involved, it'll be on me, not y'all."

"Bullshit," Ryan said, then glancing sideways at Freddie, "Sorry, pastor."

Freddie rolled his eye, his glass one following along shortly after.

"Oh, come on, man!"

Ryan looked back at Jim.

"I'm coming with you," he said. "And you'll have to arrest me if you think you're going to stop me."

Chapter Twenty-five

Norman was watching the front door of Jeremy Cook's home. Jeremy was yet another member of Revival Rock Ministries, and had been on Norman's mind a lot that day. Jeremy was a younger man, late twenties, who was always trying to get Norman to give him a chance to play the drums on the worship team. It was quite a nuisance to Norman, because he already *had* a drummer, and didn't want to be bothered by adding more people to the team. Everyone wanted to be on the stage with Norman, he often thought, and while he understood why—after all, who *wouldn't* want to share a stage with him?—he hated bringing new people on board.

Also, Jeremy was slow.

He wasn't retarded, not in the clinical sense. Not quite, anyway. But he was a few rungs shy of the average IQ. And the last thing Norman needed in his life was to have someone on his worship team who couldn't count properly. He'd never admit it to anyone, and often denied it even to himself, but Norman *did* have an issue with timing. The drummer he played with every Sunday, in his opinion, was able to follow Norman well enough, however, so the performance rarely suffered from this malady. Though most people of average or better intelligence understood that it was the band which was supposed to follow the drummer, *not* the other way around.

But this never occurred to Norman.

His head seemed to pulse then and he winced, clutching the bridge of his nose with his thumb and forefinger tightly. He recalled again the doctor telling him he needed to follow up on the X-ray with an MRI and some bloodwork to see about the mass they had found in his brain. He wouldn't though. Wouldn't show a lack of faith in his deity by worrying about some black spot on an X-ray image. As with the Apostle Paul in the Epistles when the snake had bitten him on the hand and he'd merely shaken it off, so Norman tried to shake off his own malady. Paul had been told by God he was supposed to go to Rome, and neither shipwrecks nor snake-bites were going to interfere with the work of the Lord set before him.

Likewise, Norman would let no masses on his brain distract him from the work of the Lord either. He'd been called, he'd been chosen, and by God, he was leading the Savior back into the world. He would not be distracted by the works of the enemy, and he knew his God would heal whatever was going on with his head.

The new Mary would not be stopped by the enemy.

He just had to have enough faith. His mother had always taught him of the importance of faith, the importance of keeping his eye on the will of God, his ears tuned to His voice. Anything else was a distraction to the work the Almighty had placed before him, and Norman's mother had *never* been wrong.

Still, the pain bothered him. It seemed to thrust itself into his mind like a stabbing knife, occasionally causing him to slip. Was it possible his cognitive abilities were being affected? Was the enemy so adamantly averse to his calling that it was working overtime to trip him up in his pursuit of the will of God? Why else would he have mentioned Jake to the cop? That had been a really, *incredibly*, stupid move.

Well, stupid only if you weren't a god.

And Norman fancied himself a sort of god. Why else would his mother have heaped such raving praise upon him his entire life? Telling him to embrace his call, to be *bold* as he moved forward in his fate as one of the Almighty's chosen. Gods could be bold like that because—you guessed it—they were *gods*. And gods were above the law and above everyone else. The rules didn't apply to them like they did to the rest of creation beneath them, and to suggest they should only proved one's finite understanding *within* creation, not the transcendent understandings which gods possessed of it from without.

His head was pounding as he stared at the door of Jeremy's humble home. The home of a man who, through no fault of his own, was simply not blessed with as much intelligence as the average Joe. This led the man to incessantly persist in things, things Norman didn't appreciate. Things like *please, sir, please let me play on the praise team! I'm pretty good, let me, would ya?*

It was about as pleasurable as chewing glass with a mouth full of salt. But, since the one *true* God was so providential, there was now—*blessedly*—a solution.

The pounding in Norman's skull intensified as he stared at the yellow light over the door to Jeremy's house. It seemed to glare at him like an accusing eye. Like the hideous eye of the old man in Poe's 'The Tell-Tale Heart'.

It was maddening. The way it seemed to flicker with the pulses in his temples in perfect concert with his own beating heart.

I've got to have relief from this! he thought bitterly. *I've got work to do. God's work! I can hardly see straight with this fucking headache!...Jesus, forgive me.*

He pinched his eyes shut and rubbed the lids forcefully, trying to push the pain away with his fingers if he could, or at the very least relocate it somewhere more manageable. A headache, especially a migraine—and this one seemed determined for that to be its final destination—was nearly debilitating.

He pulled his hand away from his face and opened his eyes again. As he looked at the door and its demon light perched above it, he noticed that everything seemed to have a different hue than it had just a moment before. The light still seemed to cast a yellowish glow upon all it touched, but now there was something more to the color. Like it was dampened by something else. As though he was looking at it behind a film of...

Red.

Yes, that was it. Everything had a red tint to it now. The door on Jeremy's house was pure white before, but now it had a scarlet shade over it that Norman was sure hadn't been there before.

He rubbed his eyes again with the backs of his knuckles and then blinked eight or ten times.

Everything was still red.

He cursed bitterly as he struck the steering wheel of his car, then went into his automatic prayer of repentance, which by now was simply repeated on instinct and by rote. As he did this, he stopped, looking at his clenched fist perched upon the steering wheel.

It was covered in blood.

Where the fuck did that come from? he thought, forgetting this time to ask forgiveness.

He could feel something warm and wet on his face even as he inspected his hand for cuts. There were none. He looked at his other hand and noticed now that both hands were covered in blood, as were the tips of his fingers.

A warm, wet sensation seemed to be *moving* on his face now. He pulled down the sun visor in front of him and popped the mirror cover open. He drew in an almost frightened gasp.

His face was covered in blood around his eyes, like twin rings on a crimson raccoon. Blood was flowing down his cheeks, nearly touching the corners of his mouth now, and he followed the trickles back to his eyes.

He was weeping blood.

Not really *crying*, technically, but blood *was* flowing from his eye-sockets. Right from his tear-ducts in the pointed corners of his eyes. Both sides of his eyes, too, he noticed as he leaned in closer to take a look.

What's happening to me? God, what's happening to me?

And, for a wonder, he heard an answer. *In* his mind, but not *from* it.

We're close, Norman, the voice in his head told him. It was a familiar voice, one he'd come to know quite well in the past few days since meeting his Savior and agreeing to cooperate with His grace in becoming the new Mary. *This is the enemy. Trying to stop you, to stop us! You mustn't give in to it! This will be the last one I need to become fully incarnate into the world, and the enemy knows that. He knows that and wants to stop you, so you mustn't give in! You mustn't despair! Do you really want me to walk among you in the world, Norman?*

Norman almost laughed out loud, but managed only a feeble grunt through the pain pulsating through his head and the horror streaming down his spine at the sight of the blood pouring from his eyes.

"You know I do, Lord," Norman said in a rasping whisper to the empty car. *"You know I do!"*

He thought he heard the mildest hint of a laugh in his mind as the demon-thing that Norman Reese called his Lord and Savior responded.

Then bring me meat, it said. *I need just a little more meat.*

Then the voice was gone. Norman knew it was gone as one knew when someone left the room. His mind had been vacated all at once.

He flipped up the console between the seats of his car and grabbed a bottle of Ibuprofen. He dumped five of the brown pills into his hand, popped them into his mouth, and chewed them like candy. The taste was bitter and chalky, but Norman hardly noticed. He wasn't focusing on the pain now. He was on a mission. A mission from God Himself, and he'd be damned if he was going to let the great Satan stand in his way with a goddamned headache!

Jesus, forgive him.

He was so close to the promise of the Lord walking among them, right here in the flesh, and God needed to purge the unrighteous and the unholy and the unworthy from this world so that humanity could bask in His glory and presence, and so Norman could sit at his right hand, fulfilling the calling on his life that his mother had always prophesied from the time he was just a young man, singing the praises of God and leading the masses to truth.

And there was Jake, too.

Yes, Jake was a part of the promise, as well. Seeing Jake again, after all these years. He hadn't run away as his parents had ultimately surmised, but had been banished by that bad policeman and his pals. And wasn't God cool? He was using Jake's own brother to bring justice into the world, never mind bring his brother *back* to him. The Lord knew where Jake was, he'd assured Norman of this, and when He came into our world, they would be reunited in glory and splendor, and his parents could finally reconcile with their long-lost prodigal son, so errant in his ways as a young man, but now, knowing the full truth of God, able to return to the fold.

Norman, his eyes bleeding a steady trickle of scarlet streams now even though the pain in his head was starting to abate, reached over to the back seat and retrieved his goat mask and hatchet. He pulled the mask onto his head and took a deep breath of the stale and now mildewing scent of the rubber inside. He exhaled slowly, relishing the flapping sound the mouth of the mask made as he did.

He grabbed his hatchet and slipped into the night.

PART FIVE:

Incarnation

Sunday, August 7, 2016

Chapter Twenty-six

Dinner had been wild.

Not in the respect that everyone had been drinking or eating to excess. The jokes weren't flowing, and raucous laughter was not dominating the restaurant. Elderly couples out for a quiet meal weren't glaring with the kind of contempt only the very old can muster.

None of that had happened. Yet, it had still been utterly *wild*.

Jim's big reveal had been what was wild. The nonchalant way he had snatched a chip from the basket without reaching into it, and the salsa bowl sliding into his hand on its own. Pardon the French, but that had been fucking cool.

Not that Ryan and Freddie and Honey hadn't known he was capable of this. They all remembered well the events of their childhood. Remembered Jim—then Jimmy—moving things around at will in the garage. The things he'd done at the house in the woods.

Nor were any of them under the impression that this gifting was unique to Jim alone. They remembered not only what Jim had done in their childhood, but also what Jake Reese had done, a chilling mirror image of Jim's ability, but one cloaked in malice.

What was really wild about the resurgence of the *gift*, though, was how they had all completely put this amazing thing out of their minds. And that *included* Jim himself. They hadn't *forgotten*, per se, about what he could do, they had simply not thought about it anymore. In fact, as Ryan thought back, he became convinced that since that day at the house in the woods, they had not thought about it a single time. At least *he* hadn't. And what a strange thing that was, to witness—and of course in Jim's case, to *perform*—such an amazing thing, only to then file it away in an obscure drawer inside of their minds, not to be thought of again.

Ryan thought of the words Jim had told him and the others earlier that night.

Just like that, it came back.

But why?

That was the great question. Something fishy—no, something *bad*—was going on in Winnsboro, and Jim was convinced that Norman Reese was involved, at least to some degree. But that didn't explain the gift coming back like this. All at once after so many years.

What happened at the house...that thing.

That *thing*. The Glutton, as it was called in the journal of Johnathan Michael Brogan that Freddie had found all those years ago. That *horrible* beast they had all witnessed firsthand that had changed the course of their lives forever. Driven them to the edge of madness. Three of them had medicated that madness with alcohol and sex, and the other one—Freddie—had found a higher calling in the service of God. But back when they were kids, the gift had manifested in Jimmy—and then Jake, as well—*at* that damned house. Right when *it* was trying to come through. Could that mean...

But could it really be back? And if so, how?

From what they had gathered, the thing couldn't open the doorway on its own. At least not at whim. They had speculated that the thing may have done it that first time with Mike Barton when he was in the woods with Ryan's dad, but it was also speculated that Mike himself may have had a touch of the gift and opened it inadvertently. They simply didn't know. *Couldn't* know. Maybe the thing *could* open the doorway, but only very rarely?

Ryan had no idea.

But what they *did* know was that Cloris, that furry bitch from the other world, had been the means used to come through in 1906. Then in 1990, first Jim, and then later Jake, had been used for the same purpose, albeit unbeknownst to them. The thing hadn't opened the doorway on its own.

So how is it doing it now?

Hell, he wasn't even sure it was coming through now at all. He wasn't sure the thing was even still alive. They had done quite a number on it that day. It may well have died out there in that other world.

Do you really believe that?

The answer to this was simple, and it came without hesitation: *no.* No, he didn't believe they had killed it. He remembered the beast's hissing final word to them after it stepped back into its own world, their sharpened spears sluicing out of its body, more fully formed in that other world than it had been in their own.

Soon, it had said as the portal closed. *Soon.*

Somehow, though they had put it out of their minds for all these years, Ryan knew deep down that the thing, The Glutton, was still out there, just on the other side of their reality, lurking and waiting. Exercising unknowable patience. And when the time was right, when the stars aligned and the moon was just so, it would strike. Come back.

Come through.

But how?

That, he didn't know. Maybe, if Jim's suspicions were correct and Norman really was involved, and if the thing really was trying to come through again, Norman was doing it. It wouldn't be unreasonable to assume that Norman possessed the gift if his big brother had once upon a time. But who knew?

The great question. Just who the fuck *did* know about what happened that day?

Ryan dropped his transmission into drive and pulled away from the Mexican food restaurant where they had eaten. The plan was for Ryan and Jim to meet first thing in the morning and go out to that place in the woods they'd avoided for all these years and check it out. See if there were anything to their suspicions. Honey and Freddie, along with Freddie's wife, would continue with their work of goodwill for Old Lady Johnson.

But Ryan had other plans.

He pulled onto the road and headed the hundred yards or so up to Highway 37 and turned North. He drove on through town and when he reached Pine Street, he turned left, heading West now, toward the place he and Jim were to go tomorrow.

I gotta know, he thought as he droned along. *I gotta see for myself.*

It was a damn-fool thing to do, and he knew it. If Jim was right, Ryan could be driving straight into a deathtrap. But that didn't matter to him at that moment. He had spent too much of his life following Jim, pining for Honey and doing nothing about it. Being a coward. A coward like his father, the one who had died in the asylum, raving about the thing from the shadows that Ryan knew all too well was real.

He was going to prove something to himself. He was going to prove that he was a man—*finally* a man—and he could face danger head on just like David had faced Goliath.

And it wasn't as though he were walking in empty-handed either. He had his nine-millimeter pistol in the waistband of his jeans like he usually did. You never knew when you might walk into something you can't just walk out of, and he liked being prepared. He had a fully-loaded fifteen-round magazine in the gun, and another round in the chamber, and the only safeties on this gun were his brain and his finger.

He was as ready as he could be. Well, *almost.* If he hadn't let his curiosity get the better of him, and worse yet, his *pride*, he would be going in tomorrow morning, in the light, with Big Jim Dalton, his lifelong friend and leader.

But something was pulling him. Something was *eating* at him. Not content to merely tempt him, but physically dragging him in towards this damned place full of bad memories and nightmares.

Not that he was kicking and screaming, mind you. Not at all. He was happy to be pulled in. Happy to go. Happy to prove that he was a man. *Finally* a man. After all these years.

He reached the turnoff to Mitchell Street and took it. A short time later, he was turning onto the old gravel road, the one he knew so well and had avoided like the plague for decades. His headlights danced over the rock-strewn path before him indifferently.

What are you doing? he asked himself.

Silence was his answer. He had no idea what he was doing, no matter what his ego had to say on the matter. Being a *man*. Overcoming his cowardice. Those things were there, like icing over a cake, the real substance of the matter something deeper inside of him. Only, he couldn't quite put his finger on what it was. But whatever was compelling him to come here, he knew he had to listen. Had to follow that leading where it took him and—

His headlights twinkled back to him off dark, red taillights.

There was another car out here.

Chapter Twenty-seven

Jeremy Cook was heavy.

Norman was dragging him by the leg now through the dense woods. He'd been carrying him on his shoulder before, but now he couldn't manage that anymore. Perhaps it was the pain pulsating in his head that had weakened him. Perhaps it was the lack of purely fresh air that he was breathing through his mask that he'd once again forgotten to take off on his way out here with the mutilated corpse in his trunk.

Perhaps he was just getting weak.

Norman didn't know. He *did* know, however, that he'd been ready to collapse before he'd made it halfway to the house, and had dropped the body with its congealing blood-soaked face and torso to the ground with the reverence one might give a piece of freshly used toilet paper. He fell to his knees and lowered his pounding head into his hands.

Focus, he thought. *You're almost there. The Lord can give you a healing touch when you arrive. Just take a moment, then get back to it!*

He would. He just needed a few minutes to lower his heartrate and get the pulsing pain in his skull to abate. The Ibuprofen earlier had helped for a while, but on the drive out here, the oncoming headlights had pierced through his oculus with daggers of light which had revived the headache to a level worse than it had been before. He'd also felt the warmth trickling down his face again, sticking the mask to his skin like tacky glue.

The blood flowing from his eyes was also streaking down the outer face of his mask as well. He'd noticed this after finishing Jeremy off and passing a mirror in the idiot's house. At first, he'd thought it was just splashes of Jeremy's life that had jetted from the dying half-wit, but that had only been a mist. The lined streams coming down from the eye-holes were coming from himself.

Norman caught his breath and the beating congas in his head slowed and eased their assault ever so slightly. Not all the way, and not even a lot, but it was enough.

He'd gotten up and elected to drag Jeremy the rest of the way rather than carry him. He merely had to imagine the pressure that would build in his head if he were to try heaving the dead imbecile onto his shoulder and immediately dismissed it as an option.

The woods were darker than normal that night. The moon was out, but dark clouds had begun to form which blocked its light, and that of its little cousins, the stars. He also noticed that the air seemed to be cooling, and some of the clouds pulsated with glowing yellow and pink light. It was well into August already, and should have been hot as fuck—*sorry, Jesus*—but the air seemed to be cooling to an almost pleasant temperature.

It's gonna rain, he thought.

It sure looked like it. What little light he *could* see around the edges of the dark clouds in the black sky, ringed with their faint whispers of ominous light, were soft tendrils that offered little in the way of navigation. The house, which was always dark at night but usually had the benefit of a ghostly gloom from the moonlight streaming through the windows, would be black as pitch. He had no flashlight, and he cursed himself for the lack of forethought.

Norman trudged on, doing his best to ignore the pain in his skull, trying to focus on more glorious things. Things that were yet to come, and soon. Seeing his Lord again. *Feeding* his Lord again.

And, perhaps, if he was lucky, seeing his brother.

Yes, that was really the greatest aspect of his anticipation. The Lord had promised him a reunion once the feeding was complete, and he could hardly contain his excitement. His breathing intensified once again, flapping through the mouth hole of the blood-soaked mask, and he began to smile. He smiled so widely that it caused his head to hurt even more, but he could hardly contain it.

Jake! he thought joyously. *Oh, Jake! So long gone and forgotten! Back from the dead!*

Well, the *presumed* dead, anyway. But whatever. That didn't matter to him in the slightest. He only cared that he would be reunited with his brother. The brother with whom he shared so much. Though they'd never been close in their time together as children, they shared more than most brothers ever could.

He continued like this for a time, focusing on he and his brother's glorious reunion, bleeding from the eyes and dragging the corpse along as he smiled broadly beneath his hellish mask, and finally, he saw the house just ahead.

So close!

And he was. Not only close to the house, but close to all he'd ever dreamed of. Close to his destiny. Close to his calling. To his brother.

To his *savior.*

He dragged the body up to the front of the house and dropped it again like a bothersome rock. He stood tall and arched his back, hearing his spine pop in at least four places as he did, and relishing the brief relief this translated to his pounding head.

As he stood there, looking up to the old, rotting house, he was struck again with how dark it was. How absolutely *inky* the inside looked beyond the door which hung partly open. Like the mouth to a pit that went on for an eternity without end.

He would need some light. That was all there was to it. He cursed himself once more for not thinking to grab a flashlight, and then, of course, immediately begged his phony forgiveness.

He looked around through his mask, completely oblivious to its presence on his face now, and began to think. Normally, this wasn't a difficult task for him, but with his horrible headache violently segueing into a full-blown migraine, thinking had become quite a bit more difficult. He needed light and he needed it—

All at once, the woods lit up in a brilliant blue-white glow as bright as daytime. Searing Norman's retinas was a bright, jagged shaft just in front of the house, and in the split second before the heavenly spear vanished and was followed by a deafening boom of thunder, he saw a large oak tree being split in two nearly all the way to the base of the trunk. One half cracked loudly and tumbled in three pieces to a clear spot beside it, blazing brightly with yellow flames.

Norman could hardly believe his eyes, though in the same moment he decided he wasn't surprised in the slightest either. This was his Lord's work. Norman had a need, and right when he was looking for a solution, God provided light from the sky. Now, the blinding night blazed brilliantly before him, showing him the way.

He immediately rushed to the blazing, fallen tree and began tossing dry leaves atop the flames and grabbing more branches from all around, piling them high to really getting the fire roaring so he could see.

As he stepped back, brushing dirt from his hands, he glanced over at Jeremy, as if he thought the dead idiot might jump up and run away. But the dead idiot hadn't run away. He was still lying there, his dead, glazed eyes staring out of an empty skull with milky absentness.

The branches he'd piled atop the burning tree were already beginning to catch, the fire burning brighter. Flickering light leaped out from the flames, casting moving shadows all around, and licked the blackness out of the doorway to the house. He looked in and could see the hallway beyond. It was faint, but it was visible.

He had light.

My, how God provides, he mused.

He went back to work with Jeremy, dragging him up the stairs, the dead man's head *clonking* its way up the steps as it ascended. Norman's head was starting to pound again, and he was thinking that the Lord had better hurry up and arrive soon to give him that healing touch. If he had to go much further like—

A faint, moving light caught his eye.

He froze. He had Jeremy halfway through the opening of the door when he saw it, and for the third time now, dropped the dead man indiscriminately. Jeremy's foot thumped the floorboards loudly, but after that the only sound was the crackling fire. That and...

And something else. Faint, somewhere deep beyond the trees. Like tiny snapping bones with a low rumble beneath it.

A vehicle.

It had to be. There was nothing else it could be. And that sound, coupled with the faint, trickling light trotting through the woods, was unmistakable.

He thought it was probably a truck. The low murmur of the faint engine had the distinct grumble of a large V-8 engine. Norman couldn't imagine what it was doing out here. Nobody came out here anymore. There wasn't anything out here to come *to*. But all the same, his bleeding eyes were seeing it and his pulsing ears were hearing it and they were going to—

They'll see my car! he thought in a panic.

But the fact of the matter was they would have *already* seen his car. Of that he was certain. But maybe he could make his way back there and deal with it before—

The sound stopped.

He could still see the faint light of what he now knew to be headlights through the woods, but the rumbling of the engine that had been reverberating through the trees was gone. Whoever it was had killed their engine. Probably just behind his car. Someone had come along, seen the car sitting there on the side of the deserted road, and was now stopping to check if the driver was hurt or drunk or...

Or whatever-the-fuck. Did it make a difference *why* they had stopped? Not really. None that he could see, anyway. Whether it was a good Samaritan checking on a fellow human being or a cop on patrol, the end result was the same. Norman was fucked...Jesus forgive—ah, what the hell.

Norman rolled his shoulders and pulled the hatchet out of his waistband. The flicker of the fire caused shadows to snake over him in devilish waves, and he thought, finally, that whoever it was whose lights he could see through the woods would be able to see his fire. And if they could see his fire, and found his car empty on the side of a deserted road in the middle of the night—*and* in the middle of nowhere—chances are they would either call the police, or they would investigate themselves.

He prayed for the latter.

Norman made his way down the steps, moving cautiously around the fire and towards the woods, cocking an ear towards the direction of the light, listening for any indication that the mystery person might be making their way into the woods.

Come on, he prayed. *Come on to Norman! Come feed the God of the universe!*

"Hello!" he heard a faint, hoarse cry come to him, drifting on the cooling wind. *"Is someone there?"*

Norman smiled and his knuckles cracked as he fisted the hatchet in his hand. The red hue was back in force over his vision, but it was the furthest thing from his mind. So was the painful throb between his temples.

"Yes!" he cried back in a deliberately cracked and frightened voice. "Yes, could you give me a hand? I've gotten myself in a bit of a pickle here, it seems!"

He forced a charitable laugh then, trying to covey to his late-night visitor that, *no, nothing was really wrong, this was just a silly accident, a misunderstanding, a comedy of errors. Sure, come along then and help out your neighbor like a fine little Southern Christian. Just come right along!*

A few moments later, he heard the crunching clumps of feet on dead leaves moving toward him.

Chapter Twenty-eight

Jim hit send on his smartphone and raised the device to his ear. He was calling Jack Fletcher to rendezvous with him to get to work on the sample he'd taken from Norman's car earlier that day. The sample was in his Tahoe, and he needed to get it into Jack's hands as soon as possible.

The phone began to ring, the digital buzz reverberating in his ear, and he thought about the gravity of all that was happening, though it seemed to still be just beneath the surface. He thought about the strange way his childhood friends had been reunited in the same days his abilities had suddenly resurfaced to the forefront of his mind.

It was strange, he thought, how things seemed to fall into place. He'd been coming into work just a few days prior, like any other boring day as the Chief of Police for the Winnsboro PD, which typically consisted of paperwork and phone calls, dispatching the officers and dealing with the petty bullshit that came with the job. Upset drivers calling about tickets—which, contrary to popular opinion, he had no power to overturn—talking with little old ladies who were just convinced that any sounds coming from the live music downtown after eight o'clock at night were simply criminal and should be squelched at once, and the like.

It wasn't a terribly exciting job. Not in such a small town in the piney woods of East Texas. Only two events of note had occurred here, at least that the public knew about. Several years back, there had been a series of slayings in town. All of the victims had been low life thugs—one a known junkie. One of the low life thugs, however, had been an officer he had worked with himself. Tony had been his name. And to this day, that strange case was still completely unsolved.

The other event had been a brutal home invasion at the Wade house on Melissa Lane, where Mary Wade had been sadistically and brutally raped and murdered before her husband Nathan could wrestle free and dispatch the invaders. Both incidents had been utterly shocking, but they were also total anomalies in such a small town. Aside from those two incidents, not much happened around Winnsboro, Texas, population thirty-five hundred.

But it was the bed Jim had made for himself, and most days he found it relatively comfortable. His daily hangovers from drinking entirely too much each night were usually handled with a handful of anti-inflammatories, a pair of Bloody Marys, and a pot or two of coffee, and he'd come to find this sort of existence tolerable. Not particularly *enjoyable*, but tolerable just the same.

Then, in the midst of his daily hangover and mundane existence, he'd walked into the office with a note to call Mrs. Johnson, and suddenly his power had returned.

Only, that wasn't quite right, was it?

No, his ability had never really *left*. Not really. It had always been there, he knew, but it had lain dormant for the better part of three decades. Not forgotten, just not thought of.

It was strange to him, and though he had little to no faith anymore in any deity or higher power, the words of his old pal Freddie James, the pastor of the First Baptist Church in town, continued to echo in his mind.

God doesn't call the equipped, He equips the called.

Jim wasn't sure what he really thought of that, but nothing else really seemed to fit what was happening, either. Nothing else seemed to explain how the ability had shown up in the first place twenty-six years ago, and the fact that such an amazing gift had literally just not been thought of at all after the fact until the past few days seemed too fascinating to chalk up to mere coincidence.

The Glutton, the thing they had encountered in the woods that day when they confronted Jake and his friends to save Honey, flooded his mind. And now with Jake's little brother, Norman, and what Jim was *sure* was going on and simply couldn't prove yet, seemed too much of a coincidence to be a coincidence. In fact, Jim really didn't believe in coincidences at all, not as a general reality. When something so obviously seemed to be tied together, it more often than not *was* tied, and intrinsically so. Something was going on with Norman. Norman had killed at least one person: Margie. He was certain of that. The evidence was overwhelming—albeit circumstantial—that she had indeed been attacked in her home. Now, she was missing, but he still couldn't tie it directly to Norman, in spite of the fact that he knew within his very soul the man had done the deed.

Then there were the Bowers'.

Yes, Norman was the guy. He knew it. He just needed to prove it, and Jack Fletcher was the guy who could help him do that. Jack was the best forensic specialist Jim had ever worked with, and could get things done at the speed of light when Jim really needed him to and pushed him to do so. Jack was thorough, professional, and a goddamn magician.

The phone rang for a second time, then a third. The pulsing buzz coming from the earpiece of his cell phone was loud enough to tickle the inside of his ear, and he adjusted his hand to get his thumb on the volume rocker of his phone so he could knock the decibels down a couple of notches.

Come on, Jack, he thought. *Pick up. I know it's late, but—*

"Hello?" a voice crackled to life in his ear. "That you, Jim?"

Jim exhaled with relief. He had been resigning himself to the idea that he wouldn't get hold of Jack, and was grateful to have been wrong.

"Yeah, Jack, it's me," Jim said.

"What's up, Chief?"

Jack's voice was tired, but alert. The sound of a man who'd been overworked and underpaid for the past week, but still on his game, willing and capable to rise to the occasion.

"Oh, you know," Jim said, again exhaling a sigh, "same old shit. Trying to figure this thing out."

"I'm sorry I didn't have anything more definitive for you, Chief, but all I can prove is the blood type, not the—"

"No, no," Jim said, cutting him off. "No, I've got something new I need to get to you."

There was a pause on the other end of the line. Jim could feel electricity coming through the connection as Jack's curiosity was piqued.

"Oh?"

"Yeah, I went to church this morning. Out at that Revival Rock place. Talked to that guy Norman who was dating Margie a while back."

"Right, right, I heard you talking about that..."

"Yeah. So anyway, I found something on his car just before I spoke to him, looks an awful lot like blood. But you know the drill, could have been an animal or whatever, even though I found it on the rear of the car near the trunk. The lawyers will probably throw this whole thing out for lack of procedure and warrants, but I gotta know."

"I understand. When can you get it to me?"

"Right away is the idea. If you can meet me, that is."

There was a sigh on the other end and Jim thought he heard the creaks of bedsprings expanding.

"Yeah, absolutely," Jack said. "I can head your way right now."

"You want me to meet you at the lab?" Jim asked. He was driving his Tahoe and getting ready to make the turn toward Quitman fifteen miles South of Winnsboro where Jack's lab was stationed.

"No, no," Jack said. More creaking bedsprings and heavy breathing. "I'm in town, actually. Visiting a friend. But I'm all done here. I can meet you at the PD."

"Oh," Jim said, smiling as he realized Jack was probably finishing up with a lady friend. "That works, then. Ten minutes?"

"Five," Jack responded immediately.

"Okay," Jim said, preparing to disconnect the call. "Then I'll see you—"

"Jim?" Jack asked suddenly. His tone had changed. Darkened. Grown more serious.

"Yeah?"

"You think we really have a serial killer in Winnsboro? I mean, of all places in the world, this little town?"

Jim thought about this for a moment, mulling it over. It really was a bizarre thought to have such a crazy thing happen in such an idyllic little town. One with thirty-five hundred residents in the city limits, and more churches than most small nations. Serial killers simply didn't rise from little places like this. Of course, he knew that wasn't really true. They came from all kinds of places, but in a small town you just think you know everybody, and the worst of the worst in places like this were generally rednecks who had a few too many beers and knocked their old ladies around. But killers, real *murderers*...well, that was the kind of thing that happened somewhere else, not counting the two anomalies in the town's past.

Jim took in a breath and held it before answering. Finally he said, "Yeah, Jack. I think we do. And I think I know who it is. Just can't prove it yet."

There was silence on the line for a long moment. It went on so long that Jim thought he might have lost the connection. He was about to pull the phone away from his ear to check that he was still connected when Jack finally came back on.

"You know, I've been working in the crime lab for ten years now," Jack said in a solemn tone. "And in all my time, I've never come across anything like this. I've heard of it, of course, but it's never come across my desk in Wood County. My uncle in Longview is the closest its ever come for me."

Jim thought for a moment and remembered hearing something about a killer in Longview some years before that had gone after some elders of a mega-church over there, barely an hour away from Winnsboro. Something about a coverup of molestation from many years back.

"The Charlton Fields case?" Jim asked as he sat forward in his seat, suddenly interested.

"That's the one," Jack responded. "My uncle was the lead investigator."

Jim thought back to reading about the story. The detective in Longview who'd been assigned to the case had been Harry Fletcher. Jim had never made the connection in the all the years he'd known Jack.

"I didn't realize that was your uncle," he said.

"It was," Jack replied. "Anyway, just crazy."

"What ever happened with that?" Jim asked. "They caught the guy, right?"

Jack sighed again.

"Well, they caught *up* to him. And my uncle...let's just say my uncle sort of let things play out."

Jim thought back again to when he'd read about the story. The killer had been mortally injured, but still had enough left in him to get his hands on the elder of the church who had molested the children, one of whom had been the killer's sister. Harry could have stopped him, but for some reason, he hadn't. He'd let Charlton Fields bury a knife in the man's throat and then his chest before Harry's partner—who had been badly wounded himself—had put the man down.

"Jesus," Jim said. "That's gotta be tough."

"It was. But you know, this whole thing has had me thinking about that. My uncle Harry was, well...let's just say he was a bit of a cynic. Not a bad guy, but he hated religion. He was in that church that did the coverup. Arrested the molester initially. Watched the whole thing go down. By the time it was over, he was disgusted with the whole idea of church in general, the people were all hypocrites and what have you."

Jim sat silently listening, not knowing where this was going or what it had to do with what they were dealing with here and now.

"The point is," Jack went on with a sigh, "Harry saw some things that changed him. He never told the press about it, and it was kept out of the official reports, but there was something truly evil involved, and I don't just mean that poor soul, Fields."

"What are you getting at, Jack?" Jim asked. He was completely perplexed at the shift in this conversation, yet intrigued at the same time.

"My point is, Jim, it wasn't just a case of revenge. It was much more than that. I don't know what you believe in, or if you believe in *anything*, and I really don't care. I'm not trying to evangelize you or anyone else, but my uncle was convinced that there was something otherworldly involved. After everything he'd been through, after losing his faith all those years ago—not to mention his marriage—when he finally let Fields take the last son-of-a-bitch out, he..."

Jack trailed off to silence. Jim waited for him to finish, to pick back up and continue. But he didn't.

Jim nudged him.

"He *what*, Jack?"

There was another sigh, this one longer than the others, the air whistling through the airways.

"He vanished," Jack finally said. "It was about a year later. He'd quit the force, though that was a formality. They were going to kick him out the door for letting Fields kill that man, but we still talked, you know? Not a lot, but from time to time. He was bitter, too, Jim. Really bitter. Like a thousand times worse than he'd ever been before. He'd shed his atheism, but even though he acknowledged a higher power, the situation, what it had done to him...it's like he hated the idea of God all the more once he was convinced God was real. Then, one day, poof. Gone. None of us have heard from him again.

Personally, I think the whole thing just ate him alive and he checked out somewhere, and no one's stumbled across him yet, but who knows? Point is, I don't know and don't care what you believe in, but if you have a God or a higher power, maybe you should ask for some help. If what we think is happening really is going on, if we really are dealing with our own serial killer here, you're going to need it. Don't let it do to you what it did to Uncle Harry."

Jim nodded to no one in his Tahoe as he pulled into the station and parked. He said nothing for a while, just thinking again about what his friend Freddie had told him. The only friend of the group who'd looked to God instead of a bottle to deal with what they had seen and what they had done.

God doesn't call the equipped, He equips the called.

"Right," Jim finally said after a long silence.

Jack didn't say anything else. He just remained on the line quietly, letting that sink into Jim's mind for a while.

"Well," Jim said, clearing his throat and moving the conversation along. "I'm here at the PD. See you in five?"

"Three," Jack said, and disconnected the call.

Jim pulled his phone away from his ear and stared at the police station. *His* police station. In *his* town. He suddenly felt the weight of the world on his shoulders, like Atlas, struggling to hold the planet up all on his own. How could a man carry such a burden and not collapse under the weight of it all?

He pulled the door open to his Tahoe and stepped out. The night was dark, even under the lamps of the streetlights. Clouds were forming above him in the sky and blotting out the moon and stars. A storm was coming. Jim hoped he could weather it.

He equips the called.

Jim pulled Google up on his phone and typed in a search. The search revealed an address and a phone number.

He hit the icon of the phone to place a call and raised the device to his ear.

Chapter Twenty-nine

Ryan shifted the transmission of his pickup into park and killed the engine. The headlights remained on, spraying their light upon the rear of the car parked out here in the middle of nowhere, near the place they'd played as children with their toy guns, smoking cigarettes and making lewd jokes.

But most of all, near that awful, damned place.

The twin reflections of the red taillights gleamed back at him like a pair of demon eyes. The night was silent, but he fancied he could hear the car breathing as it stared back at him with its dead, crimson lenses. Almost growling.

Ryan exhaled a shuddering gasp, rallying his courage, and pulled the handle to open the door of his truck. There was a pop and squeak, then the overhead dome lamp came on in his truck, destroying what little night vision he'd developed. He could feel the cold, comforting weight of his automatic press against his waist as he shifted and dropped out of the truck onto the gravel road, reminding him of its presence.

Will I need it? he wondered.

And that was the great question. He wasn't what you might call a *gun nut*, but he most certainly had a healthy affinity for firearms. Of course, having an affinity for weaponry wasn't exactly a rare quality in the South. Most anyone you came across was at least familiar with guns if they had a ticking heart in their chest. And at least one in three owned a gun, in the rural areas, anyway, of which Winnsboro would certainly qualify. The NRA was a household name in these parts, and to go through an entire day without seeing one of their bumper stickers on a vehicle was an anomaly.

Still, while gun ownership was a more than common thing in the area, it didn't make everyone a *nut*. Guns were no more a danger than a vehicle, speaking from a strictly statistical point of view, and the vast majority of folks who owned them were no more a threat to anyone than ice was to an Eskimo. If you know what it is and not only how to use it, but also to *respect* it, you didn't have anything to worry about. At least that was how Ryan viewed the issue.

Ryan had been carrying a gun for the better part of his post high-school life. He'd gone out and bought one on his twenty-first birthday for no other reason than he could, but soon after taking it to a buddy's place in the country to pop a few rounds off, found that he not only enjoyed shooting, but he was pretty good at it too. His first gun had been a Ruger 10/22 rifle. It was a tried and true design, and the ammunition was cheap, so he ended up finding himself slinging lead downrange more weekends than not.

After a time, he'd moved up in caliber to a variety of rifles, and then finally getting a handgun. He found his marksmanship was equally on par with the pistols as it was with the rifles, and within a year he had applied for and acquired his concealed handgun license.

Texas had since become a simple license to carry state—meaning a person licensed could carry a gun openly on their hip *or* concealed—but Ryan still more often than not elected to carry his concealed. He found that even in the gun-friendly South, there were many people who automatically assumed a person with a visible firearm was a threat, even when the gun was doing no more than sitting perched on their hip in a holster, and he didn't want or need the hassle. Folks seemed to intrinsically know that they probably interacted with a dozen or more people a day who were carrying without incident, but as soon as they *saw* a gun, they began to get nervous. And with the seemingly increasing rate of mass shootings throughout the United States, Ryan really didn't blame them. The world was going crazy.

Ryan pulled his shirt over his nine-millimeter Glock 19 into his internal waistband holster out of sheer habit, though there was no one he could see who might be alarmed at the sight of it. Out of sight, out of mind to the average Joe, but a sense of security for him if the unlikely event of the proverbial shit hitting the fan finally occurred. Of course, just as almost all carriers of weapons fail to fully process, he really didn't know what would happen if and when that shit started to fly. Would he be able to defend himself or others adequately or would he freeze? Even well-trained soldiers and police officers sometimes froze when situations went bad, and all the training in the world shooting at targets could never prepare a man for dealing with living, breathing villains meaning them harm.

Still, it was nice to have the added security with him. Ryan's history, especially in his childhood, had been littered with great stretches of cowardice with the occasional sprinkling of bravery. Since growing up, there had been fewer and fewer instances of having to stand up to others, and thus fewer and fewer opportunities for either bravery *or* cowardice to rear their respective heads. Yet, here he was, bumbling around in the dark near the woods where his worst childhood memories called home, wondering if he would be able to do anything more than revert to the fetal position if he did indeed come across danger.

Ryan made his way around the front of his truck toward the car, blinking away pinpricks of light which were attacking his vision. He was still doing this when he reached the driver's door of the car he'd found.

He peered in, the last vestiges of the spots fading away as his eyes tried to adjust to the light even as he stood in the glow of his headlamps. He was making a point of not looking into them, and trying subconsciously to avoid their reflections in the mirrors around the car.

The front seat was empty.

No surprise there, but it was still unsettling. He'd assumed as much when he saw no silhouette in the cab as he pulled up behind the car, but all the same a chill stole across him.

Where did they go?

He wished like hell he'd asked Jim what kind of car Norman drove before they'd split off earlier, but there was no sense beating the dead horse now. Besides, he could just call Jim on his cell phone if he really needed to know, only that would alert the Chief of Police to what Ryan was up to on his own without law enforcement backup, and he didn't want that.

Ryan moved on past the door and put his hand on the molding that separated the door and the windshield. He slid his hand down the smooth metal towards the hood. It was cool to the touch, but he noticed a distinct warming as he neared the hood. His palm spread wide and his fingers splayed as he swept the hood, noticing the warmth from the engine compartment.

It hadn't been parked for very long.

He pulled his hand back and reached into his pocket for his cell phone. He didn't care anymore what Jim thought about it, he needed to know right then what Norman had been driving, and if this was his car, Jim needed to know about it right away. He needed to get his ass in his Tahoe, call up the posse, and get—

A flicker of light caught his eye.

It was just the faintest waver, and it was in the deepest corner of his periphery, but it was there. At some point in the past minute or so, the light spots had finally vacated his vision, so this one stood out.

He peered into the woods, straining to see. If he *had* seen it, it was a long way off. Somewhere deep in the trees. Only now, he wasn't picking up on anything. He bobbed and weaved his head, looking through the trees for the phantom light he'd seen.

Nothing.

He sprinted back to his truck, reached in, and killed the lights. The gravel road and the surrounding woods fell into an almost pitch blackness.

Almost pitch blackness.

There was that faint flickering of light again, no mistaking it now, deep into the woods, in the relative direction of that awful place which had threatened to destroy his life.

He took a few steps toward the woods, peering at that light, *into* that light. It was as if it were pulling him, luring him like a moth to the flame.

He forgot all about the phone in his hand.

"Hello?" he called into the night, horribly aware of the absence of the symphonic sounds of insects and night creatures that should have been filling the air, which itself was even now cooling much too quickly. *"Is someone there?"*

And, to his horror, someone replied.

Chapter Thirty

He was coming. Norman could hear the crunching footsteps coming toward him in the dark, decimating the corpses of leaves which blanketed the forest floor.

Crunch-crunch-crunch.

He could hardly believe it. His tactic had been less than brilliant. Even *he* could admit that. What kind of fool came bumbling around in the woods in the dark next to a deserted gravel road? And further, what fool would actually swallow this at random without calling for help?

This fool, apparently.

But Norman wasn't going to waste time questioning his good fortune. He'd almost been found. It had been a damn-fool thing to do leaving his car parked like that in plain sight for anyone to see. Sure, he'd been doing this for several days now with nary an issue, but somewhere deep in his gut, beyond his rapture for the Lord he was serving here in the dark, he'd always known he was operating on borrowed time. No matter who your god was, reality didn't cease to exist simply because you were doing its bidding.

Crunch-crunch-crunch.

Now the question was just what to do about this intruder? He could always just wait for him to stumble by in the dark and give a few whacks with the old hatchet to the brain.

Splitty-splat, that takes care of that.

That was the most obvious approach, certainly. But who *was* this guy? And why was he here?

And who else knows?

The question startled him. Not because it was itself a startling question—he was already getting to that very inquiry on his own—but it was the direction from which the question had come that caused his breath to catch in his throat. It hadn't come from his mind. Hadn't come from his line of thought, though he was sure it would have crossed its path down the line a bit.

The problem was it hadn't come from him *at all.*

This question, like the internal conversations he'd had multiple times throughout the past few days, had surfaced *in* his mind, but not *from* it. It had come from another source, one almost right here with him.

It was the voice of God.

God was speaking to him again. But even this, in and of itself, was not what caused the faint whispers of fear to begin clenching the base of his groin. He'd been talking with God off and on now for days. Days which seemed like millennia now. He'd heard Him both in his mind and in the flesh.

No, what scared him was the uncertainty.

Why on earth would God need to ask *him* a question? Was He not God, the eternal creator of all things, uncreated Himself and all-knowing? Why would he not know? *And did Norman detect...*

Certainly not. Couldn't be. God could not be possessed of such a thing, such an emotion. And certainly not one that was so...*created.* Exactly such an emotion was a *result* of unknowing, and an all-knowing, all-powerful deity could simply not be gripped by it.

Still...

It just wouldn't go away. That gnawing, nagging feeling, now not only gripping the base of his groin, but kneading it, twisting it up in its clawed hands.

And who else knows?

The echo of the question continued to bounce around the hollows of his thought-world. He was no longer thinking of the approaching man—who was getting closer all the time, *crunch-crunch-crunch, motherfucker*—only of this question and its, its...

Its tone.

Indeed *this* was the most unsettling aspect of the whole of the business. The goddamned *tone* of the thing.

It sounded *scared.*

Norman's mind began to spin. Fresh hues of magenta coated his vision, and the world began to shift beneath him. He suddenly felt thrown off-balance, like he was tumbling freely about the cockpit of an airplane which was spiraling out of control, draining out of the sky toward an immovable rock that just kept tumbling, tumbling, *tumbling* through space.

He was going down. That was all there was to it. Nothing more to be said. He was going to collapse. Fall right to the ground, smash the leaves in a triumphant chorus of *crunch*, and smack his face right into the dirt.

He reached out to a nearby tree trunk to steady himself. Pain pulsed through his head, thrumming like the diesel engine of a battleship. Hot stickiness clenched his cheeks inside the mask. He could feel it stretching and smacking against the rubber as he breathed through the flapping mask. Oh, Christ, that flapping fucking mask! Would it stop? Would it *ever* stop? Why couldn't he see anything but red? Oh, God, how he *wished* he could blink it away! Receive that healing touch from the Lord!

And where was He? Jeremy was rotting on the floor of the house at this very minute, no doubt drawing flies and receiving nests of maggots and worms, creepy-crawling things that writhe in the mouths and eye sockets of corpses. Why was He not here? Why was He not feeding?

And who else knows?

Oh, friends and neighbors, would that question ever end? Would it ever stop bouncing off the inner walls of his skull? Reverberating off his eardrums? That pounding, pounding, *pounding—*

A branch snapped near him.

His thoughts—his *terrors*—stopped. Ceased all at once. His realization that the Lord felt *fear* at the approach of this man, this—*well, just who the hell was he, anyway?*—fled from his mind like a cawing murder of crows. The pain continued to swell, no doubt the tumor in his skull winding up for its final number in his brain, but even this sensation seemed distant now. He wasn't even aware of the red hue that was cast on everything in his sight anymore.

All he was aware of was that *crack*.

It had been close, too. The light of the fire licked up the tree he was using to steady himself, and he moved as silently as he could to conceal himself in the shadows. He deliberately slowed his breathing, forcing himself to cease the *flap-flap-flappity* going through the mouth of the mask.

It doesn't matter who he is or who knows he's here, he thought to that fearful voice within him. *In a few moments, he'll just be another slab of meat.*

Another *crack* sounded just on the other side of the tree, and he stole the smallest of glances around the trunk. He saw the man—a rather well-built man by the sight of him—taking another tentative step toward the fire and the house. He could only see the side of one eye, but he saw the distinct twinkle of fear in it.

See? He's scared, too! And boy, oh, boy! Is he ever gonna be scared soon!

"Oh, my God!" the man spoke flatly with a small croak.

Norman peered around again and saw the man's gaze was on the house. He was seeing Jeremy's corpse, lying there half in and half out of the front door, staring blankly out at him and nothing.

"Oh, my sweet Jesus!" the man said, lifting the shirt under his right arm and producing a small, black object.

It's a gun, you fuck!

That voice again. That fearful voice from his Lord. The fear was more present now, and the voice was louder.

No matter, Norman thought back to the voice. *Another few seconds and it's all over.*

Norman gripped the handle of the hatchet and slid it silently out of his pants.

Chapter Thirty-one

"Oh, my God!"

Ryan was speaking, though full of fear, with a minute croak and a flat tone. He was so scared that his voice seemed to lose the capacity to communicate his fright.

There was a dead man on the porch of the house.

A random fire—which, as it turned out, had been what had caught his eye when he was inspecting the strangely abandoned car on the gravel road—was slapping at the dark with boneless flames. It was an eerie scenario as it was, and eerie graduated into full-on terrifying when you dropped a bloody corpse on the house in front of the fire—a house that was equally randomly placed in the middle of the woods, sprouting up from the ground as though it were a part of the forest which surrounded it.

"Oh, my sweet Jesus!"

The tone in his voice was now reaching for—if not quite acquiring—the element of fear that the rest of his body was having no issues communicating.

He lifted his shirt instinctively and snatched up the Glock. The textured polymer grip felt soothing in his hand, and he subconsciously savored the feeling. Anything that helped to abate the slithering snake of terror sliming laps up and down his spine was a welcomed thing.

His phone was still in his other hand. He'd never made the call to Jim that he'd planned to make, the one that would let his friend know that he'd done the stupid, *foolish* thing of coming out to this place alone and without someone to watch his back. The one that would get the gears of the small-town police force turning and flood the place with cops and more guns.

No, he'd never made that call. Even now, as his eyes locked with that of the butchered corpse on the porch of the house, his mind wasn't sending him signals to call. To *use* the fucking thing. It was right there, in his hand, and all he could do was stand there trembling and pointing his gun—also shaking—at nothing at all. And why? Because it made him *feel* better? Because it made him feel as though that bucking, whinnying colt of horror that was pounding in his chest, pleading to be let out, begging to break free and run, run, run the fuck away from this awful damned place and this idiotic situation he'd gotten himself into and send him into a panicked flight of cowardice?

Yes, goddamnit! That's precisely why!

He managed to take a small step forward. Toward the fire. Looking over the lapping flames at the eerily shadowed house with the bloody ball of flesh lying there staring stupidly at him.

He made another step now. His brain wasn't consciously operating his feet. They were on some form of autopilot, like the way your brain reminds your lungs to take a breath every couple of seconds without thinking deliberately about it. The way your eyelids blink every so often to keep your eyes from drying out—which they were doing now with vigor standing so close to the flames.

He felt as though he were floating toward the terrible sight before him that hovered over the flames which licked the dark with their terrible tongues, their flapping tentacles that flailed aimlessly and ceaselessly into the dark night, cutting the blackness surrounding the place and casting moving shadows and waves of heat into the air that sickened his stomach to watch, though rendering him powerless to look away. Away from the poor man lying there. There on that terrible porch of that terrible house where so many terrible things had happened. The place he and his friends had vowed to stay away from forever all those years ago. The place Jake had taken Honey, and where he and Jimmy and Freddie had come to rescue her from the monstrous bullies. The place where they discovered another world filled with real monsters.

And the place where the worst monster of all had come through.

Why are you here? he screamed to himself as another shudder overtook him. *How stupid can you be? Get out of here! If there's a body lying there like that, do you think the killer is far? What if he's watching you, watching you right now, waiting for you to take just one more step and—*

As if in answer to his internal scolding, a shape moved with blinding speed in the outer rims of his periphery. It was dark, and he didn't have time to get a good look, but whatever it was didn't seem human. The shape of the head was all wrong. If Ryan had had more time to react, to behold the thing coming at him in the dark, perhaps he'd have been able to ascertain what it was.

As it was, though, he hadn't.

All Ryan had time for was to take a half-step back. That was all. A mere foot and a half step in the opposite direction from which he'd been heading. His head shifted in the direction of the shape charging down upon him, but only a fraction.

And it was this minute movement which saved his life.

He could hear an awful breathing sound coming from the thing. In the split-second his mind had to process what was happening, the sound suddenly reminded him of a whoopee cushion when the air was farting out of the rubber mouth, and for an insane wonder, he actually blurted out a single, gasping laugh.

That was all he had time to do.

A *whooshing* sound whistled past his face and there was a blur in his vision. Then the thing was running into him and he was falling. His cellphone flew from his hand and spun like a helicopter rotor through the air. His gun went in the other direction, thudded to the dirt, pushing leaves as it skidded to a stop.

Now he was falling, and whatever the thing was that had hit him, it was falling with him. The momentum and the near miss with the blurred thing that whistled past his face had thrown it off-balance, and it was going down too.

Air rushed out of Ryan as he collided with the earth. He made a loud *"ooph"* as he hit, and happened to see his phone cascading into the fire. It hit one of the burning logs with enough force to shift its position slightly, and sparks bloomed into the air.

Then the thing that had hit him tumbled into his view in front of the fire and was silhouetted in a comically flamboyant crash, arms and legs flailing around like a discarded ragdoll.

Ryan began to heave, desperately trying to pull air back into his lungs, for just a nanosecond unaware of anything else but the need to get oxygen back into his system.

"Umph!" the thing cried as it hit the ground before him and slid over the leaves and loose dirt.

Minute slivers of air were cutting their way back into Ryan's depleted lungs now, and the situation came crashing back down on him like a load of bricks. The fear leaped back up from the depths, that bucking bastard of a horse now in full revolt once again.

He rolled over, sucking in precious gobs of air every half-second, and began to scoot backwards on his butt and his back. He could see now that whatever the thing was, it actually *did* look human. At least mostly. It was pushing itself up from the ground now, and in the shadowy image its silhouette formed in front of the fire he could see the outlines of *very* human legs and arms. The torso seemed right too. Only the head was wrong.

He heard that terrible breathing sound again, and was again reminded of the whoopee cushion. Another laugh escaped him involuntarily, and he squelched it immediately.

The thing was rising to its full height now, and he could see the blurred thing which had rushed past his face just a moment before. It was gripped in the thing's hand, and the distinctive shape rang home immediately in his mind.

A small axe.

Only that's not what you called it. In his now frantic scoots away from the monster, his mind couldn't land on the right word. Couldn't pull it from the files in his mind where it *surely* resided. All he could manage were the basics of survival, to get *away* from this thing before him before it could use that...that...*whatever* you called a small axe. Oh, God, why couldn't he think?!

"You're interfering with the work of the Lord!" the thing hissed at him from its entirely *wrong* head, the words punctuated by that terrible, flapping breathing.

Ryan couldn't manage any words in response. The only thing he could do was to keep crawling away and fail at new attempts to keep from laughing at the farting whoopee cushion sound the thing kept making. The cackles rose from his chest and leaped out, Ryan no longer capable of holding them in. They were mad sounds, the raving howls of a lunatic, but he couldn't control them.

He began to roar with laughter. Terrible, horrified laughter.

This seemed to piss the thing off, but in response to this anger it kept breathing faster and faster, like rapid-fire farts spewing from its mouth, and this just made Ryan howl all the more.

Dark eyes blazed from the thing in the dim glow of the fire that was leaking around the side of its head and now his mind registered why the head had looked so wrong to him. It was a mask in the form of an animal of some sort, though the name of the animal was escaping him now too.

The thing—or man, or *whatever* it was—began to take a few steps toward him. The fire leaped up behind it—or him—like fiery wings on a dark spirit.

"Laughing at the work of the Lord?" the thing screamed now. *"Who do you think you are?"*

More farts from the thing's mouth. More laughter from Ryan. Terrified laughter, but laughter all the same.

The man turned his masked head slightly and more light was cast over the mask.

It was a goat.

The word came to him all at once, literally out of nowhere, and it drove his insane laughs to a new level. His side was hurting now, he realized, and he couldn't be sure if it was from the fall or the laughing. It didn't matter in any event. The man was moving towards him steadily, his shadow already overtaking Ryan.

He continued to scramble backwards, laughing all the while, trying to get away and knowing he couldn't at the same time. Hoping beyond hope that something would intervene at any moment and would—

A hatchet!

The bizarre realization cut his laughter off mid-howl. His mind had been working furiously in the background, searching desperately for the word, the *right* word, as if small axe just wouldn't suffice, regardless of the fact that no matter what you called the thing it would still be chopping and slicing into his flesh at any moment now, separating his muscles and tendons and bones and splashing blood all over the place.

His hand brushed against something.

Until that moment all he'd felt as he scrambled away was dirt and dead leaves. Maybe the occasional twig or branch. But this...*this* was a foreign object, alien to the environment, and as his brain was now catching up with the situation, putting the right words to the scenario, he knew what it was without even looking at it.

There was a low grumbling sound from the direction of the house, and some scraping noises. These sounds were immediately dismissed as not being relevant to the moment, but they were there, in the background behind the crackling of the fire, the crunching of leaves, and the farting of the man's goat mask.

The man was closer now, almost on top of him, fury blazing in his eyes. Ryan gripped the alien thing in the woods and brought it up.

The fury in the man's eyes changed to fearful amazement.

Chapter Thirty-two

The man's laughter was infuriating to Norman. What could possess a man to cause such an insane reaction to their impending doom?

He didn't know, but the man was laughing. And it pissed him off.

Norman began moving toward the man, gripping the handle of the hatchet so tightly he thought he might crush it to powder. His nails were digging into his palms as they were wrapped around the grip, drawing blood, but he didn't care.

The man's laughing suddenly ceased, and indescribable joy filled Norman from the deepest wells of his belly. The man continued to move away for a moment more as Norman bore down on him, but then he stopped. Norman could hear the sounds of the Lord beginning to feed on Jeremy somewhere behind him.

About time, Jesus! Where the hell have you been?

His blasphemy went without supplication for forgiveness this time. His head was pounding more than ever now, and the awful crimson hue was distracting him enough already that he didn't have time to compute other desires.

Time to die, you wretched fool!

He was smiling behind his mask, preparing to raise the hatchet over his head and destroy the pathetic, cackling idiot on the ground in front of him. The Lord would appreciate another meal on his way into the world.

Tonight was the night, after all, when the new Mary would bring the living God back into the world, birthing him onto all of mankind for the salvation of the world and the establishment of the new Earth beneath the new Heaven. And he, yes he, Norman Reese, would reconnect with his long-lost prodigal brother and reign beside the King of Kings at his right hand.

But then the man raised the gun.

Norman had forgotten all about it when he'd rammed into him, narrowly missing the man's scalp when he'd moved at the last second. He'd seen it skittering away and had dismissed it altogether as now unimportant.

But here it was. Pointing at him. Leveled on him.

No! he screamed in his head, his eyes widening behind the mask in stark terror. *No! This can't be! I'm about the work of the Lord here, you can't—*

That was all he had time to think before the gun went off.

Chapter Thirty-three

Ryan fired.

The gun boomed in the quietness of the night and fire arrowed out of the muzzle like the trail of a rocket. The recoil raised his hand slightly, but it fell back level a moment later as the slide slammed back down and chambered another round.

He was glad it had fired. When he had felt it, it was covered in dirt, and he worried that might interfere with the firing mechanism. But it hadn't. It had operated exactly how it was supposed to, and it was ready for another shot.

Good old Glock, he thought. *Not much to look at, but by God, they go bang every time.*

The man in the mask flinched backwards and there was mist which rose into the air as blood spat from the man's shoulder. Even with the close proximity, Ryan hadn't made a very good shot. It really wasn't like being at the range, popping off rounds at stationary paper targets, not when you were dealing with a living, breathing threat right in front of you. Fear had made him tremble and *pull* the trigger rather than *squeeze*, and his aim suffered for it.

He had only winged the man in the shoulder. Barely a flesh wound in reality, but it had thrown him backwards and the man was now stumbling. The hatchet fell from his grasp and to the dirt with a low *thud*, and the man began to howl in pain, something that might have been words grunting loudly from behind the mask, but in tongues only angels could understand.

Or maybe demons.

Ryan was scrambling to his feet now, all the time holding the gun out before him, ready to take another shot if the man came back at him. He would get to his feet, plant them, and get in a good firing stance, just like at the range.

Then I'll fill this fucker so full of lead they'll need a fork-truck to lift him!

Or something like that. Male ego can be a funny thing.

But even as he thought this, it became evident he wouldn't have to fire another shot.

The man in the mask spun a few times, moving backwards, howling into the night like a mad werewolf preparing to change forms, and then his feet tangled. He tumbled to the ground and his face and shoulders went straight into the fire. The awful and hilarious farting sounds of his mask stopped at once and a shriek like Ryan had never heard in all his life, be it in reality or media, rose into the cooling night. No more was the man worrying with his winged shoulder, but now he was scurrying backwards out of the fire, trying to get to his feet and swatting at his face and shoulders with wild slaps trying to put out the flames that now leaped off his entire head.

"Ahh-eeeeeeee!" the man screamed.

Ryan was mesmerized by the sight of the flaming goat-man before him, his eyes wild with fear and excitement. His heart was exploding in his chest and his breaths came in shuddering gasps. Then he noticed that other sound, the one he'd heard just before he had snatched up the gun, the one he'd dismissed as not relevant to the current situation.

It was relevant now. Relevant as fuck.

He took a few steps to the side, holding the gun on the human torch as he went, and looked past the fire to the house. The place where he'd heard the growling and the scraping.

Could it be? he thought with abject horror. *Could it really be back?*

His eyes fell on the bloody corpse on the porch and saw it lurching, its head flopping this way and that. Fresh gouts of blood were spewing from the doorway every couple of seconds or so, and Ryan could see movement in the dark beyond the door.

Then, in a horrible and revealing moment, lightning split the sky open like an inoperable wound.

For just a moment, just a split-second really, the world around them was lit up like daytime, and he could see into the doorway and see the moving shape for what it was.

He recognized the vertical mouth and the black eyes. The terrible size of the thing. It was something he'd seen as a child, when they were in that other world, and it had been seared into his mind ever since. The reason for his nightmares and for all the years of drinking, trying to drown the memory away, to cover it, all ending in failure.

It was the thing from the damned place.

Then the thing locked eyes with him and its terrible, vertical mouth seemed to shift into a sort of diamond shape that Ryan intrinsically knew was its smile. Its black eyes gleamed in the momentary light, and the raving screams of the burning man in the goat mask seemed like the furthest thing from him.

Then it roared.

Its mouth opened wide and a guttural bellow exploded forth from it. Layers of horrific octaves filled the air. It was a wet sound and the most awful thing Ryan had ever heard in his life. It was somehow more awful than he remembered it from his childhood.

Then the light from the flash was gone and the world slipped instantly back into darkness, save for the dim light of the fire. Thunder boomed overhead and drowned out the last vestiges of the thing's roar.

Then it began to rain.

All at once and in sheets, the rain was coming down. Like God Himself had unzipped, whipped out the Holy Hose, and sighed.

Nothing like a good piss.

Now that insane laughter was back and Ryan couldn't contain it at all. He was almost unaware that he was now running, dashing really, through the woods back toward his truck. His phone was gone, but he still gripped the Glock in his hand tightly. He was running and laughing, leaving behind him the burning man, who was almost put out just before the rain started and was certainly all the way out now with the sudden downpour. When he'd turned to run, he'd seen the man lying motionless on the ground. He didn't know if he was dead or alive, and he didn't care.

The *thing* was back. The Glutton, as it was called in the journal of Johnathan Michael Brogan, and he meant to get as far away from it as possible.

Lightning split the sky again and he thought he might have heard another roar, or maybe it was another howl from the man in the mask. He didn't know, and nature drowned it out anyway with another boom of thunder before he could think much more about it. It really didn't matter what it was, because either way it was horrible and he had to get away from it. He had to find Jim and Freddie and Honey. Had to get the police involved—not that they would really know what to do—and get out of there. Needed to get Honey out of there. He would tell her now—oh, yes he would—how much he loved her and that he'd loved her all along and he would take her away from this place and this town and this state and this country if necessary. Hell, he would take her to the moon if that was what it took. But they had to get *away*.

He ran.

Chapter Thirty-four

"In the name of the Father, and of the Son, and of the Holy Spirit."

The priest made the sign of the cross over himself, and Jim did the same. It had been many years, *decades* even, since he'd done this. Decades since he'd stepped foot in a church. Since he had really prayed. He couldn't remember the last time he'd done any of these things, or anything remotely religious. He wasn't even sure if he believed in any of this, or at least to what degree, yet here he was, after all this time.

He felt he had to do this now. *Needed* to do this.

God doesn't call the equipped, He equips the called.

That cliché line continued to echo in his mind in the voice of his friend Freddie, the Baptist preacher. The only one of the four who had turned to something greater than himself rather than drink to deal with their shared past. The only one who really seemed to have it all together.

Sure, Honey was a successful counselor, and Ryan was doing well in his career drilling water wells. Even Jim himself had risen to the top role in his town's law enforcement department, and that had been through merit alone. But none of this really required having it *together.*

There was something different about Freddie. Freddie had endured the worst of the physical pain of all of them, and was equally culpable in what had happened at the place in the woods when they were children, but he was also the only one who seemed to face the world, day to day, with a sober mind and a conscience that was at peace.

Ryan had lived pretty hard, enjoying the party life like any college student does, yet without any of the joy. Ryan had been drowning himself in liquor, desperately trying to forget everything they had seen, everything he'd grown up with, and had damn near killed himself in the process. He was getting better now, but only just.

Honey had done college, graduated, and built a career. Add to this that she had done nearly *all* of this while caring for a little baby she and Jim had made in a single act of desperate passion that had little to nothing to do with sex and everything to do with trying to find peace and comfort from what they had seen and done. Honey didn't stick with the alcohol like Ryan and Jim had, but she had her own demons. Daddy issues were only one of them.

And then there was Jim himself. He was in his late thirties, still drinking himself to sleep every night, and waking up to a pair of tall Bloody Marys every morning just so he could function. Yet, function he did. In spite of his severe drinking problem, he still managed to surge through the ranks in the police department and arrive in the position of Chief. A good chief, too. Most everyone in the department loved him, and even those who didn't respected him.

But none of them knew about his problem. His struggles. His crippling memories.

He equips the called.

That silly quote continued to bounce around in his head. Hadn't stopped, as a matter of fact. Not since Freddie had quipped it off to him at dinner.

Everything with Norman, the missing people and their blood-soaked homes, Norman's mention of Jake and the thoughts that had conjured of the thing in the woods...

The Glutton.

It all swirled in his mind, a perfect storm of horror, with Winnsboro directly in its path. He had a gift, something which had materialized out of nowhere when he was a kid and suddenly reappeared a few days ago, and there had to be a reason for it. He didn't buy into the *everything's-a-coincidence* ideology of some. Everything that happened had a purpose. He believed that. In the core of his being, he *knew* that.

But he still didn't know why.

When he was a child, and the gift had come upon him in the house, he had come to believe the purpose of receiving it was to *equip* him to deal with the thing when the time came. But when it had come back a few days ago, he'd had no idea why. There was no reason to think the thing—*The Glutton*—was back at the time, but there was the gift just the same. His dormant abilities had returned.

Then today, just after the insane church service, Norman had said those words which had chilled Jim to the core.

Heard from Jake lately?

Of course, he hadn't. He hadn't even thought about Jake in more than twenty years. Only, Jim had to admit that though he hadn't *really* thought of Jake in all that time, he was really thinking about him *all* the time, him and Chris Higgins and Bart Dyer. About what himself and the others had done to them.

And the thing.

That had been why he'd been drinking so heavily from the time he could get his hands on a bottle regularly. They were in his head, on his soul, all the time. And the one thing he'd found that seemed to dull their presence was drink, drink, drink...

Of course, he'd never really tried anything else.

God doesn't call the equipped.

Sure as hell not. Jim Dalton was *anything* but equipped to deal with this. He was nothing. A failure in his own eyes, no matter how well he'd done for himself or what others thought of him. He *knew* himself, and he knew that he was nothing. An all but absent father and alcoholic who made excuses not to be there for his little girl rather than efforts to be in her life more. A girl needs her father. There was no more important relationship in all the world, and he had willingly failed to nurture it the way Joanna needed. Perhaps she didn't realize that now, but one day she would, and she would resent him for it, and it was these thoughts—atop all the others—which perpetuated his cycle of self-destruction.

Yes. Jim Dalton was nothing. Yet despite this, he was thrust into a situation demanding, *requiring*, that he rise to the occasion. If he failed to do this, well...

God help them all.

So he had called the number listed for the small parish in Winnsboro where Catholics could have their Mass. It had been late when he called, and he had fully expected to get an answering machine that told him office hours so that he could come in the next day before he and Ryan went to check out the old damned house in the woods, but to his astonishment, the priest himself had answered.

"Hello?" a sleepy voice had grumbled into the phone. "Father Don speaking."

Father Don? Jim had thought. *He must be a hundred years old by now!*

Father Don Jenkins had been the parish priest when Jim had been a kid. When he'd been Jimmy. Back when his mother had faithfully taken him to church every Christmas and Easter.

Jim had thought the man was old back then, he couldn't believe that the same man was still pastoring St. Ann's.

"Father," Jim croaked, then cleared his throat. He could feel heat flush his cheeks.

"Yes?" said the old Padre.

Jim cleared his throat again. "Yes, Father, sorry. It's, uh...this is Jim Dalton."

There had been a moment of silence, and Jim had to check his phone to confirm that he was still connected to the call.

He was.

After what seemed like a long time, Father Don came back on the line, his voice lighter now and speaking with an air of familiarity.

"Jimmy Dalton?" said he. "Well, color me shocked, I tell ya. How are ya, old boy?"

Jim had been astonished that the man remembered him. It had been more than twenty years since he'd seen him, and even then it had only been a couple times a year. Calling him Jimmy had struck a chord of familiarity—and warmth—Jim had not expected.

So they had talked. Not long into the conversation, Father Don had invited him to the church and Jim had come. He knew even as he was on the way there that he needed to make things right. Set things straight. At the very least to get it all off his chest. If God was calling and equipping him, he needed to square things with the Big Man.

Jim had bowed his head when Father Don had made the sign of the cross, initiating the sacrament. There were tears in his eyes as he raised his head. He couldn't believe he was here, all this time later, returning like a prodigal son. All in preparation of facing what he feared had made its way back. The awful truth of his childhood. The awful truth about Jake and the other bullies.

The awful truth about the *thing.*

"I-I," Jim began and then stopped.

He couldn't seem to form the words. He knew he needed to. He could already feel the weight of everything trying to lift off of him, even now before he'd said a word. But the words, letting them out, he feared might break him.

He shuddered.

They were sitting in the pew at the front of the small church. The crucifix of Christ loomed over them with his painful but comforting face, and candles lit the sanctuary in a peaceful glow.

Father Don put his hand on Jim's shoulder.

"You can do it, Jimmy," he said in the kindest voice Jim had ever heard.

Fresh tears stung Jim's eyes and began to roll down his cheeks. Heaving sobs threatened to overtake him, but they passed only a moment after they started.

Jim took a deep breath. Let it out slowly. Looked up to the priest through salty, wet eyes.

He smiled.

"Bless me Father, for I have sinned."

He told the old man everything.

Chapter

Thirty-five

Horrible, white-hot pain seared every inch of Norman's shoulders and head.

His eyes shot open from where he lay on the ground in the pouring rain. He had to thank the Lord for the rain, for without it he would have surely burned away to ash. But the pain was horrific. It was exquisite. Nearly absolute. His face felt like it was trapped in a steam oven and his skin felt like it was melting from his face. It was a wonder that he could see at all, though that red hue was still cast over everything.

He struggled to his feet, relishing the rain which poured down in a torrential deluge. He looked up to it, to douse his face with the cool water.

Nothing.

There was no cooling. He could feel droplets splashing against his face, but it was as if they were hitting something else besides his skin and he couldn't—

The mask!

Of course, the mask was still on! It was no wonder his face wasn't cooling with the mask still on, the thick rubber holding in the heat.

He grabbed the top of the mask and pulled.

Fresh waves of the worst pain he'd ever experienced cascaded over him like a tsunami of agony. He cried out in a high-pitched squeal—one which sounded not unlike that of a dying pig—and fell to his knees.

His head was still throbbing, his brain beating away at the internal walls of his skull, but that pain had become secondary now. The ice picks behind his eyes seemed very far away in relation to the horrific torture upon his face.

When he had pulled, he could actually feel the skin and muscles of his face moving *with* the mask. There had been pain then, but what had made him stop pulling at the mask had been the more mature agony that came when he felt the skin trying to peel away on the inside of the mask.

The fire had melted the rubber mask to his face. To his *skin.* Removing it now would be like removing his own face. The two had fused in the flames and become one.

Terror shivered through him now at this realization. He kept his face skyward, hoping desperately that the rain would somehow penetrate through the mask and cool his bubbling flesh beneath.

No such relief came.

There was another streak of lightning and boom of thunder. In that moment, Norman saw his Lord standing over him, new skin glistening in the droplets upon him, looking down on him with the diamond-shaped smile on its terrible face.

He was here. For the first time. Out of the house, in new flesh. Standing before Norman in the rain.

All his pain retreated. It didn't diminish, but his mind had seemed to find a place to quarantine it, and it was locked away now.

"Lord," Norman muttered, but the molten rubber mask on his face made the word come out like *Norldt.*

The smiling diamond mouth stood out against the twin black eyes in the thing's head.

Then it spoke.

"Go before me," it said. *"Go, and make the way clear. Your Lord comes tonight!"*

Norman stood shakily to his feet, his whole body trembling as he did. He was nodding frantically.

"Yes!" he cried in that terrible, muffled sound through his new face. "I will go and prepare the way for you!"

"So be it."

The thing began to chuckle, a wet and guttural sound, as Norman turned and began to run. He tripped and fell a couple of times on the way, and had Norman not known better, he would have thought his Lord had begun to laugh harder. Maybe even *at* him.

But, thankfully, he knew better. He'd been raised to know about the Lord, and knew that no such thing as mockery could ever be within the God of the universe. It was impossible. Perfect love could never mock its own child.

So he ran. He had no idea how long it had been since the bad man with the gun had left, but he didn't think it could have been very long. The thought hit him that the man might still be out here, perhaps hiding behind a tree somewhere with his pistol ready. The idea made his heart quicken its pace.

Thunder and lightning continued to dance together, lighting and sounding the air around him in flickering bursts. Before long he was coming out of the woods, just a little way up the road from his car. His was the only one here. Whatever the bad man had been driving when Norman had seen the headlights was gone, and the man with it. This was a relief and he sighed awkwardly through his molten mask.

He turned toward his car and went to it, all the while still hearing the now-distant chuckle of his Lord in the woods.

He got to his car and flung the door open. He dropped himself in and then realized his keys were in his front pants pocket. He pushed his hips up and shoved a charred hand down into the pocket to fish the keys out, pulling fried skin off the top of his hand as he did so. Fresh pain exploded there, but his brain was quick on its quarantine duty and put the sensation away at once.

He thrust the key into the ignition and turned. The engine roared to life and his headlights sliced into the night before him. Lightning tore open the sky again, drowning the light from his headlamps for a moment in white light.

Norman tried to smile after this. The movement made his skin split beneath the mask and warm blood began to spill from a fresh crack in the mask. But he didn't care.

He looked into the mirror and saw himself. The mask was barely recognizable now as a goat, but if a person tried hard enough, they would get it. The horns were melted to heaps of blackened rubber on either side of the face, and everything had a strange white and black look to it, with sprinklings of blood here and there that hadn't burned off completely in the fire.

This, amazingly, made him smile even more. He thought it made him look similar to his Lord in the woods, and he wasn't wrong about that.

Norman looked over the seat to the rear of the car and pulled something out from the floorboard. What came up in his hand was a beautiful, black object. Something he'd stolen from his dad the last time he'd gone out to his house. He shifted it around in his hands and regarded it like a person regards a new tool.

His hands were burned and bleeding, but he was still able to manage to utilize all the controls with relative ease. He nodded to himself.

"That'll do," he said. It came out like *Vattle goo.*

He placed the AR-15 barrel-down in the passenger seat and dropped the car into gear. He made a pitiful turn-around, having to stop and reverse and go forward again three times in the muddy gravel road, but he made it.

Finally.

He began racing back toward town, laughing to himself now. The Lord was coming. His return was imminent. And *he* had been the one chosen to bring him into the world *and* to prepare the way! The honor alone was startling, but not exactly surprising. He'd been taught all about Jesus growing up, but he'd also been taught all about himself as well. His mother had always assured him that he was great, and he was meant for greatness, and that he was chosen by God Almighty for truly wondrous things.

And here it was! Right here, right now, he was in the midst of that calling his sweet mother had prepared him for all his life!

She really was a good teacher.

Howling bursts of laughter exploded painfully from him as he raced into the pouring rain toward town, his mission clear, his loyalty rigid and absolute.

"Prepare ye the way of the Lord!"

Blood sprayed from him with every cackling laugh.

PART SIX:

Prepare Ye the Way

Sunday, August 7, 2016

Chapter Thirty-six

Who on earth is calling me this late?

Cherry Reese was in her nightgown, a light pinkish thing—layered with multiple shirts and a slip much like all her other attire—and furry house-shoes donned her feet. Her usually stiffened hair—which typically stood out in a suspended, blasted state—was freshly washed now and hung loosely around her scalp, partially pulled back in a pony-tail except for several clusters of strands which hung carelessly about the sides of her face.

She had been getting ready for bed, her room the large master of the house and about as far from the little room George used to sleep in as it could get within the domicile. Her hair was washed, her teeth were brushed, and her large, inviting bed beckoned for her to come and lay down, letting the day and its troubles drift away to Never-Land.

But it was not to be. Not yet, anyway.

This had better be good! her thoughts hissed inside her head like demonic reptiles.

She snatched the phone up off the nightstand and looked at the bright screen. Her face formed a pronounced frown—an easily achieved look for Cherry Reese, one perfected with decades of practiced piousness—and her thumb paused over the dancing green circle with the phone inside of it.

Oh, Jesus, what now?

The caller-ID told her it was her son, Norman, calling. She knew this instantly not because it was labeled sanely with his name. No, no, nothing so quaint. She had a little nickname for her golden boy, the one who would rise to the call of all that was good and holy and change the world with his angelic voice. The one who would wipe away all memory and trace of the monster who had first slithered its way out of her vagina like the demon snake he was and would usher in not only fame and fortune to the Reese name, but also respect and praise.

Oh, what wonderful parents he must have! they would say. *His mother must be a Saint! She really must have raised him right!*

She raised him up, alright. Her little *Loving Boy.*

And for just a moment, she suddenly was slapped coldly with the dread that all of this might be crashing down, even as she stared at the delightful animation of the dancing phone in the green circle. Whatever had been happening the past few days, Norman's involvement—to what degree she still had no real idea—could be the undoing of it all. Her wonderful, called and chosen baby boy, brought down by the wretches of this world, by the wretches of this *town.*

That cocksucking Chief of Police was one of them. *And no,* she reminded herself, *that wasn't a curse.* She believed him to be just that, one of those knee-standing homosexuals opening his mouth to all manner of perversion. She had taught and warned first Jake—*that scaly serpent*—and then Norman the right and true way. She had taught them that those faggots—a word her elder boy had taken quite the shine to—were not real people with feelings and desires like anyone else, oh, no siree, not at all. These were the walking damned, abominations to nature, and they were to be shunned and sidelined until such a day that the Living God would deliver them into a new era where the laws of their great nation would finally be in line with those of The Almighty, and they could be stoned and beheaded on sight accordingly.

Cherry spent a lot of time in the Old Testament, and rather preferred it to the New. Eye for an eye, not the *Kumbaya* chanting faggotry of the latter Covenant.

She swiped the dancing phone in the green circle with her thumb and put the phone to her ear, pulling the charging cable from the bottom of the phone as she moved.

"Norman?" she almost whispered, and immediately wondered why she had.

There was a strange droning sound on the line, like an incessant hum which drummed through the small speaker next to her ear. And something else. Something that sounded like...breathing.

Heavy breathing.

"Norman?" she said again, louder this time as she shed the timidity that had come upon her unexpectedly.

"Mother?" she heard a voice say. She was suddenly no longer sure this was Norman at all. *Couldn't* be Norman. The voice was too thick, too garbled. Like whomever this imposter was, they were speaking through a wad of gel-soaked towels.

"Who is this?" she barked into the phone.

"Mother, it's me, Norman!" the voice huffed and spat. "Your son? Your *Loving Boy?*"

Her eyelids pushed together to tiny slits. No one else knew of that little nickname but her and her *Loving Boy* himself. Well, George knew, she was almost sure of it, but he was in the other room. And this call had come from Norman's phone. It *had* to be him. But something was completely off about his voice.

"Norman?" she said again, this time more softly. More loving. "Norman, are you okay? What's going on? Why are you calling so—"

"He's come, mother!" Norman shrieked into the phone, the sound of the drumming rain—*on his car?*—fading to the background for a moment when he spoke in that horrible, garbled voice.

"What's that?" she said, confused. "Norman, I can barely understand you, I—"

"The Lord!" he said, this time almost growling. Something very strange was going on with his voice. It was like he was struggling to utilize it at all.

"The Lord?" she asked back. "Norman, honey, I need you to come here right away. You don't sound well!"

"No, mother," he said and sighed. "No. You were right all these years about the call on my life, just not about the particular mechanics of it."

"What are you talking about?"

"I mean the Lord has appeared to me! He's met with me in the wilderness and given me my calling! And I've been doing it, mother, I've been doing it so well!"

"Norman, I don't understan—"

"You *will*, mother! The whole *world* is about to understand! I am the new Mary, and I've birthed Christ back into this world! And He's coming! He's coming, even now! I'm going before Him to prepare the way!"

A sick feeling sunk into the pit of Cherry's stomach. What on earth was he talking about? Had her worst fears come to fruition? Had he gone completely mad? Just what in the world did he mean he was the *new Mary?*

"Baby," she said, her voice threatening to falter, "I don't understand what you're saying. Come to me, baby boy. We'll work this out. Whatever it is. Just come home!"

"I'm sorry, mother," he said, a strange gurgle in his voice. "I've got a job to do. Most won't understand, but the Lord of creation will *make* them understand! He'll show them *all* the truth! He's come to cleanse the world of unrighteousness, and to establish His Kingdom! And He chose *me*, mother! *Me!* And I'm going to prepare a feast for His return!"

Madness, she thought. *He's gone completely bat-shit crazy! And no, that's not a curse, bat-shit IS crazy.*

"I-I don't understand," she managed to croak. Her hand was trembling on her phone now. Her lower lip began to quiver.

"You will, mother," he said. "Soon, the whole world will understand. I just wanted to let you know in case...in case I..."

He trailed off, leaving only the drumming *thuds* of the rain coming through on the call. That, and that awful, heavy breathing.

He sounded bad.

"Where are you?" she asked suddenly and with an abruptly sharp tone. "I'm coming to you right now, tell me where you are!"

She heard his voice again, coming through the drone of the rain, laughing in deep croaks.

"I'll introduce you to Him," he said as his laughter was brought under control. "All in good time, mother. I promise. In just a little while, the ways of this world will be brought under His control. And then I can bring you before His Majesty!"

"Norman Reese, you tell me where you are right this instant!" she shrieked into the phone as though she were speaking to a child. "You tell me right now!"

More horrible laughter. "I just wanted to tell you I love you, in case He sees fit for me to be martyred. I don't *think* that will happen, He's got so much planned for me, but just in case I'm wrong, I wanted to let you know I love you. I've always loved you, mother."

Then there was a loud *beep*, and the call was disconnected.

Cherry pulled the phone back from her ear and looked at the screen incredulously. *Call Disconnected* was the screen's pontification, and her hand began to shake all the more. She quickly redialed his number and put the phone to her ear.

"I'm sorry, I must be away from my phone right now—" Norman's voice mail message began immediately without a ring.

She slapped the end icon on her screen with her thumb and cursed bitterly under her breath. He'd turned his phone off.

Now what do I do? she thought. *Norman is losing it! And if he goes on like this he's liable to get caught—or worse—by that cocksucking Chief of Police, Dalton!*

A thought came to her then, the only sane thing to do at this point, but she thought it was simultaneously the best and worst thing she could possibly do under the circumstances.

But is there anything else? she thought. *Honestly, what else can you do? If you don't, he's going to end up in jail, or worse. He could end up* dead!

She cursed again, even more bitterly than before, and internally justified it to herself because it wasn't a curse. It was literally *that* bad.

She pulled her nightgown over hear head, and peeled off the layers beneath. Soon, she was stark naked, her soft belly pooching out and her aging breasts sagging, the nipples pointing to her unshaven crotch, a thicket of graying horror.

Then she was grabbing some panties and a bra, and she began getting dressed.

If you hurt my Loving Boy, she thought, seething, *I'll end your Goddamned life myself!*

Nope. That wasn't a curse. His life *would be* goddamned.

Chapter Thirty-seven

Norman powered off the phone and tossed it to the passenger seat next to the AR-15. His aim wasn't very good, and it bounced off the edge of the seat and tumbled to the foot-well.

He shrugged, knowing he wouldn't need it again. Not for a while, anyway. He didn't *really* think that his Lord meant for him to be martyred, but you never really knew. Not everything. God didn't tell us everything, and that was how one walked in faith. If you knew the outcome ahead of time, there would be no faith involved, would there?

His face began to ache and burn again, and his hand shot up involuntarily to massage his cheeks. But instead of skin, he felt the crusted and hardened rubber of his new face. He winced, more from the remembrance of what had happened to his face than from the pain, but both were present.

The rain was pelting his windshield with prejudice, and his wipers were going full speed. Even still, visibility was limited, and his vision had begun to blur again with the red hue.

My eyes are bleeding again, he thought with no real dread.

And they were. Twin streams of crimson were trailing out of the eye-holes of his mask which had fused to his face, and his headache was back with a vengeance. But all of the pain—from his molten skin, his aching head, and his burning eyes—were very distant to him now. The pain was *quarantined.* Put away. Locked up.

Mission was fueling him now, even as the tumor swelled inside his brain, on its way to causing severe cerebral hemorrhaging, probably that very night. But it didn't matter to him. He was on a mission from God. A crusade.

And he meant to see it through.

Up ahead, he could see the sodium-arc lights in front of the Police Station, and his new, rubber goat-face managed to crack a smile. And crack was *literally* the right word for it. The mask split open horizontally at the corners of the mangled and molten mouth hole, and beneath it his skin did likewise, oozing fresh blood past the cauterized wound that was his whole face. It oozed through the slits in the charred mask and dripped down upon his tattered shirt in huge, black globs.

A truck was pulling out of the station up ahead. He saw the red taillights swing across the road as the truck fish-tailed first to the left, then to the right before the tires found traction on the wet street. Norman couldn't tell much more than that it was indeed a truck through all the rain. But that didn't matter. What mattered was what was *inside* the station, and what he had to do there.

A feast fit for a King!

The cracking smile broadened and oozed.

Chapter Thirty-eight

Ryan locked the tires of his truck as he skidded into the parking space. The truck slid several feet, and for one horrifying moment, he thought he would surely be going up over the sidewalk and into the side of the brick building.

But then the pickup lurched to a stop.

He threw the gear lever into park and fumbled for the door handle. He slapped and clawed at it, his trembling hands betraying him in his panic, but after a few tries his hand found purchase and swung the door open.

He dumped himself out into the pouring rain and slipped. He sprawled to the ground, smacking his head on the concrete and wincing in pain.

"Fuck!" he wailed as he pushed himself to his feet.

He got up, and slammed the door shut and ran for the entrance, his heart pounding in his chest and in his ears. He was on the verge of *actually* exploding. Any moment now, his heart would race into warp speed. There would be stars that stretched out into bright poles before him, and his body would erupt like a volcano and spray chunks of flesh and gooey insides all over the side of the building. He would just spontaneously explode, and it would all be over. He wouldn't be able to warn anyone, wouldn't be able stop anything at all.

Just *boom.*

But none of that happened. He took a deep, moist breath from the soaking air and managed to rein the drumming of his heart down to a slightly more manageable level. He might still have a heart attack, but at least now he didn't think he would blow up.

As he reached the glass door, both hands came out to grasp the handle. There was a loud, glassy *thunk* as his right hand, and the item it held, smacked against the door. He looked down and for the first time realized he was still clutching his Glock in his hand. His knuckles were white with exertion. His hand was trembling.

Oh, fuck me, he thought. *Get it together or they're going to shoot you down as soon as you walk in!*

He took a deep, forced breath, and stuffed the pistol into his waist band. Then he grabbed the door and swung it open. He rushed into a small vestibule and to a second glass door. He swung this one open as well and rushed into the lobby, the wet soles of his shoes squeaking absurdly with every step.

There was an aging black woman behind a glass window in the wall, sitting at a desk with multiple computer monitors and large radio equipment all around her. She looked up sharply at him as he rushed in, her eyes spreading wide in alarm.

"Can I—can—can I help you?" she managed to stutter.

Ryan reached the small sill of the window and clutched it as if it were the only thing that could save him from collapsing on the floor. He held onto it like a man hanging over the ledge of a cliff two hundred feet over jagged rocks and frigid waters.

"I need the Chief, Jim Dalton!" he panted. "I need him *now!*"

The woman just stared at him over thick glasses, her mouth hanging open as she took him in fully.

"Sir, are you okay?" she asked, not addressing his demands.

"I'm fine!" he almost screamed. He took a deep breath and tried to control his voice. "I need to see the Chief now!"

"You're bleeding," she said, standing up from behind her desk. "Are you sure you're—"

"God-damn it!" he shouted at the top of his lungs. *"I need to see Chief Dalton right fucking NOW!"*

The woman's spine suddenly straightened, and tightly. Her eyes widened more than he thought might have been possible, the optical orbs appearing as though they might pop out of her head at any moment now and splat against the insides of her glasses.

"Sir," she said, a waver in her voice, "the Chief isn't in right now, I—"

But Ryan was shoving off the window sill and turning back to the door before she could finish. He didn't have a phone, didn't have any way of contacting anyone. And he didn't have time to explain things to people who could never understand. He had to move. And fast.

The *Glutton* was coming.

He rushed back out to his truck, wiping something warm and sticky from his forehead where he'd struck the concrete moments before from his eyes. He jumped back behind the wheel and started the truck.

He dropped the truck into reverse and floored the accelerator, the wheels spinning and smoking as he backed out. Then he was in drive, and went sliding out onto the street again, desperate to find someone who knew what was coming, someone who wouldn't automatically think he was crazy. He had to find one of the others. They would have a phone, some way to call Jim. Jim could get it done. He could make the other cops understand. Make them ready.

It's coming!

As his tires found traction and the truck straightened out, he was barely aware of the headlights behind him, coming up the road to the Police Station.

Chapter Thirty-nine

Barbara Leaks stared out the small window in front of her desk that looked into the lobby of the Police Department with a slack jaw, her upper lip in a sort of snarl that conveyed confusion and disgust. The drenched, bleeding asshole who'd just run into the lobby demanding to see Chief Dalton had got her blood pumping, and she could feel the after-effects of the brief encounter tantalizing her veins beneath her brown skin.

"Well, fuck you too, white-ass son-of-a-bitch!" she said to the door as it fell closed behind the man running out.

She saw a small smear of blood on the glass door he had darted through, in the shape of a hand at its outer-most points, but streaked down at an angle into a ghastly point.

"And dirtying up my goddamn door!" she exclaimed as she pushed the chair beneath her away with the backs of her considerable thighs. "Motherfucker come in here acting all crazy, I'll show *you* crazy! Just come up in here again! I'm gonna get the chief crawling all *up* in yo ass!"

She moved to a table with drawers which sat next to the window that looked out on the station's parking lot, reaching out and drawing open the top one. There were cleaning supplies in the drawer—rags, Windex, other various cleaners—and she snatched the window cleaner and a rag on top to go deal with the door to the station.

She slammed the drawer shut, a little harder than she'd meant to, yet garnished no regret from it. The crazy white man had frightened her with his wild eyes and panicked tone. But that wasn't what really had her upset. What had her upset was that he'd smeared the door up with blood, and no doubt had tracked in God knew how much rain all over the floor. And who was going to clean that up? It wasn't going to be Big Jim Dalton, she could tell you that right and straight. No sir. And sure as shit it wasn't going to be any of the other officers. Uh-uh. Not even with nearly the whole damn department in station at that very moment, sitting on their asses, telling lies to each other in the officer's lounge in back. Nope, not them.

No, it would be Barbara Leaks herself, that was who. The bitch at the desk would be the one cleaning up the mess the crazy-ass white boy tracked in, and not a damn one of the other cops would lift a finger to help.

Barbara was fuming.

"Fucking asshole!" she hissed. "I juss git rait own dis h-yea, massah! Miss Barbara juss fix dis rait up fuh-yuh!"

Lightning flashed outside and the window in front of her glowed a brilliant white. A moment later, thunder rolled heavily, and the rain seemed to intensify. She could just see the taillights of the crazy white boy's truck sliding out into the road. Hell, he was all *over* the damn road. She thought how nice it would be if one of the officers pulled him over and wrote him up a nice, fat, juicy ticket for driving like an asshole, but then she remembered that all the officers were in the lounge, even several of the off-duty cops. All back there bumping their gums and staying dry through the storm.

Nope, they wouldn't be writing that asshole a ticket, not unless Chief Dalton happened to catch the guy out there, but she knew that was unlikely. She hadn't logged a ticket from the Chief since he'd been promoted to the head job. So, no dice there.

Thunder boomed again, this time close enough to rattle the glass in the window before her. It startled her, and she stood up straight, her back arching over her bulbous behind, her face flattening against her skull and flexing her second chin out like a muscle. Had she been aware of how cartoonishly comical she looked when she did this, she would have been appalled. Barbara Leaks was a woman who prided herself on her ability to shoot straight and keep a level head. She thought it made her good at her job, especially when the tension was high and people were depending on her to get them the information they needed.

However, few people aside from Barbara herself considered her to be level-headed. They all agreed she was good at her job, but easy-going and laid back she was not.

Only Barbara wouldn't have believed that even if she had known it, and it didn't matter. She turned from the desk and the rattling window, and her eyes fell on the large, red emergency siren button located next to her work station. When the weather got really bad—like a tornado coming through—she would activate the button and a loud, wailing siren would shriek into the night, letting all of Winnsboro know to stay the fuck indoors, because shit was getting serious. She thought there was a good chance she might have to hit that button tonight, with the way the storm was shaping up.

She started to cross the office to the door at the back, next to the coffee maker, so she could head up the hall by the Chief's office to the door to the lobby. She sighed loudly and harshly, thinking of having to touch the crazy white boy's blood, even if it *was* with Windex and a rag. She didn't like bodily fluids, not even her own. Someone else's was downright repugnant. But it was part of her job. Dispatch the officers, take emergency calls, manage the office, and clean shit up when needed. It made her think of one of those jingles on the commercials on TV, as though her life and work were reduced to no more than a catchy, redundant tune while she feigned a smile for the camera and happily pushed a mop.

"I ain't y'all's fuckin' nigga, you damn straight about that," she mumbled under her breath. "Chief Dalton gonna give me a raise after this, I ain't shittin' ya!"

Then light was spilling into the office from the window behind her again. At first she paid it no mind as she waddled to the door to the hallway, assuming it was lightning again. But then the light seemed to grow, almost focus in on her from behind, and then narrow, casting her shadow on the wall in front of her. When no thunder boomed a second later—and the light remained—she stopped, turned, and looked out the window.

Headlights from a car outside were staring in at her like accusing eyes, the shadows of raindrops dancing on her face like a thousand tiny bugs. She squinted her eyes against the glare, which was very bright in spite of the fluorescents lighting the office above her.

"Who the fuck's this, now?" she mumbled to herself. "Better not be that crazy white boy come back for more. I got something for his ass, he come back in here!"

The lights did not shut off. Whoever it was in the vehicle, they were just sitting there, staring in at her, or at least she assumed they must be. What the hell else would they be doing out there sitting in the rain?

Of course, someone could be on their phone, or grabbing some papers, or something like that. But Barbara Leaks wasn't the kind of woman who assumed the most likely thing a person might be doing, never mind assumed the best.

"Just gonna sit there and stare at my black ass, or what?" she said to the window with the lights flooding in as she perched her wrists on her considerable hips.

The headlights tilted then, just slightly, first to the right then back the other way, as if they were rocking. A moment later, she heard the faint *thump* of a car door shutting, beneath the boom of the pounding rain. Barbara shifted her weight to her left leg, and pressed her wrists harder into her hips, rag and glass cleaner bottle dangling beside her like a parody of wild-west weaponry. A silhouette in the shape of a man crossed in front of the head lights then. A *tall* man, at that. She only saw him for a moment, then he slipped past the view of the window, heading in the direction of the front door. The one she was about to go clean. Where the crazy white boy had gone out just a few moments before.

She heard the officers in the back erupt in laughter then, howling and guffawing at something that had found their funny bone, and knew how to tickle.

And I'm up here dealing with this shit! she thought. *Barbara likes a good laugh too, just like any fat girl, but oh, no! I gotta sit up here like a good slave, dealing with these crazy white boys while y'all sit back there laughing your asses off, probably at some titty joke, too, no doubt.*

"Son of a bitch!" she said with a sigh and sat the rag and Windex on the edge of the table next to the coffee maker.

She began to go back to her desk in front of the little window to the lobby, and her mind caught on something she had missed before. Something she had noticed, but not picked up on right away, when the silhouette of this new guy was passing the window.

The fuck kinda head did he have? she thought.

It *had* been a funny shape. Of course, the guy had been in silhouette, it could have been shadows playing tricks on her eyes. After all, her eyes weren't what they used to be, not these days. But still, she was sure she had seen it. And nothing else about the man had seemed out of shape. Nothing abnormal. Not like his head.

She thought she had seen something like...*horns?* Certainly not. No, not even Barbara Leaks was ready to jump to that conclusion.

There was the sound of sucking air as the outer door to the vestibule which led into the inner lobby was opened. Barbara looked down to her desk and grabbed for a pad of paper and a pen to take down notes if necessary. Another eruption of laughter echoed up the hall behind her office from the cops in the back, another riot of cackles.

She pursed her lips, sighed, and shook her head as she picked up the notepad and pen. As she did this, she heard the door to the inner lobby hiss on its pneumatic hinge as it was opened.

Barbara turned to the door at the back of her office, where the laughter was still bounding through as she heard wet footsteps squeaking on the floor of the lobby just beyond her window.

"Quiet down back there, some of us got an actual job to do here!" she yelled.

As she turned to face her new guest, she stretched her most professional smile over her weathered face, being sure to peel her upper lip back to expose some of those pearly whites.

"How can I help y—" she started, then stopped dead.

Before her stood a charred horror, something out of the most terrible movies—the ones they played late at night—and one that she was sure would haunt her nightmares for the rest of her life.

Would, that is, if she ever slept again.

"Hosanna!" the aberration before her said.

Hosanna? she thought, still trying to force her brain to process what she was seeing. *Did he just say Hosanna?*

Before her stood a burned man, with charred clothing and blistered skin, holding a rifle pointed right at her. But none of that was the worst part, nor the hardest to believe. The worst was his face. His *head.*

It was a ghastly black thing with—yep, she hadn't been seeing things—*horns* on its head. Bloodshot and bleeding eyes stared out from behind two holes, and blood trickled from a split in the thing's face.

"Welcome to the Supper of the Lamb!" the monster said.

Chapter Forty

"I just don't understand where she could be!" Mrs. Johnson said through tears which soaked her face. "My Margie just wouldn't take off like this!"

Honey's hand reached out and gripped the old woman's, rubbing the paper-thin skin on the back of the lady's hand with her thumb. An empathetic look swallowed Honey's eyes, and an understanding smile parted her lips.

"I know she wouldn't," Honey said. "I'm so sorry, Mrs. Johnson. Sometimes things happen that we'd never dreamed could. I don't want to give you false hope, but I do sincerely hope your daughter is found. What's important now, though, is that you not torture yourself with all these questions. Sometimes there just aren't any answers. When that's the case, we have to learn to simply accept what is, and leave all the rest. It's the only way we can find any peace."

Mrs. Johnson managed a strained smile from behind her fogging glasses, and used her free hand to blot tears from her eyes with a tissue that was already so wet and mashed that it looked like piece of stone.

"Do you have a daughter, dear?" the old woman asked Honey in a tired voice.

Honey smiled and nodded. "I do. Her name is Joanna."

Mrs. Johnson smiled and returned the nod, wiping a few more tears from her weathered eyes.

"Well, then," she said in that same tired voice, "how would you go about accepting what is and leaving all the rest if Joanna was missing?"

The words were sharp, but not given in malice. It was a damned good question. Honey could see in the woman's eyes hope for a real answer to that. But in that moment, nothing came. The old woman's insinuation was right. There was no way Honey or anyone else in her predicament could find any real peace without some sort of closure. Knowing was the key to finding peace. Not leaving all the questions be. Her psychology professor may disagree, but he had operated in theory. This was the real world.

Honey was opening her mouth to say something, she didn't quite know what, when Freddie walked into the room carrying a tray with steaming mugs and a plate of cookies, saving her. His wife followed close behind him, a solemn smile on her face.

"Nights like this," Freddie said as he laid the tray on a coffee table in front of Mrs. Johnson and Honey, "require some hot cocoa, don't you think, ladies?"

He looked up at Honey and Mrs. Johnson then, a goofy grin on his reddish face, his eyes seeming too large behind the thick glasses he'd been donning since childhood. He looked like some sort of mad scientist, Honey thought, every time his eyes brightened behind those glasses. She had to stifle a laugh with a faux cough.

"Thank you, pastor," Mrs. Johnson said. "You and your wife are too kind, really. You shouldn't be going through all this trouble on account of a weepy old woman."

Mrs. Johnson began to shift towards the end of the couch as if to stand, and Honey gently grabbed her arm to stay her, as Freddie held out both hands towards her as if to ask her to remain seated.

"No, no, Mrs. Johnson," Freddie said in a calm, soothing voice. "It's no trouble at all, I promise you. Shelly and I are happy to be here for you, and Miss Bascom, too. Eh, right, ladies?"

Shelly James began nodding her head emphatically, her hands clasped in front of her like an infinity symbol, her eyes betraying tears that she seemed to barely be holding back.

"Oh, yes, my dear!" Shelly said. "God knows it's our duty and our honor to be here for you! This is what the good Lord expects of his shepherds!"

Honey almost winced audibly when Shelly used the word 'duty' in reference to caring for a bereaved old woman, but she managed to stifle the sound and jump in herself.

"What we mean, Mrs. Johnson," Honey said, caressing the old woman's arm in a sympathetic gesture, "is it is no trouble at all. We love you, we care about what you're going through, and we are going to find Margie. Jim is working on it as we speak, and there's no one I'd rather have looking out for me, I can tell you that."

The sniffles leveled out then in Mrs. Johnson's face, and the old lady turned her head to meet Honey's eyes. Honey could see a thankful gleam sparkling there, and also a question, which was why she wasn't surprised when the elderly woman asked it.

"You had a child with the Chief, is that right?"

Honey smiled and nodded. "Yes, he's Joanna's father."

"Babies are a blessing, all the time, no matter what," Mrs. Johnson said, turning back to the room.

Freddie and Shelly were sitting now, across the coffee table from them, in a pair of very nice armchairs. Their hands were neatly folded in their laps, and while Shelly's look seemed more forced than her husband's, Honey believed they both were doing the best they could to counsel a member of their flock in a desperate, unknowing time.

They're good people, she thought to herself. *There's some genuinely good people at that church. And they're the best of them.*

"I always tell people, even before my Margie went missing, you hug your babies, every day. You tell them you love them. Ain't *nothing* should ever stop you from doing that. No matter what they do, no matter what they say. I tell you, there's *nothing* that Margie could have ever done that would have changed the way I felt about her. You gotta love your babies, forever and always. I believe that's the closest we can get to being really like Christ in this world. Loving our little ones."

"And I say amen to that, Mrs. Johnson," Freddie jumped in.

A new batch of tears collected and spilled out of the lady's eyes then, and Honey wondered just where in the righteous hell all those tears could be held. The woman had been doing this for days now, with little reprieve. She wondered if they would ever stop. If they *could* stop.

Honey wondered again what she would do if something ever happened to Joanna, and shuddered at the thought.

They all reached out then, as if following a silent order, and fetched up steaming mugs from the tray on the table. They sipped, the warm sweetness digging directly into their marrow. Satisfied sighs were uttered all around, and they fell into silence then, a silence that Honey thought would have lasted a very long time if it hadn't been for the squealing, screaming sound of rubber on wet pavement outside which shattered it.

They all jumped, some cocoa falling over Shelly's ample bosom, probably scalding her, though she didn't seem to notice. All eyes were now looking out the window. Even Mrs. Johnson had turned, wide, wet eyes staring out into the pouring rain.

Lightning flashed then, and the silhouette of a pickup truck, sliding sideways across the driveway that led to the house, was fully visible. The outline of smoke was seen, billowing around the tires, and Honey suddenly felt a sick tug in the bottom of her gut.

Darkness fell again, all at once, and the truck vanished into the night save for the piercing headlights, but the sound persisted. It grew louder and louder, as a crackle of thunder began to rumble in the lower registers of sound.

"What in the name of Go—" Shelly James began.

That was when there was a loud crashing sound, followed immediately by a boom of thunder. The whole house shook, and Honey knew at once that the rattling of the windows and the walls was *not* happening because of the thunder. Something had hit the house, and hard.

"Jesus, fuck!" Freddie exclaimed all at once, jumping from his chair and spilling cocoa all over the room, his arms flailing wildly.

Red heat instantly flushed his face, and Honey saw Shelly looking up at him, aghast at his blasphemy, but knowing at that moment, right then, Freddie wasn't giving out any fucks. He'd said what he meant, and meant what he said.

Then Honey was on her feet. She began to sprint for the door, but Freddie had gotten going a split second before her, so she was right on his heels. Shelly and Mrs. Johnson sat wide-eyed behind them, holding their mugs of cocoa, jaws hanging to their breasts.

Freddie was first to the door and he flung it open. Lightning exploded in the sky again, making silver sheens of the falling rain, which Honey reckoned was coming down harder than she'd ever seen in all her life.

Freddie hit the light to the porch as he ran through, Honey right on his heels, and they skidded out into the downpour to see a truck—Honey instantly recognized it as Ryan's—smashed into the side of Freddie's house, the brick crumbling around the smashed front end. Ryan was spilling out of the side of the truck, a wild, panicked look in his eyes. He was already soaked through, and he was bleeding.

Freddie was flabbergasted.

"What the hell, man?" Freddie said, spreading his arms as if asking his quarry to behold something.

Ryan didn't seem to notice or care. Honey could see he was in a state of panic which bordered on shock as he rushed up the stairs of the porch to them, his eyes locked first on Freddie's, then on her own, then back again.

"It's back!" Ryan screamed. "It's back, God help me!"

Now Shelly and Mrs. Johnson could be seen standing in the window of the room they had all been sharing cocoa in just moments before, staring out at the absurd scene.

"What are you talking about?" Freddie said, his voice wavering. "I thought you and Jim were—"

Ryan snatched Freddie by the collar and pulled him forcefully towards him, until their noses were less than an inch apart.

"It's back!" he screamed again. "The Glutton! That *thing* is back, and it's coming! Where's Jim?"

But Freddie couldn't answer, it seemed. His mouth trembled and tried to form words, but none came, and his eyes were growing to outrageous proportions behind his thick spectacles.

"He isn't here," Honey said, grabbing Ryan's hands and pushing him off Freddie. "What do you mean it's coming?"

Ryan shook his head, his wet hair slinging off his forehead.

"I went out there, to that place, you know?"

Honey nodded. Ryan went on.

"There was some guy there, some *freak* in a goat mask! Fucker tried to kill me, but I got a shot off at him!"

"You *shot* someone?" Freddie started in, adjusting his soaked and unadjustable shirt.

Ryan ignored him. "There was this fire, and the guy fell into it, I think he might be dead. I don't know and I don't give a fuck! But there was something else. Something in the house!"

Honey's face shed all semblance of color. She looked to Freddie and could see that his face had done likewise.

"You went without Jim?" Honey asked, snapping her head back around to him. "You were supposed to go with him in the morn—"

"I had to know!" Ryan spat as lightning and thunder popped over their heads.

Somehow, as Honey stared into his eyes, the eyes of this man whom she'd cared for since she had met him at twelve years of age, smoking, farting, and looking at porn in the woods, and knew instantly what he meant. It wasn't that he had to know what was out there, he had to know that he was able to face it. Ryan had always been the most frightened of them all, even though he was bigger and physically more capable than the rest of them. He was afraid of becoming his father, the man who had been the greatest coward of them all. Ryan had had to know that he could face his fears.

But she said none of this.

"But none of that's important!" Ryan went on. "What's important is there was a body out there, some poor dead asshole on the porch, and when the psycho in the mask was burning, I looked up and saw that...that *thing* eating him! Oh, Jesus, *it was eating him!* You both know what that means, right? You remember, don't you?"

Honey caught a glimpse of Shelly and Mrs. Johnson in the window, no doubt hearing all of this, and they exchanged the horrified looks that Honey would expect anyone to do if they didn't know what she and these men had experienced as kids.

They think he's mad, she thought. *And I would too, if only...*

"It's trying to enter our world," Freddie said with a dazed look in his eyes, which were now focused on some point in the distance. "It's coming through."

"Yes!" Ryan screamed, nodding his head like a heavy metal guitarist. "It's through, and it's coming! We've got to find Jim, he's our only chance!"

Distant popping noises floated in through the drum of rain, only just discernable, but Honey ignored them.

"Have you tried calling him?" she asked Ryan.

He shook his head. "Lost my phone in the woods, and he's not at the station, I just checked. You have to call him right now!"

Honey turned and ran into the house then, full sprint, and went for her purse next to the couch where she'd been sitting with Mrs. Johnson. She yanked it out, all under the watchful eyes of the pair of confused women in the room and began running back out to Freddie and Ryan.

"What on earth is going—" Shelly started to say, but Honey cut her off.

"Not now, Shelly, serious shit is happening, so please just trust us!"

Shelly's face flushed red again at the obscenity, but she clammed up, which was all well and good for Honey.

Honey got to the porch again, phone in hand, holding it up for the others to see.

"Okay, got my phone, we'll call Jim!" she said, and started thumbing her way to the calling app in her phone.

That was when the wail of the city siren rose into the night like a howling demon.

Chapter Forty-one

Father Don stared at Jim slack jawed in the pew. However, while the man was clearly flabbergasted, Jim didn't think he saw any disbelief in the man's face. The Father was just, well...

Stunned.

"My dear God, Jimmy," the padre managed in a whispery voice after some time.

Jim nodded slowly, looking between his knees at his clasped hands.

"And this, this...what did you call it?"

"The Glutton," Jim replied, his eyes lifting to the giant crucifix hanging before them.

"Yes, that's right," Father Don went on, his hand rubbing on the papery, ancient skin of his chin. "This Glutton, you think it's back? Now?"

Jim leaned back in the pew, his clasped hands sliding up into his lap, and he exhaled.

"Yes, Father," Jim said. "I think it's back. I don't have any proof of that yet, but I'm almost certain. A buddy of mine is coming with me in the morning to go check out the place."

"Good, God!" Father Don exclaimed. "For Heaven's sakes, why?"

"I have to know for sure," Jim said. "I have to know for sure what I'm facing. If I *can* face it. Shit, the more I say it out loud, the crazier it sounds."

Jim noticed Father Don staring at him through slitted eyes.

"Oh," Jim said, his face flushing now, "I'm sorry, Father! Just add that one on with the rest of my confession."

Father Don dismissed this with an impatient wave of his hand. "I don't give a damn about that, Jimmy, I give a damn about *you!* Have you thought of what might become of you if you go out there? Having the grace of God on your soul is fine, wonderful even, but that won't stop you from being torn limb from limb!"

Jim looked the old Priest in the eyes, marveling at how the man had simply taken him at his word, even with how incredible the story was. Here was a very studied and learned man, a rational man, who'd listened to Jim's story, one full of other worlds and other creatures, and a monster who jumped between these worlds, eating them to the bone, and he'd just believed it. No argument, no skepticism. Just...*what?*

Faith.

It had to be. There was nothing else to explain it. Nothing else even came close.

"I know," Jim exhaled, looking back to Jesus on the Cross. "I figured if I have even half a chance, if I'm right and The Glutton really *is* back, I needed to be right with Him. Hell, I needed to, anyway. I've needed to for a long time."

Jim nodded toward the crucifix.

Father Don smiled ever so slightly at this, and nodded himself.

"Jimmy, you did the right thing, coming here. Regardless of the reasons that brought you. God never turns His back on us, even when we turn ours on Him. And you're right, you know. If you're to have half a chance here, it'll all rest on the providence of God. What you're facing down here, based on how you described it to me, is Death. You realize that, don't you, Jimmy?"

Death. Jim hadn't thought of it that way before, but he supposed it made plenty of sense. Just what *was* this thing if not Death itself? Of all the parallel worlds out there, this thing was Death to them all, or a rogue agent thereof at the very least. Coming between the worlds, using people with the gift to jump through, to feed, to grow and be born into each new world, all so it could eat it away to nothing.

Death.

"No, Father, I hadn't thought of it just that way before," Jim said contemplatively. "But you're right. It *is* Death..."

He trailed off, unsure of what to say. Father Don said it for him.

"You know, there is a remedy for Death. Did you know that? It's right there in the Good Book, too. The one thing that conquers Death, and cannot itself be defeated."

Jim's eyebrows raised. "What's that, Father?"

The old Priest leaned forward, smiling widely, exposing more than one golden cap on his yellowed teeth.

"*Love*, Jimmy," the priest said. "Only love can conquer Death. Love and Death, they're not opposites, you see. Just like God and the devil aren't really opposites. People tend to make them out to be, but it doesn't add up. God is infinite, Creator of all, He is *being* itself. The devil, he's just a creation within all that being. A bad boy, to be sure, but nothing more. Oh, I'm rambling now, aren't I?"

Jim and the Priest shared a laugh before Father Don went on.

"Anyway," Father Don continued, "what I'm driving at is this. God *is* love. The devil *brings* death. So, if God is both *being* itself *and* love, what does that tell you?"

Jim stared at the Priest for a spell before realizing the old man actually expected an answer.

"I, uh, well..." Jim started, then he fell on it. "It means love is just as infinite as God."

Father Don was smiling.

"That's right, Jimmy! And if the devil merely *brings* death, what does *that* tell you?"

Jim was nodding as he answered. "It means death is merely a created thing, a consequence to our fall in the Garden of Eden!"

"That's right!" Father Don exclaimed, pointing his finger out at Jim briskly, then bringing it back again. "An infinite thing can destroy a created thing, but a created thing can *never* harm that which is infinite!"

Jim mulled this over. The old man was right. Jim even felt what the man was telling him was key to what he was supposed to do. How he was supposed to move forward, to stop Norman and The Glutton. But...

How?

"Father, this all makes sense, but what am I supposed to do? Run up to this thing telling it I love it and sing Kumbaya?"

Father Don laughed sharply at this, then grew very serious again.

"Jimmy, love takes many forms. What you have to do is think of what form will work best against this beast. Once you figure that out, you'll know what to do."

Jim nodded again, then stood.

"Thank you, Father," he said, "I really appreciate your time, but I've got to get back to—"

Father Don was scrambling to his feet. "You're not leaving without absolution, are you?"

Jim flushed a deep hue of red at having forgotten the most important part of the sacrament he'd come to receive.

"Oh, of course not, I guess—"

"It's been a long time, yeah-yeah, I know," Father Don said, cutting Jim off and finishing his sentence for him.

Jim nodded and faced the Priest.

Father Don raised his hand in front of Jim's face and started the sign of the cross.

"I absolve you in the name of the Father, and of the Son, and of the Holy Spirit."

"Thank you, Father," Jim said, looking up and genuinely feeling an invisible weight falling away from him. "Penance?"

Father Don smirked and laughed.

"You've done enough of that already, I think."

Jim nodded again, turned to leave, and was welded into place when he heard the shriek of the city siren rise all at once.

The storm, he thought, wrestling his startled heart down from his throat. *Gotta be the stor—*

Then his cellphone was buzzing. It was Honey. A sick feeling settled into the center of his gut as he thumbed the screen and accepted the call.

"Hello?"

Chapter Forty-two

The Glutton lifted its face into the air and lapped greedily at the falling rain through its vertical mouth, a black, snake-like tongue whipping out through the razorblades of its teeth.

It's been so long, The Glutton thought with pride. *So long since a jump into a new world. And this one...oh, this one will be so sweet!*

It was standing in the woods near the old Brogan house, the place where a hundred and ten years ago it had been entombed by the sister-fucking, soft-brained Johnathan Michael Brogan. The Glutton became infuriated every time it thought of that long ago bastard, the stupid boy who'd bettered it and its dear Cloris. It was not often The Glutton could be bettered, and there had certainly been no pedigree in the Brogan boy to have warranted success against the ageless beast, but succeed he had. The boy had fed him horses and animals, and very little human meat.

And human meat is what The Glutton needed...in this world at least.

All worlds were different. All worlds had different leaders in their respective food chains. Once, several eons ago, it had been a race of what the humans of this world would have thought of as octopi. *Giant* octopi. Enormous beasts, swimming and living in a gargantuan planet covered in a kind of brine. Intelligent though they had been, these creatures—they called themselves *Ryhlectoss*—had swam about, sharing and giving to one another in a sort of commune-like culture. They knew no ownership, no private property, not even exclusivity in their sexual mating. They gave and gave alike to one another, according to the individual's needs. The Glutton had been a trifle baffled at the discovery, as it was the first—and the last—culture he'd come across whose planetary society knew no war, no chaos, and no jealousy. There were no warring factions, fighting for goods or resources. Nothing of the sort. They all simply coexisted. If a group of the beings wanted to do things differently, no one stopped them. Incredibly diverse creatures, yet they shared a genuine live and let live sort of mindset.

But as unique as they may have been, The Glutton had still found one among them with the *gift*, and had been able to turn the creature, through the help of one in the world he'd been ravaging previously—one replete with creatures that simply had no similarity to anything that the Ryhlectoss might be able to associate—to turn on his peaceful world.

After all, all intelligent beings have hearts which may be blackened.

And so, The Glutton had moved through the cosmos. One world after another, one universe after another, one reality after another. Always eating, always destroying.

It was a grand affair.

The problem was the same, however, in all worlds: finding a willing vessel who also bore the *gift*.

The *gift* was universally universal, yet still rare. There seemed to be no rhyme or reason to who might receive it, and no geological reasoning for it could be charted. One either had it or did not. And not all who had it could be turned. That was another problem The Glutton had faced in its cosmic crusade. A willing vessel who *also* had the *gift*. A black heart which could be turned, coupled with the *gift*.

Through the ages, this had been the major issue The Glutton had faced. Yet, whether by providence or sheer luck, it had always found a proper vessel. It wasn't that The Glutton didn't possess the *gift* itself; it did indeed. But its grasp on the *gift* was a precarious one. Use of the *gift* drained The Glutton, sapping it of its resources and energy, an effect that bore with it decades of dormancy as it related to its use. The Glutton *could* open the doorway between worlds on its own, but without a plentiful supply of high-meat readily present, the Glutton could never make the jump alone. It worked on occasion, but finding a thin spot was yet another issue. Thin spots in the fabric of reality were also a rare thing. To make a spot thin, something catastrophic had to have occurred, some black act whose evil intent wore away at the basic goodness of creation around it. It was these terrible acts, coupled with the *gift,* which made the jumps possible, but only if The Glutton could feast on the high-meat of the world. The high-meat—that which was the flesh of the top of the respective world's food chain—was necessary for The Glutton to rebirth itself into the world. Its soul could jump, but without a body of flesh and blood, the soul could not travel far—or for very long—away from its host.

Thus the necessity for those of the high-meat with the *gift*. Like Cloris, his most recent help. Well, most recent before the Cow, that was. The Cow, the one who'd come through and The Glutton had been feeding from for decades now, biding its time before another might come through which could deliver more of the high-meat to it so as to make the jump fully.

It liked its Cow. Both possessed with the *gift* and a black heart, the Cow had served it well. And it had provided the added nourishment to itself necessary to leap into the world, to open the door, for Norman to bring the thing its high-meat.

And now, as it looked to the sky, lapping the rain with its black tongue, The Glutton had been fully rebirthed. It had made the full jump into the new world, and it was now ready to feed.

Lightning split the sky over the abomination, and it grinned horrifically. It was time. Time to feed. Time to destroy. Time to bring death to this brave new world.

But not without the Cow.

The Glutton was many things, but a breaker of promises it was not. The Glutton had recognized the *gift* in the Cow, and had made a deal. The Glutton *never* went back on a deal. The Cow had had a very simple request, and The Glutton had granted it rather than devouring the Cow's flesh. And now that The Glutton was through, it would bring the Cow with it. The Cow would have its promise. Its reward.

A board creaked on the porch of the house behind the monster. It turned its head and beheld the Cow as it stumbled out of the house, back into this world, teetering on unsteady legs. The Cow's hair was very long, both on its head and face, and the only clothing it wore were pants that had belonged to one of Cloris's children, now tattered to rags. It was a tall thing, and very lean and skinny. Ribs showed through above its stomach, which moved in from the ribcage like a sharp V. The Cow was also covered—no, *saturated*—in filth.

Yet, the Cow gained its footing and came through. The Glutton could see nightmare scars on the Cow's arms and lower legs, its torso, and even its face. After all, The

Glutton had had to keep its strength up. In the decades since Jimmy and his buddies had humiliated The Glutton, it had been required to nourish itself, and there had been precious little high-meat left in Cloris's world. The spiders and slugs were prevalent, but disgusting to the taste and did little to sustain The Glutton.

But the Cow had been willing enough to give up chunks of its own flesh to sustain The Glutton as needed, fueled all the while by the promise of its coming vengeance. The Cow would have its day, and had been willing to make its own deal with The Glutton.

The Glutton watched as the Cow stumbled uneasily down the rotted stairs of the old Brogan house and smiled. It had been a good Cow. He would give it its day. After all, it was only fair.

And The Glutton was a fair beast.

"Come," The Glutton said to the Cow. "It's time to eat!"

The Cow managed a terrible grin, one somehow more horrible than that of The Glutton itself. All the teeth were gone, and scraps of flesh on its face were missing entirely, replaced with haphazard scarring which rendered it utterly horrific.

"It's time to eat, alright," the Cow responded with a raspy voice, mounting the spiny back of The Glutton. "Let's feast on those faggots!"

The Glutton dropped to all fours and sprinted toward town.

Chapter Forty-three

"So then I said to him, 'What the fuck you wearing, boy?'," Officer Mike Whitten said to the others in the back of the police station.

All the other eyes were on him, red-faced and teary-eyed from laughter. They had all come in, though most were off duty, just for the break it offered. All the officers, together and laughing, in the face of the issues looming over them. They knew what the next few days held for them, or so they thought, anyway. Searches through the woods, questioning of the people they had to live next to and shop next to and so forth. The shit no one liked to do. The shit that made being a cop in a small town suck the big one, as Kathy Seabolt liked to put it. She was there too, amongst the rest, mid-fifties, lines in her face and her short, dark hair hanging down near her eyes in strings. She was laughing along with them, cheerily, her soft face full of the joy of the moment, ignoring the coming storm that awaited them all.

"What the hell was he wearing?" Kathy asked Mike as the laughter abated ever so slightly.

There was a faint bark from the front of the station as Barbara scolded them for enjoying themselves, something about there being people in the world who had to work for a living. As if that bitch had the first clue about what it meant to be a cop.

"The little rat-fucker was wearing his mother's best Sunday dress!" Mike quipped, spitting laughter between his words. "Little asshole was dressed full on in his mother's black dress, this thing with tassels coming off the sleeves and even her fucking grieving white-chick sombrero, looking to all the world like a goddamned fruitcake!"

More roars of laughter from the others. Thunder boomed outside as lightning flashed through the windows, eradicating the few shadows in the room.

"What the hell was he doing in that?" asked Butch Thomson, the Lieutenant of the evening watch. "Was there a beauty show going on?"

More laughter ensued from this.

"No!" Mike chirped, trying to pull his hysteria into line. "The kid was heading to the store trying to buy beer! He thought he looked enough like his mom that the clerk would sell to him!"

Now everyone was heaving for air as the cackles ascended through the back room of the police station. Kathy Seabolt looked around the room through teary eyes, her chest heaving under her uniform in rapid rises and falls, hysterical laughter bursting from her throat.

They had all gathered here tonight without any real planning. They had simply shown up, one by one, to hang out through the storm. Only she and Mike Whitten were actually on duty—other than Barbara in dispatch—but all the others had come in off the clock, perhaps the hanging dread of the town's situation weighing on them from the missing persons which had come to surface in the past few days, along with Chief Dalton's wariness and somber tones working on their collective subconscious.

The storm raged outside, the very reason they weren't out on the streets in the first place. Not much point in it.

With weather like this, there would hardly be any citizens on the road, and why on earth would they want to sit out in the rain, writing tickets which would change nothing about the driving habits of the people of Winnsboro and only serve to get the officers soaked to the bone in the process of such futile pursuits.

No, staying in at the station was a much better idea. It wasn't as though Chief Dalton was in to push them out on the street, anyway. He'd been missing from the office the past couple days, out doing God only knew what. It wasn't like he'd told any of them what he was up to.

And so, they laughed, heartily and with the joy only found amongst the closest of friends as they shared the humorous stories that bound them together in their line of work.

Another rebuke from Barbara echoed down the hall to them. Barbara could be a real cantankerous old bitch from time to time, self-righteous and full of irate fury at her lot in life. She was solid in her job, no one disputed that, but she also seemed to think her work was much more than it was. It wasn't as though she herself were out on the streets, facing possible murder and mutilation on a daily basis like the rest of them. No, Barbara sat in the office, safe and secure, typing in license plate and driver's license numbers, squawking back the facts over the radio to the rest of them, who never knew if they were dealing with a dove or a maniac.

Yet, Kathy couldn't seem to hold it against the old cunt. All the shit-work seemed to fall to Barbara, and Kathy knew it. The dealing with the phone calls and the nuts who walked in—and there had just been one of those, they had all heard the shouting lunacy from the weirdo a few minutes before—along with the cleaning of the offices and toilets. It was a shit job, Kathy knew, and her heart went out to Barbara. The woman would never be a cop, though she'd threatened on more than one occasion to enter the academy and get her license. It just wasn't in Barbara. The hours, for one thing, but also the attitudes of the public. It was one thing to deal with the frustrations of the citizens of Winnsboro over the phone or even in the lobby, but quite another to deal with them when on the road when they may be facing a hefty fine or even jail time. She just didn't have the disposition for it.

Mike had just made another crack and the rest of the guys were guffawing in howls of laughter when Kathy thought she heard something odd up the hall. Something from Barbara. Something like...

How can I help you?

But it was cut off. Through the guffaws of laughter, Kathy turned her head to the door of the officer's lounge, and craned her neck trying to hear. It had been faint, just on the heels of one of Barbara's insults, but the way it had just stopped...

More words. This from something more muffled and distorted. The words were lost, but the cadence of them brought to mind the memories of childhood Sunday school.

What the fuck am I hearin—

Then the first gunshot rang out through the station.

It was deafening and booming, echoing off the walls and slamming into her ears. All the others seemed to shut down at the same moment, coming from gales of laughter to sheer, terrified silence in the blink of an eye.

"Wh-what was—" Mike managed to mumble before more gunshots boomed down the corridor.

Then they were all on their feet, drawing weapons and charging for the door. All humor had left the room now, replaced by dread and fear which had become a palpable thing.

"Jesus, what the fuck?" Butch Thomson managed to get out as he entered the hallway in a sprint, his gun up at his side.

He vanished out of sight as the rest of the officers rushed for the small door at the same time. There was another shot, then a spray of red mist showered back from the hallway where Butch had just gone, coating the fluorescent lights above in a terrible red hue.

Kathy came around the corner then, the first out of the door, and saw Butch before her. His head was gone, a shattered remnant of skull at the base all that remained, jetting blood and chunks of brain and bone, the pistol in his hand popping rounds off into the wall beside him, uselessly.

Terror filled her in that moment, and she took a step back, her mouth hanging open in horror. Mike rushed past her, along with Chase Barrows and Grady Hughes. They charged into the hallway, some black terror at the other end coming around as they did. Only, Kathy noticed, they weren't seeing the monster coming, because they were too preoccupied with Butch before them, now collapsed on the floor, spraying crimson and flapping around like a fish out of water, or a chicken with its head cut off, which was the more appropriate analogy.

Gunshots were still going off from Butch's pistol, harmlessly splintering the walls around them, and a moment later there were the loud, metallic *clicks* of the hammer falling on an empty chamber.

"Christ!" Grady exclaimed a second before his own head popped like a high-schooler's pimple.

Blood and brain showered the hallway, peppering Kathy's face with warmth a second before he fell.

Mike and Chase managed to remember their side arms and began to fire back, but in their panic, seemed to forget how to aim. Splinters from the walls showered and one of the fluorescents exploded near the horror that approached them from down the hall. Flickering lights then danced at the far end of the hall, flashing on and off in a terrifying display as whatever was coming for them moved closer and closer.

"Blessed is he who comes in the name of the Lord!" the thing shouted amidst a fury of gunfire.

Mike and Chase began to twist and turn, their arms splaying out in violent turmoil, as blood rained out of their bodies and screams escaped their throats amidst roars of gunfire.

Oh, sweet Jesus! Kathy's mind roared at her.

As she stumbled back, fumbling her pistol into the air, another officer rushed out. It was the rookie, she passively noticed, Rodney Chamberlin. His gun was out in front of him, his face a plaster of terrified rage and adrenaline.

When he moved through the doorway to her right, Kathy's eyes darted back down the hall where Mike and Chase were sliding and collapsing to the floor in unceremonious heaps, their falls making wet slaps on the linoleum floor which was now covered in blood. Beyond them were Grady and Butch, the former's leg still twitching, his booted foot thumping horribly against the paneled wall.

The hallway was a river of blood.

The flickering light flashed on and off at the end of the hallway where the monstrous thing was stepping over Butch's body, a rifle in its hands, aimed right at her.

Oh, my God! she thought, terror seizing her spine in an icy grip. *I'm dead!*

Then Rodney pushed past her, knocking her gun from her hand just as she was getting it up before her to fire a shot. Rodney's gun was popping rounds off, and the young cop was screaming in a pitch so high it might have been coming from a pre-pubescent girl.

Splinters flew down the hall, creeping ever closer to the monster with the body of a man, and the other fluorescent in the hall burst. A shower of shards came down just as Kathy dropped to all fours, scrambling for her lost weapon.

Shit! Shit! SHIT! she screamed in her mind, though the only sound escaping her lips was a low, whiny whimper.

The lighting effect at the end of the hall was now synced all the way down. Flashes of flickering light came and went, the brief periods between dropping them into near pitch blackness, save for the light coming from the officer's lounge.

A wet *thump* punctuated the final shot from Rodney's gun, followed by the *click* of an empty chamber. Kathy had still not gotten to her gun—it had slid through the shattered bulbs up the hall near Rodney—and she scrambled all the more frantically for it now, shards of glass digging and clawing into her hands and knees and forearms.

The pain was exquisite. Blood seeped from her in more places than she could count, and sweat was now stinging her eyes with salty fury.

"Shit!" she heard Rodney shriek in that high, feminine voice.

There were grunts up ahead, deep, muffled, wet sounds. She dared a single glance up as she waded on hand and knee through the shattered glass and blood for her pistol, pushing the pain from her mind.

The monstrous thing stood there, the rifle still in its right hand. The thing had blood running all over it, and in the flashes of the flickering light, she could see deep red and black patches on exposed skin.

Burned, her mind whispered in horror. *He's burned.*

Just before the light flickered back out, she noticed a spritzing of blood coming from the thing's left shoulder. Its charred, monstrous—*is it a goat?*—face was turned toward the wound, eyes which leaked red wide in its leathery sockets.

More sounds now. Clicks and clatters. Rodney's feet and legs were just in front of her now, her gun to the left of his boots. She saw the magazine of his gun smack the floor, bounce, and clatter away. Then another magazine fell next to this one, hitting harder and bouncing less, sounding much heavier.

He just dropped his reload! Fuck!

"Fuck!" Rodney's voice echoed in the hallway, and he was reaching down for it.

The monster seemed to notice this, because its head turned back down the hallway at them, bleeding—*yes, bleeding*—eyes glaring at them with blazing fury. The rifle was coming back up to the ready in its arms.

Rodney fumbled with the dropped magazine a moment, wincing and cursing as he managed to get his hands on it, his hand now bleeding from the shattered bulbs littering the floor.

Kathy moved and slipped in the blood which was now flowing past her hands and knees, which Rodney was standing in, now within reaching distance of her pistol. She stretched her hand out, reaching past Rodney's leg, and wrapped her hand around its butt.

Pain exploded in her hand instantly. Had it not been for the adrenalized terror she was awash with, she might have dropped it, but fear was motivating her more than pain now, and she held on. She pulled her hand back, and realized a shard of bulb was standing out on her palm. No, it was *through* her palm. She could see the other jagged end punched out through the back of her hand, the torn and shredded skin around it vomiting crimson.

She gritted her teeth, and squeezed the grip firmly, ignoring the operatic pain in her hand. She heard a slamming click, the sound of Rodney shoving the fresh magazine home in his gun. A second later was the sound of metal clamoring home and driving a round into the chamber as the slide fell into place.

"Kill it!" Kathy screamed from behind him.

But Rodney had fumbled a second too long.

The monster thing had the rifle up, and the flickering lights of the shattered fluorescents vanished as flames licked from the end of the rifle the thing was holding. Deafening thunderclaps boomed down the hall, slamming into her ears, rupturing her eardrums. Fresh warmth showered her as Rodney jerked above her and tumbled backwards.

He fell right on the top of her, his firm butt collapsing onto her back, mashing her breasts into the blood and glass, the wind whooshing out of her. Her vision blurred as she gasped for breath, but she could still make out the shape of the monstrous thing coming down the hall, stepping over bodies and crunching glass under its boots.

The thing was almost on her now, and she summoned all of her strength to raise her pistol. She'd fire until there was nothing left in her Glock, and she'd pray it would be enough. Pray the rounds hit home. Pray the—

The thing's boot came crushing down on her hand holding the gun before she'd gotten up more than six inches. Nuclear pain mushroomed up her arm from her injured hand as she felt her fingers and knuckles shattering with an awful *crunch.*

She screamed, her head jerking backwards from the pain and the top of her head hitting the paneling of the wall. But she hardly noticed that. What she noticed, through tear-blurred vision, was the barrel of the rifle not more than a foot from her face.

Kathy was pinned under Rodney, soaked in blood, much of it her own, even more of it belonging to her fallen comrades. She could barely breathe, having only just started to get her breath back when the monstrous thing had crushed her hand, causing her to scream. His boot was still standing on her ruined hand, a hand that would never hold a gun again, and she knew now would never stroke the cheek of her grandchild ever again either.

"Please!" she squeaked in a pitiful voice. "Why?"

Her eyes were not focused on the monstrous thing's terrible face, but on the bore of the barrel in her own. It seemed enormous this close. Like the mouth of a black well which went all the way down to Hell itself.

To her horror, the thing began to laugh, a wet, high, chittering sound.

"Because!" the monster thing bellowed. *"A King has to eat!"*

Before her confused mind could begin to process this information, there was a bright flash and a force of terrible strength which slammed her head down to the floor. Red filled her vision. She heard nothing now, only ringing, and her eyes lazily fluttered and looked at the floor before her. Meaty clumps stood before her, and bits of red-smeared white stuff, which looked sharp. There were other white things in front of her, small, almost like little Chicklet candies, jutting up from meaty piles of red mush.

Are those my teeth? she thought.

But before an answer came, darkness swallowed her, and she knew no more.

Chapter Forty-four

Barbara Leaks was still gasping on the floor of the dispatch office when the flurry of gunfire exploded in the hallway.

Blood was everywhere. All over the walls, the floor, on her. Even on her glasses, which had miraculously managed to stay on her despite how she'd lurched and fell when she'd been shot by...by the...

What the fuck is *that thing, anyway?* she wondered as she lay there panting on the blood-slick floor.

Well, it had to be a man. Just had to be. A very disturbed and injured man, but a man all the same. Something had melted to his face. It was likely rubber, judging from the stinking tang mixed with burnt flesh she had noticed when he had entered.

Screams echoed through the hallway alongside gunfire. She heard booms from the rifle, and loud pops from what must have been the officers returning fire with their pistols. Above and all around her, paneling was splintering and exploding, tittering to the floor in needle-thin shards. Bullets tore through the thin walls of the police station, but she was well out of the way. She seemed to be sinking further and further into the floor, losing herself in the blood-slimed linoleum. Her vision was fading too, along with the pain. *The pain...*

It had been bad at first, but it was leaving her now. Even as the warmth flowed out of her, the pain seemed to join it. Barbara knew what that meant. She was drifting toward death. She knew it the same way she knew the backs of her hands.

Bye, Felicia! she thought and gurgled a wet laugh, blood on her lips now. *Don't need yo ass 'round here no way!*

Then she thought of Jim.

Thunder exploded outside and the window she'd seen the silhouette of the goat-man through lit up whiter than fresh snow. A moment later it was black again.

Where is Jim?

More gunshots. Another scream. Splashing sounds.

Gotta do something about this, Barb, she told herself. *Ain't gonna get done by itself, you gonna have to move that big black ass. Hell, you used to it by now, anyway. Ain't nothing but the help to these honkeys, goddamned crackers can't manage to wipe they own ass without you 'round to remind 'em where they fucking belt-buckle at!*

She was nodding to herself, mumbling something unintelligible under her breath, blood oozing out of her as she began to drag herself on her stomach towards the desk with the radios and computer screens and buttons. It was a monumental effort, and she earned every inch of travel on willpower alone. Her vision was getting darker now, not only blurred but actually darkening.

Ain't much time left, Barb! her inner monologue warned her sharply. *Ain't no time to dilly-dally 'round! Get up there, do what you gotta do. Show them honkeys one last time they can't live without you. Then you go on. But not 'til then. Not 'til then, Barb.*

"Yeah, yeah, goddamnnit!" she barely managed to whisper. "I hear you, you old cunt! Pardon my French..."

Pain swept over her now, coming back with a vengeance. She gritted her teeth, wincing through them, her ebony lips peeled back over the whitest teeth anyone had ever seen. Tears stung her eyes and spilled over her plump cheeks. Then the swell of pain began to diminish, slowly. After a few moments, it was manageable again, and she renewed her efforts to move on.

She was actually thankful for all the blood. It made it easier to slide on her belly once she found purchase with her hands to pull. The desk was just ahead now, and another pull would put her up against it. After that, she would have to crawl up to her knees and reach across the desk. Then it would be done. For all the good it would do, it would be done.

What if they think it's just the storm?

It was a legitimate concern, but she couldn't worry with that right now. It would either bring help, or it wouldn't. And it wasn't as though she had a stack of other options lying around, either. No, she just had to hope for the best, and do the rest.

She fumbled her hand into the air, managed to grab the top of the desk, and began pulling herself to her knees. Pain came again now, even stronger than before, but this time she pushed through it with resolve.

Pain can go fuck itself, pardon my motherfucking French!

Then she was on her knees. Her head swirled and her vision dimmed before steadying and coming back into focus once more. Then the cycle started over.

Come on, Barb! We right here! Time to just get it done!

There was another burst of booming gunfire from the rifle and a shriek. Then she heard whimpers and some garbled speech down the hall.

Her eyes focused again and fell on what she was looking for. It was a large, red button mounted on a naked metal box with an LED light inside. The words 'CITY

SIREN' were scribbled across the side of the box on a piece of masking tape.

A final rifle boom echoed to her, and she shuddered.

Time to slap that ass, Barb!

She slapped it.

The siren rose into the night, shrieking and wailing with abandon. She began to slide down to the floor again, and she grabbed the handgun out of the under-desk holster on the way down. She slumped to the floor, and held a shaky hand up. It was only a five-shot revolver, but it was a .357 Magnum, and a .357 Magnum could fuck shit up, you bet your ass.

She heard wet clops coming down the hallway, and heard the terrible goat-man talking.

"What the hell is that?" he asked from beyond the door.

She saw his shadow in the hall and her finger closed on the trigger. The tiny handgun boomed in the office. She had meant to stop then, but exhaustion, blood loss, and all around dying in general had taken its toll on her, and her finger involuntarily continued to jerk on the trigger. The shots rang out and echoed down the hall, the only thing to absorb the sound being the corpses of the policemen and women she had served with for decades.

Click.

Then she was empty. She let the pistol drop and clatter to the floor, and her arm followed suit. A moment later, the goat-man was twirling into the room, rifle raised, eyes bulging.

"You would try to slay the Lord's chosen, you heathen?" the thing asked as he stood over her.

Barbara managed a weak smile and an even weaker laugh. Blood spat from her mouth and she began to cough. More blood came up now, and slimed her ample bosom. When the fit passed, she gazed back up at the goat-man, and met his eyes.

"Nigga, please," she said with disgust. "Just get this shit over with. Pardon my Fre—"

A four-foot flame leaped from the barrel, and Barbara never spoke again.

Chapter Forty-five

Giant, fist-sized globs of rain pelted the windshield as Jim raced for the station, his cellphone pressed tightly against his ear. The windshield wipers were doing little to help with visibility, and the curvature of the road caught large pools of water, where he hydroplaned every couple hundred feet, correcting the Tahoe each time with sharp movements on the wheel.

Still, he raced on.

"Why didn't he wait for me?" he frantically asked, his hand jerking on the steering wheel to keep the Tahoe on the road. Outside, the wail of the city siren was growing louder and louder as he neared the center of town.

"I don't know, Jim!" Honey snapped on the phone. "And it doesn't fucking matter right now! *It's back!*"

The reality hadn't struck home fully until now. As he left the old Priest at the Church, absolved of his sins and listening to the story as he raced for his truck, he'd heard her telling him the thing was back. The *Glutton* was back. It was through. And someone had *helped* it come through. But in his panicked state, Jim had initially reacted to the periphery of the situation rather than the center of it. To Ryan preempting him and going to the house in the woods alone, and tonight. Why would he do such a foolish thing? Why would—

If he hadn't, there may have been no warning at all, his inner voice spoke up.

He couldn't argue with that. He'd had a building dread over him the past few days, feeling this very inevitability looming closer and closer, yet he'd thought they had more time. He *needed* more time. He wasn't prepared yet.

But time was up. It was here. Now, today, maybe this very *minute*, and there was no more time to waste. And on top of all of this was the siren. Sure, it wasn't unusual for the siren to be sounded during a bad storm—and this storm was certainly shaping up to be just that—but the timing of everything was just all too convenient for it to be *only* the storm.

The siren. The call. Ryan going into the woods and finding the man in the mask and seeing The Glutton. All now, tonight.

"You're right," Jim sighed, turning hard onto Main Street, now only a quarter mile from the station. A gigantic rooster-tail of spray followed him closely as he sped along, only just holding on to traction. "I'm almost to the station. Y'all stay put and—"

"We're on our way!" Honey replied curtly.

"No!" Jim ordered. "I don't know what's going on there, I need you all to stay back."

"Not happening, Jim," Honey said.

He fumbled for a reply, but she had disconnected. He hissed a frustrated growl and slammed the phone down on the seat next to him. The last thing he needed was Honey out here if what he feared was really happening *was* happening. The others too, but especially Honey. The mother of his child. The girl they had all loved since they were children. Joanna was safe, for now, but if The Glutton was back, it wouldn't be long before the entire county—never mind the entire world—would be crumbling all around them. Joanna needed someone there to protect her, keep her safe. He had failed as a father, had allowed shame and self-pity to keep him from having a more active role in her life, though God knew he loved her without measure. But if something had to happen to one of her parents, it would be him. It *had* to be him. Not her, not Honey. But now she was on her way up here, walking into God only knew what.

He pulled the Tahoe, screeching and sliding, into the parking lot of the police station. The siren wailed on, much louder now. He had not passed another vehicle on the road, though this wasn't surprising in the least. With the late hour and the storm, most of this sleepy town would be doing just that: sleeping.

His headlights spilled over the front of the station, the bright LEDs cutting sharply through the halogen glow of the building's lights and the street lamps. Rain pelted down furiously, warbling and obscuring his vision as he peered out through the windshield.

He immediately recognized Norman Reese's car. He'd seen it only that morning, when he was taking a sample from the rear bumper to get to Jack Fletcher. Dread settled into his marrow as his hands gripped the wheel like a vise.

Jim was already soaked to the bone. Though his sprint from the church to his truck had been a short and fast one, the rain had been faster, and had quickly turned his clothes into a sodden mess. The leather seat beneath him farted as he leaned forward, straining to see through the deluge to something which had caught his eye in the window which gave on to the dispatch office.

There was a glow of light pouring through the window behind white blinds which were...*what?* He opened the door and stepped out with one foot from his Tahoe, peering through the gap between the door and the side pillar.

The blinds were spattered with red.

Oh, sweet Jesus, he thought, his heart rising to his throat and catching there.

A shadow moved inside the dispatch office, the dark shape dancing in the white and red glow from within. Jim's pulse quickened even more. He grabbed for his sidearm and drew it. He switched it to his left hand, and reached into his truck, snatched the mic, and flipped the loudspeaker on.

"This is Chief of Police Jim Dalton!" he barked into the mic, the bullhorn atop his Tahoe hooting out his words. They echoed back to him faintly in the pouring rain. "Barbara, if you're in there, I need you to come outside now!"

He waited, watching, trying to listen over the drone of the storm. Lightning split the sky, illuminating the scene before him in a blue hue for just a second. Then darkness fell once more with a boom of thunder.

Nothing happened. Well, almost nothing.

The shadow in the window moved. It crept and grew larger as if whomever it was had stepped in front of the window, marked by the outline of what would almost be a man, if not for the terribly misshapen blob of its head.

"Mike?" Jim said shakily into the microphone. "Butch? Rodney? Kathy? Anybody?"

He waited a second, then said, "*Norman*?"

No answer came, but as he lowered the mic from his mouth, he thought he spied the blinds—about where eye-level should be for the thing in the window—split open for just a moment. As if someone—or some*thing*—inside were peeking out for a better look.

Is it Norman? he thought wildly. *Or is it The Glutton? Is it here? Already here? Why would it come here first?*

Of course the answer to that was obvious. Eliminate anyone who might slow it down first, and the rest would be easy pickings.

I sure thought I remembered it being bigger, he thought, then shrugged this observation off. Memories of people and things from childhood often seemed much larger than they actually were. Perhaps that's all it was. But then—

Tires squealed and Jim's body seized as his head snapped in the direction of the sound. Headlights flooded his face and caused him to squint. The hand holding the mic came up to shield his vision a second before the lights were doused. He dropped his hand from his face and peered at the vehicle through the driving rain.

It was Ryan's truck, but Ryan wasn't driving. Ryan was in the passenger seat, Freddie behind the wheel, and Honey between them.

No...

Jim snapped back at the window where the shadow had been, but it was gone now, replaced with the static glow of light dancing over white shades spattered with what had to be blood. Jim tossed the mic back in the seat and turned toward his friends.

"Get out of here!" he screamed at them, waving his hands for them to go. "Get the Sherriff! Get every deputy in the county out—"

There was a boom then. For a moment Jim assumed it was thunder, but the sound of tittering glass that accompanied the boom suggested something else. As he looked back to the station, he could see the shattered remains of the window, the blinds ripped and askew now. A hand inside the room was ripping the blinds the rest of the way down. The wreckage clattered to the ground amongst the twinkling glass.

Oh, holy—

His thoughts were cut off when he heard the doors of Ryan's truck opening behind him. Jim whirled around, planning to tell them again to get out of there when the look on Ryan's pale, terror-streaked face stopped him. Ryan's eyes were peering over Jim's shoulder, up the street to the North.

"Oh, my God!" Ryan whispered.

Jim turned in time to see a dark, metal heap flipping through the air about eight feet over the road. Lights swirled and whipped around as the car tumbled end over end before smashing with a tremendous sound of screaming metal and shattering glass. The car tumbled and shrieked and groaned as it continued to flip, moving with the inertia of a tremendous force, sparks defying the rain as it slid on its roof. Jim thought he caught a glimpse of crimson inside the cab, but he couldn't be sure.

Then, the roar came.

It rose above the wail of the city siren, both deep and high-pitched at once, a hellish crescendo of octaves assaulting the night.

It's here, his mind told him in horror.

A grunting, exertive sound came from the open dispatch office window as the roar died down, and Jim turned. As he looked on in horror, he saw what was left of a large black woman who might once have been Barbara Leaks—though the condition of her ruined face rendered no indication of this—come flopping through the window, her body twisting and flailing around like a rag doll before splatting loudly on the patio landing a couple of feet from the building.

"The King has come, and it's time for the feast!" a cracked voice came from inside the office.

Then the trees next to the police station rustled, and a giant, dark shape leaped from them and crashed with colossal force atop the police station, a weighty *boom* thumping into the night. It moved on all fours, bricks crumbling and falling from the edge of the building as it moved.

The city siren horn was fitted with a rotating red warning light which spun when the horn was activated. In the dark, scarlet glow, Jim saw something riding atop the beast, but only for a second.

Another roar filled his ears and caused him to cringe back. Then the thing swung an arm and smashed the siren horn to metallic splinters as if it were no more than a pile of toothpicks.

The only sound left was the torrential downpour of the rain.

Jim peered up as lightning opened the heavens once again, revealing the greatest terror of his childhood. The greatest terror of *all* their childhoods. It wasn't smaller than he'd remembered, it was *bigger.* At least fifteen feet in height were it to stand on its hind legs. And he saw atop the monster—The *Glutton*—was a withered, pitiful looking man, his lips sunk into his mouth as though no teeth remained, but a hate gleaming in his eyes, dark and menacing.

And Jim recognized those eyes.

He spun around, waving his hands at the others, screaming for them to run, to get clear. It was all happening in slow motion. Heads turning from the monster on the roof to Jim, wild-eyed and jaws agape. Jim felt as though he were moving through molasses, his words little more than a panicked drone.

Then the gunshots began.

The windshield splintered and shattered, rounds ricocheting off the steel body of Jim's Tahoe. The front passenger tire burst with a loud *whoosh*, and the truck leaned starkly over it. Jim got to the others a second later, tackling all of them to the ground, then scrambling them all to cover behind Ryan's truck.

"MOVE!" Jim screamed.

They did. Cackling laughter emitted from the office window as the firing ceased, sending chills up Jim's spine. They all huddled on the other side of Ryan's truck, glancing back to the road and seeing the crumpled remains of the car which had come flipping down the road moments before. Now Jim could see that what he thought he'd glanced earlier was only the prologue of the horror inside the car. It wasn't just red. It was several colors. Bits and pieces of what had once been people were strewn about inside in a mess of pinks, reds, yellows, grays, and even some off-white. The people inside had been smashed like grapes, their bodies exploding inside the cabin.

Jim looked away, forcing it out of his mind, and peeked over the hood of the truck.

He saw The Glutton leap from the roof of the station to the ground, a loud *boom* accompanying its landing, the concrete around it splitting. The ground beneath them shook. He saw the man on the thing's back sliding off to the ground and taking a step away from the monster. From the look of the man, Jim would not have thought him capable of walking on his own, he was so withered and worn. Yet, not only did he move easily, he seemed to possess the strength and agility of three men.

Something glinted in the light of the street lamps. Something in the man's hand. The man whose eyes Jim had recognized in the flash of lightning a few moments before.

There was movement behind the monster and another man drew Jim's attention now. Jim could see what *had* to be Norman, though he was unrecognizable behind whatever was on his face. Red streamed out of Norman's eyes and mouth.

"God is GOOD!" Norman proclaimed as he came out and faced the monster and this other man. *"Brother, how you've been missed!"*

Then Jim knew why he had recognized the man's eyes. They belonged to Jake Reese.

PART SEVEN:

Into the Void

Sunday, August 7, 2016

Chapter Forty-six

"We should have stopped in the last town, Roger," the man's wife said to him, her words a nagging offense to his entire being. She just wouldn't stop. *Couldn't* stop. He was becoming convinced of it more and more. She just couldn't help herself. He wanted to be considerate of that, but her incessant chewing drone was working him up. He took a deep breath and hissed a frustrated but measured sigh through his dentures. His weathered old face forcing a disingenuous smile. He would need a Nitro pill soon.

"It's only another fifty miles and we'll be there. It's a waste of time and money to stop now."

His voice was even. Measured. Reasonable. At least to anyone who wasn't Rita, his wife of forty-seven fucking years.

"With this rain," Rita was going on in a flippant, arrogant, know-it-all voice that Roger despised all the way down in the atoms of his being, "you're going to get us into an accident. Doesn't matter how close we are if we never get there. Have you seen the time? What will we do if we end up in the ditch? You know your eyesight isn't what it used to be, Roger. But of course that doesn't matter to you, now does it? Men, you're all the same. You have your machismo to keep up for the rest of the world, so they'll know you're still *strong* and able. Like you're still twenty-five years old. But you're *NOT* twenty-five years old anymore, Roger, and I aim to see my grandchildren tomorrow, so you stop this car right now, at the very next motel we see. There is just no sense in this foolishness, and I've had about—"

"I've had enough!" Roger growled, much louder than he'd intended to. "Just shut up, Rita! You hear me? I'm not listening to it anymore! We're going all the way tonight, and that's how it's going to be! *Period!* Now, you can relax and make pleasant conversation with me or you can shut your fucking trap, makes no difference to me, you see. But I don't want to hear another goddamn word about stopping tonight! Get me?"

Rita sat there, aghast that her husband would *dare* speak to her in such a way, and Roger just looked back to the road, not caring. After forty-seven years, you cared about a lot less than you used to.

"Well," Rita finally said, a wavering sigh escaping her lips. "You clearly aren't willing to listen to good reason, so do with us what you will, Roger. If we're both dead in the morning, you can tell the grandchildren it was your fault."

"Tell the grandchildren?" Roger inserted, a bark of bemused laughter escaping his lips. "If we're dead, we won't be telling them anything."

Rita's cheeks flushed in the darkness, but Roger noticed them as they traveled under a streetlamp. A pair of headlights to an SUV swung violently into a parking lot up ahead.

"Well," Rita started once again, her lips a pursed plateau, "fuck you, Roger."

There was a moment of stunned silence and Roger looked sidelong at her, stunned by her use of profanity. She stared back at him stoically.

Then they were both laughing out loud, deep, genuine bellows coming from far down within them. Tears stung their eyes as the elderly couple guffawed at each other, and their hands instinctually reached out and clasped the other's. They smiled at each other a moment, and Roger thought about how much he loved her. How much he treasured their marriage and all the time they'd spent together. All the years. She was still just as beautiful to him now as when he'd first laid eyes on her at the—

Then they were in the air.

The car was over the ground and all Roger could see was the street, directly in front of him as though it were a wall. Then they were upside down and a moment after that they were seeing nothing but the stars and moon as they peeked through the storm clouds. Then it was the horizon again, but they were easily eight or ten feet off the ground.

The cycle began again.

Neither of them had the chance to register what was happening before the car smashed upside down in the street, the roof smashing in and both their skulls crushing and exploding like watermelons inside their old car as it slid along Main Street in Winnsboro, Texas, only fifty miles from Tyler and their grandchildren.

They never even heard the roar of the beast.

Chapter Forty-seven

"Oh my *God*!" Honey gasped as they pressed their backs against Ryan's truck. She'd seen the gaunt figure climbing down off the gigantic Glutton. Saw the figure greeted by the nightmare man with the horrible face.

Brother.

"It—It's—eh—eh—"

"Jake," Jim said coldly, his eyes hyper-aware but also seeming to be distant. His sidearm was in his hand and he appeared to be trying to decide on something.

There was a clatter behind them and Honey turned to see Ryan fumbling to pick something up from the ground. In the flash from a finger of lightning she saw it was a gun.

"Ryan?" she almost hissed. "What are y—"

"Quiet!" Jim whispered harshly.

The rumble of thunder rolled over them, like a giant machine, squashing them down into the earth. No one moved. Then, seeming to have decided on something, Jim leaned past Honey and Freddie to Ryan, seizing his shoulder.

"I need cover," Jim said as quietly he could and still be heard over the drumming rain.

Ryan looked confused, his eyes watery.

"What?" he responded. "Cov—"

"I've got to get to the back of my Tahoe," Jim cut him off. "I need you to shoot in their direction while I—"

A barrage of rifle fire erupted, piercing through the hammering rain with deafening *booms.* Metal rang and there were the sounds of ricocheting bullets *zinging* off the frame of Ryan's truck. The window over their head exploded and glass rained down on them in small crumbles.

"Fuck!" Freddie screamed.

Honey could see Jim reconsidering. There was no chance. He would never get to the truck and back in time. And what in the hell did he need from the truck, anyway? He knew what they were facing. Did he want a fucking flare? Did he think he was dealing with a goddamned Tyrannosaurus Rex?

As her mind raced and she heard the growls of the monster as something crunched and smacked—the sounds of a terribly rude person at the dinner table—she saw Jim looking at his hands. One held his service pistol, the other was empty.

He was staring at the empty hand.

"What is it, Jim?" she asked him.

He blinked several times before turning to her, his eyes a marvel of wonder.

"I don't need cover," he said, an astonished smile spreading over his face. "I've had it all along."

She had no idea what he was talking about, and she began shaking her head, her soaked hair flipping in tangles about her head as she did.

"I don't understand, Jim!" she spat through the rain. "What the hell do you need? Have you forgotten what we're up against?"

Jim actually laughed. It was short, and vanished almost as soon as it had appeared. But it was genuine.

"Not anymore," he said.

He turned to the back of the Tahoe, smiling.

Chapter Forty-eight

Norman turned away from his Lord as it gobbled up the fatty flesh of the bulbous black woman—the sight was giving him an uncomfortable erection, Jesus forgive him—and saw his brother looking up to the sky. Rain pelted Jake's face and Norman was touched to see the smile between his gaunt, scarred cheeks. The filth which had seemed to have become a part of Jake's flesh was running now in streaks, as though he were being reborn, *baptized* into new life by the cleansing downpour.

Then Norman saw movement behind the truck and fired several times. A window shattered and a muffled *"Fuck"* rumbled to his ears.

Nowhere to run to, boys and girls, he thought as he dropped the empty magazine from his rifle and jammed another in. He pulled the charging handle back and seated a fresh round in the chamber.

A wet, slopping sound drew his attention back to his Lord as he devoured the big black woman, and Norman saw his messiah slurping up a long string of intestine. He saw too that the beast had grown. At least another five feet in height alone, never mind the muscular structure. Every morsel of food was making it bigger and bigger, and he was awestruck at the new Christ he'd help to birth into the world.

A shrieking of metal caused him to turn back to the truck at once, his rifle seating into his shoulder. The oppressive sound continued, and his eyes darted around through the eyes of his new face, his head throbbing again and the red hue threatening to return. He couldn't tell where it was coming from. Where the fuck—*Jesus forgive him*—was that sound—

Then he saw it.

The rear hatch of the Tahoe the cop had driven up in was buckling outward. He narrowed his eyes, his head tilting to the side and the rifle coming down from the ready just slightly. The rear windshield burst on the Tahoe then as the metal buckled and bent ever more, as though something inside of it were pushing its way out, slowly but surely. But there was nothing in the truck, he was sure of it. Nothing that could possibly be strong enough to exert such force. The thought of how many foot pounds of pressure it would take to create what he was witnessing was staggering.

Norman brought the rifle back to the crook of his shoulder but kept the barrel down just slightly. Either his Lord hadn't noticed what was happening or didn't care. *What does a being of its infinite power and strength have to care about anyway?* Norman wondered. It was still slurping up the last few morsels of the black woman, smacking in satisfaction.

Jake didn't seem to notice either. He was still standing there, face upturned, his arms now outstretched to either side of him. And he was...*was he laughing?*

He was, and this forced a new smile to split the already torn skin in Norman's face even more, streaming blood.

But his admiring moment was suddenly shut down all at once with a final and intense shriek of metal and

Norman looked just in time to see the hatch of the Tahoe rip completely free of the SUV and cast itself out into the street where it clattered and clanged its way to stillness.

What the—

Then something flew out of the back of the Tahoe and to the other side of the pickup, where Norman knew the others were. There was a clattering sound and some hushed cries which sounded almost exultant.

And then silence.

Jake, finally absorbing his newfound freedom, turned to Norman, his toothless mouth wriggled apart in a horrific parody of sadistic joy.

"Let's feed the faggots to the fucker, Norm—"

A shot split the night and Norman's leg was buckling beneath him. He looked down to see blood spurting from his thigh in thin spritzes which quickly mingled into the rain. He went down with a thud and a grunt, the barrel of his own rifle clanging sharply against the concrete.

He looked up to Jake, whose face had the faintest glimmer of confusion upon it, and began to reach out to him. But even as he did, Jake's arm exploded just above the bicep with a spray of blood and meaty flesh which arced away from him.

He went down as well.

Pain swelled in new dimensions for Norman as he turned his eyes back to the pickup. There was Chief Jim Dalton, arms propped on the hood of the truck, an AR-15 of his own in his hands. He was still aiming down the sights.

Lights flooded the area then, even as the messiah finished with the woman and turned to them all with a growl of indignation and frustration.

The lights pulled around the side of the pickup, two glaring orbs piercing his vision. There were more pops from the rifle in the Chief's hands, but they uselessly thudded into the beast as it stepped past them toward the Chief and his friends, doing no harm.

But Norman couldn't look away from the lights which had just pulled into the parking lot. As though he were mesmerized by them, he stared through the molten rubber orbs of his new face with something like awe.

Then they flicked off and the door opened. Someone stood into the downpour, their hair instantly matted to them in long strings.

He couldn't believe his eyes. He blinked several times, even as his Lord moved closer to the others and the shots continued to ring out. Those sounds seemed to be coming from another country, faint and distant rumblings. He was beholding a person he loved with his whole being, here at last to meet their maker and she was witnessing her son entering into his calling.

God is FUCKING good! he praised in his mind.

Jesus forgive him.

"Mother!" Norman screamed out as he hobbled to his feet. "The Lord has come!"

Her mouth hung agape, stunned awe and terror on her face. Not what Norman had expected at all in her reaction. But she was here, ready to see her baby boy, her *loving boy*, into his new calling to the Lord's service.

"Isn't it wonderful, Mother?" he bellowed.

Jake came to his feet between them then, and Norman saw the two of them lock eyes through the pelting rain.

"Oh, God," Cherry Reese muttered, almost too softly to be heard.

"I brought Jake back too, Mother!" Norman rejoiced.

"Who are you?" Cherry shrieked as her eyes fell on Norman and her hands flew to her face in terror. "And why are *you* here? How?"

She was looking at Jake now.

"It's so good to see you, *cunt,*" Jake said with a cold kind of glee.

That was when Norman saw the glinting knife in Jake's hand.

Chapter Forty-nine

Cherry Reese couldn't believe her eyes.

There was a monstrous beast, unbelievably huge, stalking across the lot. She'd seen it, of course, just as she pulled in and stopped the car a moment after she'd swerved around the wrecked mess in the street. An unnatural horror of a creature, unlike anything her mind could associate it with.

Then she'd seen the human-sized aberration with the horrible, molten face of some sort of animal, clawing its way to its feet and holding a rifle. The thing was calling her *mother*, but she'd never birthed anything of the sort, she was sure of it. Its voice, however...that *did* seem familiar. But, it couldn't be, could it?

Then the worst horror of all seized her. It clutched inside of her, behind her breasts, squeezing with a malicious fury she'd never known before as the third monster rose from the ground. This one was somehow more horrible than the others, even with their unnatural features and the incredible size of the big one. This one had haunted her for her entire life, ever since the day it had slimed its way out of her, and all the more so since that horrible day it had slimed its way back inside.

She recognized him instantly, and horror ripped through her and caused her to shudder. She thought her knees would buckle and she might collapse, but fear kept her rooted in place like an ancient tree.

"I brought Jake back, too!" the creature with the molten face and the voice she could not dismiss intimate knowledge of said.

A scream was building inside of her as she took in the eyes of the monster she'd been all too glad to be shed of nearly thirty years ago. Those eyes so full of menace and lust.

And she saw the knife. That *same* knife, from so long ago.

"Who are you?" she shrieked at the melted creature. Then turning to the knife-wielding nightmare, she said, "And why are *you* here? How?"

The devil she'd addressed had a smile splitting its face. Mostly toothless, it was an aberration, an infernal terror. There was no humor there, no humanity. Only malice and lust and evil.

The knife glinted in a bright streak of lightning.

"It's so good to see you, *cunt,*" the thing said.

Cherry Reese released the scream which had been building inside of her, and it took with it the last remnants of her sanity.

Jake had returned. And he was coming for her.

Chapter Fifty

Jim emptied the magazine uselessly into The Glutton. The bullets did little more than create tiny pockmarks in the beast's flesh which quickly closed up with a tiny misting of something like blood.

"Fuck!" he spat, throwing the empty magazine away and loading a fresh one. "We have to stop it!"

Ryan jumped up and began firing his Glock even more uselessly into the approaching abortion of reality. The slide locked back and Ryan tossed it aside, obvious terror in his eyes.

Jim saw Cherry Reese recoiling in terror behind the approaching monster, but recoiling against her son rather than the beast, the one they'd left in the other world all those decades ago and assumed dead. And he had a knife. Jim had shot both Reese brothers, intentionally meaning to wound them, but not succeeding in slowing them down. They were up, moving, and Norman—or what *used to be* Norman—was still holding a loaded rifle.

Jim drew a bead on him.

"I am the eater of worlds!" the giant thing bellowed in a voice which was an offense to the ears. One Jim had heard as a child. One which had haunted his nightmares ever since.

"And I mean to feed!"

There was a roar then, and the thing reached down, tossing Jim's Tahoe aside, the SUV flipping and toiling through the air like a toy before it crashed into the corner of the police station, smashing away the brick and flipping sideways on an uneven trajectory, vanishing into the neighboring property behind some mulberry bushes.

The thing stepped closer and Jim saw in his periphery Freddie running to the back of the truck and beyond. The back of his coat flapped in the sodden downpour. Jim also saw Honey and Ryan, pressed against the door of Ryan's truck, which they'd been cowering behind.

A million thoughts flooded Jim's mind then, thoughts of his career, of his life swimming in alcohol, of what they'd done to Jake and Bart and Chris as kids. But the thing was here, right before him even now, and he couldn't focus on regrets. He had to do something, and something bold.

His thoughts fell to his daughter. The one he'd made with Honey, the one he'd neglected for most of his life. Tears stung his eyes as he thought of it and a grimace masked his face. He couldn't let her down, not after what a shitty, uninvolved father he'd been. No. She deserved a life. A future. And if there was anything within him which might secure that for her, he was going to do it, goddamnit, even if it killed him in the process.

Greater love hath no man than this, that he lay down his life for his friends.

The scripture echoed in his mind, bouncing off the walls of his consciousness, and he turned to Ryan.

"Get her out of here," he said, a desperateness in his voice. "And take care of my little girl."

Then he looked at Honey, the giant monster almost on top of him now.

"Tell Joanna how much I loved her," he said, a finality in his voice which caused Honey's face to twitch. "And take care of Ryan."

Honey began to protest even as Ryan began dragging her away. She screamed back at him, begging him, *pleading* with him to come, to *run*, but Jim just watched her go, tears filling his eyes and his throat utterly choked with grief.

I love you, Joanna, he thought to himself.

Then he turned back to the monster, which was almost on top of him, its giant hand swinging down and throwing Ryan's truck out of the way. It crashed somewhere a block away.

"I told you it would be soon," the thing said, leaning down to Jim. *"Only, it couldn't come soon enough."*

He could feel the abomination's rancid breath on his face through the pelting rain. But Jim didn't falter. He stood tall, the rifle in his hand. Somewhere behind the beast, Jake was approaching Cherry, and Norman was clutching his head and screaming in something which sounded a lot like pain.

Jim looked up at the Glutton and smiled.

Chapter Fifty-one

Cherry quivered as she stumbled back on uneven legs. There was some unimaginable monstrosity to her left and what must be her sweet, loving boy Norman wailing as he clutched his awful, disfigured face. But the wonder of all of this was lost as the gaunt nightmare that was Jake, thought gone or dead all these years, approached her with the gleaming knife.

"What's the matter, mom?" Jake hissed through a toothless mouth. "Aren't you glad to see your boy?"

Her trembling hand came to her mouth, her eyes horrified and bulging, and she could feel a scream trying to come. Could feel its claws ripping its way up her throat. Only she couldn't seem to release it. Her lungs were locked. Still, the clawing scream tried to build in her throat, making it feel like it were beginning to bulge outward like some macabre parody of a frog's chin.

There was movement behind her, a blur of someone running toward either her or something behind her. But she couldn't turn her head away from the nightmare of the motherfucker—*and no, that's not a fucking curse!*—lumbering toward her on legs that seemed impossibly diminished, yet frightfully strong all at once.

A truck flipped through the air and flew an impossible distance, but still she didn't flinch. The scream still tore at her throat, caught there still, her bulging eyes spilling over with tears which instantly mixed with the rain.

"Don't be scared, momma," the thing which had occupied her womb in another life said. "I just want a kiss. You can give your boy a kiss, can't ya?"

A door slammed behind her and the roar of an engine burst to life. She *still* didn't move, even when she realized it was *her* car someone had gotten into.

Behind Jake, Norman's screams changed from wails of agony to ones of fury.

"You can't outrun the King!" the Norman thing bellowed.

Shots began to ring out from his rifle.

Chapter Fifty-two

"Get down!" Ryan screamed as he pulled Honey in front of himself and tackled her to the street behind the curb where they had the slightest bit of cover.

Chunks of cement exploded all around them, some slapping their faces. Ryan's chest was about to explode and he could feel Honey's doing the same as he clutched her close to him, the old bucking steed within him braying and threatening to break loose.

No!

He wouldn't leave Honey. He'd loved her since childhood and he'd just made a promise to the best friend he'd ever had that he would protect her and his daughter and he would *not* let it win this time, not now. He would *not* become his father.

He would *not* be a coward anymore.

Lights flicked on from another car in the parking lot and the shots stopped. Ryan dared to lift his head up ever so slightly. He could see the car the woman had come in, the engine running now and lights ablaze, but the woman was not in the car. He strained to see through the rain who it was and he thought he saw...

"Freddie?" Ryan whispered.

Honey was matching his gaze now and they both were getting to their hands and knees.

They could see him there, behind the wheel, fumbling with the transmission.

"What the hell is he doing?" Honey nearly shouted.

"Come on!" Ryan said pulling her away from the scene and across the street.

But she pulled her hands free.

"I'm *not* leaving them!" she screamed at him.

Ryan could only stare at her through the rain. Eventually, he nodded.

"I love you, Honey," he said, choking back tears. "I'm with you."

Her eyes looked stunned for a moment, then they softened. Behind them there was a roar, but neither turned toward the sound. She reached her hand out and brushed his cheek gently in the pouring rain, and he brought his hand up to hers.

"I know, Ryan," she finally said, and smiled. "And I love you too."

The squealing sound of tires finally brought them out of their moment and they turned, their eyes widening and their heartrates returning to tachycardia. Freddie was driving the car at the madman with the disfigured face.

And fast.

Chapter Fifty-three

Jake could imagine the smell of her. He was close to her now, but the rain was masking her scent, making it impossible to draw in her fragrance. But he could imagine it. *Remember* it.

Her fear. How he relished the scent of fear.

It was one of the few things that made his dick hard, and now, as he drew within three feet of her, his long vacationing erection made a triumphant return to his loins.

Her car sped past them, and Jake could see his mother's eyes widen as she finally focused on something other than him.

"Don't want to miss the show, mommy!" he growled with sadistic glee.

He snatched his hand out, clutched the back of her hair, and wrenched her around. Then he held her gaze on Norman, the fucking freak.

He could see Norman's eyes, wide and...*red, maybe?* He was staring at the oncoming car, holding his rifle stupidly at his side.

"See ya, Norman, you faggot freak!" Jake bellowed over the noise.

Then Norman had the gun up and was firing again at the car, sparks flying off the metal and glass shattering.

"Noooo!" Cherry screamed in a tone which could melt iron.

She struggled in Jake's grip, trying to look away, but he'd have none of that. He *wanted* her to see this, and by God, she would. Even if he had to peel her eyelids off, she would fucking watch.

Norman folded over the hood of his mother's car. There was an audible metal *smack* as his face came into contact with the hood and Jake smiled wide and toothlessly. It was music to him. The little cocksucker was finally gone, and he'd been able to make mommy dearest watch the whole thing.

The car veered then, toward the Police Station, the engine still roaring. It bounced up over a parking block and there was a screaming of metal and a spray of sparks.

Cherry, still writhing in Jake's grasp, screamed again, something unintelligible as the car smashed into the brick wall of the building and went still. She sobbed uncontrollably now, screaming Norman's name over and over again, trying to sink to the ground but unable to with Jake holding her up.

"Wasn't that beautiful, mother?" Jake said between her moans.

He laughed again as he wrenched her around to face him. He pulled her close, his face an inch from hers. He knew his breath was rancid and he savored the revulsion on her face as he breathed deeply in her face. She quivered and jerked, but he held her in place.

"Now," he said, his mouth almost touching hers, "where's my kiss, mommy?"

Then his mouth was on hers and she was screaming into his and he could feel laughter rising in him again. This was everything he had hoped for all these years he'd been trapped with the thing on the other side and it was finally happening and his dick was *hard.*

Then she locked up, rigid as stone, and her screams faded.

Jake was ejaculating in his pants now as his blade dug deep into her abdomen, and he pulled away from her with a shudder. Her face was horrified and confused, her mouth agape and quavering. She was trying to form words or more screams, but only breathy moans were coming through. Her hand gripped Jake's bare shoulder then and her nails dug into him, but he enjoyed that as well. She knew nothing of pain and suffering, but Jake Reese did. He'd been fed on like a cow being milked for so, so long. Her little scratches were soothing to him now.

Blood began to spill from her mouth in thin rivulets and he leaned in close one final time.

"I'm glad to be home, mother."

He ripped the knife downward.

Her abdomen opened as if on a zipper and Cherry Reese's insides spilled out in a hot, steaming, tangled mess at Jake's feet. She vomited a great deal of blood, which speckled Jake's face, but the rain was already washing its warmth away. Her body quaked and shivered and, finally, she collapsed to the ground. Jake Reese got down on one knee, peering into her wide and terrified eyes as she fell over on the parking lot.

Watching her die was exquisite.

Chapter Fifty-four

The Glutton towered over Jim now.

"Your world is ending," it said, slime dripping from its open mouth. *"And I'm starting with you."*

There were screeching tires and screams behind the thing, and amazingly, it turned to look. Jim dared a glance too, and saw the Norman thing being smashed into the wall of the station. Smoke rose in tendrils from the hood of the car, Norman's misshapen face sprawled out across it along with his arms, the AR-15 still clutched in one hand.

There was another scream then and Norman and The Glutton turned to see Jake Reese quite literally emptying his mother onto the lot.

Oh, my God, Jim thought, horror filling his mind. A mind that only moments before had been filled with peace and surety. He was planning to use his power to force the thing back to the woods and banish it once and for all there at the thin place.

But suddenly he felt weak. He felt unsure. His strength seemed to be leaving him. There was so much evil in this world, never mind the universe, was it worth saving at all?

He didn't know, and all at once, doubt flooded him. Did he *want* Joanna to grow up in a world that knew so much horror? In a world where men like Norman and

Jake Reese existed? Or was it better that he let this thing before him consume them all and bring it to a stop the world over?

And besides all that, did he have the strength necessary to hold the beast back, and force it back to the woods, miles away from here?

The more he considered it the more absurd his whole plan sounded to him. It was nuts. Insane. He couldn't do that in a million years. What was he thinking?

"Well," the Glutton said turning back to Jim, a diamond of a smile contorting its face. *"His purpose was served."*

Jim fell to his knees before the thing, casting aside his rifle, and prayed.

Give me strength. Give me answers. Give me clarity. I don't know what to do. If we were in the woods, I could, but here? How could I—

There was a squeal of metal and some coughing, and Jim looked up from his prayer to see Freddie stumbling out of the car that had nailed Norman to the wall of the Police Station. His face was bloodied, and his glasses sat askew on his face, but he seemed otherwise no worse for the wear.

Their eyes met across the parking lot.

Chapter Fifty-five

Freddie sprinted from behind Ryan's truck without saying a word. He paused for a moment behind the tailgate and peeked around.

He could see the Norman thing, clasping his disfigured face and screaming, and the gaunt Jake Reese coming toward Cherry. He knew Cherry and her husband George from the monthly meetings of all the clergy of the various churches in town. With over fifteen churches in such a small town, they'd decided to try and band together for outreaches and such, to varied results. The Reeses attended regularly, but often pushed back against most initiatives the rest of the pastors—and the one Catholic Priest—tried to put forth, their reasoning suspiciously self-serving.

But now, as her monstrous son came toward her, a gleaming knife in hand, she had no self-serving and indignant posture to her at all. She was trembling in terror, and Freddie had to fight the urge to smile at her misfortune.

Breathe, he thought. *Get to the car, save your friends.*

He sprinted out from behind the truck, rain pelting him like slapping hands, and went for Cherry's car. His feet sloshed through the puddles and his breaths came in fast gasps.

He heard a crunch of metal and turned to see Ryan's truck flipping through the air and out of sight as Ryan and Honey dashed for the street. A second after, he heard the smash of the truck somewhere far away and more gunshots erupted.

Freddie ran faster.

As he approached the car and slung open the door, he heard The Glutton saying something to Jim. He couldn't make it out, but that was secondary now to what he had to do. Jim had great power inside of him, but he wasn't using it yet. Why? He could end this in a second, but he wasn't doing it.

Think, Jim! Freddie's mind screamed. *This place is as damned as the house in the woods! Look what Norman has done here!*

The engine roared to life.

Freddie paid no attention to Jake and Cherry as he dropped her car into gear and floored the accelerator. The tires squealed on the wet concrete and the car lurched forward. His knuckles were already turning white over the steering wheel as he aimed for the Norman thing holding the rifle and seeming to scream through his aberration of a face.

"Fuck with my friends and you're fucking with me, asshole!" the Baptist preacher screamed into the cab when he was only a few feet away from the goat man who was firing aimlessly into the car but missing Freddie entirely.

There was a great thud, a horrible crunch, and Norman's face smashed down hard on the hood. Blood sprayed in jets onto the windshield and immediately began to wash away in the rain. Freddie continued keeping the accelerator down and began to turn the car towards the station. He flew over a parking block, a scream of metal and sparks flooding from beneath him.

"Aaaaaaahhhhh!" Freddie screamed without end.

Then there was a sudden jolt as they smashed into the wall. Another geyser of blood jetted forth, and Freddie saw it spray the front window a second before the airbag deployed into his face, crushing his nose into a bloody lump and smashing his glasses.

"Oomph!" he grunted as his head snapped back in whiplash.

That's going to hurt in the morning, he thought absurdly.

Then the airbag was deflating, and he could see the unmoving Norman on the hood, rifle still in hand, though the hand was limp now. He'd stopped him. And with all the blood, Freddie was sure he'd killed the psychopath.

This caused him to bark in laughter, then wince at his nose. He touched it, and was instantly convinced it was broken. No matter. That's why God made doctors, right? They'd fix this up. And Norman couldn't hurt anyone else.

Then his thoughts returned to Jim. He looked in the rearview and could see the monster over his friend, reaching down for him. Jim knelt there, unmoving. Why wasn't he moving? Didn't he realize this place was thin now? He could banish this thing into oblivion and be done with it!

"Goddamnit, Jim!" Freddie moaned as he reached for the door.

It squealed open on bent hinges and Freddie stumbled out. The hammering rain caused fresh pain in his nose, but he ignored it. Jim had to snap out of it, and quick. And Freddie was the only one who could do it.

He righted himself in the downpour, and Jim's eyes looked up and leveled with his. Freddie cupped his hands on either side of his mouth and began to scream.

"It's thin here, Jim! Do it now, before it's too late! Look at this place! It's thi—"

Chapter Fifty-six

Jim's breath tore from his lungs. Tears stung his stunned eyes almost at once as he was pummeled by the deluge of rain.

Still, he didn't flinch as The Glutton towered over him, it's taloned hand coming for him.

The image was seared into his mind. His eyes couldn't quit seeing it. Somewhere behind him, a woman was screaming. Perhaps it was Honey, he didn't know. He couldn't force himself to turn around and look.

The tears mixed with the cold rain on his face, lost completely in the downpour. The monster's hand was getting closer, but Jim's eyes were welded to the spot.

Freddie had screamed to him.

"It's thin here, Jim! Do it now, before it's too late! Look at this place! It's thi—"

And then it had happened.

An unreal *crack* through the night. Not of thunder, but something else. Something manmade. It made his ears ring and his chest hitch. Freddie's glasses falling from his...*from his...*

And there was so much blood.

The top of Freddie's head came apart like a blossoming flower of red and gray and yellow. A quickly dispersed spray of red was there and gone in an instant as the rain carried it away. But the meaty debris which launched all around him flew in heart-wrenching arcs all about him as he began to fall.

His glasses tumbled from what was left of his face, if you could even call it that. It was an enormous open wound, little of it resembling the kind, caring, and brave features of his lifelong friend. Instead, it now resembled the face of the monster which was reaching down for him now.

Jim hardly noticed the scream of Cherry Reese, though in his periphery he saw her insides spilling. He was in too much shock to react to that. And the monster was right on top of him now, inches from having him and starting its worldwide reign of apocalyptic terror and mayhem. It would continue to get bigger and bigger, and if it wasn't stopped now, right this second, it never would be.

It's thin here, Jim!

His dead friend's words rang in his mind, even as Freddie's body thudded to the ground lifeless and Jim could see the maniacal, bleeding eyes of the Norman thing, pinned to the hood, some horrific cackle erupting from his awful mouth.

Look at this place! It's thi—

The screams from behind him were louder now and he saw shapes moving past him, one of them holding his rifle he'd dropped a moment before. Jim's eyes were still locked on the Norman thing, and he felt some species of rage well within him which he'd not experienced since he was a child. A child in the woods when he'd found Jake and his friends—Bart and Chris—torturing Honey in that awful house. A deep, bellowing grumble began to erupt within him, one of rage and fear and guilt. His mouth began to quiver and his lips peeled back over his teeth. His eyes became narrow slits of righteous fury as they finally turned towards The Glutton, the cosmic beast, the eater of worlds, and a rage-fueled scream exploded from his mouth as his hands came up and the air around them began to shimmer.

The Glutton's hand stopped a foot from Jim's face.

Chapter Fifty-seven

Honey's hands clasped over her mouth, hushing a monumental gasp and she doubled over. Next to her, Ryan skidded to a stunned stop of his own as the two of them watched Freddie's head come apart and his body splat to the rain-soaked lot with a small splash.

"Oh my God," Ryan whispered through the rain.

All Honey could do was stare, horrified astonishment on her face.

Behind Freddie's body was the car, smashed into the side of the station, and the Norman thing's upper torso pushed up on his elbows, the rifle clutched in his right hand.

"Glooooooooory innnn the hiiiiigheeeeeeeeesssssssssttt!" came the garbled scream from Norman, a level of insanity in his voice Honey was horrified to acknowledge the existence of.

Then there were cackles and barks of mad laughter from the pinned man.

Honey's hands came away from her face, trembling, and what was revealed there was a twisted grimace of pain, of fear, and of unadulterated fury.

"Noooooo!" she screamed and began sprinting.

She hadn't planned to move, hadn't planned anything at all, actually, but her body had taken over with pure animal instinct and she was moving now, and fast. She could feel Ryan just behind her, his breaths gasping and the repeated refrain of *"Oh my God"* coming every third breath.

Somewhere to her right, The Glutton towered over Jim, and she noticed Jake, now on his feet again, walking ominously toward the father of her child. Still, nothing swayed her. Nothing took her focus away from the psychopathic motherfucker who'd just killed one of the kindest and best men she'd ever known in her entire life.

Her eyes glanced down as she leaped over puddles and onto the curb, and she saw Jim's rifle lying there. She bent and scooped it up without thinking, and continued to charge forward.

Behind her, someone said, "What are you—"

But the drumming rain and the thundering of her heart in her ears drowned out the rest. She was pretty sure it was Ryan, but all semblance of reality was fading for her now as her vision tunneled in on Norman fucking Reese.

A shriek of anguish or fury—she couldn't tell which—erupted behind her as she closed in on the freak with the awful face, her teeth bared in an animal snarl, and she thought she heard something familiar, something she'd not heard in nearly thirty years. The sound carried with it wonderous and terrible memories. Memories of pain and loss, of horror and guilt, of shame and regret.

It's happening! she thought.

The warbling sound clawed through the thrumming rain as a boom of thunder exploded overhead.

Chapter Fifty-eight

Everything hurt. Bad.

Norman was pinned between the car and brick wall of the Police Station, and his head was singing with pain. Though the pain was immense, it hadn't taken him long to realize there was absolutely no feeling below his waist. This wasn't any good, but thankfully he knew the healer, and the healer was right there, about to snatch up that sniveling sinner of a Police Chief just across the lot. He would fix Norman up real nice, and they would move on in their glory, cleansing the world of every evil thing and basking in the righteous glow of the Almighty Father.

Hallelujah!

His hand still trembled from the recoil of the shot which had emptied the skull of the little red-headed demon who'd rammed him, and the memory—though only seconds old—made his molten face split and bleed with a smile. His head throbbed, but that would pass. It always had before. And the rain seemed to be helping the red hue of his vision as his eyes leaked blood.

Splish-splash-splish.

Norman looked up past the food for his master on the ground and saw the woman rushing, some shrieking scream coming from her like a wailing siren.

He began to chuckle in spite of himself. He was badly fucked up—*Jesus, forgive him*—pinned to a wall by a car, and was being charged by a clearly insane woman, yet all he could do was laugh. His guffaws began to increase as she leaped over the curb and snatched something up off the ground. Something long and black. Something which looked a lot like...

A lot like his *rifle.*

She'd snatched up the Chief's rifle on her way, and suddenly fresh barks of mad laughter erupted from him then, higher in pitch now than before, as he took in the futile absurdity of her attempt.

Splish-splash-splish.

What did she think she was going to do against the Lord's chosen? And never mind that, *he* had his rifle, right here in hand, and she was going to charge him like a wild animal?

Ha!

Norman raised his rifle, forcing his cackles to abate so that he could aim. He nuzzled the stock against his shoulders and peered down the sights. His bleeding grin split wider as he watched her wet breasts sway as she came, and he was disappointed to find there was no stirring down below. There was *nothing* down below. No feeling at all.

Splish-splash-splish.

His head throbbed.

Doesn't matter, he thought as he slipped his finger around the trigger. *My King will set all this right.*

She was closer now, and Norman thought he heard a strange warble, and the periphery of his vision caught something strange. Like a strange light, only that wasn't quite right. It was the air. Almost as if it were...were...

Shimmering.

But he couldn't focus on it now. He had business to deal with here and—

He saw Jake approaching the King and the Chief. He was approaching them slowly, deliberately, his bloody knife hanging loosely at his side.

Bloody knife? Why is his knife blo—

Then he saw it.

His focus was completely off the charging woman now as he saw the messy, steaming heap on the lot just behind Jake. His chest seized and his breath caught, his heart hammering in his chest now a million beats per minute.

Is that...is that mother?

"Moooommmmmmyyyyy!" he screamed in an uncharacteristically high pitch, his throat turning raw from the effort.

Jake paused then in his stalking approach, turned to Norman, and smiled widely.

Norman's mangled jaw hung agape. He couldn't believe it. After all he'd gone through, all he'd sacrificed and worked for to birth their Lord back into this world and bring Jake back, he'd *killed* their mother? Their loving mother? How could he do such a thing? What kind of monster would kill his own mother, and Norman's as well, of all things?

An insane scream, a high-pitched wail of fury and agony, tore from Norman's throat then, shredding his esophagus as it escaped him, and suddenly the rifle was turning toward Jake. He still stood there, smiling, now waving the bloody knife at Norman. The woman charging him was very close now, almost on top of him. But Norman was fast. He was good. He'd been target shooting his whole life. He could get two rounds off in time.

Splish-splash-splish.

Still shrieking, everything within him in a black rage at the betrayal of his big brother, Norman squeezed the trigger, a madness in his eyes.

Click.

The lack of discharge shocked him and his torso jolted. He'd been so ready for the *crack* of the shot and the recoil, the utter lack of it had caused him to spasm.

Eyes wide now behind his new face, he began fumbling with the rifle, turning it over in his hands, a stupid look of confusion in his eyes. That was when he noticed the open chamber, which locked open when the magazine was empty. He'd fired all the rounds he had and not realized it. Never reloaded. Sent the last one home through that Baptist bastard's—*Jesus, forgive him*—skull.

"Oh, my God," he mumbled as the woman pulled up a few feet from him and raised the rifle in her arms.

His eyes met hers, then the open bore of the barrel.

"Lord," he screamed to his unmoving King, eyes never leaving the barrel in front of him, *"deliver me from mine enemies!"*

"I'm delivering you straight to hell, motherfucker!" the woman screamed.

Her rifle was not empty.

Chapter Fifty-nine

Jake's smile broadened as he looked away from the sight of his brother's head exploding and bullets pummeling his torso. It was a delicious sight, one *almost* as satisfying as seeing his mother's entrails spill to the sodden ground.

Now to settle the score with Jimmy.

He heard a faint curse as the little bitch—now a grown bitch—pulled the trigger on an empty chamber of the gun she'd used on Norman. This amused him even more as he laughed now, marveling at his luck. He'd been brought back after decades of torture and imprisonment, being fed on in tiny, but excruciating removals of his flesh by The Glutton, as it used him like a cow to feed itself just enough to remain viable for when the right moment came, while he'd fed on the eyeballs and soft insides of giant insects. And to find not only his sniveling, faggot brother, but also his cunt of a mother in the same place and being able to watch them both meet their end...*oh, what a glorious thing.*

The head honcho son of a bitch was just in front of him now, and seemed to be using their shared power to hold his captor's blade-like claws at bay, but only just. The air was shimmering and the familiar warble was in the air, but it was faint. As though Jimmy-boy were having trouble making it happen. Perhaps exerting too much energy into holding the monster back to affect the tear between worlds.

"Long time, Jimmy," Jake said through toothless gums.

He stood there, next to Jim now, holding the bloody knife in his hand. The rain seemed to intensify then, and lightning ripped the sky apart above them in a fantastic explosion of light. Thunder boomed immediately overhead.

The policeman's eyes met his, a species of terror there, but also a form of determination. The man was trembling, on his knees, arms outstretched above him, holding the beast back merely a foot away from him.

"Kill him," The Glutton uttered.

Jake moved his gaze from Jimmy to the monster, meeting its black eyes. There was a desperation there he'd never seen before in all his time with the creature, and it brought unavoidable joy to him to see it. The beast which had kept its promises to him, yes, but at the cost of great and prolonged physical and psychological torture was now...what? It wasn't quite scared, that wasn't it, but it *was* worried. Concern leaked from its gaze like water from a dripping faucet.

Jake's smile turned malicious.

"Kill him and we can move on to the rest," the thing said, diplomatically.

Jake turned to Jimmy, raising the knife. The taste of copper filled his mouth as he licked the blade, tasting his mother's blood, and he felt a tingle in his loins. He'd waited so long for this, *dreamed* so long of this, and now it was finally here. The lead faggot, on his fucking knees, no less, and Jake towering over him ready to strike.

But the look in the policeman's eyes caused him to pause. The terror and determination seemed to have vanished now, replaced by something Jake had a hard time processing. All those years ago, this sniveling little fucker—not so little anymore—had had nothing but disdain for him. Nothing but disgust and hate. But now, what Jake was seeing in him was causing him to hold back.

It was...*compassion?*

No. It couldn't be. Jake was incapable of the emotion, and there was no way this piece of sh—

"Help me, Jake!" Jim pleaded.

Jake couldn't move. His breath caught in his throat and he froze in the downpour. His face took on a confused quality and his head cocked to one side as his eyes narrowed on the helpless cop.

"What did you say to me?" Jake growled.

"Help me," the cop repeated. "I can't do it alone, and I know you went through hell with this thing. Together we can put it away forever!"

The beast roared then, causing Jake to flinch slightly. It seemed to lean into the cop more, fighting against the invisible force of mind and will Jimmy was using to hold it back, and it gained some ground. An inch, maybe two, but it was getting closer. Jimmy seemed to be trembling more, his face contorted with effort as he pushed with all his will to hold the thing back.

"What we did to you was wrong!" Jimmy almost screamed as he strained to fight back the thing leaning into him. "What we did to *all* of you! I'm sorry! We were kids, but we knew it was wrong and we did it anyway!"

The Glutton's back was writhing, its hooves clawing into the ground as it pushed harder against the force of Jim's will. The octave-layered roar sounded again.

A wretched sound.

"We were wrong! I know there's no forgiveness for what we did, but I want you to know *we were wrong!*"

Jake couldn't believe his ears. He blinked several times, staring almost stupidly at his nemesis on the ground before him, unable to believe what he was hearing. He hated the man, yes, all of them. But this plea for forgiveness baffled him all the same. The monster next to him had never made such a proclamation. In fact, in all the years he'd spent with it, screaming as the thing would take a chunk of flesh from his thigh, his arm, his back, it seemed to enjoy every moment of it. Never an apology, never a single ounce of regret.

All it wanted was to feed. And it had *used* Jake for that purpose. Nothing more.

"I don't give a fuck about your apology," Jake said, though his voice wavered in spite of himself.

Jim nodded almost imperceptibly. "I know you don't, but I still had to say it. You deserve that."

Jake's jaw fell open. The knife was extended from his hand, about waist level, but he couldn't move it. He'd never been so blown away by a turn of events in his life. Both in this world and the other, all he'd ever been told was how everything was *his* fault. *His* doing. No matter the cause, it had been *he* who endured the punishment. But now to hear *this*, and from all people...

"Kill the fucker, cow!" The Glutton screamed in its awful, layered voice. *"Kill him now!"*

Jake's eyes fell to his knife, the blood nearly washed clear of it now. He let it drop to his side as he turned to look at The Glutton.

Jake's smile returned.

"You're scared," Jake said to the thing.

As he peered into the creature's eyes, Jake saw real fear in them for the first time.

Chapter Sixty

What the fuck is he thinking?

The Glutton struggled in the invisible bonds the human was holding it in, and hissed and snarled loudly in protest. But it couldn't move. It couldn't wriggle free. It would have been nice to have Norman mowing the food down for him, but he was dead. It was no great loss to The Glutton. It didn't care. But it needed assistance now, just as it had needed both Jake—its cow—and Norman—its feeder—to come through into this world. And this world was so ripe for the picking. So full of high meat. It was deliciously full of meals. The power it would achieve by the time it had finished dining on the—

But it couldn't move.

This human's power was strong. Stronger even than Cloris had been, and the thing had never seen such power before it had encountered her. The Glutton *was* breaking through, however, though slowly. It was inching, ever closer, to the human's face. When it got there, it would tear him apart and slurp down his insides, increasing its power. It would never be able to turn this one, it knew, but that was what Jake was for. His cow.

Only the Cow seemed to be having thoughts of its own now. The fucking human was turning him, swaying him to help. It wasn't as though The Glutton hadn't realized the need for Jake all these years. But it had to feed. It had to keep just enough strength for a jump the second it detected a presence on the other side. Surely the Cow understood. Certainly the Cow could see the necessity. And hadn't The Glutton kept all its promises? Brought him back and delivered him the balm of bloodlust he'd always desired.

But still, he was considering. The fucking human holding him back was convincing Jake to turn on it. And it was a dangerous notion to consider. Should they both come after it, there was nothing it could do to stop them from driving it back into another world. An empty world. One where all its strength would vanish and fade and it would be forever trapped. Or perhaps an even worse place. The burning place it had escaped eons ago, before it had gone on its excursions through the universes and cosmos.

No, it thought. *This will* NOT *happen. Not now. Not here.*

The Glutton leaned against the force of Jim Dalton's will with all its might.

Chapter Sixty-one

Jim was losing. The Glutton was inching closer and closer to him, the razor talons slithering through the pouring rain toward his face, hungry for blood.

"Jake!" he said more forcefully now as something warm and gel-like began to ooze from his nose. "We can get rid of it! And then you can have me. You deserve that for what we did. I'll be all yours, but we *have* to send this thing back!"

He moved his gaze away from the encroaching talons to Jake. Jim was trembling now with the strain, and he had no idea if he was getting through to Jake or not. Jake kept looking from him to the creature, then back again. He was considering. Jim was a sitting duck right then. He could just slit his throat and be done with it. But Jim could see Jake had been through unimaginable torment these past decades and would very much like a little revenge on The Glutton as well.

"He's right, you know," Jake said, turning his eyes from Jim to the monster. "Together, we could send you back."

Jim saw the creature's eyes widen. In their black, inhuman depths, Jim could see something like terror and rage warring with each other for dominance inside the thing. It was scared. Scared of *them*.

The talons came another inch closer. Jim's trembling evolved into shaking. Warmth oozed from his nostrils and he felt the same begin leaking from his eyes.

"Jim!" he heard Honey scream and saw Ryan holding her back.

He couldn't focus on that right now. He had to focus every inch of his will on holding the creature in place.

"I will have my meat!" the thing bellowed, its hot, rancid breath piercing the deluge and stinging Jim's face. *"I don't need the Cow anymore! I'll eat you ALL!"*

New pressure seemed to press on Jim as his shaking transformed into a near quaking shudder.

"Jake!" Jim screamed.

"Cow, you say?" Jake said addressing The Glutton.

There was a momentary respite from the incredible pressure as the beast met Jake's gaze. Terror spilled from its godless face.

Jake began to laugh. A maniacal, psychotic laugh laced with malice. He snapped the blade back into the hilt of his knife.

"Fuck you," he hissed at The Glutton.

Then Jake Reese, lips peeled back over vacant gums, raised his hands toward the monster. The creature began to howl in layered octaves and Jim could feel the pressure moving back toward The Glutton.

The air around them began to shimmer and peel away, revealing another world.

Chapter Sixty-two

Ryan pulled on Honey, his arms around her waist, as she struggled and screamed, her arm outstretched toward Jim.

"Jim!" she cried as they both collapsed to the wet parking lot.

"There's nothing we can do, Honey!" Ryan gasped into her ear as he pulled her close. "We'll get ourselves killed! Think of Joanna!"

This seemed to register with her, as her struggles abated and she leaned back into his chest, a hand covering her sobbing face.

Jake had appeared to be about to kill Jim, but whatever Jim had said to him seemed to sway the gaunt psychopath. Now, Jake was glaring up at the giant monster and thrusting his hands towards it.

The air began to waver and Ryan saw a portal shimmer open like he had seen all those years ago at the damned place in the woods. Dusty roads and dilapidated old buildings were just visible behind the giant Glutton, the ruins of a world that had experienced the full force of what this cosmic beast was capable of were it to be unleashed.

Both Jim and Jake's faces were strained, their mouths open and contorted, and Jim's nose and ears were bleeding. Whatever exertion he was using to push back against the monster was causing his body great stress and bursting capillaries. Ryan wondered if Jim's eyes might pop from their sockets if he continued pushing like this.

The air continued to waver and shimmer, the warbling sound rising as the portal grew larger around them, revealing more of the apocalyptic wasteland of the world beyond it. That was what was waiting for them all—the whole world—if Jim and Jake failed to cast this monster out.

But as he watched, holding the sobbing love of his life in his arms, his eyes wide and heart hammering, he was filled with an odd sense of hope. His best friend and his worst enemy were tearing through to another world.

Freddie had been right. This place had become thin.

Chapter Sixty-three

The screaming howls of the Glutton were ear-splitting. Jim gasped as the sounds assaulted his hearing, but he pressed in all the more. Jake was doing the same beside him, hands outstretched toward the beast, and Jim could see the other world appearing around them. The desolate, foggy landscape, so similar to their own, but so different as well. What had it been like before this cosmic terror had come and destroyed it, he wondered? Had there been a police station, or something like it, in this same spot over there like there had been the house and fort in the woods?

He reckoned it was likely, but quickly turned his thoughts back to the monster and Jake when he felt the pressure surge against him with renewed vigor.

"Never!" The Glutton roared in their faces and inched closer to them.

Jim didn't have time to consult with Jake anymore, he could only hope his old nemesis was thinking as he was.

Give it all you got.

As Jim pressed back, he found himself rising to his feet again, the warmth running from his eyes and nose. He saw in his periphery that Jake's eyes and nose were gushing blood, and only then did it register that *that* was the warmth he felt pouring from his own face.

The force is tearing us apart from the inside, he thought.

But it didn't matter. This thing could *not* be allowed one step further into this world, and if it tore him apart in the process to stop this thing, it was worth it for the sake of his daughter, his friends, and the world.

Greater love hath no man than this, that he lay down his life for his friends.

The scripture resounded in his mind and gave him new strength. Strength he hadn't known he possessed until this very moment, and he felt it surge through him like a tidal wave.

He was screaming, but he was only vaguely aware of this. The air around them began to shimmer even more, the warble intensifying, and the beast's howls became all the more desperate.

And what he saw was beyond his ability to process.

He'd been able to see the other world before, the one The Glutton had leaped from, but now the fabric of *that* existence was changing. A portal within the portal tore open, revealing yet another world. This new one was bright, full of green, but nothing seemed to live there other than plant life. At least in this particular spot.

Then yet another portal tore open within the third world. The power was thundering through him as he was faintly aware of another lightning strike in his own world.

Another portal, and another. As he witnessed multiple tears in reality splitting open within themselves, he realized he and Jake and the Glutton were moving. Almost as if they were falling, but horizontally through these universes, being sucked toward the next and the next. The scenery was flying by. Many of the landscapes were desolate and void. Perhaps The Glutton had already visited these worlds. But others were vibrant and alive. He saw what he thought might have been some sort of dinosaurs in the briefest of flashes as they hurtled from one world to the next, though these dinosaurs had fur and faces of human-like skin.

Then they were on to the next and the next. He caught glimpses of landscapes and beings his mind was unable to associate anything with. Things with lashing tentacles and beaks, things like men covered in pink fuzz, a strange trunk drooping from beneath square eyes in colors he'd never seen before. And there was more, but they were moving faster and faster, and everything around them began to blur.

Jake was screaming next to Jim now, and their wails rose along with the monster they were banishing. The terrible howls, both their own and that of The Glutton, were nearly deafening.

Jim felt weightless all at once. He was still flying toward something, but the landscapes and creatures he'd been seeing before had vanished and there was a blank void around them now, almost like space, but without any starlight. The only light in this place was a faint red hue, one which was intensifying with every passing second.

He looked over to Jake and saw the psychotic man still screaming, though his hair had gone snow white. He also looked thirty years older. Had they aged in these past seconds as they hurtled through the worlds? Was time accelerating? Or was it sheer terror which had drained the man's hair of color and withered his flesh?

Jim didn't know and didn't have a mirror to check his own condition. The red hue continued to intensify, glowing brighter and brighter, and Jim finally caught sight of its source.

There was another portal ahead of them, but there was no hilly landscape beyond it. There were no fantastic animals waltzing around within this new world. It was like looking down on a red ocean, waves of what appeared to be flames ebbing and flowing. There was a sound of terrible wailing, like the sound of torment which rose as they neared the awful place.

A lake of fire, Jim thought and shuddered.

The Glutton was screaming now, thrashing its weightless body through the space, unable to combat the inevitable trajectory towards the place.

"No!" it screamed, at once petulant and terrified. *"I'll not go back! I cannot go back!"*

Gooseflesh marbled Jim's entire body. If this place was indeed what he feared it was, did this thing come from there? Had it escaped and gone rogue?

Then he thought, *am I about to be swallowed in there, too?*

He released his force of will on the monster and tumbled through the void, flying closer and closer to the portal. He realized how gigantic it was, as the nearer they drew the larger it loomed before them. More than fifty feet high now, where it had been merely the size of a man before. They were beyond reality now, between all realities, tumbling in the great void towards not another universe, but another dimension. One of torment, wailing, and the gnashing of teeth.

Oh, God, Jim thought.

Jake had released the Glutton as well, and was tumbling near him, weightless. Their speed must have been phenomenal, but there was no wind, almost no air here to slow their acceleration.

"Now you're mine!" Jake screamed, bringing Jim's awareness back to the moment.

Jake was rolling and tumbling towards him, the knife in his hand, a madness in his eyes so cold Jim physically shivered.

"Sorry, Jake!" Jim bellowed, drawing his pistol from its holster. "I may have stretched the truth a bit!"

Jake's insane eyes widened as they were drawn to the barrel, and his face snarled.

"You fucking fag—"

Jim fired.

Jake's chest bloomed with red and a swatch of meat tore away from him, his eyes so wide they nearly dropped from his gaunt face, and blood began to pour from his mouth.

But he was still tumbling toward him, the knife still in hand, and Jim instinctually threw his other hand out. The air shimmered and Jake's surprised, dying face vanished into yet another portal and then was gone.

Jim closed the portal and turned back to the beast before him, which was still screaming. The fiery portal had almost swallowed them now, and stood at least a hundred feet high. Maybe more. The searing heat was scalding his skin, feeling like a terrible sunburn which set in within seconds.

The Glutton met Jim's eyes and reached out for him.

"You're coming with me!"

Panic was thrumming through Jim's body now and he frantically tried to think. The monster almost had a taloned hand around his foot. He looked at the gigantic portal and wondered if he could close it. He had to make sure the beast went through first, but they were so close now, he'd better get started.

As the portal began to close before Jim's eyes, The Glutton grasped his foot.

"Eternity will be a good start to your suffering!" the thing hissed, its awful tongue snaking out and licking its face.

The portal continued to close, and they were almost inside of it. The heat was enormous. Jim wondered if his skin would begin to bubble soon. The air was thick and smelled of Sulphur.

The portal was closing.

"Eternity!" the thing howled.

Jim peered behind the thing and saw what appeared to be a giant, rotting worm rising from the sea of fire before them, and a mouth which could never be described opened from the abomination as it rose to meet them.

No greater love, Jim thought as he shut his eyes.

As the portal continued to shrink, there was a horrific scream as Jim began kicking at the taloned hand which grasped him.

Chapter Sixty-four

Honey couldn't process what she'd just seen. She'd seen a lot as a child, including an ageless, cosmic monster. But this, she simply could not process.

Jim, Jake, and the monster had vanished into the portal as though being sucked out into the vacuum of space. Then several minutes had passed and the portal closed, leaving nothing behind of them.

She had stood then, Ryan finally letting her go, and together they stumbled toward the spot on uneven feet. Their jaws hung open in identical stupors of awe.

Then the air had opened again, and a body tumbled out, splatting to the pavement mere feet in front of them with incredible velocity.

Honey had cried out, clasping her hands to her mouth and taking a step back involuntarily. Ryan had reached out to steady her as he too cried out similarly.

Whoever it was who'd come through the portal had come with an incredible speed. When they hit the pavement it had been with enough force to almost explode the body and crack the concrete. The skin burst on either side of the man—she could see now it *was* a man—and intestines and blood were leaking out in grotesque form.

Then she saw the knife. It was Jake's knife. Even as she fought back the urge to vomit, doubling over and holding her mouth in a death grip, she knew it was him. And the wound on the back of the body she could tell had nothing to do with the high-velocity impact with the parking lot.

It was an exit wound from a bullet.

"Where's Jim?" she wailed, turning to Ryan whose wide eyes told her he had no answers for her. "Oh God, what did he do?"

She began to collapse then, heaving sobs exploding from her, and Ryan caught her, sinking to his knees with her and holding her tightly. She embraced him back, crying and screaming all the while.

"What did he do?" she bellowed over and over again.

Ryan stroked the back of her head, crying himself as he thought of Jim, and he saw Freddie's lifeless body across the lot.

"He saved us," Ryan said through his tears. "He saved us all."

"Goddammit, *NO!*" Honey screamed through her sobs, her face buried in Ryan's shoulder.

But Ryan continued to stroke her hair and shush her sweetly, rocking with her as they sat on their knees in the terrible place beneath the pouring rain.

"He just saved the world, Honey," Ryan whispered to her.

But she shook her head violently, pulling back from him slightly to look him in the eye.

"But he has a daughter!" she hissed. "*We* have a daughter! What about her?"

Her shoulders hitched up and down as she buried her face in Ryan's chest. But his hands cupped her face and she allowed herself to be directed back up to look at him.

"I'm still here, Honey," he whispered through the downpour. "I've always been here, and I always will be. I promise. I promise that to you, and I promise that to Joanna. Jim asked me to take care of you."

She stared at him a moment, her tears indistinguishable from the rain, and a faint smile spread across her saddened face.

"He told us to take care of each other," she said.

Ryan nodded. "And I mean to do just that."

As they sobbed and distant sirens wailed from miles out of the city, Ryan and Honey leaned in and kissed.

It had all the passion of a decades long wait.

Epilogue

Saturday, September 15, 2018

Honey, Ryan, and Joanna Dalton walked through the cemetery, all holding hands. Joanna had a somber look on her face, but she'd grown stronger in the past years since her father had given all to protect them. Ryan had made sure she knew what a hero he was, even if Sherriff Brock had been more skeptical.

In the wake of the events at the police station, some neighbors had heard all of the gunfire and had called 9-1-1. Since there had been no one to answer in the Winnsboro Police Station, the calls had rolled over to the County Sherriff's office, twenty miles away. All available units had been dispatched, the Sherriff himself roused from sleep, and all had descended upon Winnsboro in a flurry of red and blue lights. Only two people had been left, Ryan and Honey. The bodies lying around, and the carnage inside had left the lawmen slack jawed and bewildered.

Ryan and Honey had told them what they knew, leaving out the parts about the cosmic Glutton. There was no way anyone would believe it, and though there had been absolutely no explanation for the flipped car with the elderly couple inside, nor for how Ryan's truck had been found upside down a hundred yards down the street, and likewise they'd had no explanation for Jim Dalton's Tahoe being smashed and on its side next to the station. Luckily for them, no one spent a lot of time on these matters.

The only officer of the Winnsboro Police Department who'd not been slaughtered by the maniacal Norman Reese—he'd been identified in autopsy, along with his mother and a man presumed to be the long missing Jake Reese—was a reserve officer named Robert Jenkins. He had been on vacation with his wife of twenty-three years in Arkansas, and had been appalled to hear of the carnage when he returned.

He left the department, leaving Winnsboro officially without a police force.

The county had compensated, pulling several of their officers in to watch over the town, though it was quiet and sleepy after the horrific events of that night in August of 2016. Eventually, the city had hired a new Police Chief and reinstated a local Department, and things had gone back to more or less normal.

The disappearance of Jim Dalton had left the Sherriff perplexed. There had been no real explanation for it, none Honey or Ryan could give, anyway. They'd simply told him they didn't know where he was. That they'd assumed he'd been killed in the murder spree inside.

Lots of speculation arose, some people even murmuring that he'd run away like a coward when the diabolical Reese brothers fell upon the station. Others speculated he'd been kidnapped and murdered by them before the massacre and his body had simply never been located.

But Ryan had made sure Joanna had known the truth.

"Your daddy was a hero," he'd told her. "Your daddy saved the whole world."

The light in her face when he'd told her this—which was the absolute truth—had sealed his belief it was right to tell her all that had happened. Honey had agreed, and it seemed that Ryan's care for her daughter had caused her to fall completely for Ryan. They had married the following Spring, and shortly thereafter Honey had given birth to Jimmy Jr., the second child born to Jim Dalton and Honey Bascom, after only the second time they had made love. Ryan raised him and Joanna as though they were his own.

Revival Rock Ministries had not been long for the world after the deaths of Norman and Cherry Reese, and the long-lost Jake. George Reese had been unable to hide a near sense of joy at the passing of his entire family, and when it had come out that a seventeen-year-old girl in his church's youth group was pregnant with his child, the man had vanished. In the course of a single day, his bank accounts had been emptied, and no one had heard from him again. Most were tickled pink with that fact. Others, such as the teenage girl's father, had been infuriated. Perhaps he would turn up one day, but the authorities weren't really looking anymore.

"Shh-shh, baby boy," Honey said to the whimpering infant—almost a toddler now—in her arms as they weaved through the tombstones.

Ryan reached a hand out and stroked the baby's face.

"Easy now, Jimmy," he said. "We're going to pay respects to your daddy and then we'll get home.

The official story taken up by law enforcement had been that Chief Jim Dalton had been murdered, but never recovered. Without a body, there could be no official declaration of death, but the Mayor had elected to give him an officer's funeral and the city had paid for the grave marker.

Ryan, Honey, Joanna, and Jimmy Jr. stepped up to the grave they were looking for. Ryan and Honey knew the truth, knew that Jim had vanished on the other side, somehow sending Jake back dead, and that he was in all likelihood dead himself now. To them, the grave was appropriate.

Joanna knelt down before the marker and placed a flower at its base.

"I miss you, daddy," she said as she stepped back, putting her hand in Ryan's.

He gave it a gentle squeeze and she returned the gesture, looking up at him with a sad smile. Ryan smiled at her, then turned to Honey. She didn't meet his gaze, merely continued staring down at the marker.

"I'll never forget you, Jim Dalton," she said, a strain in her voice. There were tears in her eyes. "And we'll keep our promise to you."

She took Ryan's hand then and gripped it tightly. Ryan turned to the grave, nodding to it as if to say hello to an old acquaintance he'd seen on the street.

"Big Jim," he said, his voice cracking. "I miss you, buddy. I always will. But you have my word, no harm will come to your daughter or your son. And I love Honey with all of my heart, the way I know you wanted to."

He stopped then, tears streaming his face, and he fought them back. Both Honey and Joanna leaned into him and he released their hands and put his arms around them. He kissed Honey on the forehead.

"We love you, Jimmy," he said. "And we miss you."

They took a few more moments and then moved on. They had one more grave to stop at.

They found it quickly, and they all gazed down at it somberly. It was Freddie and Shelly James's graves. Side by side. She'd fallen to pieces at the news that her husband had been murdered that night, two years ago, and had slashed her wrists in the bathroom. The First Baptist Church of Winnsboro had been shaken to the core by the news, and it had taken nearly a year for the board of deacons to hire a new pastor, but they'd finally moved on.

"You know," Ryan said, squeezing Joanna's shoulder, "your Uncle Freddie was a hero, too. He and your dad were the bravest men I ever knew. I always admired them for that. They make me want to be a better man."

Honey kissed the side of his cheek and said, "You're a wonderful man, Ryan Laughton. Don't you ever tell yourself any different."

He smiled at her, then looked down to Joanna. She looked up at him and smiled, her cute and crooked teeth gleaming in the light. They would have to get her braces in the next couple of years, but right now, they were the most precious sight Ryan or Honey had ever seen.

"I wish I'd known Pastor Freddie," she said. "He sounds like he was a cool guy."

Ryan squeezed her tighter to his side.

"Me too, baby," he said. "Me too. He was the best."

They took another couple of moments to gaze down at the marker and then headed for their car. Their future was bright, and the world was safe. Ryan would make sure of it, as well as Honey. No one would ever harm their children, not so long as they had breath in their lungs.

As they neared their car, none of them noticed the warble in the air behind them or the shimmer around the grave of Jim Dalton.

And no one noticed the flower by the marker disappear.

About the author

Chris Miller is an active member of the Horror Writers Association and is a native Texan who has been writing from an early age, though he only started publishing in 2017. He attended North East Texas Community College and LeTourneau University, where he focused on creative writing courses. He is the superintendent of his family-owned water well company and his first novel, A MURDER OF SAINTS, has been met with acclaim from both critics and readers alike, as has his second novel THE HARD GOODBYE his novella TRESPASS, and THE DAMNED PLACE. His short stories–found in numerous anthologies–have likewise been praised. Chris and his wife, Aliana, have three children and live in Winnsboro, Texas.

Website: **http://www.authorchrismiller.com**

www.blackbedsheetbooks.com

A deadly virus spares only those of fairest skin,
but humanity's fate rests in the hands of one black man.
Ask for it
wherever
books are sold!
SKIN
SKIN
The debut novel by
Rick Dallison
Rick Dallison
ISBN: 978-0-9984427-0-9
www.blackbedsheetbooks.com

Beware not the storm, but the ancient evil it brings...
WHITE OUT
TOM SAWYER
The author of
Dark Harbors
Ask for it
wherever
books are sold!
WHITE OUT
TOM SAWYER
ISBN: 978-1-946874-00-9
www.blackbedsheetbooks.com

A new legend of SLEEPY HOLLOW
Ask for it
wherever
books are sold!
AnnMarie
MARTIN
www.blackbedsheetbooks.com
The Hollow
AnnMarie
MARTIN
ISBN: 978-0-69225829-3